BEACH BODY BOOGIE

Timothy Fagan

 *Fireclay Books*

Published in the United States by Fireclay Books
Winchester, Massachusetts
www.fireclaybooks.com

Cover design by damonza.com.

Library of Congress Control Number: 2018907389
ISBN-13: 978-1-7324596-0-1 (paperback)
ISBN-13: 978-1-7324596-2-5 (ebook)

First Edition

To my dad.

ONE

Three years ago

The bomb pop. *Ta-da!*

Pepper Ryan grinned—he'd finally chosen his winner. The original bomb pop was the greatest ice cream truck treat of all time.

It was a tough call, and no disrespect to his semi-finalists (Choco Taco and Klondike Bar—well fought!), but the cold sting of cherry, lime and blue raspberry *was* a hot summer afternoon, deep down wherever the simplest memories of his childhood were stored. Just thinking about a bomb pop made Pepper's mouth start to water, all these years later.

Pepper was now a twenty-six-year-old police officer, sitting on an overturned plastic milk crate in the back of a dirty old ice cream truck, waiting. Hence the frozen treat debate, even though its coolers were completely empty. He'd been on stakeout since 11 PM, so almost an hour. And for three hours each of the last two nights.

He was parked on the edge of Shore Road, just short of a beach parking lot at Rogers Lighthouse that his super-confidential source (Pepper's best buddy, Angel Cavada) had tipped him *might* be used as the handoff location of a hell of a lot of little blue pills at midnight, some night this week. Angel was an entrepreneurial spirit. He knew all kinds of people who heard things from all kinds of even worse people…this gossip was so thin it didn't include names. But *supposedly* the pills would be dropped by a Rhode Island scumbag in a blue Honda to a more local scumbag in a red Jeep Wrangler Sport. The local scumbag being—Pepper believed—the source of the benzo analog pills poisoning New Albion's middle school and high school for the past three months.

Pepper's patrol shift had ended at 6 PM, so his current activity was a bit of unofficial, unpaid overtime. He didn't inform his boss, New Albion's Chief of Police Donald Eisenhower, about the tip or his stakeout. Eisenhower would have told him to go home. He'd have handed it to his School Resource Officer investigating the pill epidemic, who would have shared it with the county and state police on their task force.

But Pepper's theory was either the local scumbag was a very lucky dude, or else the task force had an info leak. So what was wrong with testing his little theory? Pepper was way too pumped to care how Eisenhower would lecture him after the bust. Pepper fucking *hated* drug dealers and the misery they sold. It wasn't at all about competing again with his dad's old legacy, or even worse the raw memory of his brother Jake, no matter what some would inevitably say.

Outside the truck's split back window, a bit of moon dimly lit the parking lot, the beach and the Atlantic Ocean beyond. A blinding sweep of the lighthouse's beam across the sky occasionally turned midnight to noon, then flashed away. It was early June and chilly, both in and out of the truck.

Pepper waited, happy but impatient. All bottled energy. He realized he was whistling the beginning of Led Zeppelin's killer summer song, "Dancing Days"—its electric guitar riffs of adrenaline—over and over... He should have brought his guitar on the stakeout, he could have jammed with himself.

Finally, just after midnight, a blue Honda Civic with tinted windows cruised by but didn't enter the parking lot. Pepper watched it slowly disappear around a curve further along Shore Road. A minute later, a red Jeep came from the opposite direction and slowly pulled into the lot without using his turn signal. Okay, clearly a bad guy. The Jeep backed into a spot with its rear end to the ocean and killed its engine. And waited. Pepper crawled forward to the ice cream truck's cab, shaking pins and needles from his legs. Staying low, he used his phone to record video of the Jeep.

After five minutes the Blue Honda arrived again, from the same direction as before. The driver had made a loop. It pulled into the lot (signaling!) and pulled in nose first next to the Jeep, real close. Its lights stayed on.

Arms holding a backpack, followed by a head, poked out of the Honda. A black baseball cap and arms emerged from the Jeep, taking the backpack.

Without stopping recording, Pepper dialed the hot number for the New Albion police station. Barbara Buckley on Dispatch answered.

He gave a quick description of the vehicles and the situation, requesting backup.

"Uh, Pepper?" asked Barbara. Pausing, maybe trying to figure out how to deal with Pepper's foolishness over an open channel. "What're you—"

Pepper missed the rest because he dropped his phone in his lap as the Honda backed out of its spot. Pepper started the engine of the ice cream truck and jammed it into gear. It lurched forward, blocking the lot's only way in or out.

The Honda slid to a stop, almost hitting the ice cream truck. Pepper could see a woman behind the wheel— somewhere between thirty and fifty, lean, pale white face. Curly brown hair. Her mouth and eyes were wide open with fear.

Then two developments happened at once. The woman backed up the Honda and raced at an extreme angle at the lot's curb, aiming to jump the curb onto the sidewalk then to the open street. And the Jeep was also moving across the lot now in a slow wide circle. As if watching.

Pepper could hear a police siren, far in the distance.

The Honda's front left tire hit the curb and it went airborne, flipping over on its roof. It slid across the asphalt, spinning like a kid's toy.

The Jeep completed its circle and hit the curb on the beach side. Its oversized tires had no problem with the curb and it bounced onto the grass then disappeared down the walkway to the beach. With the backpack of pills.

So Pepper stomped the clutch and yanked the ice cream truck into reverse gear. He backed about fifty feet in a swaying line as fast as he dared, then yanked the truck forward onto a service path with beach access.

Pepper roared forward down the packed dirt and sand path, snatching his phone from his lap.

"Dispatch! The Honda's disabled in Rogers Light lot. Female driver, maybe armed. Ambulance needed. I'm pursuing the Jeep."

A pause, then Barbara asked, "What's your twenty?"

The service path ran out and the ice cream truck hit deep, loose sand and beach grass. The truck slowed hard, its engine whining high and rough. Pepper could see the rear lights of the Jeep disappearing down the beach.

"I'm ah, off-road. Driving north on Roger's Light beach." Pepper flipped the toggle for the ice cream truck's music and its loudspeakers crackled into full volume, "*Da da Da da Dum, da da da da DA da Dum*"... the same tinny, hissing tune he remembered running after in his youth with his brother Jake and their buddies. He realized it was the goofy old song "Do Your Ears Hang Low".

I miss you Jake, thought Pepper. His brother Jake had died a little over a month ago and it still felt unreal. Like it was part of a nightmare from last night that haunts you the next morning. "Tell backup to follow the music," he said.

"Goddamn Pepper! What—"

But Pepper dropped his phone in his lap again, needing both hands to control the steering wheel that was jerking wildly from side to side. The ice cream truck was lunging and rocking over the sand. Not good. So Pepper angled toward the wet, packed sand of low tide, closer to the waterline.

Which turned out to be nice and almost firm. He had the gas pedal pinned to the floor and appeared to be gaining on the Jeep, which was having a much easier time with the sand but kept slowing as if looking for a way off the beach. Pepper knew the Jeep's next good choice was a half-mile further along—a pedestrian right-of-way between beach houses.

He snatched the phone from his lap. "Send a car north to the beach access path next to the Kendalls' house. Suspect's in a red Jeep."

But no response from Barbara. Pepper saw he'd disconnected the call somehow during the chase. Fuck.

The Jeep was only 100 yards ahead of him now and was nearing the pedestrian walkway.

The ice cream truck hit a tide pool and slid to the right, Pepper dropping his phone again. The truck almost stopped but with tires spinning furiously Pepper forced it forward. Smoke was now coming out from under the hood, swirling in his headlights.

If it wasn't for the smoke, Pepper was sure he would have seen the motorboat. But he didn't. He t-boned its large, curved side—a dark black, twentyish-foot boat beached on the sand, waiting for the tide to come back in. The boat shattered in a burst of fiberglass. The ice cream truck jerked to a stop on the remains of the boat's stern. Pepper was thrown forward, his waist seatbelt jackknifing him to smack his forehead on the steering wheel.

Pepper felt a quick, fiery pain and then instantly he was almost completely lights-out unconscious.

From a very far and small place in his mind, Pepper was still conscious enough to realize he had right and truly fucked up this time—the stakeout, his job, his life. And he also knew he wasn't dead because he could still hear the ice cream truck's relentless music, but somehow fainter: *Da da Da da Dum, da da da da DA da Dum--*

Not dead, just a damned sight worse…

TWO

Now

You wouldn't believe the stuff that ends up on a Cape Cod beach. Some just nice to look at, like a fancy shell or a chunk of sea glass. But sometimes valuable stuff too. An old coin or a watch. An engagement ring. Whatever gets carried, then dropped in the sand by some moron. Or even stuff lost at sea, until someday the waves and tide spit it back on shore.

Bert and Sherry Tucker liked to get there early for the best pickings. Sure, it was maybe a bit chilly on Dill Beach, a little past 7 AM on that Sunday in June. Most people in New Albion were lazing around in bed, or at least their kitchens. But even in their sunset years, the Tuckers were still the kind of folk who don't miss the best part of the day.

The sky was already light blue. Easy waves were lapping at the seaweed line. *Like a scene in one of those reverse mortgage TV ads*, thought Bert. He laughed, drawing an indulgent little glance from his wife. Bert promised himself he'd remember that line and share it at cocktail hour with the Wolsons and the Fischers. But he never did, and never thought of it again. Because that's the morning they found the clambake pit.

The Tuckers stopped when they saw it—abandoned, still

pinned down with its shiny brown tarp. And sure, they didn't have the full noses of their youth, but what was that funky smell? Bert kicked away the driftwood pinning down the tarp's edge. He peeled back the corner, releasing a briny gust of steam. He rooted around in the seaweed with a thin piece of driftwood. Exposed a swollen, red hand.

A little more exploring confirmed it was, for flip's sakes, connected to a dead body—a man with a face that, despite considerable bloating, was grinning up at them.

As Bert later repeated multiple times to the Wolsons and the Fischers, he'd been in the Marines, he knew his civic duty. He pulled the tarp back over the situation, even carefully pinned it down with the driftwood to keep the body warm. Then he called 911 on the iPhone their daughter gave them last Christmas.

* * *

The New Albion police don't get many 911 calls and obviously it was important to get someone's butt there ASAP when they do. So when Officer Pepper Ryan heard Dispatch send a patrol car and Lieutenant Dwayne Hurd to a reported dead body on Dill Beach, he decided it was his sworn duty to skip out on a second consecutive day of manning the Rogers Folly Road speed-trap and all the boredom that offered. Instead, he sped to the shore with lights and siren.

Pepper had left the New Albion police force three years earlier after a disastrous beach chase of an alleged drug dealer, followed by even more disastrous arguments with his chief of police, Donald Eisenhower, and his own dad, Gerry Ryan, the town's former chief of police. His whole life went up like a fireball that night and Pepper just frickin' quit—he left town, didn't come back for three years. He had only returned to New Albion and rejoined the police department that week.

Pepper was the third officer to arrive at the scene, a bit behind the patrol unit with two officers. It was 7:32 AM. Clear sky, light wind, no sign of rain to muck up the crime scene. Since he hadn't been sent by Dispatch, *per se*, he radioed in his location before he climbed out of his car. Zula Eisenhower, the Chief of Police's daughter, was on the dispatch desk but Pepper didn't quite hear her quizzical response before his car door shut.

Pepper had only recently met the junior, Jackson Phillips. But he knew the senior, Randy Larch, from the old days. Liked him fine. *The kind of cop that hits singles all season*, his dad had said once as a compliment, when he was still chief of police. His dad hadn't actually said *unlike you*, but Pepper had heard it anyway, being more the kind of cop who either hit a grand slam or struck out and got tossed from the game, then the ballpark.

Larch was just finishing the last knot of the crime scene perimeter, having strung a rough circle of police tape using trees, rocks and driftwood as posts. "Hey, Wonderboy!" Larch greeted Pepper. "You're back in uniform two days and the kooky shit's already started."

"Yeah, what're the odds?" Pepper said. Because a real pro doesn't take the job personally, or so he'd heard. And because he knew his fellow officers had started a pool to bet how long Pepper would last with the New Albion force this time. Funny but disappointing. Especially since Pepper couldn't get in on the action.

The police tape perimeter was already attracting random civilians taking phone videos of the crime scene and each other, with the most fuss around a shaggy guy in a purple hat and clothes that looked like they were from the lost and found box at a medieval festival. And better yet, a Channel

Four truck was now backing up to the beach. A reporter hopped out and started brushing her hair vigorously. The news truck must have been in the Lower Cape area for some other reason, just their luck.

But Pepper ignored the growing circus and went right to the victim's body which it appeared was half buried in...a clambake pit?

"Looks like expert work to me," said Larch. "You do a clambake right, it takes like half a day. Digging the pit, lining it with rocks, heating them for hours under a bonfire. You got to gather seaweed, layer it in there. Cover it up nice with a wet drop cloth, then a tarp like this one, all pinned down to hold in the steam."

"So you're thinking the perps are locals?" asked Phillips.

Larch gave a noncommittal wave. "What I'm saying is, you can't cut corners or it comes out shit. It's a lot of work to do it the right way. With dead bodies, you don't usually see this much effort."

"Real New England craftsmanship," said Phillips. "Maybe a tuna fleet hit job?"

Larch was giving Phillips the hairy eyeball. "Seriously? The fishermen would settle their beefs offshore at Stellwagen Bank. But somebody saw something. You can't spend half a day steaming a guy to death with nobody noticing. Not on Cape Cod, even before the 4th of July."

Pepper was trying to tune out Officers Laurel and Hardy and study the crime scene. Yep, it was a goddamn clambake pit, with all the fixings. Pepper could see the tarp, the canvas drop cloth pulled part way back, the seaweed. Even some quahogs and other shellfish poking out around the half-revealed body.

"Maybe not that expert," Pepper said, pointing. "Who puts a starfish in a clambake?"

It was a bright red starfish, sitting on the dead man's chest, almost blending with the man's red athletic jacket. Not even seagulls eat starfish, they're one of the most disgusting food sources in the ocean. Definitely not people food.

"Good catch Pepper!   You channeling Jake?" joked Larch.

Jake, his older brother.   The finest young homicide detective in Boston in the last twenty years, everyone agreed. Right up until a little over three years ago, when he stepped in the path of that damned jewelry store robbery, off duty and under-armed. The Ryan curse, taking the job too far…

"Sweet jumpin' Jesus," said a voice from right behind Pepper's shoulder. "New Albion just made tonight's news." Lieutenant Hurd had arrived.   Hurd was a medium-sized white guy. Wiry. His nose was *way* too long for his thin face and the small mustache under it didn't help. Hurd had joined the New Albion force during Pepper's absence so Pepper didn't have a good read on him yet.

Pepper stayed bent as close as he could get without touching the body.   Studying the dead guy's swollen face. Definitely a guy, maybe late thirties. Black hair. And the guy looked a bit familiar…

"Ah shit," Hurd was muttering in Pepper's ear, so softly probably only Pepper could hear him. "Ah shit, ah shit, ah shit…" Like a meditation.

Then Hurd seemed to collect himself. "Is an M.E. on the way? What about Barnstable? And where are the wits who phoned it in? I'll interview them myself."

"Sir, this was weird enough we thought the General would wanna call the shots before we bring down the M.E. and any, er, outside resources," said Phillips. They all called Chief Eisenhower 'The General'—meaning it as a kind of compliment, and maybe also to be funny, since he didn't

11

resemble the original General Eisenhower at all. But no one would ever call him *that* to his face.

Pepper knew it was usual for murder scenes to bring in the Cape and Islands District Attorney's Office from nearby Barnstable, which would send a team of state police detectives. But turning this over to the staties before the Chief of Police was in the loop would probably not be appreciated. Like his predecessor Chief Ryan, the General took a pride of ownership in criminal activity in his town, despite the limits of his resources.

Phillips was wringing his hands. "And our witnesses are over on that log. Oh, shit!" The elderly couple wasn't on the log anymore, they were being interviewed by the TV news lady.

"Larch, get 'em away from that reporter," barked Hurd.

Pepper was still fixated on what he could see of the body. The dead man's face. A face he was 90% sure he'd seen once before... But since he'd absolutely promised himself to be less impetuous this time, for once in his checkered law-enforcement career, wouldn't it be better to keep his lips zipped, for now?

"As for the body," continued Phillips. "His pockets are empty except for a big cigar tube. Weird for a guy in a jogging suit, right? But no I.D."

"You *touched* the body?" asked Hurd, his nose in too close to Phillips. His face flushing red.

"Lieutenant, about this victim?" interrupted Pepper, surprising himself. "I think he was a fed."

"What?" asked Hurd and Phillips, simultaneously. Phillips wringing his hands.

Pepper focused on the lieutenant. "I'll bet he was a federal officer."

Hurd tilted his head. "Pepper, you know the vic?

What's going on?"

"No, never met him. But a few days ago I saw four men in suits walking down Shore Road, right past the driveway to my family's house. Like they were surveying the road. I thought maybe reconning for the upcoming presidential vacation at Eagle's Nest, since it's about a mile further down? Unless he has a brother in town, this man was there."

Lieutenant Hurd was giving Pepper a look, like it sounded pretty thin. Hurd might have taken lessons from Pepper's dad—he had exactly the same skeptical scowl, plus the bonus impact of his long pointy nose. But finally he said, "Ah, shit... Phillips, check it with the station. Any missing, ah, federal officers. But on your cell phone."

Phillips trudged down toward the shoreline to make the call. Pepper saw him striking a pose by the water's edge as he talked on his phone, gesturing dramatically with his free hand. The TV crew was filming his whole act.

Two minutes later, Phillips came trotting back and slapped Pepper's back with an attaboy. "A Secret Service agent named Keser was just reported missing—Zula was about to put out a BOLO. He hasn't been seen since yesterday morning. You think it's him? And the reporter asked, can she have a quick interview with Wonderboy?"

"Nice catch again, Pepper," said Larch. "You sure you're the guy who flamed out last time? I may need to go change a bet."

But Pepper didn't smile, because he could feel Hurd 's eyes still on him. Like he suspected Pepper knew something more than he was saying.

THREE

By late that afternoon, Pepper was waiting alone in the New Albion police station's only conference room when Zula led in two Secret Service agents.

The Secret Service had arrived at Dill Beach a few hours earlier and immediately taken over the crime scene. After a brief call with the General, Lieutenant Dwayne Hurd conceded jurisdiction, which made good sense to Pepper. The Secret Service wasn't going to negotiate—that was one of their guys in the clambake pit. A team of state detectives had beaten the Secret Service to the crime scene and had adopted a more territorial attitude. Less cooperative. Until the Secret Service called the staties' boss elsewhere on Cape Cod and had them pulled off, along with the local M.E. A while later, the Secret Service had requested this meeting with the New Albion police and to Pepper's surprise he was asked by the General to sit in, despite being the newest hire and low man on the department's totem pole.

"I thought we're ah, meeting with the Chief?" asked the younger guy, his hands gesturing what looked like fake confusion. He was tall and too thin in his shiny blue suit. He had blond hair, shaved shorter on the sides but a little too long and styled to one side on top. Handsome, but not as handsome as he probably thought. The older guy, heavier, gray temples, a long pale scar on his cheek, made a *relax* gesture with his hand.

They introduced themselves. The skinny guy was Special Agent Dan Alfson. The older guy was a big dog—Special Agent in Charge Daylan Hanley. He carried himself like Pepper's dad always did—with casual but absolute authority.

Zula Eisenhower left to get her dad, with a parting eye roll to Pepper and a flip of long black hair. Pepper had to admit she'd grown to be an attractive woman, reflecting her African-American dad and Malaysian mom. But more than unofficially off-limits to any New Albion officer looking to keep his job and his nuts. Pepper had heard that Jackson Phillips took her out for ice cream soon after joining the force and ended up on speed-trap detail for six months.

But Pepper saw Special Agent Alfson tilt his head for an exaggerated appreciation of Zula's rear end as she departed. Practically whistled. Alfson noticed Pepper catch him gawking, reddened a bit, then started fumbling a pad and pen from his black briefcase.

"So, you met the Chief of Police's daughter?" Pepper asked him with a chuckle and a nod to the door.

Alfson smirked, said, "You don't—" but stopped when Hanley stood as Chief Donald Eisenhower came through the door, accompanied by Lieutenant Hurd. Chief Eisenhower was a big man—even taller than Pepper. And much thicker. Freckles on his broad African-American face. A gray fringe of hair, which Pepper knew he'd contributed to over the years. The General's gravitas dominated every room he was in, even with heavy hitters like these Secret Service agents.

Eisenhower introduced himself and Hurd to the agents, but also picked up on an awkward vibe, raising a quick eyebrow at Pepper as if to say, *have you already screwed things up?*

But they all found seats and settled in, the locals on one side of the table and Secret Service on the other.

"I appreciate you taking the time, Chief," said Hanley. He gave a quick summary of the facts so far. The body was Arnold Keser, an intelligence officer on the Secret Service's advance team for the POTUS's vacation. Keser had gone for a run on Saturday morning, went missing. Turned up in that clambake pit. He was shot in the gut with double ought buckshot but didn't die from that wound. He'd been steamed to death.

"And then there's this," Hanley continued. He lifted a laminated photograph from a manila folder, spun it around so it was facing them. Tapped it instructively with his pen.

"This is a copy of a document found tucked in Keser's pocket, folded and rolled up in a cigar tube. You may recognize it."

It was the Declaration of Independence. Pepper remembered it from history class. He squinted, tried to follow the small handwriting. There were a few phrases underlined, so Pepper focused on those:

--We hold these truths to be self-evident, that all men are created equal, that they are endowed by their Creator with certain unalienable rights, that among these are life, liberty and the pursuit of happiness.--

--But when a long train of abuses and usurpations, pursuing invariably the same object evinces a design to reduce them under absolute despotism, it is their right, it is their duty, to throw off such government, and to provide new guards for their future security.--

--Such has been the patient sufferance of these colonies;

and such is now the necessity which constrains them to alter their former systems of government. The history of the present King of Great Britain is a <u>history of repeated injuries and usurpations</u>, all having in direct object the establishment of an <u>absolute tyranny</u> over these states.--

Then on and on, but no more underlining. A long list of grievances against bad old King George III. And then the kiss off—declaring the split from Great Britain. Followed by the many politicians' signatures, all dwarfed by John Hancock's sprawling alpha male signature. But off to the right, someone had hand printed the planned start and finish dates of the president's vacation, drawn a crude picture of a starfish in red ink, and printed below it: *R.I.P. Garby. U took my candy!*

"Pretty fucking weird," said Chief Eisenhower.

"Let me open the kimono," cut in Alfson, clicking his pen. "The POTUS gets around ninety death threats a year, more in election years. Most are drunken scrawls by nobodies who piss themselves when the Service pays them a visit. But our folks in Forensic Services study every note. The handwriting, the quality of paper, the ink. Scan for DNA, the whole nine yards."

"So?" asked Pepper. Which earned him a hard cough from Chief Eisenhower.

"So a couple dozen threats every year are treated as more credible, for one reason or another. A few really get our attention, like this document. We read it as a direct threat to kill the POTUS. We only have a preliminary report, but so far? No helpful DNA. We have an unsub or group of unsubs who've proven they're willing to kill. And the weirdness worries me. The crazy bit about the candy— what's that all about? Why a clambake grave? Why shoot

17

Keser? It appears he was paralyzed by an injected drug, then shot while lying in the clambake pit."

"Sounds like he might've pissed someone off. Any thought there was something personal between Keser and whoever shot him?" asked Hurd.

"Maybe," said Hanley. "Or maybe they think they're clever. Breaking that old saying, 'Don't shoot the messenger'? And our intel is there's something weird going on big picture too, with the upcoming POTUS visit to this town. Many more activist and protest groups than usual are chattering about traveling here during the presidential vacation. And in much bigger numbers. It's got the hairs on my neck standing up. And that's why we need two favors."

Ah, thought Pepper. *The punch line.*

"First thing, Chief," said Hanley, "I need you as point on media relations. But for national security, don't mention the POTUS death threat or that the victim was Secret Service. Just give the media as little as possible: all leads are being followed…no information's available yet about the victim, but any witnesses are encouraged to contact you. That kind of play."

"But in practice, your town officers will need to stand down on the case, hard stop," added Alfson. With just a drip of condescension?

Hanley put a hand on his agent's shoulder. Almost," he said. "Our theory so far is maybe the unsubs have some local connection. That whole clambake thing, and the way Keser was grabbed so cleanly, like they knew the best spot. So if you have an officer with real local knowledge, I'll take him on loan. A local liaison. And it'll help your optics—you can tell the press he's your lead investigator."

What they call, thought Pepper, *a fall guy*. And for once Pepper would let someone else have the honor of blowing up their career...

"We'd be happy to help," said the Chief. "This is New Albion's most shocking murder since... well, probably ever. With the President vacationing here, the media'll be thicker than sand fleas. There'll be a lot of local panic, what with the public not knowing who the victim is. The impact it'll have on summer rentals if we don't catch this nut."

"So if I need to borrow someone who's familiar with all the native troublemakers and lowlifes, who's the best you've got?"

Lieutenant Hurd gave a thoughtful grunt. "Can we chew on it, get back to you? We're stretched past breaking already, schedule-wise. But we'll free up someone and let you know."

Special Agent Alfson was eyeing his boss. Maybe trying to decide whether to complain about recruiting a local in front of the actual locals, or to save his whining for later?

Chief Eisenhower leaned back, put his hands behind his head. "How about Ryan?" he asked, with a nod toward Pepper.

What?!? Pepper's stomach tightened like he'd been punched. He was too shocked to even object.

But Hurd dragged forward his chair with a squeal. "Chief, he's been back one week!"

"Maybe someone with a *tad* more experience?" asked Alfson.

Did he intentionally sound like he was talking patiently to stupid people?

Eisenhower crossed his arms. "This is Ryan's second tour with us. And investigation's in his DNA. His dad was chief of this town, before me. And he's as local as it gets. He grew up here, knows all the scumbags and they know him."

"Aren't you the one who flagged Keser as a federal officer?" Hanley asked Pepper.

Pepper nodded. He still couldn't speak, his mind was racing too fast. His plans were going out the window. In fact, it might be a complete disaster.

"Sir!" complained Alfson to Hanley. Ignoring everyone else. "Shouldn't we take this offline with whoever you're sticking him with?"

"Not to worry Dan, he'll be partnered up with you."

"What?!?" asked Alfson and Pepper at the same moment.

"See? They're already on the same page," said Hanley. He and Eisenhower stood, shook hands.

"Thanks again," said Hanley. "We briefed the POTUS about the threat against his life and he didn't even blink. He's determined to come here as previously scheduled. So let's catch these assholes before he arrives."

FOUR

It was four days prior to the clambake murder scene that Pepper Ryan had seen the dead man. And only in passing. But it was at the crucial moment of Pepper's homecoming after almost three years away from New Albion. So the man's face was glued to Pepper's mind, by association.

Pepper had driven home to Cape Cod from Nashville in two days. He'd made one stop on the Tuesday afternoon and then passed a semi-restless night in a motel in Virginia. On the next day, Pepper had driven through almost nonstop for nine hours. By evening, he'd crossed the Sagamore Bridge. Then hit the New Albion exit around thirty minutes later, bone tired with an aching butt. Pepper hadn't called ahead to tell his dad that he was coming home, let alone his return to the police force. Of course, his dad was close buddies with Chief Eisenhower, who must have been tempted to spill the beans, despite promising Pepper he wouldn't.

Pepper hadn't seen or talked to his dad in almost three years. Memories of that final day were still raw in Pepper's chest—the damn ice cream truck chase, leading to a shouting match with Chief Eisenhower, leading to Pepper quitting the force. The anger and argument had carried home, become an even louder confrontation with his dad, who took his old lieutenant's side, of course. Pepper had walked away just a twitch short of punching out his dad—he'd grabbed his guitar, a backpack of clothes, not much else. Driven away and stayed gone.

So it was with a dull ache of anxious hostility that Pepper cut down to Shore Road a couple streets early. The scenic route. And it seemed nothing had really changed. Mostly Cape-style homes, a little on the larger side. He rounded the bend past Rogers Lighthouse, then along the stretch of significantly larger houses. Pretty much mansions, mostly, on estate-sized lots. Except one smaller, low Cape-style cottage tucked away on a small peninsula, a long stone's throw removed from Mansion Row. The Ryans' snug home.

From the road, it appeared nothing had changed. The house was small but to Pepper, perfect. It was lopsided in shape since the left side had been raised decades ago to add a second-floor dormer for his and Jake's bedroom. The home was covered in cedar shingles washed to gray by the Cape Cod weather. The windows were framed by neat white shutters.

On one side of the house, his father had planted roses for his mother, many years ago. Pepper could faintly picture her tending them in a big straw hat and a red dress. Pruning shears in her hand, turning to smile at Pepper as he ran across the lawn to her. But he knew he'd been way too young when she'd died for the memory to be real. Maybe it had been Jake's memory, had he told Pepper? The rose bushes were now climbing wildly, almost blocking the dining room window. A thick collection of low evergreen bushes ringed the house.

But before he could turn into the Ryan driveway, Pepper had to wait for four men in dark suits who were walking past his driveway opening. Pepper felt a flare of irritation. The men were all wearing white shirts and bland ties. Matching shiny round pins on their left lapels. They were gesturing at both sides of Shore Road as if assessing the roadway. Unusual pedestrians to be strolling along the sandy edge of their street at sunset. One man stopped in the middle of the driveway, gesturing and saying something to the other two, ignoring Pepper's truck. After a long three count under his breath, Pepper lightly honked his horn, like hey, wake up.

The man in the driveway tilted his head as if noticing the truck for the first time. He took off his sunglasses and made a little comic "I'm walking here" gesture, laughed at himself for the benefit of his companions and said something to them. After a couple more seconds, he slowly moved from the opening, giving Pepper a little mock wave.

That man, Pepper now believed, had been Arnold Keser.

But at the time, Pepper had dismissed the four walking men from his mind as soon as they cleared the driveway entrance. He'd been exhausted, stiff and totally focused on being home and what would happen next. How his dad would react.

The long driveway was still worn dirt with a smattering of crushed oyster shells. Pepper eased his pickup truck slowly all the way down to the house and parked in the little turnaround in back. He paused a moment, looking eastward over the Atlantic, took a very deep breath, let it out slowly. The blue snakeskin of the ocean gleamed back at him.

Pepper walked up the side porch's creaking steps. For the first time in his life, he rang the bell. Waited.

A bit later, the door opened and there was his dad, Gerald Ryan. A little older. His head of white hair was still full, meticulously combed. A little smaller now than the six foot of his prime, but still solid in his early seventies. Still had forearms like Popeye. He was wearing green work pants and a thin multi-colored flannel shirt with the sleeves rolled up. His serious face peered back at Pepper through thick glasses, tilted up a little.

"Shit Pepper," his dad said after an awkward pause. "For a moment I thought you were Jake. You look more like he used to, with that Sox cap."

They stood there, staring at each other.

"Home for a visit?"

"No sir. Home for the summer. And a job."

His dad finally stepped back, made a little gesture. "I guess you'd better come in."

What dummy said you can never go home again?

They sat at the old yellow Formica table in the kitchen. It still had the same minuscule wobble. Pepper noticed a Christmas card with two little boys stuck to the fridge with a magnet. Patrick and Little Jake, his brother's sons. They must be around eight and ten years old now.

"They're getting big," said Pepper, getting up and plucking it off, studying them. They both had the Ryan blue eyes, but their smiles were more like their mother's. Cautious.

"Little hellions. Chips off the Ryan block. I only get to see them a couple times a year. Julie gets too busy, now she's teaching again."

"I've got to get up to Boston and see them soon, if she'll let me in. She any less mad about me?" Part of Julie's mourning for Jake included anger toward the other Ryan men--particularly Pepper.

"Julie's still Julie. But keep your butt out of trouble for a little bit and I'll put in a good word for you."

His dad began clattering around the kitchen, making coffee, and Pepper just stayed silent. Building whatever strength he had left.

His dad came and sat at the table while he waited for the pot to percolate. He tossed a box of oatmeal cookies on the table, the same brand he'd favored since Pepper was little. Maybe even the same box—Pepper remembered them as unpleasantly hard, tasteless and liable to suck all the moisture from your mouth.

"So," his dad said, somehow biting into a cookie. "There must be a hell of a story...home for the summer? Something to do with that?" Pointing to a band-aid which covered a pretty good cut above Pepper's left eye. "You running from someone, handsome? Maybe a girl or her boyfriend? And you said, a job?"

Pepper definitely wasn't going to get into the story behind the band-aid, not right then. But was that what his dad still thought of him? "There's no girl. I've signed up with Eisenhower for the summer."

His dad actually recoiled. "You what!?"

So the General hadn't tipped off his dad. "Just for this summer. Gives me time to figure out what's next. "

His dad had gone red. Was shaking a bit. "I don't understand. What about your music?"

"That wasn't going so hot. It was time for a change--a simple job with a steady paycheck."

His dad grimaced. "You disappear for three years, the wandering bard? Threw away family and friends? Career prospects? Now you're Mr. Steady? Where'd you come back from, the nuthouse?"

"Nashville, most recently. Austin and L.A. before that." Pepper hated that his answer wasn't completely honest, though it wasn't exactly a lie.

His dad got up, poured two cups of coffee. Put one in front of Pepper. The mug said 'Got Crabs?', with a picture below of two New Albion green crabs.

"So why're you *really* back...second chances?" asked his dad. He was now standing behind his chair, leaning on it, looking like a cop trying to bully a murder suspect into confessing. Which would have been more intimidating if he didn't have an oatmeal cookie crumb hanging from the corner of his mouth. "Finally feel guilty for taking off? Or hoping to bring the Ryan name back to our former glory? No, don't tell me you're actually trying to pretend you're Jake again?"

Right, and there it was. Cold anger flooded Pepper's mind. He almost didn't recognize his own voice when he spoke, it sounded so measured, clinical.

"I'm just here for a job. Temporarily. And Eisenhower needed extra help this summer, with President Garby coming to town."

His dad chuckled. "You know the papers say that'll be a real shit show. How'd the president piss off so many voters that quick? You sure you want to get caught up in his hot mess?"

Pepper stood and walked to the kitchen window. Looked out to the gray wooden deck and the beach fifty feet in the distance. The silvered water beyond, reflecting the last of the day. He yawned violently—the long drive had completely fried him.

"Speaking of messes," Pepper heard himself say. "I heard from the General that things aren't so hot for you these days, financially? I can chip in, pay some rent, if you can put up with me moving back in here?"

His dad flushed an even deeper red. Started shaking again. "Eisenhower and his big fucking mouth!"

"So it's true?"

His dad huffed, dislodging the cookie crumb. "It's just the property taxes. They've tripled in the last ten years. The town assessor's been hitting me just like the bigger houses on the road—the damn price of this ocean view. So I've had to take out a home equity line."

"And?"

"And I'm maxed out, all right? Upside down with a balloon payment due. So the writing's on the wall—I'll have to sell. The bank'll force my hand this fall. Maybe sooner. Unless you made a couple million bucks on your songs?"

Pepper hadn't.

"I'll figure out something. Or not. But it's my problem and Eisenhower shouldn't have said anything to you." His face was creased with betrayal—Pepper recognized the look.

But Pepper felt betrayed too. "Dad...I'm glad he did. This is my home too, right? Jake's and Mom's. Our memories of them. Why didn't you tell me yourself?"

His dad laughed. "Well, I guess I was waiting for the phone to ring. You forget the number?"

Pepper's stomach tightened into a knot. He bit off a response, knowing it'd be so easy to make his dad explode. But that was the great thing about being a Ryan--the fight would be waiting in the morning. He yawned so hard he felt his jaw click a mini-dislocation. He was too exhausted for coffee to help. "You have any problem me sleeping here?"

His dad paused. Finally he said, "You've always been welcome here, Son, no matter how you left. No matter how many times you've... But good luck with the job— Eisenhower's going to need any help he can get."

Pepper said nothing more. Instead, he gave a luxurious yawn and stretched. Left his dad alone at the table.

Pepper went out to his truck and grabbed his guitar case and a backpack. He'd only owned the guitar, a Taylor acoustic-electric, for two days. He'd bought it at Gruhn's in Nashville to replace his dear old favorite Gibson, which on

Monday night—his final night in Tennessee—he'd smashed across the face of the owner/bouncer of the bar he was playing in. A different story.

His other things could wait. Pepper went back inside and climbed the steep, narrow stairs to the small bedroom where he'd bunked for so many years with his older brother.

The room was as they'd left it. Baseball gear in one corner, hockey sticks in another. Curling-edged posters of Bruins and Red Sox players who were long retired. The half-assed repair job of fishing stickers covering the hole in the closet door made by Pepper's head, thanks to a surprisingly effective wrestling move by the bigger, stronger Jake, too long ago.

How could his dad have been planning to sell the Ryan home without telling him? That concept had never even remotely occurred to Pepper. He wondered again if coming home had been a big, fat mistake.

Pepper had leaned his guitar case in the corner and dropped his backpack. Taken off the Red Sox cap and hung it on the bedpost. He'd looked out the bedroom's small window at the Atlantic one more time, which had gone deep gray under the early moonlight. Then he'd slowly climbed up to his top bunk, still fully dressed, and stretched out, pressing his face into the musty pillow. He'd been asleep before his eyes closed.

FIVE

I'm the most powerful man in the world.
I'm the most powerful man in the world.

Wayne Garby kept repeating this to himself, softly but firmly. When he felt like he exactly believed it, he pulled himself to his full five ten and three-quarters inches and stepped from the White House's West Sitting Hall into the master bedroom of the most powerful man in the world. His bedroom.

As summoned.

The First Lady, his wife Lulu, whirled at her Chippendale writing desk and threw the Hamilton biography at his head.

Damn! He barely ducked it—great arm for a tiny woman. "Lulu honey!" he protested.

"Don't honey me, you *shit*. I just heard about the security briefing. There's some wacko assassin running around where you're forcing us to go to on Cape Cod? *I'm not going!*"

Uh oh. "Lulu, you're talking crazy," he said with open palms and the low whiskey tone that had helped him win 54.5% of the popular vote eighteen months earlier. His *trust me* voice. But he casually slid to the left, behind the Italian carved settee, just in case. He was heading to Japan and

Vietnam for a quick trip before their Cape Cod vacation and couldn't afford facial bruising.

Then he tried again. He didn't want to imagine the media, political and financial fallout if he couldn't get every damn family member to show up for the First Vacation. "I was going to tell you at dinner," he assured her. "I don't want some weirdo to ruin our getaway! A real family vacation, for all the baloney you put up with every day. Your long hours. The hardest working first lady since Jackie O!"

"Family vacation? Don't make me laugh," she said, but with a tiny bit less vitriol. He knew she secretly measured herself against Jackie O. All the first wives did.

Garby noticed the slight drop in her fury and jumped on it. "The four of us, honeybee. Walks on the beach. Bike rides to get ice cream. A good old-fashioned family vacation. And a chance to reconnect with the girls and each other. Put that Jimmy Fallon thing behind us. And clear our heads from all the Washington talk and nonsense."

Garby knew Washington got on her nerves, same as his. He'd just spent thirty minutes straightening out his press team about the latest cheap shot at yesterday's press briefing—questions about a rumor that Garby had a stake in some offshore entity Garby'd never even frickin' heard of! Snarky innuendo about money laundering and Iranian oil. His press secretary was blindsided and botched it, the putz— his answer sounded like guilt or evasion, especially the clip everyone ran. But the rumor was total balls-out fiction! Garby could defend financial ties with a borderline smell— you gotta do what you gotta do in a complicated world—but he'd be damned if he was going to get torpedoed on crap he never touched!

His wife was staring at him, reading him. Weighing which way to take this. "Can't we just change our plans?

You knew I wanted us to go to Paris this summer."

Huh? Garby knew she'd watched a *lot* of French Open tennis this spring. But the City of Lights was now her newest thing? He suspected that Republicans who hope to be re-elected don't vacation in Paris... "Honeybug, my approval rating's the lowest first-term since Jimmy Frickin' Carter. If I vacationed in Paris now, we'd have to ask the French for refugee status!"

She didn't break even a little smile at that one. "But why Cape Cod?" she demanded. "Why not home, see our friends?"

Running home to Kentucky would be retreating, make him look like a pussy. But he knew Lulu wouldn't understand. "Acker Smith invited us to stay at his compound and you know I had to say yes, honey bunch. I'll need his super PAC again for my reelection. Think of our legacy! And Smith's really sick."

She was giving him her full glare, but at least he had her attention.

"Actually," he continued, lowering his volume. His confidential voice now. Full eye contact. "Lulu, he's dying. There's probably no next year for him...I have to lock up his money this summer. For the re-election *and* our presidential library. We've got to stick to the plan."

If there was one thing that got through to the First Lady, it was the never-ending need to feed the financial beast. And she knew they'd had no more generous billionaire on their side last time than Acker Smith. Garby held his breath. He had to nip this in the butt--he was already late for a drop-by with the Turkish ambassador.

Finally she sighed. Her martyr sigh. "Well, *you* get to tell the twins about the beach assassin," she said. "If you can get them to stop partying long enough to listen. And Wayne?"

31

"Yes, dear?"

"Speaking of Washington talk and nonsense? If I hear there's a fake-boobed redhead named Alexis anywhere on Cape Cod during our old-fashioned family vacation, I'll stab you dead in your sleep. Save the assassin the trouble." Lulu smiled sweetly at him to make it clear she wasn't joking.

Garby swallowed, flashed back a moderate smile. He quickly closed the distance between them, gave his wife a lingering but wary hug.

And made a mental note to ask Alexis to go blonde.

But Garby was humming lightly as he made his escape to the Turkish ambassador. He scored this a win for himself, Washington-style: slightly more victory than defeat.

And hey, he was headed to Cape Cod in the summer. Golf, sun and sand. Bikinis.

What could go wrong?

SIX

A yellow Porsche convertible came around the bend fast, probably going twice the thirty miles an hour limit on Shore Road. Startled the crap out of Pepper Ryan. He shook off his surprise, hit his rollers and took off in pursuit.

Pepper had parked his squad car on the shoulder of Shore Road to call his brand new partner, Special Agent Alfson. Pepper had been on his way back to the police station but knew when the General saw him he'd expect an update on the Clambake case.

Which was nada, so far on that Monday morning, unless Alfson's little army of investigators had made some progress. Unfortunately, Pepper was having trouble getting a clear cell signal along this stretch of Shore Road, the smallest bar on his phone blinking in and out. But the speeding Porsche had interrupted and also pissed off Pepper.

Pepper had the Porsche pulled over within half a mile. He typed its license plate into the laptop strapped to his cruiser's dashboard. It came back as registered to a Delaware corporation named Fulmar Limited. No citation history.

Pepper radioed in his location to Dispatch, said he'd stopped a car for a speeding violation, then spelled out the license plate number. Zula Eisenhower's sweet voice piped back over the radio, repeating his location, then she added, "Use caution, Pepper!" Zula was way too chatty for open radio, but better to let her dad smack her down--anything Pepper said would just make her worse. "10-4, Little Ike," he replied, because he was pretty sure she hated sharing a nickname with an old white president. And she was wicked fun to tease.

Pepper was surprised that he got an adrenaline kick as he cautiously walked up behind the idling convertible, his sunglasses on, hat low. Everything a cop should be. He unclipped his newly-issued Glock 23. He didn't need Zula's nagging to remember even a routine stop can turn deadly.

The Porsche held two people but it was hard to notice anyone other than the driver. She was a wavy-haired honey blonde, big red sunglasses, about Pepper's age, late twenties. Maybe a bit too thin for her own health? But attractive enough to probably expect to smile her way out of speeding tickets. Too bad she'd caught an officer who could steel himself against such charms. A model lawman, who could spit out tickets to miscreants like a human Pez dispenser.

A pretty boy type was sprawled out fake-casual in the passenger seat. He had light brown hair, two-day stubble on his cheeks. Probably a touch younger than the woman. Pepper noticed he was wearing a graphic tee with his own smug face on its front. Wicked ironic.

All four of their hands were in sight. Pretty Boy was puffing on a vape pen, nonchalantly exhaling vapor. He was also fiddling with his bright red cell phone like he was trying to stealthily record the police stop, angling back and forth between his own profile and the rest of the scene. God bless the TMZ generation.

The woman driver leaned forward to get her license from her purse, while maybe also trying to give Pepper a long

wink of tanned cleavage. Pretty Boy didn't miss her move--
he puffed up his chest and blew vapor toward Pepper.

Pepper saw the name on her Florida license and his
subconscious unease clicked into realization. Madeline Smith.
Maddie! Pepper actually felt his stomach tighten, his
breathing quicken, but as if he was watching himself from
outside his body. Get it together dude.

"You know the speed limit along here?" he asked in his
lowest voice.

She smiled like a toothpaste commercial parody—
perfect white teeth with just a hint of a smirk. She started to
answer, but Pretty Boy put his arm across her chest.

"Hey hey," said Pretty Boy, with a little finger point
toward Pepper. "We have the right to remain silent, we know
our First Amendment rights." He vapor puffed victoriously.

She pushed his arm away. "I'm sorry officer, Justin's
from California. It must be about forty-five here, right? Was
I going a little fast?" She even bit her lower lip a bit.

"It's thirty along this stretch. But you were pushing
sixty."

"This is like profiling," complained Justin. "Harassing
the famous."

"Excuse me?"

Justin pulled himself to full height in his bucket seat, like
he was really going to say something important this time. But
Maddie cut him off. "Officer, don't pay any attention to him.
He's going to shut up now."

"Good idea," said Pepper, taking off his sunglasses and
slipping them into his pocket. "Well, you need to slow this
rocket down. Lots of kids on bikes along here, too many
blind curves. But I guess I'll have to let you off with a
warning this time. Since we're married."

Pepper didn't know whose reaction was funnier,

Maddie's or Justin's. Pepper had knocked the flirty little smirk off her mouth, which was now hanging open in confusion. Justin immediately turned red, his eyes darting back and forth between her and Pepper, anger and confusion dueling for control. He slid low in his bucket seat, snapped a defiant selfie with his phone, another victim of The Man.

Maddie slipped off her sunglasses, flipped back her honey blonde hair, stared up at Pepper, finally really looking at him. Studied him. "No damn way...Pepper Ryan?" And then she smiled for real this time, with her eyes, all playful joy and energy. Like her smile when they were young.

"You're married?" howled Justin.

"It was fourth grade," said Maddie. "Married in the playground, at recess. I had a maid of honor and everything."

"And a tin foil ring," said Pepper.

"That isn't even legal..." protested Justin weakly, slipping his phone into his pocket, but they weren't listening to him anymore.

"And don't forget those two summers in high school," smiled Pepper.

She laughed back. "Never! I should have *known* you'd find me—I just got back to Eagle's Nest. Daddy's dying. And I'm helping host the president's daughters next week. God Pepper, I haven't seen you since that summer before twelfth grade, when I was still a brunette!"

That Saturday night in late August, before she'd gone away to a new boarding school in Switzerland, to be exact. At the insistence of her daddy, the billionaire a-hole Acker Smith, who was less than impressed with her wild, local boyfriend.

Pepper knew her father was sick, but dying? And he knew Smith was a political bedfellow of Wayne Garby, the most hated president in modern U.S. history. So Smith had recruited his own daughter to host the president's notoriously social twin daughters? That actually made sense.

"Right, not since the summer your mom died," Pepper agreed quietly. But his mind was racing with memories from that last summer. And racing with adrenaline—he suddenly felt seventeen years old again. "I just got back too. But I want to hear everything you've been doing all these years. I'll catch you later Maddie." When he handed back her ID, his fingers touched hers, almost accidentally, and she jumped a little.

Back in his cruiser, Pepper sat for a bit. Madeline Smith. Pepper faintly remembered the teenaged loss and emptiness that'd hit him that final August night, when Maddie told him on the beach below their houses she was going away. And Eagle's Nest was always a mile and a half down the beach from the Ryan home, a faint reminder whenever he drove past. Like catching a whiff of an old love's perfume. Especially when he heard the infamous noon ringing of Eagle's Nest's bell tower, her father's obnoxious sentimentality imported from the south of France for his French wife. Pepper had thought about Maddie a lot in the first years after she'd gone, then less often, then less intensely when he did.

But now Maddie had reopened the door and so of course he'd take her up on the invitation. It was serendipity, right? Pepper smiled, recalling how pissed her buddy Justin had appeared. That was okay with Pepper too. He decided he'd be visiting Maddie at Eagle's Nest absolutely as soon as possible.

Pepper hit his mike, informed Dispatch he was clear of the stop and was coming to the station.

"Roger that," replied Zula. "The Chief requested you touch base when you get in."

As feared. And Pepper hadn't connected with Special Agent Alfson.

"So, first ticket of the new week?" continued Zula's voice. "Our taxpayers will be so grateful..."

"Negative. Reduced to a warning."

"Oh, she must have been pretty! Was she, Pepper? Did you get her phone number?"

What could heart-of-stone Officer Pez say? Pepper just clicked off.

* * *

Oliver Young and his 'colleague' Croke were driving slowly in thick traffic along Route 28 late on that Monday morning, both quiet. Passing a seemingly endless parade of nautical mini-golf courses, ice cream stands and tacky restaurants.

Actually, Croke—a white-haired guy about a million years older than Oliver—was driving their Chevy Impala. Croke was a bit of a legend in their line of work, but the stories about him were all decades old. What was he—sixty? Don't hitmen retire? The brokers of this murder contract—a mob family in Queens, N.Y.—had paired Oliver with the dinosaur Croke, saying it was too big for a solo job, but maybe trusting the old-timer more than the new guy Oliver. Oliver had only completed one job for *them* before. Oliver had never seen Croke until two days ago and looked forward to never seeing him again after this job was in the can. The guy smelled like nervous body odor.

Oliver slouched down in the passenger seat. After a normal hit job, he would quickly be long gone. Goodbye, Cape Cod. Hello, Atlantic City? St. Louis? Wherever the road took him, as long as it was far away from the scene of the crime. And his karma had been shaky recently—why push it?

But this hit had been special—the jogger was some kind of cop—and the pay reflected it. And their bosses had instructed up front for Oliver and Croke to stay somewhat nearby because more work would soon follow. Maybe enough for Oliver to accumulate a haystack of cash so he could take a long deserved break. What he'd heard called 'fuck you' money. Oliver liked the sound of that.

So Oliver and Croke were guests at the modest Sanddollar Motel in Hyannis, about a half hour west of New Albion. And today they needed to check in with their bosses down in Queens, which was typically accomplished through quiet, mostly unused web chat sites. Phone calls with *them* were rare. Discouraged. Like many who earned their living in the discreet world of organized crime, *they* liked the internet's dark veil.

Free wifi was the Sanddollar Motel's biggest sales point on its sign since *POOL* had at some point been crossed out with a thick black line. But Oliver didn't want to shit where he ate, so to speak, and so he wasn't going to access the internet from their motel to chat about murdering people. Not even using coded language. Croke had grudgingly deferred to Oliver's suggestion to drive eastward along Route 28 and find anonymous internet access.

When they'd arrived on Cape Cod on Thursday, Oliver had expected to find a patchwork of cute little towns and villages. The footprints of wherever European settlers chose to set up, many centuries ago. Not the pilgrims exactly, but probably not too far after. Instead, he'd found Cape Cod was in fact just one long traffic jam.

Then Oliver saw a sign: Entering Chatham. Incorporated 1712. Yep, so practically pilgrims. Oliver nudged Croke who carefully parked on the little main street just after noon, practically in front of the stone steps of the Eldredge Public Library.

In Oliver's opinion, libraries were awesome. Total anonymity, privacy and protection for the general public. And librarians usually refuse to roll over for law enforcement efforts to monitor or track folks who used the library's computers, on principle. Ideal, right?

Until they got to the front door. Locked. They both tugged the door, peeped inside, all dark. Them Oliver saw the sign. Doesn't open until 1 PM on Mondays.

"Good thing they aren't trying to make any money..." Croke grumbled in his crabby Eastern European accent. Oliver's bosses had told him that Croke was from an area which used to be part of Czechoslovakia, or Slovakia, or somewhere in between.

Whatever. So they went and ate lunch nearby, pretty decent pizza. At exactly 1 PM, they were standing at the library's door again when a small, very elderly woman in a green pantsuit unlocked the front door and opened it as if they were her grandkids, finally coming to visit.

Oliver was a bit thrown and a confusing conversation began. It smoothed into what they were there for: computer access? She ushered them in and pointed them to the computer room near the magazine racks. A little peeling sticker on the computer said: *No water permitted in computer areas.* A little sign on the table said: *No food or beverages. One person per computer.*

Oliver sat at the furthest of three computers and Croke wandered away into the stacks of books. Oliver fired up the library's secure Tor Web browser. Logged on to the correct obscure, anonymous chat site.

And let out a quiet groan. The message said:

Charlie is unhappy...last surgery unsuccessful. May need corrective surgery to clean up something witnessed...will know soon. Pray...check tomorrow.

'Charlie' being their Queens bosses' weird codename for the client. Surgery unsuccessful? What was the client's problem—did the message mean there was a goddamn witness? Should Oliver and Croke call in and talk it through with *them*? But he knew *they* hated that.

The client had requested a splashy murder, the kind that gets lots of press. So sure, Oliver showed off a bit. Took the job to the next level, big time. Tried to show *them* how lucky *they* were to have Oliver on the assignment.

And yes, the clambake motif had been Oliver's idea. The client had told them to bury the body on a particular beach where a big hole would be waiting. They were also instructed to leave on the body an item that was delivered in their drop package: a red starfish. But inspiration had hit Oliver in his motel room bathroom while thumbing through a free tourism magazine, taking a dump. It had a big article with lots of pictures spelling out the ritual of a New England clambake, breaking down every step. The sheer charm of the clambake had caught his imagination. It seemed so...native.

And Oliver had never felt anything like the media response to the clambake murder. The newspaper headlines! The breathless anchorwoman leading with the story on the Boston evening news. It was more than a murder--it was a sensation, just because of the clambake angle. Even though there was no mention who the victim was, yet. And no mention about the cigar tube or the mystery note it probably held. The tube had been sealed shut when it arrived in the drop package with their boring but reliable Impala.

Sure, Oliver had murdered before. Four times. But always discreetly. Nothing to excite more attention than any other sad little crimes happening every day across America. It was just business, until now. The media coverage gave him a taste of what it'd be like to be famous. No, infamous...

But the word *'witness'* in the chat room message had left Oliver cold. The client's instruction had been clear—there could be no witnesses, no fuck-ups that could lead back to Oliver and Croke, let alone the client. What'd gone wrong?

Only a few people had entered the library since Oliver and Croke arrived. The librarian seemed to have forgotten them and was away from her desk, somewhere among the shelves. Croke reappeared at Oliver's side with a book in hand. "So hey? Everybody happy?" he muttered while flipping through the book, as if to act discreet.

"Our patron requested we stand by," said Oliver.

"Our who?"

"Our patron. The client."

"Stand by?" Croke repeated, his accent sounding heavy with skepticism. Maybe the older man was still reluctant to concede leadership to Oliver.

"Stay in the area and check tomorrow."

Croke paused, thinking. "Huh, so we are coming back tomorrow. I think I'll borrow this book. Keep me busy tonight."

"Croke, you're saying you wanna apply for a library card? Where we do our anonymous online chats with *them*?"

Croke looked hurt. "It seems pretty good...all about the history of salt. But it's *really* about how people in older times got rich, I think. And also about food."

What? "Well, you're not getting a library card. Obviously. So let's go."

Croke nodded grudgingly. He stretched, then pretended

42

to be tucking in his shirt. What he was doing, to Oliver's disgust, was slipping the damned salt book down the back of his pants.

"Okay, we go," said Croke.

What a partner-in-crime.

Old Lady Pantsuit was now back in her chair at the main desk. Oliver nodded innocently to her on their way out but she was doing something complicated with paper slips and didn't seem to notice their escape.

As Croke reversed from the parking spot in his jerky-jerky style, Oliver fished out of his pocket the special cell phone which had also been in the job's drop package. Small, blue and cool-looking. Expensive. Apparently with all kinds of encryption and other security, like the CIA uses in their spy network. A phone they'd been given in case, and only in case, the client suddenly needed to talk to Oliver and Croke directly. Which really, really should never happen. Their bosses said the client had required this special direct link, that it was a deal breaker.

But their bosses said Oliver and Croke shouldn't even think about using this blue phone to make any calls. Don't order a hooker. Don't even order a pizza. *They* hadn't been joking, because *they* don't joke. And don't fiddle with it, he'd been threatened--you try to crack open the phone case, maybe even breathe on it wrong, it self-destructs. Oliver thought *they* might be exaggerating about that part, maybe?

Oliver turned on the special phone. It'd been off since they received it. Not that the client would soon be calling them directly, right? This wasn't *that* kind of emergency. But maybe better to leave it on from now on. Just in case.

Oliver felt a surge of excitement and power. Electric, pounding adrenaline. He thought back to the crime scene, where he'd loitered anonymously for a while in the mob of gawkers, soaking in the big drama he'd created.

He decided to make the most of his time on Cape Cod. Sure, keep *them* happy, but completely hands off. Keep old man Croke under control and himself in charge. And if they got any follow-up assignments, Oliver would completely amaze the client, ignite the media and horrify the public.

Show the world something a little different...

SEVEN

Zula Eisenhower was in her pop's office when Pepper Ryan stopped in, as requested. Returning stud. Returning troublemaker. Pepper had lost his boyishness during his three years away, but that'd only made him more darkly handsome. Great hair. A big, white smile that spread from his lips to his light blue eyes. Wherever he'd been, he'd found time for workouts or hard labor—he was even stronger and leaner than he'd been during his college hockey career. Zula could see his neck muscles disappearing under his uniform shirt. She knew Pepper had been much swooned-over during his past in New Albion, and this new, mature edition of Pepper—more confident, more charismatic? He was going to be all kinds of trouble for the ladies of Cape Cod this summer...

She'd known Pepper since they were kids and had always felt close to him, although he was almost six years older than her. Maybe even kinda liked him over the years, except when he made her so mad she wanted to strangle him. But now? When she'd first seen Pepper again after his return, she'd instantly felt something different. Part raw itch, part wildfire. Zula had wanted to just grab Pepper and take him somewhere private. Or even better, have him do that to her... Her reaction had surprised, scared and exhilarated her.

"Missing Nashville yet, Pepper? That's where you came home from, right?" asked her pop.

"Just glad for a clean slate, sir. The chance to prove myself." Pepper's voice was calm and smooth, with just the right amount of bass.

Her pop snorted. "Why do I feel smoke blowing up my butthole? Sorry, Zula."

Yeah, like butthole was a new one to her. Did her pop think she was ten years old?

But he was already ignoring her again, laser-focused on Pepper. "But that's not why I called you in. What'd your new partner Alfson have to say this morning? You two making any progress on the Keser case?"

"We haven't talked yet today. But I have some ideas I'm headed out to look into."

Her pop shook his head. "That explains why I have these." He waived two old-fashioned red phone message slips. "One from Special Agent Alfson—does Officer Ryan have another number? And one from Special Agent in Charge Hanley—call him ASAP. Is your phone working?"

"Yessir."

"Well when you leave my office, use it. Call Alfson. Speak into the bottom, listen at the top. Communicate, cooperate. I'll wait thirty minutes before I call these gentlemen back and I want to hear they feel happy and loved by their local liaison."

Zula could see Pepper was wrestling internally to say something other than another 'yessir'. From the flex of his forearms, she guessed he was opening and closing his fists under the table. She could pretty much imagine what he was thinking. But ultimately—good thing—he said nothing. Just nodded, his face having reverted to stone.

"You want to redeem yourself, the Ryan family name?" her pop said in what Zula knew was his deadly serious voice. "Put away that guitar and make your dad proud this time? Here's your chance. I'm doing you a favor—this summer job...the clambake case. But I'm really doing it for your dad. So don't blow it again."

"Got it."

"You think it was funny, last time? Destroying that boat with the ice cream truck? Your one-man shitshow?"

"No sir."

Zula didn't know why her pop was poking Pepper about *that* again. "But that drug dealer left town and the pill problem at the schools dried up, right?" she asked.

Her pop gave her a glare to shush her. "The world's coming to New Albion this summer. Our town'll be overflowing with Secret Service. And Homeland Security, the FBI...you name it. And with the POTUS staying waterside, the Navy's here too." He grimaced. "Sure, we're the smallest turd in the bowl. The Secret Service is responsible for protecting the POTUS. But God-forbid anything goes wrong here? More dead bodies? Riots? Or heavenly-God-forbid someone takes a shot at the POTUS? It's New Albion that goes down in history with the black eye. Like goddamn Dealey Plaza. So you know what this means?"

"Overtime?" asked Pepper.

Zula choked back a smile.

Her pop stayed dead serious. "It means, get along with your Special Agent Alfson better than you have so far. I hear he's on the fast track, being groomed for Hanley's level. Maybe that's why he wasn't such a fan of working with you. Maybe you look like a danger to everything he's been working for. But just cooperate. Catch those clambake assholes, quick. And whatever you do, keep me up to date."

"Yessir." Pepper paused, thoughtful, then his eyes locked on hers. "If I need a hand when things get busy, can I have Zula? Maybe for some NGI searches or other research?"

Zula sat upright. Research? She liked the idea of helping Pepper with the Keser case, but who did he think she was, his assistant?

Her pop was shaking his head *no* anyway. "Zula has a full load on Dispatch. The Secret Service has all the researchers you'll need if you ask politely. And Pepper? You're starting with strike two. If you get the urge to think outside the goddamn box, and that box is local, state or federal law, just quit first. Again."

* * *

Pepper had invited Special Agent Dan Alfson to meet him at the police station to touch base and was surprised when Alfson arrived accompanied by five Secret Service investigators. Pepper would have brought a bag of bagels.

The meeting was super serious, professional and not very productive. The youngest agent walked them through the case book—initial reports from the New Albion police, evidence and medical report, witness statements. The crime scene area had yielded a mishmash of potential evidence— cigarette butts, footprints, hairs, etc. But each much more likely to have been left there by someone other than the unsubs or the victim. The autopsy had yielded a couple tidbits. Gravel was found embedded in Keser's hands with related hand scrapes. Road rash. This supported the theory that Keser was grabbed mid-jog. He also had a fresh bruise on the back of his head. They watched overhead video of the clambake pit and beach area that the Secret Service had taken with a drone but Pepper didn't pick up anything helpful from that angle. Cool to see, though.

Another investigator shared progress on Keser's movements prior to his death. The last part was easy—he'd been seen by another agent heading out for a run, which he was known to do five or so days a week. The investigators were reconstructing the forty-eight hours leading up to Keser's death in case his work or other activities somehow related to why he was killed, but hadn't identified any connections yet.

A team at Quantico was analyzing the note found on the body. Alfson said they didn't have any solid theories yet about the Declaration of Independence or the odd accusation that the POTUS took the unsubs' candy, but they should have a profile completed soon.

"The candy thing creeps me out the most," said Pepper. It's so juvenile and...personal."

"Maybe," said Alfson. "We'll wait for our pros to tell us what it means, if that's okay."

Which bugged Pepper, but not as much as that the Secret Service team had pretty much nothing to run with, so far.

"Can I get a copy of your case book?" Pepper asked.

After a pause, Alfson approved that with a short nod. "But the local angle, Pepper—let's peel the onion. What've you got so far?"

To which he had to admit the truth—not even bagels. But Pepper had a plan...

* * *

Pepper needed to bring local genius to the clambake homicide investigation, right? He used to know most of the

49

wack jobs and lowlifes in lower Cape Cod. But having been away for three years, he didn't have any confidence in his grasp of the current players. So Pepper went to see a guy who would know. The only question was whether the guy would still talk to him.

Pepper pulled into the parking lot of the waterfront restaurant and bar that in Pepper's youth had been a restaurant called Sandy's Seafood. The big blue sign now read Malecón. His father had told him this place was the new venture of Pepper's oldest buddy growing up, Angel Cavada. Another person Pepper had flaked out on, when he'd taken off three years earlier, not long after Jake died. It still made Pepper sick to his stomach, how he'd treated Angel. Had he forgiven Pepper?

The teenage hostess said Angel was expected soon, so Pepper took a stool at the bar by the back wall to wait. Behind the bar was an enormous painting of a harbor waterfront. Somewhere in Cuba? Pepper ordered a jack and coke from a Latina bartender with a name tag that said *Summer*.

Malecón was cool. A blend of styles between Cuban and Cape Cod. Lots of wood. Light colors. Pepper knew Angel's parents had arrived from Cuba on a scrap wood and plastic bottle raft thirty years ago, before Angel was born, so it'd be beautiful if Angel made his American millions by tapping his Cuban heritage.

Angel came through the front door ten minutes later. Maybe a few extra pounds on his five foot nine frame, but pretty much unchanged. A quick back and forth with the hostess, followed by Angel's signature laugh. Deep, loud and infectious. Pepper saw the hostess laughing along--what choice did anyone have?

Angel saw Pepper at the bar. Angel did a little double-take, then sauntered over, his face having dropped its smile. This Angel was more serious. More guarded?

"Hey, *Mano*, I heard a rumor you were still alive..." said Angel. "I thought maybe you went Wonderboy for real, but I never saw you in the movies. Or maybe over to Milan, modeling, making millions in your underwear?"

Pepper got off his stool, started with a handshake that morphed into a half hug and a backslap. Kinda awkward.

"Angel, you did it man! This is the place you always used to talk about!"

Angel gave a nod. "Opened a year ago. Had to go for it, right? And so far so good. The food's the real deal. But the waitresses!" Angel kissed his fingers. "I pick 'em myself. Sweetest on the Cape! But the real magic's out back, you got a minute to see?"

So Pepper followed Angel through a door into a back patio which was bigger than the restaurant. Part garden, part patio bar. With a stage tucked away at one end. And an amazing view of the Atlantic Ocean.

"This is the key to the whole place," said Angel. Pepper could hear the quiet pride in his voice. "I took down a ton of trees and bam, there it was--the big blue ocean! I would have invited you to the opening, but no one knew where to reach you. What the fuck?" A simple question loaded with disappointment.

Pepper told his story. Said he'd been kind of freaked out by Jake's death and then getting suspended. Said he was sorry for not keeping in touch, which sounded hollow and strange even to his own ear. He added that he'd been playing music in Nashville most recently.

"A Nashville star! I could have predicted it. *Mano*, tell me you know Blake Shelton!"

"I sure do! Unfortunately, he doesn't know me..."

Angel laughed a little louder, a little more like himself. "Well, tell me you've come home to do a musical residency, right by the ocean. Music five nights a week out here. All I'm missing is a rugged scamp like you to sit on a stool and play Jimmy Buffet, Kenny Chesney, all those island booze songs. You used to play guitar decent enough. But your voice, kid, and your pretty face—the ladies'll line up all the way back to the Sagamore. You still got perfect pitch?"

Shit. Pepper pictured how the General would react if he heard Pepper was moonlighting. "Angel, I'm back with the Albion police. It's a favor to Chief Eisenhower. I won't have much time to serenade tourists."

"Whoa!" said Angel. Visibly recoiling.

"Really...I'm back to do a job. And I was hoping you could do me a solid? Fill me in on some info?"

Angel was just studying him, maybe a little too hard. "Home ten minutes and you've already broken my heart again." Another pause, then: "What do you need?"

Pepper explained he was gathering unofficial dirt on criminal groups in the area, especially those that hid behind legitimate fronts and so might be cruising under the police radar.

Angel yawned. "There's still the low-key drug dealing. Some folks selling meth. Some oxy or synthetics. The usual B&Es at vacation homes. All petty shit—near the lowest end of the food chain. Are those the types of folks you're looking for?"

Pepper took a deep breath and thought, *fuck it.* He explained to Angel about the clambake victim being Secret Service, how they were testing a theory he was killed by one or more locals with a hatred for President Garby. Maybe a radical activist group—what the feds would call domestic terrorists. "But they'd cut off my nuts for telling you, so keep this secret, okay?"

"Whoa!" said Angel, shaking his head. Then he sat thinking a bit. "I don't agree you're chasing homegrown lowlifes. Not much fuss from extremist groups locally. Maybe the worst of the environmentalists, like the PLANT folks over in Wellfleet, but murder? Not really their gig. My gut, I think you're after vacationing lowlifes. I'd check with Nancy over at New Albion Realty. Remember her? Black hair? Big...eyes? Maybe better you don't use my name. Anyway, dust off the old Pepper Ryan charm and get a list of homes rented in the general area to a single party for multiple weeks."

Not a bad thought. "Buddy, I'm glad to see you're still a genius."

"Oh, and have you been tracking down a witness too?"

"Witness? No, why?"

"I heard somebody saw the clambake victim getting grabbed. Maybe just a rumor."

Pepper tried to get more out of Angel but he couldn't recall who he'd heard it from, or anything else to help chase the rumor back to its source. But Angel promised to keep his ears peeled and call Pepper right away with any further gossip.

"Oh, speaking of gossip," said Pepper. "You'll never guess who I saw the other day!"

"Madeline Smith?"

Good fucking guess. "How'd you know?"

Angel laughed. "You think Pepper Ryan being back in town's a big deal? *Mano*, Madeline Smith is the hottest of hot tickets—she's international gossip page one. They take her picture in a restaurant, its booking system gets blown out the next day. She dates someone, he becomes the media's 'It' guy. And she's entertaining the presidential twins when they arrive… So hey, do me a solid bro—get Maddie to bring the twins to Malecón? This place'll be legendary. And I think she had a thing for me, back in the day…"

Instead of an answer, Pepper gave him a hug. "I missed you, pal. And I appreciate your help."

Angel just gave him a light punch on the shoulder. "There's millions to be made on the Cape bro, all kinds of ways, except driving around in a cop car chasing down mouth breathers. Now you're back, you and I should own this town by Labor Day. At least tell me you'll think about it!"

New Albion would never be the same, thought Pepper. "I'll hop onstage sometime when I can. I promise. And damn, I miss performing almost as much as I've missed your evil laugh. It's great to see you again, Angel. I'm glad you're living the dream."

"Fuckin' A. You hear I'm on the Chamber of Commerce?"

* * *

Pepper strolled into the New Albion station house a bit later that afternoon. He had a five-page list of all multi-week house rentals on Cape Cod, courtesy of Nancy from eleventh-grade homeroom. Yes, he was back in town. No, he hadn't heard about her wedding. But she'd been happy as a clam to help him out.

Zula was on the desk with Barbara Buckley, the Dispatch Supervisor, nearby in her wheelchair. Barbara was chatting away on her headset and Zula wasn't, so Pepper pounced.

"Busy?" he asked Zula with a smile.

She studied him with her big brown eyes more than a little suspiciously, then gave a quick glance over at Barbara who was still chatting. "What'd you have in mind?" she asked.

He pulled the list from behind his back. "I know what your dad said, but this'll be quick. Is there a way you can check a list of local addresses against the dispatch blotter to find any matches? It might be super important, for the clambake case."

She held up a hand, took a call. Dispatched EMS.

Barbara Buckley was still on her call but she caught Pepper's eye, grimaced. He'd known Barbara since he was a little boy and that's how she still treated him.

Zula clicked off her call. "How'd you get this list?"

"Expert investigation, my methods are classified. But it's too many addresses for me to visit and time's, you know, of the essence. I hoped maybe the scumbags have already gotten some police attention. And one other little thing?"

She gave him a long sigh.

"A red starfish was in the clambake pit, on the body. I've never seen a red starfish around Cape Cod, and no one in their right mind eats starfish anyway, so why put one in the pit? Ignorance or maybe something else? Can you google around, see if there are any red starfish locally? I'll text you a picture of the one from the crime scene, maybe it'll help you figure out what type of starfish, where it came from? And if it's not local, maybe who sells them?"

"Shouldn't the Secret Service be doing this?"

"They probably are. But they don't know the Cape the way you do. They might not connect the dots on something a native soul like yourself would see, no problem. Please?"

"Push off, Pepper," said Barbara, having finally finished her call. "Sniff around my girl after hours, would ya?"

Zula tucked the list under some manila folders and gave a bigger, more dramatic sigh. "These favors are adding up, Wonderboy. You're going to have to make it up to me somehow, big time. And don't think you can get free favors by having your dad ask again!"

"What?"

"The inventory of all the seafood found in the clambake murder pit, that your dad said you wanted? He asked me to get it from the feds, said you'd owe me. I gave it to him half an hour ago."

What the hell? Pepper tried to hide his surprise. And Barbara was still glaring at them, so with a final smile to Zula, he pushed off.

Because he needed to find out what his dad, the supposedly retired Chief of Police, was up to now...

* * *

"You just missed him," grinned old Mr. Kierce at Orleans Seafood Market. Flashing what locals call "summer" teeth (some're there, some're missing).

Pepper's dad hadn't answered his cell phone or the home landline, so Pepper had taken his hunt to the open road, guessing the ex-cop would begin with Kierce—his favorite seafood proprietor—when searching for the source of the seafood in the Keser clambake.

Pepper thanked Mr. Kierce and headed back to his police cruiser. Unless his dad had changed, Pepper had a good guess where he'd have headed next.

And yep, bingo! Pepper found his dad sitting on a picnic bench at High Seas Ice Cream Hut, which was too close in proximity to the Orleans Seafood Market for him not to stop in for a quick cone. Ice cream was one of his dad's very few human weaknesses.

"Hey Pepper!" his dad said, with a little wave of his cone. Looked like vanilla infused with red sauce...Raspberry

Ripple?

Pepper joined him on the bench. Pepper didn't say anything—he just gave back the kind of look his dad had given Pepper so many times before. Disgust and Disappointment Ripple.

But his dad only chuckled. "I guess Zula spilled the beans?"

Yeah, hilarious, but Pepper tried to keep his cool. "I've got a question…when you were chief, what would you've done if a civilian decided to get involved in solving a murder?"

"Civilian?" his dad sniffed. "I'm a sworn deputy of Barnstable County!"

Which was true, barely. About a year after his dad had resigned as New Albion Chief of Police under the financial and political cloud of an embarrassing lawsuit, he'd quietly been sworn in as a deputy by his close friend, the Barnstable County sheriff. It'd been a gesture of respect, an honorary role.

Pepper put on a Barbara Buckley-quality grimace. "You're retired."

"And you're a hard guy to help."

His dad wanted to help him? Or did he just want to show Pepper up? But Pepper's curiosity was getting the better of him. "So did Kierce think they sold that shellfish?"

"Nope. He said the list was a real mishmash of low-end product, not right for a good clambake. Probably a New Yorker or other mental defective, he said. Classic old Kierce! But I know all the other stores and docks that the perps could have bought it from in this part of the Cape, so I'll check around some more. A clerk might remember them and there might be security tape. Maybe they even left credit card info, if they're as stupid as Kierce says."

Pepper suspected they weren't. They'd probably bought the mussels, quahogs and other shellfish in small batches from different stores, paid in cash. He'd have to ask Alfson whether his small army of investigators had begun chasing this seafood angle yet. Same for the other stuff used in the pit—the tarp and the canvas, if the Service thought they were new. But Kierce's comment was interesting—it made Pepper question whether the clambake pit and murder were actually the work of a local. Something to consider further.

"But seriously Dad, you need to stop."

His dad grunted. "Kierce said no one'd been in yet to even ask about the seafood list. So maybe you and the feds need all the help you can get? 'Cause if I solve this case first, everyone wins, right?" said his dad, sounding tough and unrepentant, but the raspberry ripple had melted onto his hand and he had a crooked smile on his face.

EIGHT

Smith Enterprises' Gulfstream G650 jet landed gently at Barnstable Municipal Airport on Monday afternoon. Its only passenger, Lizzie Concepcion, was in a limousine ten minutes later. Depending on traffic to the Smith estate in New Albion, Lizzie figured she might have about forty-five minutes left to her career as Special Assistant to the billionaire fund executive Acker Smith.

She worked at Eagle's Nest daily, but the sight as she came up the long driveway never failed to impress. It was a French Chateau style mansion in the tradition of "*Mangez la merde*, you peasants". Totally over the top. Mr. Smith had built it for his late wife, a minor French actress named Sophie Bissonette. Gray stone everywhere, like a castle. It had fifteen bedrooms, one which had basically become Lizzie's. The mansion also had a cute bowling alley, an oversized swimming pool and tennis courts on a twelve-acre wedge lot with private beach.

The limousine parked in front of the main house beside the large, round spewing fountain with a giant, naked Greek nymph statue. Lizzie stared up at the nymph and made a little fist pump. *You and me, sister.*

Lizzie was completely stressed out over the pending

arrival of the President of the United States. Did Mr. Smith invite President Garby to vacation at his compound or did President Garby invite himself? The origin was a little muddled, but Mr. Smith's true feelings about President Garby were unambiguous. Mr. Smith was seething. He was fixated on how betrayed he already felt, a little more than a year into Garby's presidency. Now the president was coming to Eagle's Nest with an agenda that was crassly, pathetically transparent—to beg Mr. Smith for more money. Lots more. And with a new level of urgency, apparently driven by reports of Mr. Smith's imminent death. Lizzie would have to be on top of her game...unless Mr. Smith fired her in the next few minutes?

Lizzie hurried up the broad staircase as quickly as her four-inch Jimmy Choo heels would permit. But then she stood at Mr. Smith's bedroom door for two minutes. Paralyzed by strong emotions. Agonizing over what to say. And whether Mr. Smith's legendary temper would take over, shoot the messenger? She took a deep breath. Raked her fingers through her shoulder-length, chestnut brown hair— her nervous tic. Turned the doorknob and entered.

It was dark in Smith's bedroom, as always. Smith couldn't take much light in his condition, it gave him blinding headaches. An overdose of lavender scent permeated the room despite the open balcony doors.

Her boss was sitting in a chair out on the master balcony under a broad awning. He was wearing large, dark sunglasses. He looked...well, he looked like he was dying. Waxy pale, but with darkened patches of skin. And so thin now.

"Good morning, sir. How are you feeling?" she asked tentatively.

"A little better today."

She made the appropriately supportive noises, even

though feeling a little bit better wasn't going to help him in the end, right? "Let me get your tea."

Mr. Smith had begun to feel sick quite suddenly four months ago. It started with stomachaches. Some nausea and vomiting. Progressed to liver and kidney damage. A rapid fall from the picture of health to someone who didn't have the physical strength to walk across a room. His mind was still strong sometimes, but often distracted. Only his infamous temper remained intact, exploding when people didn't expect it, showing flashes of the legendary hedge fund leader's fire and intensity.

Lizzie had brought in a parade of men in white coats to Eagle's Nest. They'd examined their patient exhaustively, she'd made sure. They'd drawn his blood multiple times, reported back every result. They all told Mr. Smith the same thing. He had Stage IV pancreatic cancer, caught way, way too late. It had metastasized to distant organs. Surgery was not an option. Realistically, the only focus was to manage his pain and other symptoms. Maybe reduce his jaundice, help his appetite. A steady dose of opioids for the pain. Maybe a few months to live. Maybe only weeks.

After returning with his special tea, she gave him a little space. The balcony faced east and the morning sun was still rising over the choppy Atlantic, casting its orange glow. It contrasted dramatically with the estate's green lawn and towering white flagpole, fifty-four feet high, with its colossal American flag twisting and flapping in the morning wind. Oddly, there was not a person in sight, from the long swimming pool and low property outbuildings to the broad lawn and the beach beyond. She squinted past the harbor's island breakwater to the fishing boats and sailboats coming and going. She saw Mr. Smith's superyacht, *Madeline Too*, waiting at anchor in deeper water a bit further out.

Lizzie had been Acker Smith's right-hand woman for two-and-a-half years. Her title was Special Assistant, but she was more than his *asistente*. She had an MBA from Tuck. She had her CFA. She'd survived five years in Washington D.C.'s lobbyist jungle working for the National Mining Association, where she'd learned way too much about the mining industry. But more importantly, she'd learned how power worked and why the weak stayed weak. Everyone in Smith's financial empire knew she was his proxy—especially since he'd grown sick. She knew many of them didn't like to take orders from the new Latina with Smith's ear. And she guessed what gossip they spread. But she couldn't count the many times Mr. Smith told her she was smart, talented and indispensable.

Smart enough to fear this morning she was about to be fired.

As Mr. Smith sipped his tea, she quickly recapped her trip. A weekend in Miami, where the work being done to the hull of *Madeline*—Smith's other superyacht—was going well. *Madeline* was an identical twin vessel to *Madeline Too*. Mr. Smith had said she didn't need to check on the work herself, but as she'd gently pointed out, this was the level of attention that'd made her so successful. Mr. Smith's right-hand woman had to be there. That's how she got things done. She'd been right down in the guts of the ship with an independent expert—a very expensive friend of a friend—at her side during the most delicate work, making sure no corners were cut and everything was absolutely perfect. The shipyard idiots resented her intrusion, but she got her way, as always. That was her superpower...

Then she'd flown in the Gulfstream to Stamford, Connecticut. To the headquarters of Smith Capital Management Group LLC, the golden heart of Smith Enterprises.

Acker Smith was one of the original, revolutionary hedge fund specialists. Smith Capital Management reflected his maverick style and aggressive investment strategies. They ran multi-strategy funds. Credit funds. Collateralized loan obligations. Real estate funds. Or any other alternative investment vehicles that could make him a buck.

But Mr. Smith's time at the headquarters had almost completely stopped as his illness progressed. Lizzie had become his proxy. And she'd spent a very busy Monday morning there, which was the delicate topic.

"Mr. Smith, I have some bad news." She tried to deliver it as gently as possible. That two of his traders and his Chief Operating Officer had been meeting with Ben Yang, Principal at the Winn Funds. A top rival for Smith Capital Management. She told him their conversation was exploring two paths: a merger between the two hedge fund families or a lift out of the traders, the COO and some key portfolio people. And a deal was going to be cut very soon—not waiting for Mr. Smith's death. Smith would be hit with an ultimatum: merge with Winn, or else the three ringleaders would take so much of his team that Smith Capital Management would be crippled. She knew this fear had been on Smith's mind for weeks—everyone knew he was dying and so it was open season to try and pick off his top people, his clients, his whole operation.

Smith's waxy face paled even whiter. He was trembling. Lizzie knew the only thing Mr. Smith valued more than money was loyalty.

"Arrange to fly them here," he said in a weak, raspy voice. "I want those people to look me in the eye. Tell me to my face."

But now the really delicate part. "Sir, I hope I didn't do something wrong but I told HR you wanted their positions terminated. And told Security to remove them from headquarters this afternoon. It's all happening right now."

Lizzie's voice cracked, but she pushed forward. "Mr. Smith, I should have talked to you first! But if they found out you knew, they'd have jumped. I made sure HR is terminating for cause. A long list of misbehaviors. They'll be in no position to steal any performance or position data or recruit away anyone. I also instructed Legal to file suit against Winn for interference with employment contracts. That should make Winn back off from hiring those traitors."

Mr. Smith was still too pale, still shaking. But he was drinking his tea. Thinking. Having moved from shock into a low boiling rage. Balancing out Lizzie's independent and bold actions. But also the need for quick vengeance.

Would she be next to be fired?

Mr. Smith's cell phone rang. He slowly found it in his bathrobe pocket and pulled it out, put it on speaker.

It was the heads of Legal, HR and Security, two men and a woman, calling from Stamford. They were about to act and wanted to confirm the plan with Mr. Smith himself. Maybe to make sure his legendary temper hadn't cooled. Or that his pushy *asistente* hadn't overstepped her authority?

Mr. Smith sat studying Lizzie like he was counting up her many mistakes. Lizzie's heart was in her stomach. The wind kicked up, swirling her long dark hair. Over the shoreline she could see a tern riding the wind, quickly flying sideways. Effortlessly. The sight made Lizzie jealous.

"Pull the trigger," Mr. Smith said. "And make it as painful and embarrassing for them as possible. I want you to claw back their last two years' bonuses. Levy against their bank accounts today."

"Ah," said the General Counsel. "We do have the power in the employment agreements to do that, technically. But—

"

"Fuck but!" yelled Smith in a broken, half-scratch voice. "Today! And if their bank accounts don't have the money, file liens against their homes. Take their goddamn cars. Scorched earth. And anyone with FINRA licenses, you list plenty of damn cause in their U-5 filings. Make them fucking unemployable."

Another voice cut in. The woman, the head of HR. "We hear you Mr. Smith, but can I suggest—"

"Today! Show everyone else how I treat traitors. I'm not dead yet, goddamn it!" The last sentence was intense but quieter. He sat back in his chair. He was sweating and his face was contorted. "And make sure Brandon Blacklock knows *exactly* what happened to them."

Blacklock was Smith's star portfolio manager, especially in his own mind. Lizzie'd told Mr. Smith that Blacklock had been exceeding his authority at the Stamford headquarters in recent months, acting almost proprietary. Throwing around his considerable weight (the slob had to weight over 300 pounds). Lizzie was actually surprised Blacklock hadn't been part of this coup. She jotted Blacklock's name and direct office number on a yellow sticky note, beneath an unrelated to-do she'd already recorded. She was so darn busy she could barely keep track. But she needed to make sure Blacklock had gotten Mr. Smith's message: *know your place*. Blacklock had been paid tens of millions in recent years, but he was one of those singular assholes whose appetite for money—and power—had no earthly limit. She'd unfortunately learned all too well about *that* type during her D.C. years...

"Ah, screw 'em all," whispered Mr. Smith. Maybe too faintly for the phone people to hear. But it was done. Mr. Smith reached for her hand, squeezed it to reassure her. Or himself? Then his hand slid loose and shifted to her knee, rested there.

But Lizzie still had her job.

"Sorry sir, but I have one other piece of news," she said. "The body they found on the beach? It was a secret service agent doing advance work for the president's visit here."

"What?"

She told him the basics of the story she'd heard from locals with inside access. "I wanted to make sure you're still comfortable with *your* plan."

"Screw Garby too," said Smith, more weakly now. "No changes...I still want our fucking president to have as miserable a vacation as you can arrange without breaking the law or getting caught. If someone's distracted the Secret Service, well, that'll only make it easier for you, right?"

Lizzie said nothing more. She would bury herself in preparations for the president's arrival at Eagle's Nest. She would keep her head down, focus on execution. Leave worrying and sleep to those with spare time.

"Daddy? Am I *interrupting* something?" Madeline Smith stood in the balcony doorway. Her manicured hands hooded her eyes against the sunlight, a look of concern (or suspicion?) spoiling the undeniable charm of her face.

Lizzie's own face burned. She reflexively stood and stepped a bit away from Mr. Smith, his hand falling off her knee. Lizzie immediately wished she hadn't. Who did Madeline think she was, the spoiled little brat? The daughter's recent arrival at Eagle's Nest, her first time in Lizzie's years with Mr. Smith, had been nothing but another headache for Lizzie, another problem to juggle. And she suspected the girl was only home for more money—a fat reward to host the notorious First Daughters, or maybe even bigger? To confirm her precious inheritance was safely intact?

But Lizzie choked back indignance and pride. She forced herself to smile at the girl. This was *not* the time to make new enemies, unless provoked...
Focus on execution.

* * *

Pepper was finishing a couple of slices at Broken Dreams Antiques and Pizzeria when Special Agent Dan Alfson entered. Broken Dreams was a big, uncluttered antique store, with a pizzeria in the back. You could sit anywhere among the antiques with your food and everything in the place was for sale except the brick oven. Alfson wove through the aisles of old furniture and curios to Pepper's place at an iron French bistro table with three chairs, sat down. Cast judgment over Pepper's pizza with a short glance and a sniff. Maybe not the ham-and-pineapple type, so another strike against him.

"I've got a bone to pick with you, Ryan," Alfson began. "Don't you answer your phone? It's almost five o'clock and we need to touch base. Hanley's been all over my ass." He flicked an invisible bit of lint off his suit jacket sleeve.

"AT&T's a little spotty in parts of New Albion."

"Well, no surprise. But you heard our bosses. We're supposed to be working together and I can barely track you down. Maybe too busy talking to the press?"

"What?" asked Pepper, mouth full.

"It's all over the news the clambake body's a Secret Service agent. Do we have you to thank?"

What? "Alf, I haven't said jack to any reporters. Not a word. So maybe check your own team?"

Alfson snorted. "You're my only wild card. And it's Dan. Only my friends use Alf."

Ouch. But Pepper let the pain go. "Has your team found where the seafood came from?"

"The seafood? Ryan, just a guess—the ocean?"

"But did the unsubs harvest it themselves? I bet they probably bought it. Did your lab say how fresh it all was? How many types of clams? Maybe they purchased it from somewhere nearby on the Cape…"

The agent pulled out his phone hastily, then more casually got up and wandered away. Came back.

"Probably a long shot, but my folks'll chase that down for you."

Pepper tried a little Zula-mindfulness breathing, so he wouldn't strangle the guy. "Okay, so have you confirmed Keser's last hours yet? What advance work he'd handled? I was wondering, did he have run-ins with people on your watch lists or with any terror groups in the area?"

Alfson shook his head. "Nothing like that. Keser had been at Eagle's Nest for six days with nine other agents. He'd been verifying the compound's vulnerable points. Handling interviews and background checks on Smith's staff, the usual. Inspecting the bulletproof windows installed in the Guest House. Lots of moving parts. We had other agents working off property, following up some security threats and logistical problems for emergency evacuations. They contacted people in the area on our Class Lists, people who'd posed a past threat. But Keser wasn't in those interviews. Why?"

Well," said Pepper through the last mouthful of his slice. "If I told you a militia group visiting town had more than a few sandy shovels on their front porch, what would you say?"

Alfson blinked, as if in disbelief. Stood up again. "I'd say you've been holding out on me."

NINE

Pepper gave Special Agent Alfson a lift out to Murray Road in his squad car.

Pepper really hadn't been holding out on Alfson very long. Not on that particular news. Maybe fifteen minutes before Alfson had interrupted Pepper's meal, Zula Eisenhower had called Pepper. She hadn't worked her way through much of the list yet, but she'd recognized one rental property address at first glance since it was on the overnight blotter for a noise complaint. A patrol officer named Dooley had stopped in briefly, asked the occupants to lower the volume, and had gotten out of there.

Zula said she'd called the officer to get more details. He said he'd gotten a pretty hostile reception—maybe they hated redheads? One man had reluctantly produced ID and although it looked like a driver's license it wasn't issued by any of the fifty states. "Do militias take vacations?" Dooley had asked her. "Because if yes, that's what we've got." And the officer recalled there was a sizable cluster of shovels covered in sand leaning on the porch railing. More than might be normal.

Alfson was rubbing his cheeks and his left knee was unconsciously bouncing up and down. Trying to come up with alternate, innocent explanations of the shovels? But Alfson phoned someone on his team to let them know where they were going.

As they drove, Alfson riffed on a topic he clearly loved: himself. He was a former detail guy, now back in the field. He'd been assigned by Hanley as a back up of the intelligence squad. He didn't necessarily agree with Hanley that anything too unusual was going on, because trouble was routine for them.

"Our license plate scanners have picked up at least nine groups in town so far," said Alfson with a yawn. "Several militia, anti-government or anarchist organizations. Let's see, so far your little town's got the Green Mountain Free Militia, the Black Stand, the New River Front, the KKK, the list goes on. All the usual shit disturbers and media mosquitoes. They usually do more damage to each other than create a security risk for the POTUS, but we'll be watching. And I suggest you locals get your ducks in a row."

What would Pepper do without him?

At the rental house, a heavyset man answered Pepper's knock. He was wearing only a pair of gray boxer shorts whose elastic waist had surrendered the fight. They drooped low on one fat hip, somehow not slipping to the man's ankles. But shockingly, he was not in charge. Droopy-drawers went to get someone else.

Pepper craned his neck to peek in. He could see all the way to the kitchen. The hallway had a small table that was empty except for a sleek blue cell phone, some model Pepper didn't recognize.

A different man came down the hall, picking up the cell phone mid-stride and slipping it into his pocket. He stayed on his side of the screen door, didn't invite them in. He said his name was Brian Edward Westin. A short white guy, probably late fifties. A belligerent tilt to his face. Pepper could tell Westin was in charge because he was wearing both a t-shirt and pants.

Alfson had grudgingly agreed in the car to let Pepper take the lead. It made sense to keep this visit from sounding like part of a federal investigation, for now. So Pepper introduced himself, flashing his badge, and said he was following up on the noise complaint from last night. He introduced Alfson but didn't mention he was Secret Service. "We heard you had quite a gathering last night. Are you guys some kind of club or organization?" Pepper asked Westin through the screen door.

"Why, you hoping to sign up?"

Pepper heard laughter from back in the house. Westin was playing to a peanut gallery.

Pepper tried to stay calm. "Are you planning to hold any public demonstrations while you're in town? Maybe get a permit, that sort of thing?"

More laughter from back in the house.

Two trucks pulled into the long dirt driveway side-by-side behind Pepper's cruiser but no one climbed out.

"How long have you folks been in town?" asked Pepper.

"Since last Saturday."

Pepper was surprised the group hadn't hit the police radar earlier. "What's the deal with all the spades?" Pepper asked with a nod across the porch, where a group of flat tipped garden spades was tossed in a loose pile, as the patrol officer had remembered. They were crusted with sand. "You guys into building sandcastles?"

"Spades? Nobody here but us whites, officer."

More laughter from the back room.

But Westin had more. "You really here about that clambake stiff? Did somebody say we did him?"

"Did you?" asked Alfson.

"No way. Where we come from, we would just shoot him and leave him. If someone's pointing at us that's a lie I'd take pretty personal."

"Good to know," said Pepper. "But you got any weapons on the property?"

Westin smiled. "We're free men, gotta protect ours. You know how many Americans are killed by illegal immigrants each year?"

"I'm not here to debate, Mr. Westin," said Pepper. "I'm here to tell you how it works in our little town. You break Mass firearm laws or get out of line with public demonstrations? You'll be finishing your vacation at MCI-Cedar Junction."

Westin spat on the front hall floor. "You think we're here just to hear ourselves talk, while illegals flood what's left of our fine nation? We got Garby elected but he hasn't done anything to solve the problem. So he *is* the problem. Why should he have a peaceful vacation while our nation's going down the toilet? You think you intimidate me? Coming on our property with just this scarecrow for backup? Bring a war to my doorstep, try to embarrass me? In my country, son, your kind always gets what it deserves, times ten. Now run along and have a nice fucking day."

The men who'd arrived were now out of their trucks, milling, staring up at the screen door conference, discontent. About to join them on the porch maybe.

Time to go before they had to shoot someone. "Well, if you have questions about how to do things right in my town, you give me a call," said Pepper. He tucked in the edge of the screen door a generic New Albion Police business card with his name and cell number written in on it.

Westin just smiled. "Come back anytime. But, hey?

Bring better backup."

Pepper and Alfson walked back through the cluster of men, not stopping when one of them, a guy with a curly mop of hair, said something. Not stopping when some of them laughed.

The two trucks behind his cruiser meant he couldn't back down the driveway. And he wasn't going to ask them to move because he knew what their answer would be.

So Pepper drove forward onto the grass and did a turnaround on the front lawn. Maybe hit the gas a little more than he had to, because his rear wheels spun and slid, ripping up the lawn and spitting dirt toward the front porch as he swung around the trucks, back to the road.

"Hey!" yelled Alfson.

"Oops."

As they drove back toward downtown, Alfson made a call. Pretty quiet, Pepper couldn't hear much of it. A couple minutes later he got a call back. Info about Brian Edward Westin.

"He's got a hyphen between his first two names," shared Alfson. "Brian-hyphen-Edward Westin. He's the leader of the New River Front. What they call a "sovereign citizens" group. American patriots fighting a complex government conspiracy that most Americans are too stupid to understand. Champions of the effort to change the fourteenth amendment that grants citizenship to anyone born on U.S. soil. And deny birth certificates and Medicaid to children of illegal immigrants. They're also working to create an alternate currency because, you know, the American currency is doomed."

"That brand of patriotism," said Pepper.

"Also known as an anti-government extremist group. Ties to white nationalist groups. Good old-fashioned conspiracy theorists. And Westin seemed like a jackass, but don't take him too lightly. He's ex-military—75th Rangers. More dangerous than he looked. Plenty of training to be our killer. And he left the army OTH—bad papers. I'm having someone look into why they tossed him…maybe that's part of his grudge."

Pepper was surprised by that news. He knew their quick retreat from the rental property would be interpreted as weakness, like blood in the water for sharks. Despite Pepper's obnoxious lawn job. Give the New River Front confidence for whatever shit they were planning to disturb. Not Pepper's finest moment, but what was the alternative--a shootout?

"Pretty unprofessional back there, destroying property. And I'd say that was the worst interview I've ever seen, except for one thing," said Alfson.

Pepper didn't ask. Just stayed silent.

"Except I think they're Keser's killers. Now we just need to make the case. I'll get some resources assigned to them. Start with surveillance and then work toward probable cause for a warrant. But we'll keep the investigation wide open for now—just in case for once my gut's wrong."

* * *

Pepper, with Alfson, drove to a few other rental addresses listed on the police blotter but their work yielded no positive results. Pepper dropped Alfson back at his car at Broken Dreams Antiques and Pizzeria. Enough kumbaya and condescension for one day. And they both had to make their reports. Pepper was salivating but was proud he resisted a second trip inside the pizzeria in one day.

And Pepper had to fight not to laugh when he saw

Alfson's little Ford Focus displaying an orange violation ticket for parking longer than one hour. "I'll take care of that, partner!" said Pepper.

But Alfson just scowled, stuffed the ticket in his suit jacket pocket.

Pepper drove off by himself past the Fudge Castle, the candy store that'd been there since Pepper grew teeth and which made the best saltwater taffy on the Cape. Pepper had been spanked by his dad after shoplifting a handful of taffy at age six, one of his earliest acts of rebellion. He was driving toward the police station, scratching his armpit where his bulletproof vest had been rubbing too much, when Dispatch crackled on and broadcast a "help the officer" request. This was a very rare emergency message asking all law enforcement in range to assist an officer in extreme physical danger. Pepper knew it would bring every lawman in radio range as fast as they could get there. A rare tidal wave of weapons and badges.

Barbara Buckley said in her neutral, clipped tone that multiple 911 calls reported an officer was being assaulted. She stated the address as 32 Front Street. McLennen's Bar.

Pepper hit his lights and siren. He was only a block away. He took the corner onto Front Street then yanked his cruiser to the curb. He spat into the radio that he was on the scene and was going inside.

Sergeant Weisner radioed she was ETA one minute and to wait for her backup.

But a minute's a long time when you're being assaulted. Maybe too long...

Pepper sighed as he hustled out of his cruiser. He drew his Glock, then pushed through the heavy steel door. He paused inside to let his eyes adjust to the dim lights and a scene of mayhem.

TEN

McLennen's was the beer and a shot dive bar in town. Not Pepper's favorite hangout in his younger times. Even on a good night, it was mostly alcoholics, bums and troublemakers, as opposed to the suntanned, fresh lipsticked summer girls Pepper and his pals tried to chase at the more touristy watering holes.

The layout was long and thin, with a scarred wooden bar running half the left wall. Beer signs were attached to almost every inch of brick wall space. A pool table took up the back area. The right wall was lined with beat-up, red leather booths. Scarred tables ran down the middle.

But right now, with a couple of smashed chairs and an overturned table, McLennen's was in a state of suspended chaos. Broken glass littered the floor. A dozen customers were scrunching back from the trouble, in booths or huddling behind the bar. Pepper was shocked to see those guys from earlier in the day: Brian-Edward Westin and a couple other New River Front housemates, including Mr. Droopy-drawers, who was now sporting shorts. Was their presence a coincidence? Did the NRF like to get out and party?

The only customer defying the violence was a scruffy man in a purple fishing cap, apparently homeless by his layered, eclectic clothing and long greasy brownish hair covering much of his face. Pepper thought he'd seen him before, but at the moment couldn't remember where. Unlike the others, he'd remained on his stool at the bar, cradling his drink defensively.

Toward the back, a giant man in a wifebeater t-shirt covered in blood was standing over a semi-conscious Lieutenant Dwayne Hurd. Large knife in his right hand. Pepper recognized the giant: Marcus Dunne. They'd played high school hockey together for a couple of years until Marcus dropped out to work full-time on his father's boat. He hadn't missed many meals since then. Always tall, by his late-twenties he'd filled out with muscle and fat. His hair was greasy and matted. He looked like a bear who'd just killed his prey. He had some kind of milky coating on his lips.

"Hey Wonderboy," said Dunne, quick and hard through his teeth. "Long time. Heard you was back."

"Hey Marcus," said Pepper. "You terrorizing the village?" Hurd was still in a heap at Dunne' feet, but moving just enough for Pepper to tell he was breathing. Pepper kept his Glock pointed directly at Dunne's chest.

"This little guy tried to cuff me. Haul me out of here in front of my wife, like a bitch."

"Oh yeah? You and Marie finally marry?"

"Her little sister Trish."

"Hey Trish," said Pepper.

"Hey Pepper," said a woman's voice from behind a booth table.

"Trish, he on anything I should know about?" Pepper asked, keeping his eyes on Dunne.

"A little meth Pepper. I told him--"

"Shut the fuck *up* Trish," interrupted Dunne, shifting around from foot to foot. "Shut up everybody. You too,

Pepper. You're not Wonderboy no more."

"I don't want to shoot you, pal," said Pepper. "I was heading to have a beer myself. Shift just ended. But I'll take you in, make sure you get a fair shake for this mess."

"Nobody's taking me in. We need to make a deal. I tell you who did that clambake body thing. Get a free pass here. But you put your gun away first."

"Were you part of that, Marcus?" asked Pepper, slowly circling Dunne to his right. He slipped his Glock into his holster, snapped it closed.

"Fuck you! But I know what I saw and I know it's worth—"

Two other uniformed officers--Sgt. Weisner and Officer Phillips--burst through the front door, handguns pointed and screaming for everyone to get down.

Dunne reeled back then squatted over Hurd's body, dropping his knife and fumbling at the Lieutenant's belt. At the snap on Hurd's gun holster.

Pepper didn't have time to think. Impulse took over. Pepper was on Dunne in three steps, tackling him just as he straightened up. Pretty good football tackle, for a hockey player, except his cheek collided with something hard as stone, probably Dunne's elbow. But he'd caught Dunne off balance and Dunne went down sideways, heavily. The handgun flew from Dunne's hand, somewhere left.

Luckily Pepper ended up on top of Dunne. But unluckily, he was now close enough to be enveloped by Dunne's sour b.o. stench. Really ripe. Pepper had learned how to box in high school, but he'd learned how to fight a year later playing in the British Columbia Hockey League. Pepper began raining punches on Dunne's face.

Dunne recovered, reaching up and getting both hands around Pepper's throat. His eyes, inches from Pepper's, were like big black pools. But before Dunne could get a good squeeze on, Pepper pulled back from his grip. He swung down his forearm full power on Dunne's nose, felt it pop and saw blood spurt.

Then Dunne tossed him off, like Pepper was a child. A little meth, right. Dunne was lit up like a Christmas tree, feeling no pain.

Pepper crawled under the pool table as Dunne came after him howling and foaming blood, while Weisner and Phillips inched forward from the other side, guns pointed at Dunne, still screaming for him to get down. Pepper felt broken glass digging into his hands. He got clear to the other side of the pool table as Dunne stumbled around to cut him off, ignoring the other officers. So Pepper rolled back to the side he'd started on and scrambled to his feet.

As the big man cut around the pool table's corner, sliding on the broken glass as the other two officers closed in, Pepper had just enough time to grab a pool cue off the table and hit Dunne as hard as he could with the fat end right in the nuts. Two balls, corner pocket.

Which thankfully was game over. Dunne went down with a long howl and curled up in a tight fetal position.

A woman screamed and scurried to Dunne's side. Must be Trish, but with a bunch of tattoos Pepper didn't remember. Other officers were coming through the door.

Pepper noticed Westin and his hate buddies were nowhere to be seen. They must have slithered out the back door as more law enforcement came through the front. Obviously not big fans of the boys in blue...

And the homeless guy in the purple hat at the bar was laughing and laughing like the whole world was his personal comedy show.

ELEVEN

On Tuesday morning, Pepper found Zula plugging away faithfully on the dispatch desk. She was radioing instructions to a patrol officer so Pepper made it to her elbow before she noticed him, making her jump.

"Damn, Pepper!" she said, then muted her mike too late. "You scared the *piss* out of me, Frankenstein!"

Pepper had fresh stitches on his cheek, where it'd been split in the bar fight. "Hey Little Ike," he said with a smile that hurt. "You on a call? I got your message—what's up?"

Zula sighed, flipped back her black hair. "That call was about the damn peeping tom, again."

Pepper knew the station had been getting two or three calls a week for the past two months about a very active peeper. More since the story in the *Cape Cod Times*.

"An older lady, this time," said Zula. "Said she saw a man gawking in her bathroom window. Maybe just her imagination, but who knows?" Zula gave an eye roll like *don't underestimate how weird the world can be.* "Anyway, I finished researching your red starfish. It's definitely foreign, probably from the Indian Ocean. I sent a picture to a buddy who's an oceanographer at Woods Hole and she agreed with me."

"Cool. I'll get Alfson's folks to dig deeper—maybe

there's a limited number of importers. Anything else?"

She paused, then frowned. "Did you hear the press got wind that the clambake victim was a Secret Service agent? Alfson's boss Hanley joined Pop at his press conference this morning about the clambake murder investigation. Pop told the world that you're leading the investigation for the department so now everyone knows you're the man, including the bad guys... Then Hanley announced you've located a witness and Pop got a choking fit, right on camera."

Damn! What could they be thinking, using Marcus Dunne as bait to lure out the unsubs? Hanley hadn't struck Pepper as being a moron or reckless...

"But that made me wonder," she continued. "Could someone else have seen something, it being a Saturday night?"

Pepper didn't know where she was going with this, but gave her an encouraging nod.

"Maybe someone parked that night at the Dill Beach lot?" she explained. "It's kinda isolated. And really popular with the sixteen and seventeen-year-olds to park, make out. All that hormonal stuff, you know?" Then she blushed, which made her look a lot like a teen again.

"Great idea--did someone call in?"

"That's just it. No teens would stick their necks out, call the cops, say they were sucking face or worse, down in Dill Lot at night. Get their parents mad, all that hassle. A patrol car stops through sometimes when everything else is quiet, shoos them away, but I checked with the patrol officers on duty that night and no one checked the Dill Lot on Saturday night, things were too crazy around town. So I hoped maybe some teens were parked and saw something. But they're too scared to say anything. Just an idea."

Pepper squeezed her shoulder. "Pure genius! Now I just

have to figure out how to get word out to teens. Maybe have Justin Case put out a social media clip…"

"How do *you* know about Justin Case?"

Pepper preferred not to bring up Maddie Smith and the ticket he didn't give her. "He's here in town," Pepper said. "Do you know much about him?"

"Hey hey!"

"What?"

"That's Justin Case's signature line. *Hey hey!* He's super cute but a *baaaaaad* boy. Where've you been hiding yourself? Justin Case's quite the hot online reality star."

"I must've been in some other reality. But now he's here, sponging off the Smiths at Eagle's Nest."

Zula filled him in on Case's background. His breakthrough on the YouTube clip series, *Spring Splash*, about twenty-somethings acting like idiots. How he went solo— Twitter, Instagram, Facebook and YouTube, the whole deal. "He's posted thousands of videos of himself, has millions of subscribers," she said. "And billions of views. So yeah, he's hot."

Huh. "What's the guy actually do?"

"That's just it. It's what he *doesn't* do. He's made an art form out of acting laid back. Like the world's crazy and he's too cool to get taken in. Pull up his clips and look—he just makes a few dry comments. Maybe shrugs. People go nuts for it. And he endorses his own Lazy Style merchandise, like headphones, but sometimes he doesn't even bother mentioning them. Doesn't have to. His viewers jump on it. And he gets lots of money for the views and from advertisers."

More evidence that the world was going crazy. "Does it say how he got involved with Madeline Smith?"

Zula raised an eyebrow. "Aha, so *that's* what this is

about. You know Justin Case posted a clip about you pulling them over, hassling them? It was pretty funny. Well, People Magazine said they met at a New York exhibit of her paintings. Her art's pretty good, for a spoiled brat. And they're the hot, hot couple right now. But she's quite the man-eater so it shouldn't last long."

"Zula!"

"Just saying! Hold on a sec." Zula took her mic off mute and dispatched a patrol car to check on a house alarm.

"Sorry," she said. "Anyway, so Justin Case isn't quite A-List, yet. But he's pretty big competition, Pepper, if you're hot for Madeline Smith."

Pepper didn't want to get into *that*. "Can you run a check on him?" he asked. "Convictions, arrests, anything? It's important background info, for the Keser case, and totally kosher since Case's staying at Eagle's Nest."

"So, maybe it won't be illegal for me to check him out?" she snorted. "Just piss off my pop if I help you? Sure, why not? But, seriously—you think Justin Case is trouble?"

"I know he is," said Pepper, and he meant it. "I just don't know whose yet."

* * *

"Are you holding out on me again?" Special Agent Alfson asked Pepper.

He'd ambushed Pepper right outside the New Albion police station. Was leaning on Pepper's truck, arms crossed, in a tan suit and tie that was pretty much as out of place as any suit on the Cape.

This was really turning out to be a bad day. Pepper's cheek felt like it was on fire, where it'd been stitched up. And he'd just had his rear end chewed up by the General—

Sergeant Weisner requested Pepper be suspended for ignoring her order to wait for backup before charging into the bar. Pepper had admitted to the General that he'd heard Weisner's order, which pissed the Chief off even more...not accepting the easy way out, pretending he hadn't heard her order on the radio. The General had been more disgusted with Pepper than usual. About an eight on his disgusted scale. And now, here was Alfson with a self-satisfied curl to his lips.

"Holding out what?" asked Pepper, sipping his cup of coffee from the station with a little extra defensiveness and innocence. Since he was holding out, but not on anything Alfson could have figured out, right?

"The guy you assaulted in the bar. Dunne. Did you know our advance team interviewed him recently? He threatened the POTUS's life about six months ago. Something about a big section of offshore fishery being shut down, destroying his God-given constitutional right to fish. Threatened to use Garby for tuna bait. Called it self-defense."

"A letter?"

"No, a phone call to the White House switchboard, which was re-directed to one of our agents. Then someone from our Boston office drove down to put a scare in him. Threatened him with five years in prison and a quarter million dollar fine. Maybe Dunne was high when he called—he didn't seem to remember much, but didn't deny it. Our folks in Protective Research concluded he wasn't a credible threat. Dunne went on our lowest level Class I Watch List, but our advance team interviewed him again last week since he lives near Eagle's Nest."

"But not Keser?"

"No, two other agents. And they assessed him again as

not a credible threat. But your lieutenant—his report about the bar incident says he just happened to be arresting Dunne for having a couple papers of crank? Yeah, right. So Mr. Local Expert, what do you know about Dunne that you didn't share with me?"

Not a fucking thing, asshole. Pepper had been holding out on totally different topics than Dunne. "First I heard about it, partner. Thanks for sharing the info with me. But I was surprised to hear the Secret Service gave a quote to the press that we have a witness in the clambake murder? What're you doing, using Dunne for bait?"

"Since *someone* leaked that the victim was Secret Service, we're getting a lot more involvement from D.C. Including PR decisions we might've handled differently here on the ground."

Classic federal reflex—pass the buck. "Well, while info's flowing freely, what more details can you share about Keser's work at Eagle's Nest in the days before his murder?"

"What?" Alfson was now drumming his fingers on Pepper's truck's hood. Pepper was wishing he hadn't washed it so recently.

"You said he was assigned to review the people who'd be inside Eagle's Nest? Must have been from Acker Smith right down to the gardeners, right? Maybe Keser hit a nerve about Smith or one of his people, something nasty enough that they would kill him to bury it?"

Alfson just stared at Pepper. Shook his head sadly...dismissively. "That sounds pretty exciting, but it's all make-believe, hard stop. Keser didn't uncover anything like that about the folks at Eagle's Nest in his interview. I already told you, his work was routine—a security review of the buildings and personnel at Eagle's Nest and Smith's huge yacht. Confirming bulletproof windows were installed at the

Guest House, that kind of thing. And coordinating the security perimeter with other agencies, like the Navy with their dolphins sweeping the harbor. No red flags were tripped."

Alfson said it so smoothly, so condescendingly, that Pepper almost believed him. Even about the dolphins.

"But you guys had to vet the people at Eagle's Nest pretty hard, right? Security checks, financial backgrounds, all that? To let Smith host Garby?"

Alfson guffawed. "The Secret Service doesn't *let* the POTUS do anything. We aren't calling the shots. We just jump in front of them."

Pepper gave a weak chuckle for partnership's sake. "Maybe it'd still be helpful for me to read Keser's work files. See what he might've focused on."

"Sorry partner, the advance team's work is classified. And since I doubt you have any security clearance, you'll just have to trust me. They didn't produce anything about Smith or anyone else at Eagle's Nest that'd lead to Keser's murderers. And they didn't identify any new security risks to the POTUS. Smith's rich, he's an asshole, he's dying. But he's the POTUS's rich dying asshole and his whole team checked out. Now I'm meeting with Hanley in half an hour, so if you have any other leads I can share which don't imply we've been sitting with our thumbs up our asses?"

Pepper didn't. "If I get any solid info, I'll call you right away," lied Pepper. "But one other thing? Can you put me on the gate list for Eagle's Nest? I'd like to talk to Smith, maybe his staff. With you, of course."

Alfson shook his head. "You really trying to get close to Smith? Or is this maybe about his smoke-show daughter? I hear there's some history between you two? Sorry buddy, that compound's now a federal security area. Locked down, land and sea. Even the shoreline—like I said, the Navy's had their trained dolphins working the area for underwater explosives, the whole nine yards. It's big time. And if a local cop shows up and starts harassing the POTUS's host? It'd take one call to D.C. before I'm freezing my nuts in the Anchorage field office and you're back on a street corner somewhere just as far away, playing your guitar for pocket change."

Right now, that wasn't sounding too bad, Pepper with the guitar and Alfson with iced nuts. Pepper knew he still needed to try to talk to Dunne, one on one. But his priority was to get into Eagle's Nest to move his investigations forward. So he'd have to get through those gates soon, even if he had to get inside without his dear buddy Alfson…

TWELVE

Later that morning, Pepper waited at New Albion's town pier. Wearing boat shoes borrowed from his dad, for God's sake.

He'd called Maddie and after a little *how you been* and *remember when*, Pepper offered to show her something out in the bay that'd change everything she knew about the world.

"It's fate, you calling," she'd said. "Because I've got a big problem and you're the only one who can save me."

It was the kind of clear, warm day which makes Cape Cod legendary, with just a light breeze to keep him coolish. At a quarter past eleven, a low sleek tender boat approached the pier. With a beaming Maddie. Short white skirt, striped blue tee shirt. Blonde hair flying. Again with the big red sunglasses.

But unfortunately, Justin Case was onboard too. He was not beaming. More of a smoldering scowl, very expressive. Probably practiced it in front of a mirror every morning.

The tender was captained by a tall thin balding man. Bristly blonde mustache. Crisp white uniform. With economical moves, he steered the tender to a stop inches from the dock.

Pepper stepped aboard and got a lingering hug from

Maddie, followed by pecks on both cheeks. European style, nice. But no kisses from Justin. He was playing with his sunglasses, ignoring Pepper.

"God Pepper, you grew up into *quite* the hottie!" said Maddie, giggling and squeezing Pepper's arm.

Justin was giving Pepper a death glare, which Pepper pretended not to see.

"But what happened to your face?" gushed Maddie. "Anyways, I'm *so* glad you called. What's your big surprise?"

"I'm sure you've seen dolphins before...but I'll bet you've never seen trained Navy dolphins!"

"Say what?!?!"

"Sure. I heard all about them from Alfson, the Secret Service special agent I've been helping out. All very hush hush. The Navy taught a special team of dolphins to do all kinds of things. They search for underwater explosives, watch for hostile swimmers, even attack America's enemies. The feds are using them to patrol right offshore of Eagle's Nest."

"How would dolphins know if a person in the water was like, America's enemy?" scoffed Justin.

Maddie laughed, way into the idea now. "Training, silly!"

Over the rumbling idle of the tender's engine, Pepper explained the Navy had been training dolphins and seals that way for decades.

"What if they have little uniforms!" Maddie exclaimed. "Let's go Vinter!" She was practically bouncing as the captain slid them away from the dock and motored off parallel to the shore, then angling gradually toward deeper waters. "I just gotta get out of these clothes," declared Maddie, and she shimmied down her white skirt to reveal a yellow bikini bottom. Off came the shirt, and there was the matching yellow bikini top.

Wow.

"That's my honey!" yelled Justin over the engine noise, and he made a grab for her, but she eluded him, giggling.

"Eyes on the water!" she yelled. "First one to see an attack dolphin gets a big fat kiss!"

"I got your big fat--" yelled Justin, but a surge in the tender's engines drowned him out as the boat leaped forward. It also threw Justin off balance, and he fell back in a tangle of ropes and clothes. Pepper was holding on to a seat back and barely avoided ending up on top of Justin. Score one for the townie!

When Justin finally staggered back to his feet, he was checking out a long nasty scratch on his arm welling with blood. Pepper noticed his cursing was pretty energetic--not so lazy style. He wrapped his arm in a big white towel and sat off toward the back, apparently wounded inside and out.

They cruised back and forth off the coastline near Eagle's Nest. Pepper had to admit he wanted to see a Navy dolphin too. They saw a pod of humpbacks that almost made Maddie forget about the dolphins. Vinter killed the motor as they approached and the whales passed by pretty closely: four adults and a calf. Maddie hung out over the rail toward them like she couldn't stand to be so far away, eyes and teeth flashing, long blonde hair whipping in the offshore breeze. Ridiculously cute. And easily mistaken for a teenager again, at least to Pepper.

They didn't see any dolphins but, as Maddie reminded them, that didn't mean they weren't down there. Eventually giving up the search, their boat curved away toward an enormous yacht anchored a half mile offshore. Mirror black hull with a red stripe and a white bridge. The name stenciled on its bow was *Madeline Too*.

"Permission to come aboard?" asked Pepper with his

flirtiest smile. And enjoyed Maddie's yes and Justin's scowl.

It was the nicest 193-foot yacht Pepper had ever set foot on. Cost ninety-five million dollars to build, Maddie said with a shrug. It had ten staterooms. Eighteen crew. Was comfortable with twenty guests. Even more comfortable, she giggled, for just two...

That caused more not-so-lazy glares from Justin. He was taking Maddie's attention to Pepper pretty damn hard. Which Pepper didn't give a fig about. But Pepper had to admit, it was dizzying to see wealth on display at this extreme level.

"You want to know the punchline?" said Madeline, leading them through sliding doors into the main cabin. "Daddy built two of these boats a few years ago. Two! Hired the Vinter brothers fresh from Norway, one to captain each boat. And they're identical, even the furnishings, except for two things. The other yacht is named *Madeline*, not *Madeline Too*."

"What's the second difference?"

"The other Vinter doesn't have a mustache. He can't, says so in his contract. Daddy wants to be able to tell them apart," she giggled. "Otherwise the two *Madeline's* are identical twins."

"Why two yachts?"

"One for the Mediterranean, the other one for the Caribbean and the east coast. Obviously!"

"Sure, obviously."

"But the Med boat's in Florida right now anyway. They had to swap out a generator or something."

Pepper remembered his truck was overdue for an oil change. Who said the rich are different from you and me?

* * *

Justin went to find a bandage for his arm so Pepper grabbed the chance. "Maddie, why'd you never come back after you went to Europe for senior year?"

She frowned. Even her frown was sexy. "This place is just too small! And daddy was such a tool, I stayed as far away, and had as little to do with him as I could. Except spend his money. Hey, I think I bruised my tush when Vinter gunned the tender's engine...can you take a look?" She bent over a bit, stuck out her rear end, pulled her white skirt up.

Pepper didn't see any bruise. But she was so tanned, he had to examine her backside extra carefully to be sure...

"Hey hey!" Justin thumped back down the stairs and gave them the hairy eyeball. He had a series of little band-aids on his arm. "Girl you need to keep that thing covered, you'll make Officer Friendly here do something he's gonna regret!"

"Just a health check," smiled Pepper.

"Hitting on someone's girl might be bad for *your* health," sniffed Justin. "I'm getting a beerski—come on Maddie!" And he limped off up the stairs without making any further threats, which was probably good for *his* health.

But Maddie didn't follow Justin. She stepped in close to Pepper and her eyes narrowed. "It's been great seeing you, Pepper! Reminds me what I was like, just a silly kid. Before..." She made a hand gesture to finish her thought. Then grinned. "But I feel like a *bad* girl today," she said. "Justin told me last night to stay away from you. He should have known—that's *such* an aphrodisiac!" And she grabbed Pepper by the shirt, pulled him close for a peck on the lips, then ran off laughing up the stairs to the deck.

Pepper didn't wag his tail and follow. Instead, he peeled

off, went down a long hallway. One of Agent Keser's last official acts before he was killed had been to do a security review of this very yacht—could Keser have seen or done something that led to his death? He still doubted that Keser's snatching was random or opportunistic. Was the answer—or at least a damn smidge of a clue—onboard?

So Pepper did his own mini-sweep, checking rooms to the left and right. Mostly bedrooms, with absolutely nothing suspicious or helpful. Toward the back, he found what must be the master suite. Enormous bed. Giant bathroom. And a little alcove serving as a kind of office. An expensive but functional desk, of dark mahogany. No computer.

Pepper quickly opened the desk's stack of drawers. They were mostly empty. Nothing interesting.

He gave a tug on the top drawer. Locked. He pulled out his penknife, slipped it into the crack above the drawer, where the lock mechanism should be. Wiggled the knife's tip around as best he could. Pretty tight fit. Jiggled the drawer. If the many movies he'd seen were any guide, the lock should pop open. Which would almost make up for the minor damage he was causing to the drawer's edge, flattening and scraping the shiny finish.

But the lock didn't pop open.

Pepper regrouped, knowing time was short. He could be caught at any moment. Pepper checked the big drawers again, more carefully. On the left side of the middle drawer, way back and high up, hung a little key on a tiny hook. And yep, it unlocked the top drawer which held only three manila folders.

The first folder held insurance info for the ship. The ship was registered to Fulmar Limited, with a Delaware address. Had Fulmar also been the registered owner of Maddie's Porsche? It rang a bell...

He'd have to check into the corporate name and Delaware address. Pepper took a picture of the top page with his phone. The rest of the document was a form contract. He was flipping through the other folders and not seeing much of interest when he heard footsteps in the hallway. Getting louder.

Pepper shoved the folders closed, then the drawers. Locked the top drawer and pocketed the key, no time to rehang it from the little hook.

Ripped off his tank top, threw himself across the master bed.

And Pepper was lying on his side, shirtless and flexing like a jackass, when the bedroom door pushed open and Captain Vinter's face peered in. Then jerked back. Then he stepped into the room.

"Ms. Smith is looking for you," he said in his roller-coaster Norwegian accent. Almost made the name Smith sound exotic. But his blonde mustache was twitching suspiciously.

"I was hanging for Maddie," said Pepper with his biggest fake pout. "She's not still on deck with that hippie, is she?"

"This is Mr. Smith's bedroom, the door should have been locked. You'll please..." Captain Vinter gestured for Pepper to vacate, like someone would command a particularly stupid dog.

Pepper didn't overdo it. Groaned a bit, rolled his eyes, sighed. Slipped his tank top back on, stretched, sauntered out.

Saw Captain Vinter standing in the doorway, shaking his soup-catcher in disgust. And dialing a little silver cell phone.

So, not quite how they investigate in movies. Pepper was pretty sure he hadn't found anything on the yacht that would help figure out why Agent Keser was killed...but in the real world sometimes the only progress was eliminating dead ends.

* * *

"Oh, listen, it's noon! My mama's bells!" Maddie exclaimed. Pepper had rejoined them on the upper deck. He could hear Eagle's Nest's bells ringing, faintly across the water. Maddie, standing next to Pepper, suddenly and fiercely hugged him, melting against his side. Then they all were silent, even Justin. Pepper knew that Smith had installed the bells decades earlier as an indulgence to his first wife, homesick for her native French village where similar bells rang to mark every hour of the day and night.

The details were New Albion lore: lawsuits back and forth between Smith and neighbors, between Smith and the town. The old town manager had joked that million-dollar bells should come with an off switch. Eventually, the lawsuits were settled, Smith had bought out his angriest neighbors at a fat premium to end up with a sizable compound, and the bells were reprogrammed to normally ring only once per day, at noon. Locals passing by at midday barely noticed them anymore, they were such a part of the town's fabric after so many years.

But Pepper remembered how they'd rung, on and on, the evening Maddie's mother died when Pepper was seventeen. That the town had let their strange billionaire grieve for his dead wife—no one complained. Maybe they'd rung for an hour straight? Longer?

Maddie asked Justin to go down to the lounge for her sunglasses and he grudgingly clomped off.

"Wanna hear something totally poetic?" she asked Pepper. "When Daddy got a pacemaker last year, they added a special transmitter. When he dies, a signal goes to the bell tower and it makes them ring one final time, like they did for Mother."

Crazy! "I didn't know he was such a romantic." *Or was it just narcissism with a matching budget—a kind of crazy caused by too much money?*

Maddie gave Pepper another hug. "I'm *so* glad you're here!"

"Me too. Sweet boat," he answered, into the top of her blonde head.

"No, I mean *here*. In New Albion. I need someone I can trust. It's just me and Daddy. And a bunch of fucking vultures, you know?" Maddie had pulled back without breaking her embrace. She was looking up into Pepper's face. And moisture was welling in her eyes.

"Maddie, what's wrong?"

She took away one hand to wipe the tears. "It's her! Daddy's secretary. She's after his fortune, I know it. What if she gets him to sign a will leaving everything to her, something like that? I just know there's something going on, the way she looks at him when she doesn't know I'm looking."

"Elizabeth Concepcion?"

"Yes! She just *appeared*, a couple years ago. I called Daddy from Paris one day and she answered his cell phone. The gossip is she seduced him before he got sick. And now that he's dying, she practically controls him! Almost never leaves his side. I tried to talk to Daddy about her and he got mad and took her side."

"Well, he's even less likely to listen to me." Acker Smith had hated Pepper when he was the teenage boyfriend—a no-good local, dragging down his daughter— and Pepper doubted whether time would have made Smith's heart grow fonder.

"I need you to do me a huge favor and check her out. Where'd she come from? Any criminal record? And maybe help me figure out if Daddy's got a new will tucked away, something she tricked him into."

Huh. That'd be Pepper's ticket into Eagle's Nest, and a good excuse to paw through Smith's underwear drawers, for his other, more official investigating. "Of course, Maddie, for you? I'll see what I can do."

"And I'll totally make it worth your time," she whispered in his ear. Then she hugged him again, more fiercely this time. But Pepper didn't mind because at that exact second Justin came back on deck, twirling Maddie's big white sunglasses triumphantly. He froze, mid-twirl, and the crabby look on his face made Pepper wish he had his phone camera handy, and an Instagram account...

* * *

It was around 2 PM on Tuesday and Oliver was in Croke's room at the Sanddollar Motel. Room sixteen. Oliver had insisted on having a separate room, for his own sanity. Croke's room had light blue walls. Tile floor, like in a hospital. It was a little worn out, battered around the edges. Sort of like Croke. It had two smallish beds. Croke always slept in the one closer to the bathroom, so Oliver had claimed the one nearer the door as kind of a visitor's couch.

Oliver had just come back from a quick solo run to the Chatham library to check for chat room messages from their bosses in Queens. He'd driven their new ride: a Ford Taurus snatched from outside a muffler repair shop where it'd been left with its keys in the ignition. The Taurus now sported license plates from a Ford Escort. They'd dumped the old Chevy Impala a little further down the Cape.

Oliver had made the trip alone since the elderly librarian seemed to have a thing for Croke. She'd actually gotten up the last time and asked if Croke was looking for anything special. Was that...flirting? Oliver preferred her slumbering behind the checkout desk. And Croke hadn't returned the Salt book—he still had his nose in it whenever the opportunity arose, slowly grinding forward.

But there had been no new chat room messages from the bosses in Queens. Oliver didn't know whether that was a good sign or a bad one. So he was just sitting there on the crappy little bed, imagining all the ways *their* silence could be bad...

Oliver was startled from his funk when the special blue client phone rang. Oliver knew it was the blue phone because it was a foreign ring, one he'd never heard before. A high-pitched buzz, like insects fighting. He fished it from his pocket and stared at it. It continued to ring.

"Shit," he said, and figured out how to activate it. "Uh, hello?"

The caller didn't give a name, just identified himself as their recent client, calling with another job. Must be super security conscious—his voice was disguised by some kind of electronic device. In case Oliver and Croke were recording the call? Or in case law enforcement had a way to listen?

The client got right to it. He wanted them to make the witness to the clambake job disappear. A fisherman named Marcus Dunne.

Oliver wondered if it was the crazy fisherman from the cop incident who got pool-cued in the nuts...New Albion was still buzzing about it.

"Why aren't you commissioning this, er, *cheese order* through our bosses, like last time?" asked Oliver, not entirely trusting the super secure phone was actually super secure. And not entirely trusting the client, either. Their bosses used a cheese shop in Queens as their front. Oliver could see Croke exaggeratedly nodding in agreement from his little bed.

The client spat out a grainy string of curse words. Said time was too short. That they had the phone for this very reason. Then the client stated the pay: double what they received for the last hit, to be wired to whatever accounts they instructed.

The pay was a very big number—had their bosses been keeping an oversized cut of the last fee? Oliver knew the criminal family who brokered them for the first hit would bury him and Croke in a deep septic field if *they* ever got wind of them freelancing. But hey, Oliver needed to make the client happy, right? Wasn't that the American way? So this time, it required cutting out the middlemen.

"Okay," said Oliver. "We can deal with that guy but we'll need some special equipment. A powerboat. Not, ah... stolen."

From the corner of his eye, he could see Croke pantomiming alarm and confusion.

The client asked a question.

"Size?" repeated Oliver. "Small. Big enough for, say, three people." Oliver thought a bit. "No, just for two."

THIRTEEN

Pepper wanted to find out if Zula's hunch was right—that teens may have parked at Dill Lot the night of the clambake murder. He had, at that age—with none other than Maddie Smith.

So first thing the next morning, Pepper drove to the Holbrook home, rang the bell. His heart suddenly racing. He hadn't seen anyone from that family since his return to New Albion.

The mother answered the door. Denise Holbrook. She was a thin, tall woman in her early forties. Mid-length brunette hair and a Cape Cod tan.

Her hand came to her throat, she froze, then she came forward, hugged him fiercely. In a bit of shock from seeing so unexpectedly the man who'd saved their nine-year-old daughter from the back of a sex predator's van.

"Pepper Ryan!" Mrs. Holbrook sobbed into his chest.

In Mrs. Holbrook's arms, that night from eight years ago hit Pepper again, suddenly and intensely. He was that twenty-year-old police cadet again. The wet evening just at twilight, seeing what might have been a backpack in the tall grass, watching a brown van turn, slowly move away... And Pepper's outrageously reckless decision to run that van off the road, into a tree.

More than just remembered, Pepper actually felt what had followed next, like being in a PTSD nightmare: his hands on the van's cold, slick door handle, the burn of the first two bullets that'd had hit him—one in the ribs, one in the shoulder... He was suddenly looking again into the pale, bloodshot eyes of the man he'd wrestled in the middle of that wet street, both understanding that one of them was about to die. And he felt again the searing pain and raw itch in his left thumb's missing tip—the man's third, final shot had blown off the end of Pepper's thumb and the side of the man's throat. The man had bled out in less than a minute, soaking Pepper in metallic stench. But worst of all, Pepper heard again that muffled *thump thump thump*. The sound that Pepper first heard lying in the street, under the dying man, then followed to the brown van's rear. The terrified kicks of little Leslie Holbrook.

"I'm sorry," he said. "I should have called first, but I had a question for Leslie."

Mrs. Holbrook stepped back, wiping away tears. "A question? About the van?"

"No, nothing to do with that. Something I'm working on—I was hoping she'd do me a favor? How is she?" Leslie must be almost finishing high school.

"She's great. We're all great. We heard you were back in town but didn't want to..." She made an apologetic gesture. "She's at work at the Chatham Bars Inn right now. Would you like to come in anyway?"

Pepper thanked her but said no, he was working too, had to get back out there. If he could have Leslie's cell number, he'd leave her a message?

Of course, whatever he needed.

"Pepper, would you come to dinner sometime soon?"

"I'd love to," he said, and meant it. He said goodbye and Mrs. Holbrook gave him another long hug. Pepper could see she was crying again.

As a twenty-year-old police cadet, Pepper had been a lot more pain-in-the-ass than hero, even that night with the damn brown van. He wasn't the type to be self-sacrificing. People who knew him best would have described him as rebellious and angry. Mad at his dad. Mad at Jake. Mad, probably, at himself. And a lot more of his strength that night had come from rage than he would ever admit. But to the Holbrooks? The media, when they nicknamed him Wonderboy? Everyone who didn't know the true story? He'd been raw justice, or vengeance, or whatever the hell people prayed for when predators were loose among them.

And Pepper wished he believed those fairy tales too.

* * *

Pepper could still feel the adrenaline from the Holbrook visit burning through his blood as he reached the police station. That may be the true explanation why Pepper said what he said to a reporter from the Boston Herald who approached Pepper on the station's front steps.

"Any developments on the clambake investigation?" the reporter asked.

The prudent answer would have been a smile with 'No comment at this time'. Instead, Pepper said, "I'm confident we'll have the murderers in custody shortly. They made some really dumb mistakes. Truly moronic. They may be among the stupidest criminals I've encountered in my career."

So, probably adrenaline. But officially? He'd tell his bosses he was trying to provoke the unsubs into making a misstep…

Kicking himself for opening his pie hole, Pepper went into the station. He wanted to informally interview Dunne before he came up for arraignment, see what info he could get from him about the clambake murder. If Dunne was withdrawing from meth, that could either make him extra chatty or shut him down completely. But it was worth a try and Pepper believed Dunne might open up a bit to him. But not if Alfson was there too, Pepper suspected, so he didn't call him.

Pepper didn't view this as freelancing away from his Secret Service partner. Was there anything wrong with stopping in to see how his old high school teammate's nuts were feeling? Pepper guessed the General would have already passed the word to the SAIC, Hanley. And they would note Pepper hadn't filled in Alfson, the way any good partner would. Which wouldn't be great for the General's blood pressure.

"I'm going to borrow the interview room," Pepper told Gerry Forrestal, the duty sergeant. "Can you grab Marcus Dunne from lockup?"

"Sorry Wonderboy, no can do," said Forrestal.

Okay...what? Had the General anticipated Pepper's request and left an order to block it? "No sweat," said Pepper. "I'll pull him myself."

"Not here you won't."

Pepper didn't know Forrestal well at all; he was a career cop from Boston who'd only joined the New Albion department two years earlier.

"Sergeant, do you and I have a problem?"

"Nope. Just you."

"Which is...?"

"They released Dunne this morning. Own recognizance. A white shoe lawyer drove all the way down from Boston to spring him."

"That doesn't make any sense. Did the Secret Service interview him?"

"Officer, I just work here. You want the skinny, talk to the General."

Chief Eisenhower was at his desk, staring into a cup of coffee like he didn't know what it was. Pepper sat without invitation. "Chief, why'd you release Dunne? I wanted to continue the conversation he started while trying to kill me. About the clambake murder. I think he'd talk to me, we go way back."

The General sighed. "Dunne's lawyer says he'll talk about what he saw…if we let him off for shitkicking Hurd."

"You didn't take that deal!"

The General finally looked up from his coffee. "Of course I didn't. I can't have citizens shitkicking my guys without consequences. Bad for morale. We're going forward with all charges. But to build a little goodwill, I got a weekend approval from the bench to release him on his own recognizance. Every day's valuable during bluefin harpoon season, so Dunne owes us one.

"And somehow he got a lawyer from Scheren & Cabot to slither down from Boston. She was threatening to tearing the DA's team a few new holes. She argued Hurd didn't have probable cause to take Dunne into custody so everything after that moment was our bad. She was flinging around terms like 'police brutality', 'false imprisonment' and 'loss of consortium'. Sounded expensive for us. We'll negotiate something to get Dunne to talk, but I won't agree to let him off for what he did to Hurd."

Hmm. "You mind if I visit him at home, ask him some questions? I think he'll talk to me, for old time's sake."

The General just gave him *that* look. "Pepper, we know

he's represented and his lawyer told him not to speak without a written agreement. The Secret Service is having their lawyers type something up, ASAP."

Pepper wondered to himself why ASAP never felt fast enough. "Alfson told me Dunne threatened the POTUS a few months ago, so they think he might be involved in the Keser killing as more than a witness. But the feds were okay with releasing him?"

"They must have patience, Pepper. Try it, it comes in handy in life sometimes. And I'm not happy I didn't hear about the Secret Service's theory about Dunne until now. I said, keep me informed!"

At which perfect time Lieutenant Hurd poked his nose in. His face was multi-colored and his arm was in a sling. "Ryan, you still talking about your skill with a pool cue, or are you back to business? We've gotten reports of at least three major activist groups in town already. Have you interviewed them yet for the Keser case? Any of them?"

"One group, the New River Front, and they're definitely persons of interest."

Hurd made a face. "Well, don't get blinders on so quickly—check out the other two groups. Zula's got the info. One's an eco-wack group called PLANT. It's an acronym for something stupid. The other outfit's an open-border lobby, I forget their name. And you know the POTUS arrives in only three days, right? I guess we could ask him to delay a bit if you're too busy taking boat rides?"

Shit. Who'd ratted to Hurd about Pepper's boat ride with Maddie? Was Hurd embarrassed about Pepper saving his butt, so he was giving Pepper a hard time, trying to tear him down in front of the General?

Pepper decided he'd spend the rest of his day running down the known activist groups in town. See if any of them felt like confessing to the Keser murder. He'd even invite Alfson along (while hoping he'd say no thanks).

Then, if Pepper happened to find himself in the right neighborhood, he'd stop by Dunne's home. Maybe Dunne would offer him a beer and voluntarily tell what he'd witnessed. He hoped Dunne had actually seen something helpful and wasn't just bullshitting to get a free pass on the charges he'd be facing. Pepper's instincts told him he could get Dunne to open up. If Dunne wasn't still pissing blood…

FOURTEEN

Special Agent Dan Alfson surprised Pepper by agreeing to join him on the activist group welcome wagon. He must have been getting a lot of flack from Hanley. Or maybe it was Pepper's magnetic personality? He hoped not.

This time Alfson left his little Ford Focus Hybrid in a New Albion police parking spot. Probably didn't want to collect any more parking tickets.

"I've been checking you out," said Alfson as Pepper drove them in the direction of the first address on their list.

"I'm flattered, but I'm straight."

"Ha, funny man! No, I was surprised you're a Harvard grad. Kind of slumming here in local law enforcement, hey? You come back to snatch up the lovely Zula, or what?"

Alfson was better than coffee for getting Pepper jacked up. So Pepper changed the topic by asking for an update.

Alfson shared that the forensic evidence from the clambake site hadn't produced any leads, yet. His team of investigators had grown to twelve agents, but none had found strong leads yet.

Their first stop was an ecology rights group called Planet Liberation Action Now Trust that had set up in town for the week. A little tortured of a name, but with a groovy acronym:

PLANT. Alfson's research folks had verified that the group rented two houses in New Albion, side by side, a few blocks from the beach. Not a cheap neighborhood. And the Secret Service had identified a possible affiliation between PLANT and a domestic terror cell that were the prime suspects in the arson of a waste-to-energy facility in Maine ten months earlier.

The interview went smoothly, at first. Alfson and Pepper sat down in the living room of the larger of the two rental houses with a man and a woman who were careful to explain they were not the leaders of PLANT. PLANT, they explained, was a grassroots organization—a leader-free resistance. The woman, a lawyer, suggested they think of her as a kind of spokesperson. The man didn't explain what he thought he was.

"A leader-free entity?" confirmed Pepper. "Like a starfish?"

"You bet!" said the woman. "They even call our type of group a starfish organization. Independent parts with a shared goal to support ecological and environmental causes. Do you know what happened historically when fishermen tried to get rid of starfish here on the Cape by chopping them up?"

Pepper nodded. "The pieces regenerated, so the fishermen ended up with a lot more starfish."

"Exactly! So don't mess with us!" She talked a bit about their plans for holding nonviolent protests, making it clear that she knew more about demonstrations and permits and the first amendment than Pepper did. Seasoned activists, the kind that pre-negotiated the number of arrests to ensure the police had enough transport wagons for the experience to be civilized. Orderly. But Pepper was pretty sure the blue cell phone sticking from the woman's purse was the same unusual model that Pepper had been glimpsing all week...

"Just one other question," said Pepper. "Have either of you pacifists visited any waste-to-energy plants in Maine in the past year, maybe burned it down?"

The man appeared stunned, then reddened with anger, started wagging his finger at Pepper. "Playing by your rules doesn't always get our planet the protections it deserves. We're willing to pay the price for what we believe in. Are you?" He was half-standing now like he wanted to smack Pepper. So, maybe not completely orderly. The woman had her hand on his shoulder, trying to calm him down or maybe even to hold him back.

She flipped into lawyer mode. Full attitude. Showed them right out.

"You get that reaction a lot?" asked Alfson, as they walked back to the police car. "I still think those New River Front punks murdered Keser, but these PLANT assholes deserve a closer look too."

Pepper had to agree so he nodded—some surveillance wouldn't hurt, right?

* * *

Pepper's stomach was growling so he pulled into the parking lot along the beach seawall and parked his cruiser near a blue food truck called Captain Lefty's Fish and Chips. Food trucks were one of the few changes to New Albion in recent years that made perfect sense, filled a gap.

"Hungry?" he asked.

Alfson laughed. "Not for grease. But I have to touch base with my team anyway, see if anyone has caught any leads. You knock yourself out."

So Pepper radioed in his location and checked his phone.

Nothing important. As he left his car, Pepper saw a man hustling across the parking lot toward the food truck. It was the purple-hatted homeless guy who'd been sitting at the bar in McLennen's on the afternoon of the Dunne arrest. Purple hat firmly in place--must be his signature fashion statement. But to be honest, the man might be wearing exactly the same outfit as in the bar, from hat to shoes. Hard to judge how old he was, maybe early thirties?

Pepper joined the food truck line behind Mr. Purple Hat. The man seemed to sense him, turned with a surprised gawk, then stepped away.

"Whatta *you* want officer?" Purple Hat asked Pepper, shaking his long mess of hair. Between the unruly brown hair and his large white sunglasses--women's?--it was hard to see the man's expression. His voice was a little high and a bit cracked.

Pepper just smiled. "I think the fish and chips--must be their specialty right?"

The homeless man cracked a grin. "Glad you weren't here to arrest me like you did the big crazy man in the bar. My grapes hurt just thinking about it!" The homeless man was grinning but also sizing Pepper up. "Hey, you wanna make a bet? Loser buys lunch?"

This was getting interesting. "Okay."

The homeless man took a stance, dirty hands on hips. "I bet I can tell you where you got them shoes!"

What? Pepper had bought them so long ago even he couldn't remember. "Okay, it's a bet." Just seeing where this was going...

Purple Hat grinned, confident. "Officer, you got them shoes...on your feet!"

Pepper laughed. Never underestimate a man who wears a purple fisherman's cap. So Pepper ordered and paid for two fish and chip specials, served old-fashioned style in newspaper cones. After they loaded up their food with ketchup and salt, they sat together on the seawall's edge. The fishing boats had already returned for the day; they rocked below them on the battered commercial pier. Motorboats and sailboats slid back and forth around the bay, some heading out to deeper water, but most just cruising. Pepper could see just a hint of the *Madeline Too* on the horizon. It was a million dollar day, warm and clear with a light breeze. Pepper didn't feel bad at all, leaving Alfson in the stuffy patrol car on his conference call. After all, Pepper had cracked a window for him...

"They call me Rowboat Willie," the man said, offering his hand to shake. It was softer than Pepper expected.

"Pepper Ryan."

"Oh, I know who *you* are!" laughed Rowboat Willie. "*The* Pepper Ryan. And nice moves the other night. I think your buddies woulda shot that man."

Pepper didn't say anything back, just grunted with his mouth full. The fish was perfect, crispy on the outside, hot and moist on the inside. The newspaper cone was thick with grease and ketchup. To their right, two seagulls sat just out of reach, shifting from foot to foot with their characteristic impatience, calling dibs on leftovers. Pepper unsnapped his Glock threateningly but the birds didn't seem to care, so he closed the snap. Rowboat Willie chuckled again, didn't miss a thing.

Rowboat Willie's long stringy hair was working against him, dangling in the way of his plastic fork as he shoveled fish and chips into his mouth. Little bits of ketchup stuck in his hair. "You officers getting close to catching your clambake killer? You see me get interviewed on TV? That lady didn't pay me but hey, it's all good publicity in my line of

111

work, right?"

So *that's* where Pepper had also seen this character—the circus gathered at the crime scene police tape. Willie really got around. "What line of work's that?" asked Pepper, trying not to watch Willie's eating style too closely.

"Fashion designer!" winked Willie, underarming a few fries down the beach. The gulls sprang after them.

Then Pepper had an idea. "Hey, back at McLennen's Bar? Did you hear the big guy say anything before I came in?"

"Oh, I wasn't too close. Maybe just close enough to hear...something..." He grinned, and yep, there were the bits of fish and chips on display. Pepper lost the rest of his appetite.

But Pepper fished a twenty from his pocket, displayed it to Rowboat Willie. "I'll bet you can tell me twenty dollars worth of something, right?"

Willie snatched the bill with a high-pitched chuckle. "It's a bet! I heard just a little. The big guy, he was drinking like a fish. Down toward the other end of the bar, with a woman. Three guys came in, made their way over, invited themselves some conversation. But I couldn't hear much..."

"You haven't won that twenty bucks yet."

Willie was silent a bit. "I think I heard the big guy say something to the three guys, like he was repeating it back to them. I shit you not, I think he said 'nude river front'."

"Hmm," said Pepper. "What else?"

"Something about Saturday."

"Upcoming Saturday? Or last Saturday?"

"Maybe last Saturday. Things that'd already happened. They got in closer, were talking more quiet, you know? Then that cop came in and the other three guys cleared away. Pretty soon all shit broke out."

Pepper handed the homeless man his business card. "Well, that part I know," said Pepper. "But if you remember anything else Dunne said, can you give me a call?"

"Dunne's the big dude? Why's he so important anyway...did he waste that clambake guy?"

That was a rumor to nip in the butt. "No, no, Dunne's just a fisherman with a bad attitude. But think some more about what he said, you might win another bet or two. And until we catch our killer, be careful out there."

Rowboat Willie tucked the card somewhere into his outfit and then nodded past Pepper's shoulder, like Pepper had missed something. And he had.

Pepper had been so busy with the conversation and with rescuing his last fries from the ketchup puddle in his newspaper cone that he hadn't noticed the busload of Weepers who'd pulled into the parking area a few hundred yards further down the lot.

It was a brightly colored school bus with four loudspeakers pointing forward like horns. Their full name, the Weeping Church of Peter, was painted down its length. It parked lengthwise, taking up six parking spaces along the beachfront.

Fuck.

Pepper crumpled the newspaper into a ball and three-point shot it toward the battered blue garbage barrel next to the stairs down to the beach. His shot bounced off the rim and tumbled down the staircase, stirring up a few bees buzzing around the garbage barrel's opening. More laughter from Rowboat Willie. Without dignity Pepper retrieved his trash and settled for a dunk this time.

"Gotta go, Mr. Rowboat," Pepper said. "Thanks for the company."

"You get 'em, Officer!" Willie was a hot ticket and

someone to keep an eye on—he'd either end up in jail or in business with Angel.

Pepper went back in his cruiser and saw Alfson still deep in his conference call, saving the free world one agenda point at a time. Pepper grabbed his ticket pad from the front seat, pointed toward the bus and made an 'I'll be right back' gesture. Alfson gave him a little salute.

FIFTEEN

Pepper paused at the front of his cruiser and fully wrote out six parking tickets. He then walked across the lot to the bus.

"That didn't take long," laughed a tall, lanky man with an unruly head of sandy brown hair who was leaning against the front bumper.

Pepper didn't reply. He just smiled, nodded, and checked the parking meters alongside the bus. Of course, they were all expired. So he went over to the bus and tried to hand the parking tickets to Lanky Guy.

"Not me, man," L.G. said, "I'm just along for the ride."

So Pepper walked to the driver's side, got on his tiptoes and slid them under the windshield wiper.

"Excuse me officer!" yelled an older man, hustling up from the beach, with two younger women in tow. One in her twenties, the other a teen. "What seems to be your problem?"

Pepper recognized him immediately: the infamous Reverend Michael McDevitt. Pepper knew enough about him and his 'church'. The Weepers' headquarters was in Fall River, only an hour and a half away. His poison had done awful damage in New Albion in the past, but to give the

Reverend credit, his garbage had risen to the national stage in recent years.

"No school today?" Pepper asked the teen.

"She's homeschooled. More quality family time," said McDevitt.

Pepper knew everything he needed to about the Weepers and their qualities. The Weeping Church of Peter was, effectively, a hate church. Their greatest skills were getting media attention and pursuing lawsuits. They picketed dead soldiers' funerals—Reverend McDevitt explaining to the media they weren't there to pass judgment on the deceased, because God already had. The media had given a lot of press to the series of court rulings which upheld the Weepers' constitutional right to picket near funerals.

But Pepper had to admit, their church stood on clear principles. They opposed interracial sex and any other racial mixing. They also fought abortion and homosexual rights. They were often at the heart of demonstrations that became violent when opposing groups showed up. Such events were typically followed by the church suing everyone else involved. Oh, and they opposed taxation of individuals who allied themselves primarily with their church, not the USA. Funny how so many of these groups had a thing against taxation.

"Where'd you get that bruise on your arm?" Pepper asked the teen, ignoring McDevitt.

"Sports," she said.

On TV, McDevitt appeared huge. Not quite so big in person, without his microphone and hate signs. His only distinctive feature was his black hair. It was thickly gelled into an elaborate coif that would withstand the beach breeze. Maybe even a hurricane.

"Did you just give us a parking ticket?" he asked with great indignation, playing to his two women companions and

Lanky Guy. They were lapping it up.

"Nope. I just gave you six. One for each spot you're taking up."

The man got agitated. "*The Lord shall break in pieces the oppressor. P*salms 72," he said. Finger poking the air at Pepper to emphasize his words. Luckily for his finger, a safe distance from Pepper's chest. "You harass us and your runt-ass town'll spend the next three years getting taken apart in court. Again. It's been a while since I got one of your police chiefs canned, so pick the fight carefully. I'd be happy to teach that lesson again."

Pepper remembered all too well.

More church members were trickling back from the beach to watch the confrontation. The Weepers had been picking a public battle with President Garby in recent months, showing up to disrupt his East Coast appearances. Through megaphone ridicule and prayer barricades, they'd been trying to advocate for President Garby's salvation. Which seemed to be connected to him becoming more in line with the Weepers' holy agenda. Is that why they'd come back to New Albion?

Then McDevitt froze, squinted at Pepper. At his name tag.

"Dear Lord," he said, now chuckling. "Officer *Ryan*? Don't tell me you're the son of your disgraced Chief Ryan? I thought I ran your family out of town—guess I'll have to try harder this time. *Gather me the people together, that they may learn to fear me, and they may teach their children.*"

Pepper's blood was nearing the boiling point. "Is that a threat?"

"No, it's Deuteronomy." McDevitt's followers laughed.

They were in a staring contest now, neither willing to break away first.

"Well, enjoy your visit to our runt-ass town," said Pepper. "And I'll be back in an hour. Like clockwork. Six more tickets if you're still here at expired meters." Smiled extra politely, walked away.

* * *

Lizzie just needed to get the darned documents signed. She'd spent the past twenty minutes standing at the edge of Mr. Smith's enormous mahogany bed, trying to get him to approve the seemingly endless stack of documents needing his personal signature. He'd always liked it that way for money movements, corporate actions, all the decisions which kept his extensive empire spinning nicely in orbit. And his lack of delegation was a nice mechanism for keeping himself solely in control of his empire. But it made her life much, much harder.

So when Mr. Smith's daughter Madeline walked right into his bedroom, no knock, no appointment, maybe Lizzie made a mistake. Lizzie had almost had a child, back when she was young and married. She often wondered if the baby would have been a boy or a girl, if she hadn't miscarried. Either way, she knew her own sweet little child wouldn't have been a selfish brat like Madeline Smith. Lizzie had grown up hard, in the LeFlak housing development in Queens, New York, and she had no tolerance for soft, spoiled princesses.

"He's not available right now," Lizzie said. This time Lizzie consciously didn't step away from Mr. Smith. And not from Madeline either. "Come back in an hour," ordered Lizzie, as firmly as she would the other employees at Smith Enterprises.

And the little snot sailed right past Lizzie. Even bumped her as she passed. "He's never been *available*," scoffed

Madeline. "But why don't *you* come back in an hour? Or, never? Daddy and I need to have a family discussion. Maybe you should get some sun?"

And the daughter actually gave her an eye roll...

"Great news, Daddy!" Madeline said. Plopped herself on his bed's edge. "Pepper Ryan's back! You remember him? Tall, dark and scrumptious? He's got a badge and a gun and everything. I made him promise me to nip in the butt all the, you know, *dirty stuff* going on."

"What dirty stuff?" asked Mr. Smith. He was sitting up taller now, but still pale. Still weak and confused. But louder.

"He's close to catching the murderers of that poor agent on the beach. He called them morons, it got retweeted a billion times. The Secret Service is *so* grateful for his help. But I told him I'm worried about maybe some other shady things happening at Eagle's Nest. He guaranteed me he'll take care of it."

Smith pulled his blankets higher. "You mean—"

"Sir?" interrupted Lizzie. "The Secret Service is handling all security issues for the presidential vacation. We shouldn't be inviting in the local police—think of the gossip and bad publicity!" Not that Mr. Smith would mind any bad publicity if it was limited to President Garby—like confirming the stubborn rumor of Garby's latest mistress stashed away somewhere nearby on the Cape! The president deserved all the mud he stepped in since he created it.

"*Daddy* has nothing to worry about," laughed Madeline. "Pepper's the best and he'll do anything for me. But I wouldn't want to be the dirtbags trying to pull anything around here! Just watch!" Finished with a smirk.

"Well thank you, Madeline. But your father needs rest," said Lizzie as sternly as she dared. "So if you'd *please*..."

Madeline reached forward and pulled her father's

blankets even higher. Almost to his chin. And Mr. Smith let her. Then he smiled, maybe for the first time that day?

Then Madeline left them.

Lizzie made sure the bedroom door was closed.

Smith looked furious. "Pepper Ryan..." he said. The way she'd say 'yeast infection'.

"Mr. Smith, did you mention to Madeline any of the, er, special arrangements you asked me to make in connection with disrupting the president's vacation? Could she have been talking about those groups?"

"The protesters and other shit disturbers?" he smiled. "I haven't said a thing."

"Fine, sir," she said, relieved. She couldn't be sure from one day to the next that he'd remember what they'd discussed and why it was happening. Hopefully he recalled it was *his* idea, and she was just following orders.

It was dangerous and unprecedented, the plan to disrupt. To spend significant money—millions—to make the President of the United States as miserable as humanly possible on his vacation. Payback for his disloyalty to Mr. Smith, right? All technically legal, of course—she was almost absolutely sure? Lizzie caught herself combing her brunette hair with her fingers. Forced herself to stop.

"Good," said Smith. "Garby's a weasel and a coward. That narcissist deserves all the suffering he gets."

Lizzie almost laughed—barely caught herself. Stayed silent.

"It's like all the idiots say—you have that epiphany when you're dying. Did I give it my best and was it a worthy cause? And how'll I be remembered... Well, I hope Garby remembers me with great pain. And Lizzie? Everything has to go *perfectly*. So don't let anyone get in the way. Especially Maddie's goddamn high school sweetheart."

* * *

Oliver didn't spend much time at marinas. But this one, Murphy's Hole Marina, was as Oliver would have pictured. Rows of weatherbeaten wood docks, boats of all sizes and shapes. A little store. All Oliver cared about was this was the right place.

They'd walked down onto the far dock, past the little yellow rope with the sign which told them not to. Oliver was trying to play as dumb a tourist as possible. Croke should have been a natural at looking dumb, but instead appeared uneasy behind his too big black sunglasses. And he seemed bothered by the floating dock's small movements.

But now they were standing by one particular fishing boat. They'd interrupted its captain who was performing one of the little tasks every boat owner always seems to be doing. Something with a rope, grimacing like the activity was a bit painful. And the captain wasn't as interested in talking to them as Oliver had hoped.

"It's our last day," Oliver said to the captain, with a little hand flourish. For emphasis. "We're headed back to Rochester this evening. But I thought, hey, wouldn't it be great to get out for a couple hours, maybe catch a big tuna myself, like on that TV show?"

"*Wicked Tuna*," said the captain. But still pretty much not interested. Still half dealing with what he was trying to do with the rope.

"So," said Oliver. "Maybe you know a boat I can charter for a little while? Just me. My brother here, he's not going. He's scared of deep water."

Croke grimaced at him. "Not scared. But I'm not feeling so good, today."

"I'd pay cash. A full-day rate for three hours," said Oliver quickly. "For the trouble, since I didn't, you know, make a reservation..."

"You could try *Cape Crusader*," said the captain, gesturing back toward the marina's other side.

"What's the fair rate, $1,800?" asked Oliver. Setting the hook.

"You said three hours?" repeated the captain. Definitely thinking about the money now.

Croke was pointing toward a large cabin cruiser, not a fishing boat. "Is that *Cape Crusader*?" Was he playing dumb or was he actually confused? Frickin' Croke.

"$1,800? Be a shame if you didn't get out on the water, your last day. I'm Marcus Dunne, captain of *Sure Thang*, at your service."

"I'm Will," said Oliver. Then he had to hold back a grimace as the captain shook his hand too hard.

"I could take you out as soon as I borrow some baitfish. When'll you be ready?"

"Oh, he's ready," said Croke, giving the captain what he probably thought was a warm smile. But the captain was already counting the $1,800 Oliver had handed over, didn't notice anything else.

SIXTEEN

While heading back to the New Albion police station where Special Agent Alfson had left his car, Pepper filled him in on his encounter with the Weepers.

"You wrote them tickets?" Alfson chuckled. "Pepper, you're a classic. Did you order them to leave town before sundown?"

Pepper didn't mention his dad's prior incident with the leader of the Weepers, since Alfson might laugh that off too.

"Reverend McDevitt and his hate cult have built up quite a war chest with their act," said Alfson. "Millions of dollars, from their lawsuits and tax-free donations from people even more nuts than they are. Which they've been quite happy to spend to keep stirring up more shit, but as a matter of religious principle I bet they don't pay parking fines. But I'd have liked to see McDevitt's face when you gave him those tickets..."

Pepper left Alfson back at his car, then with a friendly toot toot and guilty conscience drove off to swing by Marcus Dunne's house before he headed home. He knew the General--not to mention Alfson—would tell him not to. But Pepper also knew he had a better chance of getting quick info from Dunne. If they had to wait for the lawyers to negotiate a deal, it might be too late to act on whatever info Dunne had.

Dunne lived in the cheapest corner of New Albion. As far from the ocean as you could get and still be in the town. Small lots, older houses.

Dunne's house was a dump. Weed patches, fishing equipment and toddler gear were scattered around the yard. The clapboard siding had long needed repainting. Two cars were parked in the driveway, both covered in dust and grown around like they hadn't moved in a while and didn't expect to.

Pepper was still in uniform. He stepped carefully around a tricycle and an empty boat trailer and climbed the steps to the front door.

Trish answered the door. Cutoff jeans and a black lacy top that might be more for sleeping. Blinked at Pepper. He saw her eyes narrow and her face harden.

"We got a lawyer," she said. "You get your ass off our property, Pepper Ryan."

"Hello to you too, Trish."

She was out the door now, in his face. "You put Marcus in the hospital and come here for a hello? You stay away from us."

A little girl—three, four years old?--poked her head around the door and smiled at Pepper.

"This your daughter?"

Trish's face eased for a second. "This is Kaylee."

"Hello, Kaylee!" Pepper gave the little girl his super-friendliest smile.

"Get inside!"

Kaylee studied Pepper, then slid back from view behind the door.

Trish's fists were balled, she was breathing heavier. Looking more than a little pissed. "Pepper, whatta you want?

Marcus isn't here."

Pepper spread his empty hands, palms out. "I'm not trying to cause him any trouble. But he knows something about the clambake murder. Or said he did, right? So if the wrong people hear, he could be in danger."

Trish glared at him. Weighing the level of his bullshit. "You think he's stupid? That I'm stupid?"

Pepper hadn't known Trish well. She was maybe three or four years behind him in high school. Her older sister Marie had been a little wilder but a little less naturally pretty. Trish had gotten the looks in the family but it appeared the last few years had been wearing on her.

"Trish, you know Marcus was about a half-second from getting shot when I whacked him. It had to be done."

She grinned despite herself. "He's still pissing blood. Probably good for you he's not here. He's still pretty mad about it. And not sitting comfortable, neither..."

Pepper grinned back. Okay, progress. "Trish, I'm not going to screw you guys over. But Marcus needs to tell me what he knows. He'll be safer once the info's out."

Trish sighed. Looked about ten years older than her real age. She crossed her arms over her chest but was rubbing her upper arms like she was cold. She fished in her pocket and pulled out cigarettes and a lighter. Sparked up. "Want one?"

"No thanks."

She blew out a long stream of smoke. "Well, you take it up with Marcus. He went down to work on the boat. He's taking it out to Stellwagen early tomorrow and well...something always needs fixing."

"Murph Hole Marina?"

"Yeah. His boat's in an outside slip, all the way to the left. The *Sure Thang*." She shook her head. "And I can never get him to admit if it's named after me or Marie." Pepper saw her green eyes well with tears, but the water didn't make it to her cheeks—it stayed there in her eyes like perfectly crowned shot glasses. "Pepper, you gotta help Marcus. If anything happens to him..."

"I'll go down there right now. Hopefully he'll talk to me."

Trish stepped in for a goodbye hug but Pepper kind of botched it, being distracted by a car pulling up to the curb.

Three men got out. One was Westin, the top banana from the sovereign citizens outfit, New River Front. His two companions were wearing pants, so their visit must have been premeditated. Then they saw Pepper on the porch with Trish. They whispered among themselves and then Westin pulled out his fancy blue phone, made a call.

"They know you?" asked Trish.

Westin got a little more animated as his call went on, like he was arguing with whoever was on the other end. Then the three men climbed back into their car. As they were pulling away, Westin rolled down his window and gave them the middle finger.

"Yep, I guess they do," Trish said, with a little grin.

Pepper gave her a kiss on the cheek, suggested she be extra careful. Not open the door to any strangers unless they show a badge.

"My dishwasher may not work, but my shotgun's fucking tip-top," she said, smiling.

Pepper decided to pretend he hadn't heard the last comment. He was back in his truck on the street and had started his engine when a car passed and pulled into the driveway. A Ford Focus Hybrid. Two somber gentlemen in suits climbed out—part of Alfson's growing team on the Red Starfish investigation. Trish had gone inside. He figured the agents would hassle her but she'd be safe, as long as she didn't open with the shotgun.

Pepper was more worried about making his own clean exit. If the agents reported back to Alfson they'd seen Pepper at the Dunne's house, the day's kumbaya with Alfson would be undone. Pepper considered making a quick call to him but Pepper didn't have any info he wanted to share with the federal agent, quite yet. He needed to get something concrete first.

The two agents hadn't seemed to notice Pepper yet. He pulled away from the curb and was almost past them before they reacted.

"Hey!" yelled the agent Pepper recognized, who was waving to flag him down. But Pepper just waved back, friendly but busy. Drove away smooth but fast.

* * *

Pepper suspected the two Secret Service agents would be close behind him once they talked to Trish, maybe joined by a pissed-off Alfson, so Pepper headed straight to the marina.

Murphy's Hole Marina was at the far edge of New Albion's shoreline, tucked behind a man-made breakwater. Pepper had spent a lot of his youth with his buddies and Jake in little boats around the marina, fishing and swimming and screwing around.

Nothing much had changed here. Maybe it was a little more spruced up. What was the word--gentrified? Less fish blood stains on the dock. He made his way to the far left and walked down the ramp. The marina held a mix of commercial fishing boats, sailboats and motorboats. Most of the slips were full and not many people were around.

He didn't see *Sure Thang*. But three outside slips on the far left were empty.

Pepper strolled over to a teenager who was sitting on an upside-down white pail, deep in concentration while tying an O'Shaughnessy hook on thick fishing line.

"Excuse me, you know where *Sure Thang* ties up?"

Pepper could see the teenager taking in his police uniform, deciding whether to be helpful.

"You Pepper Ryan?" the boy asked, now making eye contact.

Pepper nodded.

"I'm in Leslie Holbrook's grade... Yeah, *Sure Thang*'s slip's the middle empty one over there. He was just going out when I got here. Picked up a half-day walk on."

"When was that?"

"'Two hours ago. But funny you're here. I heard from Leslie, maybe I should talk to you?"

* * *

Pepper had left his voicemail for Leslie that morning. Requested she get the word around—if anyone was parked at Dill Lot on Saturday night, they needed to call Pepper. That it was super important.

The boy asked Pepper, can they keep it confidential? Pepper said he'd do his best to keep him out of it, but they really needed to know whatever he had to say.

"So, I was at Dill Lot on Saturday night," the boy admitted. "Just past dark like 9:30, for a while. I'm not saying with who, okay?"

"That's okay for now. What'd you see?"

"Just a car. It came into the lot and we scrunched down as it passed, thinking it might be a cop car, since it kind of looked like one."

"What color?"

"Maybe blue. Dark anyways. It backed in, far down by the end, near the path to the beach, you know? So I decided it wasn't the cops, because you guys just cruise through, shine your lights. But I didn't think anything of it yet, right? Just like they were parking too, wanted some space. But four men got out—"

"You sure they were men?"

"Definitely. They were bigger than girls and how they moved, you know? They were men. But I didn't see their faces or anything. It was too dark and too far away."

"So what'd the men do?"

"They popped their trunk. I saw them take out shovels, head down to the beach. They had to be digging a hole for that dead guy!"

"Maybe. Did you see anything else?"

"No. Jamie—I mean, my friend—was getting kinda freaked out, us hiding down low, watching the other car. I was trying to talk her into sticking around. But when a cop car came through the lot too, that made her even more freaked out. Her parents are low-key crazy."

"You sure about the cop car?" Zula had said every officer confirmed they hadn't patrolled Dill Lot that night. He'd have to ask her to double-check, had she missed somebody?

"Definitely. It was marked and everything. It cruised right through, then stopped for a minute by those guys' car. Then my friend...she wanted to split, too much traffic that early in the night. So we did." Then the boy thought a while. "Be nice if you'd catch those murdering sons, like you did that fucker in the brown van. Because Dill Lot used to be a great place to park..."

SEVENTEEN

Pepper and his dad came from the Fenway Park tunnel near first base into bright sunshine. They paused, blinking, and taking in the spectacular infield. The razor straight chalk lines. Pesky's Pole. The Green Monster looming in left.

"A grass and dirt church with eight dollar beers," said Pepper. "Remember? That's what Jake called this place."

"Amen," said his dad.

Pepper was taking that afternoon off—his first break since starting again with the New Albion police. Someone had dropped off at the police station a couple Red Sox tickets with Pepper's name on them. A rare 1:35 PM game for that Wednesday. An anonymous welcome back. The public dropped off food, tickets, all kinds of gifts to the local police and firemen from time to time as a thank you. Especially since 9/11. But Pepper suspected the secret angel this time was his buddy, Angel. And the General had insisted that Pepper take his dad to the game. Basically ordered him to do it. Chief Eisenhower and his dad were tight enough for his boss to know how uncomfortable things remained in the Ryan home since Pepper's return. And this game was the perfect chance to find a way to somehow reconnect with his dad, right?

And Alfson? He was tied up with three teams of Secret Service investigators and had said he *might* have a window of opportunity to touch base around dinner time. Which lessened Pepper's guilt for an afternoon off, just a tad.

Their seats were twelve rows behind the Sox dugout, and like all the best days at Fenway, the weather was clear and warm. Anyone who knew right from wrong loved the decision a while back to renovate historic Fenway instead of replacing it. They'd preserved its essence while wedging in some extra seats and a few more executive comforts. Like the seats they were in--a little wider than the vintage seats, a little bit more curved and comfortable for an adult rear end. Discomfort was one tradition Pepper was happy to sacrifice.

Pepper felt a bit older today than his twenty-nine years, kind of beat up. It had only been a few days since the bar fight and he had various aches and pains from things he'd sort of pulled wrestling with Dunne. His cheek had gone black and blue around his stitches, but was hurting a little bit less.

The Fenway crowd was into the ballgame. Tons of Sox fans wore replica game jerseys, even the grown-ups. A level of commercial support way beyond Pepper's worn red cap with a white B.

"We didn't do this enough," said Pepper. "In the old days." It'd been a rare treat in Pepper's youth to make the pilgrimage up to Fenway with his dad and Jake.

His dad was silent a bit. "I did the best I could, Son. The job never stopped..."

Shit. Pepper took a gulp of beer. "I didn't mean it that way."

"In fact, I was amazed you could take the afternoon, what with being on such a hot case."

Frickin' touché. Pepper's gut tightened a bit. This outing was off to a wrong start... "Speaking about the old days, I had a little run-in yesterday with your old buddies. The Weepers."

"McDevitt? He came to town?"

"I gave him six parking tickets. He didn't take it well."

"At least you didn't punch him in the face."

And they sat, each thinking about his dad's career-ending punch six years ago. The Weepers had been picketing a dead soldier's funeral. The chaos was captured on video from three angles. The Weepers had broken the police line in several places and the reverend got too close to the grieving widow and her parents. She'd turned, her face pale, running with tears. Eyes wild with fear and grief, shrinking away as Reverend McDevitt leaned forward, spitting his insults into her face. Chief Ryan's right cross had caught the reverend on the ear mid-taunt, knocking him unconscious before he hit the ground.

Pepper had seen the footage so many times on TV afterward, it was embedded in his brain more than most childhood memories. "Well, it was a hell of a punch. For an older guy," said Pepper, grinning a bit.

His dad cracked a little smile back. "Not as creative as a pool cue to the nuts, but it did the job."

From the next section over, the peanut vendor kid tossed a bag of peanuts over Pepper's head perfectly to a fan who'd waved for them. More accurate than today's Sox starter. The kid reminded Pepper of the teen from Dill Lot so Pepper quietly told his dad about the witness and what the boy had seen. "But something's not right," confided Pepper. "About the cop he saw drive through the lot? Zula talked to all the officers on patrol that night and confirmed they weren't there that night. Someone's lying and it better not be someone with a badge…"

His dad laughed. "You sound like Jake, with that line. But maybe there's some other explanation. Did she check with the sheriff for county cars? Or an officer could have popped over from Chatham…maybe trying to locate his own teen parked in the dark?"

None of which Pepper had thought of.

"I can check with Kelly over at the sheriff's office and Melanie at Chatham," offered his dad. "I can get quick answers--they both have crushes on me."

The old man was probably only half-kidding. "Thanks, but let me think about it first."

By the bottom of the fifth, the score was Tampa Bay 5, Boston 4. But Boston had runners on first and second with no one out.

Pepper's phone rang. Special Agent Alfson.

Shit. Pepper had left a message for Alfson that he'd be out of town for the day, hadn't said why.

Pepper didn't answer the call, but he gave his dad a grimace. The Sox's left fielder struck out a moment later, so Pepper took the chance to get up and do the Fenway shuffle past the row of fans to the aisle. He walked down through the tunnel to the concession area under the seats. Then called Alfson back.

"Partner, where're you at?" asked Alfson.

A deafening roar from the crowd above him drowned out Pepper's reply. A home run? At least a hit. But Pepper was trying to muffle the noise by covering the bottom of his phone. With a pinkie stuffed in his other ear. Didn't help much.

"I'm up in Boston."

"Don't tell me you're up at Fenway?" Alfson's voice was dripping with incredulity. Or maybe disgust? "What're you--

part-time?"

Pepper didn't take the bait. Instead, he filled in Alfson about the teen witness and everything he'd told Pepper. The four men, the shovels, the sedan that might be blue, everything the boy saw. But not his name. "Find Dunne for me and maybe I'll be less paranoid," said Pepper. "I'm not putting that kid's life at risk too."

Alfson sputtered and blustered, but Pepper wasn't budging.

Alfson finally gave up, for now. "Well, enjoy your vacation day. By the way, one of my crews just got back the toxicology for Keser. The lab found two drugs: Atricurium and methadone. The unsubs probably shot him up with atricurium…it's a short-term paralytic. Followed later by a big whack of methadone, which basically kept him paralyzed while he steamed to death. Maybe they're not as moronic as you told the press. If you were hoping the unsubs would overreact to your insults, I guess that failed, huh?"

Pepper had heard of methadone but not the other drug. Were the unsubs pros, or crazy? How did the drugs fit the profile?

"By the way," said Alfson. "My boys went by yesterday to check on Dunne and thought they saw you?"

"Yeah, I was doing the same. But he wasn't around— probably decided to sleep on his boat, offshore."

Pepper promised to call Alfson first thing in the morning, then hung up. He bought four Fenway franks then returned to his seat. The roar had been a three-run homer so the Sox were now up by two.

Pepper and his dad didn't make much small talk now. They kind of focused on the ballgame's rituals. But the Ryan men were never the chatty types anyway. Pepper relaxed, getting into it. Even the syrupy sing-along to Sweet Caroline before the Sox batted in the eighth didn't annoy him as much as it used to.

Top of the ninth, Tampa had runners on first and third with two outs. Pepper and his dad were on their feet with the rest of the Fenway faithful when Tampa's catcher struck out to end the game.

As they joined the afternoon rush on 93 South, Pepper realized that maybe for the first time he was glad to be home again. But he knew he and his dad were both conscious of the empty space in the truck, where his older brother Jake would have been. Hell, Jake would have been driving.

"I was thinking," said Pepper. "Maybe you could give me a hand a little, with the clambake case? Like those calls to the county sheriff's office, and to Chatham? Quietly, so the feds don't throw a fit."

His dad paused a little longer than Pepper would have expected. "I wouldn't be interfering?"

"No way. I still think they might be right that a local connection's the key and who knows the Cape better than us? But two things, Dad. This time, I'm in charge, okay? You let me know what you're up to, before you do it. And anything you find, you tell me, even if you think it's not important. That'll be my call, what matters. Oh, and you'd better ask for the General's blessing--I'm already too high on his shit list."

"That's four things," said his dad in his old cop voice, but from his peripheral vision Pepper saw a hint of a smile.

So okay, the beginning of a new beginning...

And Pepper was trying to keep the big picture in mind. This crisis was just temporary. The case would be solved soon, or at least the President would have safely come and gone. A couple of weeks, tops. It'd be all good before they knew it...

Within ninety minutes they cruised back over the

Sagamore.   Hit the New Albion town limits by 6:30 PM. Rolled up Shore Road to their cottage a few minutes later.

Except the cottage literally wasn't there anymore.   Where their house had been that morning when they'd left, there was nothing now but a sloping lawn of grass and a landscaper watering newly-laid sod from a hose attached to a truck with a big water tank in the back.   The house was just gone: demolished, trucked away and the foundation had been filled in and sodded over.   No sign there'd ever been a home there.

Pepper and his dad just sat in his truck at the roadside, stunned.   Pepper thought he must be asleep, having a nightmare, was this for real?   Next to him, his dad had gone pale white, clutched his chest, let out a muffled little sound like he was being crushed.

EIGHTEEN

The ambulance raced through traffic to Cape Cod Hospital in Hyannis, with Pepper following too quickly behind in his truck. An endless thirty minutes.

That began a long night. The doctors were still trying to figure it out. His dad had symptoms of a heart attack. They'd found cardiac enzymes in his blood, which meant his heart muscle was damaged. The EKG showed abnormalities. But they couldn't find any blockages in the arteries that supply blood to his heart.

They said it was maybe something called Takotsubo cardiomyopathy, his left ventricle wasn't working due to a surge of stress hormones after severe emotional trauma. A medical term for your heart just got broken. They had his dad pumped up on a number of medicines but weren't going to operate if they could avoid it.

The New Albion dispatch desk must have picked up the ambulance transport details because half an hour after Pepper arrived, so did the General and Zula.

"Two hospital runs in one week, Pepper?" asked Zula. "You making this place your second home?"

Ouch. Pepper told them about the Ryan house having been demolished. About his dad's reaction.

Zula's hand covered her throat.

The General was too mad to sit after he heard Pepper's story. He went to call a patrol car to check whether the landscaper was still there to be questioned. Zula stayed in the ER waiting room with Pepper, working her cell phone. She checked in with every officer who'd been on duty. Hit pay dirt with the younger guy, Jackson Phillips.

Zula squeezed Pepper's arm and relayed the story. How Phillips had been at the site all day. That he'd gone to the address for construction detail he'd been given: 76 Shore Lane. That there'd been no construction there, just a quiet house on a quiet street. How he'd taken a little initiative, drove a few blocks over to 76 Shore Road. That the demolition was in full swing, with a snarl of construction vehicles and other traffic. So he'd figured it was a typo and jumped right in and worked traffic detail there all day. No, he hadn't bothered Dispatch with the typo. No, he didn't know it was the Ryan house. And no, he hadn't checked the demolition company's paperwork, why would he? But he remembered part of the logo stenciled on the six or so dump trucks that carted away the rubble after the bulldozers completed the demolition. Some name with Rhode Island under it.

* * *

Soon after sunrise on Thursday morning, his dad in stable condition, Pepper drove back from the hospital to the Ryan home site and parked streetside. They'd even resodded the driveway path. It was all grass now, the entire fucking lot, like a park. He stood above the slope where his family's house had been. Where his mom had lived, before she'd died giving birth Pepper was four. Where he and Jake had grown up. Pepper could feel his face burning.

A BMW convertible pulled in behind his truck. It was his buddy Angel Cavada. Pepper hadn't talked to him, but Angel must have heard and known Pepper would be back to survey the disaster. Knew Pepper like a twice-read book.

"Well, on the bright side," said Angel after he slipped from his convertible, "your lawn never looked this green."

"Makes a nice pretty place to bury the assholes who did it," snapped Pepper.

Angel just grunted, held his tongue.

A wave of anger, embarrassment and frustration was washing over Pepper now he was back on site and could see it all starkly in daylight. This couldn't be fucking real! His dad could have been killed in the demolition. And Pepper. "What the hell am I doing wearing a badge?" he asked. "I can't even protect my own home."

"*Mano*, I get it," said Angel. "This is a mortal bitch-slapping. Looks like a real attempt to wipe your family off the map. Literally. But you guys'll get up, fight another day, right?"

Pepper was still almost too angry to respond. "Dude, I gotta tell you, I never felt like this before. Beyond pissed. Heartbroken. Embarrassed--this was my *HOME*." And Pepper had to ask. "Angel, you didn't drop off two Sox tickets at the station for me, did you?"

Angel shook his head no, watching Pepper. Confused.

"I was so full of myself," Pepper grumbled. "Some anonymous benefactor drops off two tickets, welcome home, native son! And I took the hook like a freakin' tuna!"

Pepper kicked the fresh sod hard enough to rip it up. "Maybe it was a mistake for me to come home. Maybe I need to quit the force, get the hell away from the Ryan curse. Start fresh, somewhere else, doing something completely new."

"Couldn't blame you either way bro. Even before this shit."

But Pepper couldn't fool himself. "Realistically? Screw that. I have to find whoever did this. And they'll be getting off easy if they just end up in handcuffs."

Pepper and Angel walked all the way to the new lawn's end, where it gave way to a strip of scraggly beach grass, leading to the beach dunes and shore. And it was funny--just getting a little closer to the ocean seemed to calm Pepper down a little bit.

"How the *hell* did they get the whole demolition and cleanup done in less than six hours?" questioned Pepper.

"Well, they did. Always quicker to destroy than build, right?" said Angel. "All it takes is some extra equipment and manpower. And the whole thing was just a sucker punch, really, when you think about it. What were you supposed to do? Those trucks came out of nowhere."

True. Pepper couldn't have done anything to prevent it from Boston, not if he was being fair to himself. "But I can do something to find out who did it. Find the trucks. Follow the paperwork."

"And from the other angle," said Angel, "any idea what wack job would hate you or your Dad enough to do this?"

Pepper studied the gray, gray water. "I've rattled a few cages since I got home. The other day I embarrassed Dad's old punching bag, Reverend McDevitt. And Dad had two decades as a cop here to make his share of enemies."

"Any chance it could just be a stupid mistake?" mused Angel. "A paperwork screw-up? Like someone did the right job, wrong location?"

"Sure. But I doubt it. My guess? Good old-fashioned revenge. Or maybe an attempt to distract me? Other than the Weepers, I've had a few run-ins with activist groups who might be criminals or terrorists, once we figure out what they're really up to. But—"

Pepper's phone rang and he answered quickly. It was Lieutenant Hurd, hopefully with news about catching the bastards who demolished their house. Where they were sitting, Pepper couldn't get a great signal, but he pressed the phone as hard as he could into his ear. It sounded like Lieutenant Hurd was saying...but he couldn't be saying?!?

"Lieutenant, did you just order me to stay clear of my home demolition case?"

At his side, Angel's eyes went wide. Quizzical surprise.

Hurd's voice was 51% static, 49% attitude. "Wonderboy, I hope you're hearing me," Hurd repeated thinly in Pepper's ear. "You're too close to the case. You're the victim. But we'll have our best people on it. Hell, I'll be on it too. We'll catch the scumbags, I promise. But we need a clean case to get a conviction. No way we can let you help-- you're the victim! And Chief Eisenhower agrees."

At that moment, Pepper almost quit again. He even opened his mouth, cleared his throat, started to form the words. Fuck Hurd, fuck 'em all. No way was he sitting this one out. But as he started to say so, he saw Angel gesturing wildly. The cut-off motion, across Angel's throat.

And the damn cell phone connection was getting even more unstable and thin.

So Pepper just hung up. Considered throwing his phone as far into the Atlantic as he could, but stopped himself.

"Well there's insult to injury," said Pepper, dazed. "The lieutenant ordered me to keep out of this investigation! As if that's even possible!"

"Unbelievable!"

"Maybe I should just quit, because I'm not sitting this

out. I'll keep working on the clambake case but no way I won't help run down the assholes who did *this*. And could I get your help?"

"Always, *Mano*. I'll chat around town. See what's the buzz."

"Thanks, I owe ya pal…"

Angel gave him a too-hard punch on the shoulder. "You get on the stool some Thursday nights, belt out 'Margaritaville' for my sunburned tourists, and we're even."

Good word, thought Pepper, studying the Atlantic's morning surf and the low bank of early summer clouds choking the shoreline. *Sums it right up, buddy. Time to get even.*

NINETEEN

Pepper headed straight to the police station to requisition a new uniform, since his had been in the demolished house. Luckily his Glock had been safely in his truck's lockbox during the Fenway trip. But when Pepper arrived at the station, Trish Dunne was sitting there, waiting for him.

"And only you, Wonderboy," said Sergeant Forrestal, with an annoyed head shake.

Trish's daughter Kaylee was kneeling on the floor, using a chair as a desk for her coloring book. Crayons had spilled across the floor. They'd been there a long while. And Trish looked like she hadn't slept. Hadn't eaten. Hadn't showered. Pepper thought maybe she was wearing the same clothes as when he'd been at her house yesterday.

"Officer Ryan shouldn't even be talking to you," said Forrestal. But Pepper took Trish and her daughter back into a small interview room.

Trish didn't waste time. "Pepper, you've gotta find Marcus. Something terrible *must* have happened! This isn't like him. Sure, he sleeps out on the water when fishing's hot. But he almost always checks in on the radio. But he's not answering!" She was shaking and started crying, eyes closing slowly.

"Trish, how'd you guys get that fancy Boston law firm to represent Marcus?"

"The lawyer? He just showed up. Said he was *pro bono* because of their work with the fishing industry. Which Marcus said mighta been bullshit. But she got Marcus out, right? You think that lawyer has something to do with Marcus disappearing?"

"I don't know," said Pepper quietly. Taking Trish's hand, giving a squeeze he hoped was supportive. "Trish, did Marcus tell you what he saw, about the clambake murder?"

Trish shook her head.

"Nothing at all?"

"Just what he said at the bar. Or was it earlier... About the asshole car?"

"Marcus didn't say anything about a car to me."

"Or the guy with a ball cap?"

"Who?"

"Well that's all he said. He saw a car that morning, broke down right where the news said the jogger was snatched. A big blue car, some American make. Marcus kept calling it the asshole car. And he saw two guys. One had a ball cap, but not a sports logo, you know? An Interstate Batteries hat."

"What else did he say?"

"Something I didn't get. Something about cashing in. But he was kinda high, I don't know what he meant. Or if he was joking? But Pepper, I just need him back. I need your help. The rest of the cops, you know, whatta they care? But if I don't get him back..."

Cashing in? Asshole car?

Pepper promised Trish he'd do his best. That lots of local law enforcement were on the lookout for Marcus too.

All the right things. Trish had stopped crying when she led Kaylee away but her eyes were harder and her face was set. Already accepting the worst. Like that's how it went in their world so why would it go differently this time?

* * *

Pepper felt pretty damn frustrated. He was sidelined from hunting down the people who destroyed his own home and effectively put his dad in the hospital. And he remained on the outer circle of the Secret Service's homicide investigation. How was a Wonderboy supposed to do his job?

Pepper also suspected that the Secret Service wasn't sharing everything they knew about the long list of activists and their organizations in town for the POTUS's vacation. Pepper's own list had grown to thirteen groups, with known activities ranging from clean, legal protests to acts of domestic terror. But the other Secret Service agents referred Pepper's questions to Alfson. And Alfson seemed to delight in giving Pepper the narrowest answers possible.

So enough of that. Pepper found an empty office, closed the door and called the FBI's National Security Branch. Their analysts would have literally written the book on the thirteen groups Pepper was wondering about...

Pepper explained who he was and the general situation in New Albion, then the intel and analysis he needed on the thirteen groups. Far more information than he believed he could access through the usual interagency law enforcement databases. Could they help?

The clerk passed him to an agent, so Pepper told his story all over again to her. Finally the agent said she'd see what she could do, she'd have to clear it up her chain of command.

Pepper didn't hear urgency coming back through the phone. He heard jadedness, weariness. So he played a card he'd hoped not to. "Have your boss chat with Deputy Assistant Director Edwina Youngblood, in your Criminal Investigative Division. She owes me a little favor."

The pause that followed may have been caused by the agent trying to decide whether to ask what favor Pepper had performed for Ms. Youngblood, but eventually she just promised to be in touch.

Pepper thanked her, wishing she'd said *soon*...

TWENTY

Later that afternoon, Pepper Ryan made the drive back to Hyannis to help his dad leave the hospital. Pepper arrived to find Jake's widow, Julie Stowe-Ryan, already at his dad's bedside. Pepper hadn't seen her in three years, since Jake's funeral. She was unchanged: tall, athletically slim and pretty, despite her severe blonde hairdo and hard eyes.

Jake and Julie had been married for six years when Jake was killed. She, Patrick and Little Jake still lived in the house in Boston's Jamaica Plain neighborhood that she and Jake had bought as newlyweds.

"He's coming with me," said Julie, arms crossed.

"Hello to you too, Julie," said Pepper. "How've you been?"

His dad was sitting in a chair in the corner, tying his shoes. "Angry. That pretty much sums it up," he said. "She's been cursing at me in French, which Jake always said was a bad sign."

Jake had met her a year after she'd received her master's degree in teaching at Tufts. A man had been murdered a floor above her apartment and Jake interviewed her when going door to door, leaving her apartment with no worthwhile information except her phone number. They'd married four months later in Las Vegas after a quick, crazy romance, to the horror of her wealthy Connecticut family.

Pepper had heard that Julie went back to teaching French at a Boston high school after Jake died. In the first year after the funeral, Pepper had tried to send postcards and birthday presents to Jake's boys, but Pepper had never heard back. 'Papa' Ryan was allowed to visit his grandsons but his invitations only came just once or twice a year. Pepper didn't understand it.

"It's settled, Pepper," she said. "I'm getting him away from whatever Ryan disaster you've unleashed this time. He's lucky to be alive! He could have been at the bottom of a dump truck!"

"Your call, Dad," said Pepper, gritting his teeth, making eye contact with his dad. Who gave him the smallest nod back.

His dad stood slowly, stretched, then walked over to stand at Pepper's side. "It'd be good timing to visit the boys—I don't have anything to pack. But that house was everything I had left of my wife. And Jake. All the pictures, everything... Sorry Julie but I need to stay, help figure out who destroyed our home. And I promised Pepper I'd help with another case, so that's two good reasons to stick around. Eisenhower said I could bunk with them."

Pepper had an unhelpful mental image of his dad and the General in bunk beds. He laughed out loud, which earned him a glare from Julie. But she quickly refocused her anger on his dad.

"Help?!?" scoffed Julie. "You're retired! What can you do?"

Pepper's dad looked right at his son's widow, saying, "I can help track down the dirtbags—if they're in my town, I'll find them. Always could. And even better, I still know a lot of people with badges who owe me favors. So I guess it's time to collect."

"Why did I even come down?" complained Julie. "And I won't even imagine where *you'll* be sleeping!" she said to Pepper with a toss of her short hair.

Pepper said nothing. Angel had offered to take him in, but Pepper felt in his gut he had to stay on the Ryan property, even if that meant sleeping in a tent. Angel had promised to do better than that and they were meeting up later that day for Pepper to learn Angel's surprise solution. None of which would impress Julie…

Julie's eyes were wet but her voice had no shake when she said, "Well, that house wasn't all you had left of Jake. Don't forget you have Patrick and Little Jake too. And I'll be praying for you both. Praying that my boys won't need to go to another funeral."

* * *

Zula Eisenhower couldn't get Pepper to answer his damn cell phone. As usual. She tried his number for the eighth time. Finally, he picked up.

"Hello?" Pepper's voice was scratchy. Far away.

"Pepper it's Zula. I've got some--"

"Hold on, Little Ike--"

She heard his voice even fainter, yelling to someone else. Then he was back.

"Sorry kid, I was just trying to back a trailer over Angel. What's up?"

What? "Sorry to interrupt whatever nonsense you boys are up to, but we just got a call from the Coast Guard. They found Marcus Dunne's fishing boat about eight miles offshore. It was half sunk with no one onboard."

Silence from Pepper. Then a burst of creative swear words.

She filled him in on the water search efforts to find Marcus Dunne. The Coast Guard had sent a response boat crew from their Base Cape Cod. A helicopter and an HC-144 surveillance airplane from Air Station Cape Cod were both assisting in the search. As well as the New Albion harbormaster and the New Albion police boat.

"Any other bad news?" he asked.

Zula could hear a voice in Pepper's background. "Some good news," she said. "An outfit from Warwick, Rhode Island called A&M Demolition saw the news story about your house and called us. After maybe spending some time chatting with their lawyers. Said they had the contract to demo the house and fill the site. They were hired by email and paid in advance by wire transfer. They subbed out the utility shutoffs and landscaping to an outfit from Fall River. Their position is they received copies of all the paperwork and permits, so what's the problem. They weren't willing to share the correspondence unless we get a warrant."

"They said 'so what's the problem'? Zu, what's their address in Rhode Island?"

"Pepper, no! Pop would *kill* me if you showed up at their office. We've got to do this by the book. Get a warrant. Follow procedure."

"You ever notice the good guys are the only ones following procedures? We don't have time to screw around with interstate warrants. What's the address?"

"I know my pop ordered you not to investigate this yourself. I've given all the info to Lieutenant Hurd and he'll take it from there. Trust us, Pepper. We're not the enemy."

But if Pepper was within reach right then, she would have strangled him.

150

* * *

Oliver joined Croke at his room at the Sanddollar Motel and filled him in about two messages that had been waiting on the chat room site when Oliver stopped in at the Chatham library. First, telling them that the client had gone silent. And second, instructing Oliver and Croke to wait for further orders from *them*.

"Uh oh," said Croke.

Oliver'd had the same reaction. Had *they* caught wind of Oliver and Croke's moonlighting for the client?

After a while, Croke said, "I might take off in the morning, somewhere inland. What with all these bodies piling up here."

Oliver pulled out his favorite knife, a folding Gerber. He opened it, closed it. Opened. Closed. Just fiddling with it, but conspicuously. He needed to handle this development right—keep Croke in place. "Take off? You want me to leave a message in the chat room, tell *them* you're out?"

Oliver and Croke both knew *they* wouldn't be happy. And when *they* were unhappy, even more dead bodies than usual tended to pile up...

Oliver pocketed his knife and stood. "I'm going to bed. You get some sleep too. We'll talk it over in the morning and figure out the next step, like professionals."

By talk it over, Oliver meant convince Croke, even if that meant threatening the old-timer. And by figure out the next step, Oliver meant somehow figure out whether the cops were even close to them, so he'd know if they could hang on for just a bit longer. If not, Oliver would split immediately...there was no point being infamous *and* incarcerated, huh?

TWENTY-ONE

Pepper Ryan had received Zula's news about Dunne's boat late Thursday afternoon, just as he was finishing parking his new home. A 1963 Airstream Globetrotter trailer. It was either really ugly or really cool, depending on your personal style. It looked like a baked potato wrapped in silver foil, on wheels. Angel had arranged it through his underground local network for Pepper as a cheap rental for the next few months without sharing too much info about its history. At least it was spotlessly clean.

Pepper had hauled it down from Wellfleet with his truck and parked it at the grass lawn's end, just shy of the beach. Angel was unhelpfully waving his arms and shouting contradictory directions as Pepper made the final forward and backward adjustments to position the trailer in the perfect spot. He'd angled it so the first thing he'd see when he came out the door was the ocean.

So it'd be home, for now. Before they figured out whether insurance covered whatever happened to the house. Before they would hopefully rebuild the Ryan home. But this would keep the weather off his head in the meanwhile. And maybe deliver a message to whoever took down their house, that Pepper wasn't going anywhere.

And then the shitty news came about Dunne's boat. Pepper unhooked, saluted goodbye to Angel and headed out in his truck and civilian clothes, following Shore Road south to the marina to join the law enforcement gathering there.

Pepper joined Chief Eisenhower and Lieutenant Hurd on a lower dock, where they were interviewing the captain of another fishing boat who shared the outside dock with Marcus Dunne's *Sure Thang*. The captain had been out with a charter yesterday afternoon, never saw Dunne or his charter clients. As they finished, Special Agent Alfson appeared on the ramp so they walked to meet him away from the boat captain's earshot.

"Too bad about Dunne's boat," said Alfson. "They find him yet?"

"The Coast Guard's hard at it but no news yet," said Hurd. "But look at this." It was a picture from a batch forwarded by the Coast Guard. It showed the fishing boat's stern, pretty low in the water, but clearly showing a large red starfish attached to the boat's transom, right next to the name *Sure Thang*. Hanging there like a weird decoration.

"We don't know Dunne's dead yet," Eisenhower reminded them. "But that red starfish guarantees this is foul play..."

Hurd yawned. "The clerk at the marina store saw Dunne talking to two men, one a bit older and heavier. One a bit smaller and younger. When Dunne came in to bum some baitfish, he told the clerk he'd picked up a half day with a solo tourist. A real sucker."

"I'll have an artist stop by," volunteered Alfson. "See if he can sketch up something to help identify them."

"The press is gonna pile on this," said Eisenhower. "You watch. They'll tie in that shark sighting next door in Chatham, the public'll be picturing Marcus Dunne being

153

eaten by Jaws."

The regional press had been hyping the presence of a great white shark spotted off Chatham's South Beach yesterday. It'd probably been chasing seals around in the channels but was trapped near shore for hours after the tide went out. Estimated over fourteen feet long.

They were all walking back up the docks to the parking lot now in a small, unhappy cluster. And yeah, picturing the big Chatham shark tearing into Dunne—how could they not?

"Well, my money's on the New River Front for both the Keser murder and your house's demo," said Alfson. "And the Dunne disappearance. Just our gut so far, given their body of work. By the way, my team got nowhere with the seafood angle. They drilled down at over forty seafood stores, supermarkets and roadside stands. They couldn't find anywhere that sold that shellfish combination found in the Keser clambake pit. Our new theory's the unsubs bought it in small batches from multiple locations, being hyper-careful. But my team bumped into something else funny. Every store they went to, someone else had already been there asking the same questions. An older guy, posing as a cop."

"Yeah, funny," said the General.

Pepper thinking, *Dad!*

Alfson sighed, long and pissy. "I told my guys if they catch up to that clown to arrest him for obstruction. Anyway, the POTUS arrives tomorrow and Hanley's calling me for hourly updates at this point... So Ryan, can you please—pretty please—call me if you pick up any info even remotely helpful?"

"Of course, partner. And speaking of pickups, that's Dunne's truck," Pepper said, pointing to a beat-up red Chevy truck parked next to a split rail fence. "We told his wife your folks'd probably want to sweep it before she can drive it home."

"Thanks Ryan, we will. Hey, by the way, that story you're so famous for, the brown van? Some of us were wondering, how'd you know there was a little girl in the back? Nice work and all. Heroic, despite the wrongful death suit. But how'd you know?"

Eisenhower and Hurd were watching Pepper now too, waiting for his answer.

"Just luck," Ryan shrugged. "I'd seen the BOLOs, from the other two missing children. The driver didn't stop fully at a red, before he turned right. Then he panicked." Sticking exactly to what he'd written in his report, eight years ago.

"Good luck he was so sloppy, with you right there watching him. Well, I gotta run. President Wayne Garby and family arrive tomorrow morning. So if all this chaos in your town's really been about him, then buckle up, friends. It's about to get much worse."

TWENTY-TWO

Cape Cod is a great place to get away from it all. Unless you're the President of the United States. Then it all comes with you. But Wayne Garby wouldn't have had it any other way.

As he sat in the leather comfort of his helicopter seat just before noon on Friday, he imagined what the little people on shore were seeing. He pictured their eyes growing to saucers as the five Sikorsky S-92 helicopters appeared over the ocean horizon and shifted in formation as they swooped toward New Albion. Four helicopters eventually spread in the sky but did not land. The fifth, only now identifiable as Marine One, approached shore and gently landed on Eagle's Nest's wide lawn. President Garby knew how to make an entrance.

He allowed his in-flight security detail to exit first, then his twin daughters Brianne and Skyler, then himself with his wife. He loved being *the man*. And what better way than the air display to show Smith that Garby was the true big swinging dick and Smith was just lucky to know him?

The remainder of Garby's entourage had preceded him to Eagle's Nest, although most would be staying in hotels, motels and rental homes nearby. Fifty-five staff members. Eighty-four secret service officers. 100 or so reporters and other media schlubs would be haunting the vicinity, like buzzards. And of course the protesters, camera hounds and miscellaneous nutballs. So, a circus of hundreds.

Everyone knows the President of the United States can't do anything right. He can't even go on vacation right. The press had been sautéing him for the past two weeks, of course. The standard outrage: with all the crises going on in the world *at that exact moment,* how did Garby have the gall to take a vacation? The stock market was too far down, unemployment was too far up. And now he had the historic opportunity to nominate two Supreme Court members at the same time, to fill one justice's recent retirement and another's fatal stroke only two weeks later. The press was incredulous—instead, *his* priority was a beach holiday with his billionaire backer? Proving again beyond a doubt that Garby was irresponsible, out-of-touch, a money whore, etc.

Well, it takes one to know one... And Garby's actual priority at that moment was to locate a nice, dry gin martini.

On the plus side, both of his daughters had actually shown up. His poo-pooing of the assassination threat and his cajoling had, as expected, been largely unsuccessful. But he'd sold them on Smith's daughter, a jet-setter and money burner of the first class, being there as their personal hostess. With her London and Miami trash nightlife friends. It would be a scene. They knew her a little. And a little more by reputation.

They would do it for the fam.

Acker Smith and his daughter Maddie met them on the compound's Guest House patio-- handshakes, hugs and kisses. Smith looked like shit. Pale. Thinner. Death warmed over-easy. Which was accurate, Garby guessed. His daughter was Cape Cod delicious. Long wavy blonde hair. Thin where she should be, curvy where she should be. Little white shorts, the perfect fit between classy and obscene. Like she'd stepped from a Ralph Lauren ad. He noticed her studying him but she didn't look away when he caught her—she just smiled mysteriously, boldly.

He toyed with the idea--could he? No, to even think about nailing Smith's daughter would be a disaster on all fronts. Garby had to keep it clean. For the sake of the millions he needed to secure from her daddy this week. And to not tempt Lulu to carry out her threat to assassinate him herself...

When Garby had been briefed about the Red Starfish Wacko, the Secret Service Director had actually advised him to cancel his vacation. And Garby might have canceled if he could, but he *really* needed to ask Smith for a ton more money, this week. And almost as important, he needed to keep looking strong. Even if he was actually pretty damned scared.

Fuck it, done was done. Garby wondered whether his favorite pal Alexis had arrived on the Cape yet. She'd be staying with a lady friend in Chatham, the next town over. He'd have to ask his chief of staff when they got a side moment—Alexis was one of his unwritten responsibilities. Garby imagined Alexis' newly blonde hair which he hadn't seen yet. He smiled. Sure, she was older than Smith's daughter, but she was like a mint condition vintage Corvette. Full speed on straightaways, exciting on curves.

Garby smiled. This vacation would be exactly what he needed. Screw the protesters and troublemakers. He'd take his family out for the ice cream, window shopping and photos. And tomorrow afternoon he'd be headed to Eastward Ho! Country Club in Chatham for 18 holes, after a quick stop en route to welcome Alexis to the Cape. He hoped she'd have little white shorts too. And he hoped when

Lulu heard the name of the golf course he was headed to, it wouldn't coincidentally make her suspicious. He'd have to bring Lulu a complimentary visor from the pro shop.

Garby had missed the thread of the group's conversation and didn't know why everyone was now staring out to sea.

"The *Madeline Too*," announced Smith's daughter. Madeline did a ta-da move, kicking out one long tanned leg for extra emphasis.

A cargo ship was cresting the horizon. Crowding the horizon, a leviathan.

But it wasn't a cargo ship. Garby could see now it was a yacht. The biggest motherfucking yacht Garby had ever seen--long, black and sleek. The five Navy helicopters were flying seaward and as they passed the yacht, they seemed like little fucking seagulls.

Smith's yacht. The best money could buy. Like Garby himself... Smith's message couldn't be any clearer. Feel free to mooch off my home. Feel free to beg for my money. But don't forget who owns who...

Where was his goddamn martini?

TWENTY-THREE

Pepper Ryan spent the early morning in a Robinson R44 Raven helicopter, an exercise in necessary futility. He'd hired the helicopter and pilot out of his own pocket to take him in a starburst pattern from the spot where Marcus Dunne's abandoned boat was found. Hoping what—that he would see Marcus Dunne floating in the water, alive? Despite no such success by the Coast Guard's helicopter, seaplane and boats? Pepper knew that his effort was irrational, but he had to do *something*.

The sunrise provided a blood-orange mess of light, bouncing off of the low cloud cover, setting the ocean aglow. His pilot kept the helicopter incredibly low to the water, and Pepper kept his binoculars glued to the helicopter window. The water was calm enough that he should be able to see any significant object floating on the ocean's surface, but he knew with tides, currents and time, Marcus Dunne could have floated a large distance by now. And they didn't know whether he was even in the water, dead or alive.

Pepper felt angry, anxious and powerless. His gut was unwilling to accept what his brain was telling him. Why would the Red Starfish Killer have let Dunne get into the water alive?

He was glad that the helicopter pilot wasn't the chatty type. Pepper just scanned and scanned until the pilot gave him the high sign—fuel was getting low. Failure.

What was he going to say to Trish Dunne, and their little daughter?

* * *

Zula Eisenhower was covering the front desk while the sergeant took his lunch break. And the foot traffic was constant—citizens lined up, ten deep. A queue of unbroken misery. *Where do I bail out my boyfriend? Where do I report my missing car?* Zula was experienced enough to handle their questions easily, but still young enough to be bummed by their misery. So she really didn't have time for Pepper Ryan's nonsense when he appeared at her shoulder.

Pepper looked like crap. Like he hadn't slept. Like he'd slept in his uniform. But still looking good enough to get that damn tingle going on the back of her neck. *Idiot!*

"Zula, do you, ah, have plans later?"

Later today? What was he thinking about—work or... pleasure? She made a face, asked the lady at the front of the line to please hold on a sec. Turned to look up to him, grinning down at her. "Why?"

"Well, two things. Angel's throwing a bit of a bash tonight at Malecón. A welcome for the Garby twins. There's even a VIP list, and Angel was kind enough put me on it. With a plus one. So, interested?"

Of course she was, but she feared it was for a different reason than Pepper, the idiot. So play it casual... "I heard about his big event. Like everyone else within a hundred miles...party with the First Daughters... Do I need any shots first?"

The waiting lady was tapping some paperwork impatiently, so Zula ignored her.

"I'll buy you all the shots you can drink. Oh, and one other thing. I'm trying to make sure Agent Keser wasn't killed for something related to his work at Eagle's Nest...could you do a full search on a company called Fulmar Limited? Maybe start with corporate record databases, confirm where they're registered, who're the officers? And bounce those people against NCIC, iCORI, whatever you can access. Also OFAC, if you can. The whole nine yards..." Pepper looked at her—tired, worried, almost pleading.

So what was a girl to do?

"Whatever you need," she said. *Just please please don't take me for granted, bub.*

* * *

Pepper left his Airstream around 9:30 PM on Friday, maybe dressed a little sharper than usual. It helped that almost all of his clothes were newly purchased, due to the house destruction. He arrived at the Eisenhower home a few minutes later to pick up Zula.

Tonight was all about getting in tighter with Maddie Smith and her so-special guests, the First Daughters, because Pepper needed to get free roam of Eagle's Nest, ASAP. There was nothing on the water that he could do to help find Marcus Dunne or to get to the bottom of all the other chaos that had been going on in New Albion. So he would focus his energy on trouble on dry land.

Maddie wanted him to investigate her daddy's assistant, but she hadn't gotten Pepper on the Secret Service's gate list, yet. Someone was delaying the approval and Pepper suspected his dear partner, Alfson. The special agent didn't know about Maddie's request to make sure daddy's billions were safe from his assistant's claws. But Alfson knew Pepper wanted to look into the work that Keser was doing before he disappeared in case it pointed Pepper toward the killers. Pepper wasn't going to share all his plans and motivations with Alfson—he needed to do his own snooping, not blindly trust the feds did a thorough job. Nor trust they were sharing with Pepper everything he needed to know...

Mrs. Eisenhower answered the doorbell. Tiny, Malaysian and with a joyful smile on her lovely face. She enveloped Pepper in a hug despite not being a bit over five foot four. She'd always mothered him and Jake and he still loved every bit of it.

"Zula will be right down," she said with a wink. "Are you skinnier, Pepper? How about some nice rendang while you wait?"

Pepper did love her cooking. And he hadn't had rendang for years... But he thanked her no, said he'd already eaten. Which had been an Italian sub, standing over the tiny sink in his Airstream.

Pepper found Chief Eisenhower in the den with his houseguest, Pepper's dad. The two men had been friends since their army days, surviving Eisenhower's time as lieutenant to Chief of Police Ryan, then Eisenhower's taking over when Chief Ryan suddenly resigned six years ago after he KO'd Reverend McDevitt. The kind of friendship which transcended such mistakes as well as rank and reporting lines. They both had their feet up and had been talking about the presidential vacation while sipping scotch whiskey with the TV news on mute. Pepper suspected Lagavulin 16, with one measly ice cube each. He declined a glass.

The General was staring at Pepper and finally he said, "Zula tells me this is work tonight?"

"Yes sir, kind of undercover," answered Pepper, immediately regretting that word choice.

Without really moving, Chief Eisenhower seemed to expand and somehow grow more menacing. "Well, be extra careful. If Zula gets hurt…there'll be another murder in this town."

Pepper's dad chuckled. But Pepper swallowed, then nodded. Message received, boss.

President Garby's face appeared on the TV screen and the General broke off his glare to turn on the volume. It was a news story recapping how the First Family had tied up New Albion's picturesque little main street. How dozens of regular families had their vacations ruined for his photo op and stroll. No consideration for the voters. Shouldn't he be back in DC, working to fill the two Supreme Court vacancies? That kind of snarky pounding. With a snort, the General clicked off the TV.

"Did you hear yet about our progress on the house demo?" Pepper's dad asked him. He shared that a sheriff in Warwick, Rhode Island had obtained and served a warrant on A & M Demolition earlier in the day. A Warwick judge had agreed there was concurrent jurisdiction between Massachusetts and Rhode Island since the alleged illegal activity—the home destruction and removal—continued all the way to the Warwick landfill.

"The sheriff and I go back a bit," said his dad. He explained he knew the sheriff from a case ten years earlier involving a Warwick politician with a suspiciously large vacation house in New Albion. He'd assisted the sheriff despite pressure from some pretty wired Massachusetts politicians with ties to the suspect.

"Saved us weeks on the warrant," grunted the General. "The demo company is probably just a pawn—we need to figure out who moved the pieces."

His dad winked at Pepper. "So I'll drive over to Warwick in the morning, collect copies. Good thing I've got the Barnstable deputy badge. Because our Lieutenant Hurd doesn't seem to have much time to lead this investigation..." Pepper knew his dad had been a workhorse as New Albion's chief of police, but he'd never known that his reputation—and web of friends and influence—extended so far beyond his corner of the Cape.

The General started to respond but then stopped, his eyes glued over Pepper's shoulder. So Pepper turned.

Holy shit.

It was Zula standing in the doorway, but not like he'd seen her before. She was wearing a mid-length black skirt and glittery black cropped bustier which left her narrow waist and belly button exposed, with a winking little diamond piercing. The bustier clung to her upper body, showing every curve, and just a hint of dark cleavage. Her brown eyes looked bigger than ever. Her long, straight black hair was loose on her shoulders, except one thin braid at the side of her head. She was wearing slender high heels which brought her up to the height of Pepper's lips. And he could smell her perfume faintly from across the room, like sweet vanilla smoke. Zula Eisenhower, all grown up.

Zula gave a mock pose. "I figured it's going to be hot tonight?" she said.

The General put down his scotch on the table with a little bang, causing it to slosh over the side.

Zula's mother appeared at her side in the doorway and smiled. "Just let me get my camera," she said.

"Mom!" Zula pulled Pepper out the front door and closed it, with her own little bang.

TWENTY-FOUR

When Pepper and Zula neared Malecón, they found the streets in gridlock. Way more cars than usual and all maneuvering for parking spaces. He hooked a left down an alley, parked behind Tootsie Griffin's dark insurance agency.

When they walked around the corner and saw Malecón, Pepper stopped in his tracks. Malecón's electric blue sign was mostly covered up by black fabric, leaving just three letters glowing in the night above the crowd: **ecó**. With expert staging by one of Maddie's South Beach friends, Malecón's patio had been reborn for one night only as a Miami-style ultra-lounge in honor of the First Daughters' arrival. A Cape Cod first.

The mob by the front door was everyone on the Eastern Seaboard trying to get in.

There was a blue velvet rope blocking the door and a broad line overseen by a very large, bored bald dude with scars crisscrossing his face. But according to Mr. Scarface, Pepper was on the VIP list, he and Zula could go right in. Accompanied by grumbling from the waiting horde until the bouncer quieted them with a raised eyebrow.

They entered, Pepper blinking to sort out the confusing layers of light. The patio was unrecognizable. Little lamps with colored bulbs were strategically arranged around the patio, with ominous shades. The light was inconsistent--warm, then missing. Shadows danced in and out of Pepper's eyes until he didn't know whether he was tricking himself. The fence and portable walls were slashed by vertical, fluorescent tubes in ambers, reds and burnt oranges, not unlike an angry sunset standing on its side. The long bar was framed in purple fluorescent tubes, covered by a smoked plastic case.

Pepper found himself grinning. This was not his typical scene, but it was pretty cool. And the crowd was electric—mostly young, but a mix of ages. And in that twisted lighting, mostly attractive.

The stage was lit a bit differently. It was lined with drip-scarred candles, which flickered wildly in the swirling crowd, always in danger of snuffing out, but always springing back with taller flames than before. Behind the flames was a DJ with equipment stacks, playing house music. His head's left side, including his eyebrow, was shaven. All hair on the right side was blue. Again, including the eyebrow.

"DJ Bad Smurf?" laughed Zula, her eyes, teeth and hair shining in the lights.

Pepper squeezed her hand and led her toward the patio's middle, where Maddie Smith was center of the universe in a silver, flapperish dress, long legs shimmering in green nylons. Maddie was loosely surrounded by a good-sized group, including internet star Justin Case, who was puffing his vape pen and entertaining his own posse of admirers. Their clique seemed to be watched by, and somehow above, the rest of the crowd.

Pepper was already more than a little sick of Justin Case. Word of his presence in New Albion had spread from YouTube to other social media. Justin was sighted buying a slice at Broken Dreams, and looking not quite *meh* about it—his highest endorsement. Broken Dreams had been overrun since that moment. Tweets blasted a rumor he'd been attacked by a shark but escaped mostly unscathed. Teens and twenty-somethings were spontaneously traveling to the Cape hoping to meet Justin Case. To beg a selfie. Or the ultimate, a lazy snippet of video with their cyber-idol.

At the moment, he was holding Maddie's hand but was facing two other women. Identical brunettes, in matching white leather minidresses and flip-flops. Early twenties. Pepper recognized them from pictures—President Garby's twin daughters, Brianne and Skyler. Secret Service codenames: Freestyle and Funsize. But he didn't know which was which. One a touch shorter, so would she be Funsize? Pepper saw two men hovering nearby who were clearly out of place and uncomfortable in jeans and blue blazers, matching five-point star pins on their lapels. Close but not too close, what they'd call loose surveillance. God bless the Secret Service...

Justin was telling the twins some story and they were hanging on his every lazy gesture, every carefree word. As Pepper and Zula joined the group, Pepper overheard Justin say, "And that's why I have a passion for beauty."

"Oh my *God*, Pepper, you look even better dressed up!" screamed Maddie, giving him a hug and a kiss on each cheek. Her light perfume was spicy. Invisible fire. Then Maddie noticed Zula, gave what Pepper figured was her best smile. Zula smiled back, a tad extra fake? Pepper introduced them and Maddie repeated the French cheek pecks, taking her in and pronounced, "*So* exotic!"

Quickly, Maddie had each of them by the hand and interrupted Justin's spiel to introduce them to the Garby daughters.

"Ohhh, I *love* your bustier!" said Brianne. It turned out the twins loved **ecó**. Loved the music. Loved everything.

"Pepper?" asked Skyler, the slightly shorter twin. "Why do they call you Pepper?"

"Because he's hot!" said Maddie. The twins both shrieked.

Pepper could see Zula watching their antics, her arms crossed and her mouth tight, then maybe realizing it, correcting with a too-big smile.

Maddie told Pepper and Zula she'd flown in the DJ from Miami. DJ ChilEboy, with a capital E. *The* hottest DJ of Latin house and EDM.

"Sounds *so* Cape Cod!" exclaimed Zula. Pepper gave her arm a squeeze.

"He gets a hundred grand a night," said Maddie. "But Daddy doesn't mind—we just *had* to have him. And he's killing it!"

"How'd you talk Angel into all this?" Pepper asked Maddie, gesturing around the patio.

"Angel? He still does what he's told," she laughed. She probably didn't know Pepper had planted the idea with Angel for a First Daughter welcome party.

Maddie had Pepper by the arm as she introduced him and Zula to a few more of her group's inner ring—good friends up from Miami. Dear friends from New York. Others in from Spain and Russia.

"But you guys aren't a *thing*, right?" Maddie asked Pepper and Zula.

"Us?" said Pepper lightly. "No, we work together."

"And it's just as fun as you'd guess. *Super* fun," said Zula, again with an over-the-top smile.

"He always was!" Maddie laughed, grabbing Pepper's arm, squeezing. Which brought Justin right to her side.

Which made Maddie laugh more, and louder.

"I know what you're really doing here," said Justin, now standing too close to Pepper. Borrowing courage from his posse?

"Do tell," said Pepper. Zula was watching them while pretending to listen to something a Garby twin was saying. She now had one hand pressed lightly on the small of Pepper's back.

"You pretend you're investigating stuff. Mr. Top Secret. But you're really chasing after Maddie. How about you take your jackboot hormones somewhere else?"

Jackboot hormones? Sounded like a good band name.

"Not that I'm worried," continued Justin, waving his vape pen near Pepper's nose for extra emphasis. "Maddie's crazy about me."

"She'd have to be," said Pepper.

Maddie giggled. "Enough J," she said, tugging at Justin's arm. He was turning a very uncool shade of red. "You don't want Pepper to kick your ass in front of your adoring fans!"

A few of Justin's hangers-on were lurking too close, in what they probably thought was a menacing herd, eavesdropping for an opening to get involved. These gents were not as polished as the others in the Maddie/First Daughters/Justin group. Pepper thought he recognized one, a guy in a tight black v-neck t-shirt and long curly hair? A local from Pepper's misspent youth? He couldn't recall. Did Justin roll with hired muscle? Or were they just disciples itching to prove their value and share the light of cyber celebrity?

Justin finally pulled his arm free from Maddie and headed toward the bar with a laugh. After a few parting glares, his entourage followed. Probably to do some lazy shots.

Then Pepper heard that one in a million laugh. Angel Cavada! Turning, he saw Angel was standing at his side, watching. He was wearing a black suit and his hair was slicked back Desi Arnez style. He gave Pepper a bearhug.

"*Mano*, the Pepper I knew would have fed him that vape pen! You must be mellowing as you age, like cheese. But I'm starting to like Justin Case. You can't fake that kind of self-enthusiasm. But speaking of *hey hey*—" Angel took a dramatic step back. "It's Pepper *and* Zula Eisenhower! Oh, man."

"Nice bash, Angel," said Zula.

"Really happening," he agreed. "And girl, you—" He stepped back, shaking his head. "If I wasn't already in love... Which reminds me, Pep, I need you to meet someone special. She was just here..."

Angel went on tiptoes, searching around everywhere but couldn't spot her. "Maybe she's in the ladies. See you guys in a bit." And Angel darted off to keep the party spinning.

DJ ChilEboy's low bass twirled with higher synthesizer, like a spell. The twins were right behind Pepper talking to Maddie now, so he could overhear snatches of what they were saying.

"He's a cute one," said one twin.

"I'd climb that," said the other.

A cocktail waitress with short, spiky pink hair arrived with a tray full of mojitos, compliments of Angel Cavada. Good man. Pepper was surprised how many people he knew in the crowd. He saw Lieutenant Dwayne Hurd in a light green flowered shirt at the bar, ordering a drink with a woman at his side.

Zula had seen them too and was chuckling to herself. "You know who's with Hurd? That's Lizzie Concepcion. She almost pulled off the town manager's ears last week when he followed up about some event permits during the presidential vacation. She's Acker Smith's chief of staff...rumor is, maybe more."

Maybe Maddie hadn't been nuts when she asked him to dig into whether daddy's riches were safe from any chicanery by his faithful assistant... Pepper almost mentioned that side job to Zula but stopped himself—for some reason Zula didn't seem to be a big fan of *anything* about Maddie.

"Really?" he asked, instead. "Smith's so much older!"

Zula laughed. "Some women are crazy that way."

Pepper knew Hurd had gotten divorced about four months ago and word around the station was that Hurd got the worst of it, really took it on the chin and wallet by his ex. But good for him—he must be getting back out on the swingin' singles circuit? Lizzie Concepcion was peering over at the Maddie clique and combing her medium-length brown hair with her fingers. Too nervous to come over and say hi to the boss' daughter? Or just irritated about being seen in public next to Hurd's Hawaiian shirt?

Then Pepper's dear partner, Special Agent Alfson, strolled up with a frozen drink in hand. His pretty blonde hair was just a little out of place, very unusual. And was his thin handsome face maybe a little flushed?

"Ah, I *knew* you'd be off-duty!" he said to Pepper with a too big smile. Maybe the drink in his hand wasn't his first. Or even his third.

"And the lovely Chief's daughter. Chief's lovely daughter. Zula." Alfson took her hand and kissed it.

"Enchantée," said Zula.

"That your first Daiquiri, partner?" asked Pepper.

Alfson waved dismissively. "No worries, I'm not working tonight either. I'm just keeping an eye on things." Smiling at Zula. "My lucky night."

Zula smiled back.

Was Alfson naturally that obnoxious, or was he just trying to irritate Pepper?

Plenty of the crowd was headed toward drunk. Pepper saw two middle-aged women in short dresses, a bleach blonde and a redhead, had climbed onstage and were taking selfies with DJ ChilEboy. The DJ pulled them both in tight and the three were laughing uproariously.

Pinky the cocktail waitress re-appeared, handing over test tubes of blue alcohol to the twins and Maddie, who quickly drank them with maximum flair and hooting.

A while later, Angel reappeared with a tall, slim dark woman with brown eyes and long black hair braided like a rope. The missing woman—Angel's new flame, Marisol. Quite a beauty but older than Pepper would have predicted. Angel bragged that she was second-generation Cuban too. A filmmaker. Marisol shared she was headed to Havana in a few days for a documentary she was shooting about an endangered species of Cuban orchids. She started to describe the changes happening there since the U.S. relaxed its embargo a bit. Lots of stealth business activity, lots of challenges dealing with Cuban officials. The next wild west.

Angel hovered proudly but couldn't stay in one place. It wasn't easy, hosting the most happening night spot to hit Cape Cod in anyone's memory. He hustled away to talk to his security team.

"You keep him clear of trouble while I'm gone," Marisol said, laughing, flashing white teeth. "Some women misunderstand Angel's hospitality!"

* * *

Pepper had just headed into the men's room, still

chuckling about Angel and his many romantic highs and lows, when he stopped short, staring incredulously. A large, crude five-point star was drawn on the bathroom mirror in what looked like red marker or lipstick. And roughly colored in. It looked like a big, red starfish. Below it was written: *Where is my candy!*

An overweight man in a Tommy Bahamas shirt was washing his hands. He saw Pepper stop and stare. "Yeah, some fucking people, huh? Just say no to drugs..." the man said.

The significance of the red starfish from the Keser and Dunne crimes had never been mentioned publicly. So only a person involved in those killings would leave this sign. Did it mean another attack had happened, or was about to? The First Daughters were just steps away, in a big, wild crowd...

The Tommy Bahamas guy tossed his paper towel at the black garbage can by the wall and walked out as three other guys came in. Three of the Justin Case disciples who'd tried to join the stare down with Pepper earlier. Pepper almost didn't recognize them, his mind was racing so fast. He had to go tell the Secret Service about the mirror—

"Hey, shitface," said one. The tallest, farthest to the left. Maybe the wittiest.

"Not now!" said Pepper, and he started forward to move around them toward the bathroom exit.

"We just need to talk to you," said the middle guy, sliding to block Pepper's way, arms out wide, with a smile that suggested he was lying. The guy with the long curly hair. Where had Pepper seen him before tonight? Was he...one of the knuckleheads who'd been in the driveway at the New River Front house?

"Guys, I'm a cop and I've got to go prevent a crime. So, seriously, get the fuck out of my way." Pepper was getting angry. Frustrated. He didn't have time for this! An attack on the First Daughters might be happening out there, that very second! Pepper wished he was wearing his handgun tonight.

"You can go in a bit, asswipe. Once you promise to stop hassling Justin Case," said the shortest. But thickly muscled. Heavy black boots. "And once your ambulance gets here."

They came at him at all together, in a sudden bum rush. To surprise and overwhelm him. Probably planning to get him down, stomp him.

But Pepper moved too, at the same moment. He moved forward and left, hitting the tallest guy with a straight right punch to the face. Stunning him for a moment, just long enough for Pepper to yank him into the path of his two buddies, tangling them.

Pepper's hand was on the bathroom door handle when he was grabbed from behind. It was Curly, yanking him back toward the other two. Toward his beating.

But Pepper went with it, throwing himself backward. Curly fell on his ass from the lack of resistance and Pepper landed on him, twisting as he fell, and hitting Curly with a headbutt at the moment they both reached the floor. He caught Curly right across the bridge of his nose, which collapsed and erupted. An immediate bloody mess. Curly's eyes were open but unfocused—stunned, maybe part way unconscious.

Then Pepper really lost it.

Maybe it was a combination of his anger and frustration about being delayed while the First Daughters were in danger. Maybe it was too many times of suppressing his instincts and trying to not rock the boat. To do things the right way. But for whatever reason, Pepper's vision was now a white flash. And the rest of the world was slower, a thick liquid. Pepper was both in the action and above it, almost an observer. He watched himself punch Curly in the face twice, then scramble to his feet and slip sideways to avoid a booted kick from the shortest of the attackers. He grabbed the boot at the highest point of the kick, charged forward, and the man was bowled over backward, his head cracking against the black ceramic sink.

The tallest guy tackled Pepper and they both slid on the wet floor as they fell. They rolled together across the wet tiles, crashing into the black metal garbage can in the corner. Pepper broke loose and found his feet first, so as Tall Guy rose, Pepper kneed him in the chin as hard as he could. The man tumbled backward into the garbage can, which collapsed and tipped, covering him under a little avalanche of crumpled paper towels.

Pepper sensed another guy coming up behind him so he spun into the man, grabbing his shirt, pushing him to his heels, pulling back his other fist—

"*Mano!*"

Pepper came out of his rage, found himself holding Angel by his tie and shirt in one hand, the other fist just starting to move forward. Pepper froze, let go. "Sorry brother! These guys jumped me but I've gotta— I think there's gonna be—" Pepper gestured at the red starfish scrawled on the mirror, yanked open the door and left Angel standing openmouthed in his rumpled suit, surrounded by the bloody mess of bodies on the bathroom floor.

And as Pepper burst from the men's room back out to the patio, he heard a loud scream cut through the music.

TWENTY-FIVE

Pepper immediately saw Maddie Smith's silver dress near the bar. And the twin white leather dresses. But Pepper was pretty sure that's not where the scream originated. More like from the direction of the stage.

So Pepper ran that way, saw the blonde and redhead still up there, but the DJ wasn't in sight. The women were part way bent over and looking around the stage in panic.

The DJ must have collapsed?

Pepper made it to the stage before Malecón security. The DJ was lying on his back and his face was covered in vomit. His body was convulsing violently.

Then the convulsions stopped.

DJ ChilEboy was unconscious and not breathing. "Call for an ambulance! Call 911!" Pepper yelled at the blonde and the redhead above the music's heavy bass. The two women stared wildly at him, then the redhead finally pulled out her phone.

Pepper used two fingers to clear the man's airway, then began CPR.

Lieutenant Hurd arrived at Pepper's side, knelt to assist. Then did a double take. "Ryan, why're you covered in blood?" Pepper didn't interrupt his counting to answer.

A doctor in a leopardskin miniskirt came onstage and took over. Pepper and Hurd following her orders.

The paramedics arrived very quickly. In less than twenty minutes from the time of the scream, an ambulance departed with the still-unresponsive ChilEboy accompanied by the leopardskin doctor. The crowd was unsettled, rumors swirling. Had ChilEboy drunk too much? Shot up, sniffed or swallowed too much? Another ambulance had arrived, the rumor was there'd been a mugging in the men's bathroom. The gossip fueled the crowd's chatter. But as soon as the stretcher with ChilEboy had left the stage, Justin Case stepped up with a *hey, hey* into the microphone and kept the music spinning. Or the play button playing. However club music works. But his presence on stage seemed to reassure the crowd that everything was going to be lazy, hazy and cool.

Pepper quickly filled in Hurd about the bathroom attack and they hurried to the men's room. They found Angel standing by the door, arms crossed. With a pair of paramedics impatiently standing by. Angel had locked the three assailants inside and was waiting for Pepper before he'd unlock it.

Hurd drew his handgun and led the way into the bathroom. But the room was empty, other than a mess of blood and paper towels. A window above a stall had been smashed.

"Fuckers!" said Angel. "And what the hell's that on my mirror. Some wacko wants their candy? Jesus...your bad guy's either nuts or a kid."

Pepper was just as unnerved by the lipstick words. Was the red starfish killer just messing with them, or did the repeated references to candy have some significance?

Everyone went back outside. "Should I shut down

early?" asked Angel. His night had gone from triumph to disaster.

"I'll get a BOLO out for three white guys covered in blood," said Hurd.

Pepper quickly gave him a few more descriptive details of his attackers and suggested that the lieutenant also try to locate the Tommy Bahamas guy who was in the bathroom when Pepper entered it, to get a statement. The lieutenant left.

Special Agent Alfson joined the group and saw Pepper's blood covered face and shirt. "Ryan, what the hell happened to you?"

"Trust me," Pepper said, with a wink. "Most of it's not mine. Did you get the girls out of here?"

Alfson grimaced. "Freestyle and Funsize? They wouldn't leave! The DJ thing spooked them for half a second, but a little more liquid courage and they bounced right back."

Pepper filled in Alfson about the red starfish graffiti and the agent went to inform the protection detail about the danger, then to take a look at the bathroom mirror.

"Angel, we need to interview your staff about ChilEboy," said Pepper. He'd seen a GHB overdose before and ChilEboy's seizures and vomiting made Pepper suspect that drug, or something similar. Which wasn't so hard to accept, a DJ overdosing from a club drug, right? But did the DJ take the dose himself, or was he poisoned? If it was a coincidental accident, why else had someone drawn the red starfish on the mirror?

"*Mano*, you mind washing up first?" asked Angel. "All that blood, you're going to scare the crap out of my girls. My guys too."

Angel set them up in the stock room and pulled

employees in to be interviewed, one at a time. Bartenders, security and waitresses. Pepper and Lieutenant Hurd asking the questions. Alfson was there, leg tapping impatiently. Zula too. Pepper had washed his face off with a wet bar towel and stripped his shirt off. Put on a shirt which Angel threw him with a grin—a Malecón staff t-shirt, at least one size too small.

The story came together from staff interviews. The blonde and the redhead women on stage had ordered a round of shots for themselves and ChilEboy, but when Pinky the cocktail waitress delivered them, the DJ had grabbed and drunk all three. "Like a joke, you know?" said Pinky. Whose real name was Joan. "Then they ordered another round, but I was slammed. So I didn't get back to them with the second round before, you know, he collapsed." Her eyes were full of fear and excitement.

"We need to talk to the blonde and the redhead," said Pepper.

"I'll go see if they're still here," volunteered Alfson, slipping out. Much more sober now.

"One last question," Pepper said to the waitress. "If someone wanted to spike those three shots, did they have a chance?"

"I put in the order from my tablet, but it took me a few minutes to get back to the bar. So yeah, they would have been made by Kyle or Summer and just sitting there with other orders. You think they were spiked?!?"

Alfson came back a couple minutes later and reported the blonde and the redhead were long gone.

At that moment Zula received a text from an ER nurse she knew: DJ ChilEboy had been declared dead on arrival at Cape Cod Hospital.

* * *

Angel left to pull the plug on the night. No last call, just a quick, polite shutdown of the music, raising of the lights. More police were arriving by the minute.

"You think the DJ was poisoned by the Starfish Killer?" Hurd asked the others. "Why the hell would he want to kill ChilEboy?"

Alfson shook his head. "I'm guessing he didn't. I bet ChilEboy drank shots meant for Freestyle and Funsize. Looks like the whole First Family's being targeted, not just the POTUS. And Ryan, did I hear this ultra-lounge circus was your big idea? We got lucky this time but please, no more bright ideas involving the twins, huh?"

Hurd had his phone out now. "I'm calling in state resources. This fucking place is going to get processed like a crime scene. Multiple crime scenes."

Out on the patio, the crowd was filtering out. Maybe witnesses slipping through their fingers, but they didn't have the manpower to stop the mob exit. Pepper found Maddie and her group with the First Daughters outside on the sidewalk. The twins were shrieking with laughter. Blowing kisses. Hugging Angel. Hugging everyone in their group or near them. ChilEboy's death wasn't killing their buzz. It only made the night more epic.

But Pepper hadn't secured his free pass into Eagle's Nest yet... "Hey—," he yelled to the First Daughters as they started to walk away. This might be his one last chance this week for an invite inside Eagle's Nest. But he had to stay at Malecón to help Hurd for a while... Then a question came out of Pepper's mouth that even surprised himself. "Do you girls like waffles?"

Of course Brianne and Skyler did. Loved them. Now

that he'd mention waffles, they wanted to go for some right now. Had to!

"We have the best waffle house on the East Coast right here in New Albion. Aunt Anney's Kitchen. But it's closed this late. Tell you what. Get those Secret Service gentlemen to put my name on the gate list and I'll bring you a big bag of them in the morning. Practically breakfast in bed."

They loved it. Aunt Anney's Kitchen, the whole idea. So awesome. Pepper would be welcomed with open gates, they'd take care of *that*. But not *too* early...

"Thank you, *Officer*!" winked Maddie, then turned to the twins. "Ok, darlings, let's go, go, go! Hey, what happened to our third Suburban?"

From behind her, Justin grinned right at Pepper. "Congrats, man—you got yourself an honest job?" Pointing at Pepper's borrowed Staff shirt, laughing. "Now, I gotta get me some velvet." Taking Maddie's hand and leading her away toward the first Suburban.

"Velvet?" asked Pepper.

"Don't ask, *Mano*," said Angel. "Don't even think about it..."

The two black Suburbans filled to capacity, then slowly drove away into the night.

"Pretty important sardines. What happened to their third ride?"

"My doorman with the skin problem told me a skinny Secret Service guy commandeered it to send two drunk ladies home. A blonde and a redhead. It was probably a more exciting night's work than my celebrity bouncer expected."

Pepper found Zula back inside the Malecón patio, sitting on a black leather couch. Fatigue had set in on her face and she greeted Pepper's arrival with an annoyed yawn. Alfson was standing at her side, talking to her.

Zula stood slowly, then leaned on Pepper's arm as she adjusted her shoe strap. "I'm not going to wait around for you, okay? My feet are killing me and I'm on Dispatch at 8 AM."

"I can give you a lift," offered Alfson.

You got another Suburban handy? Pepper gritted his teeth. "Sorry, Zula. Hurd'll keep me stuck here a while."

Alfson grinned. "No worries, partner, I'll take care of her."

And only another yawn from Zula, not even a peck on the cheek when they left. Pepper was pretty sure she was pissed at him. But thanks to Freestyle and Funsize's waffle cravings, his name would finally be on the Eagle's Nest gate list. The perfect chance to sniff around the big house to figure out if Maddie's old man being bilked by his Girl Friday, while maybe giving Pepper room to move forward his own little investigation...

So finish at Malecón, then drown in sleep. Tomorrow would have to go better, right?

TWENTY-SIX

Not *too* early the next morning—practically noon—Pepper arrived at Eagle's Nest. He had to pass through two checkpoints along Shore Road with their deadpan agents coming out from the shade of their cheap white tents, and then a third checkpoint at the Eagle's Nest main gate itself. At the first checkpoint, he had to confirm his social security number and the agent checked her computer, maybe a criminal database? His name was on their gate list, he wasn't a criminal, he passed. At the second checkpoint, a German Shepherd sniffed around, in and under his car. At the third, the agent kept Pepper's I.D. and would have taken his handgun too, which was why he hadn't brought it.

So, if the waffles were cold, the twins would have to take it up with the Secret Service.

Pepper hadn't been to Eagle's Nest since he was seventeen but it was as over-the-top as he remembered. Pepper knew Acker Smith had built Eagle's Nest for his late wife—Maddie's mother. Pepper parked his truck in front of the main mansion by a large, round fountain with a statue in its middle of an oversized Greek nymph, acting surprised to be naked. The mansion's front doors were solid wood, twelve feet high. What would it feel like to call a place like this home?

Pepper took the long walk around the house's side, to the backyard. The twins were sunning by the main house pool with the First Lady. Big smiles, small bikinis, on all three. Maddie Smith and Justin Case were there too, with a couple others, and were about to go down on the beach. Did Pepper have a bathing suit?

Pepper held up a backpack, said he'd go change, meet them down there. The twins were already tearing into the waffles with ooh's and ah's. Loved the waffles, loved his plan.

Maddie gave him an exaggerated wink, with a hint of a smirk? She waved toward the main house. "Anything you need, *Detective*, you'll find upstairs…"

So, time to toss the billionaire's mansion for clues. Pepper made his way in through the rear entrance. Marble, gold, glass. Everything was larger than in a normal house, the entire scale was over the top.

At the end of the hall, he climbed a broad staircase, nodding to two house staff—a woman and a man—as he passed them going the other way. One called up after Pepper, but he kept climbing with purpose. He had plenty to get into before his bathing suit. Agent Keser had begun his review of this building on the day before he died and ended up in the clambake pit—was there any connection, at all? Priority one was Pepper's official business—anything that might help his investigation. But hey, if Pepper bumped into any dirt that proved or disproved Maddie's suspicions about her daddy's assistant? That'd be a lucky bonus.

As he reached the landing, he almost collided with a woman in a nurse's uniform who'd just left a room on the hall's end. Pepper stepped aside with smiles and apologies, let her take the staircase down. He waited a few seconds—

the hallway was now deserted. So he gently opened the door she'd left and went in. Blind curiosity, for lack of a better plan...

It was a bedroom. Larger than any Pepper had ever lived in. Pretty dark. A kingsize bed was kitty corner, near the windows with curtains drawn firmly closed.

A man was in the bed. Acker Smith? Pepper tried to recall the billionaire as he'd last seen him, almost a dozen years before. This man looked...well, he looked diminished. Close to death. He was almost unrecognizable. His face was sunken and he had less hair now—the hands of cancer? The man was deeply asleep.

There was a machine on a long table close to the bed. It held a number of tubes of blood. Freshly drawn by the nurse? There was a medical folder labeled Acker Smith. Pepper opened it but understood little. Quick glance at the sleeping man, then he took out his phone and took pictures of the medical chart's first few pages. Each picture's click sounded like a little slap breaking the room's silence and the flash was blinding, but necessary in that dark gloom. With one eye on the charts and the other on the man in bed, Pepper finished as quickly as he could.

Some other device was on the table, maybe medical? It was a small rectangular box with a wire attached, looked like a headphone wire. Pepper took a picture of that too, nice and close. Click, flash.

There was a large ceramic penguin on the table, near the blood machine. Pepper was a big fan of penguins so he rubbed its head. Then was startled when the penguin started to vibrate. What the hell?

It vibrated, stopped, vibrated again. Like a cell phone with its ringer turned off. He held down the penguin with one hand and tugged up with his other. The head popped free. And he saw a cell phone with its screen lit up, on a pile of glassine envelopes. It was another of those strange blue phones and it was still ringing.

Pepper picked it up and clicked it on. "Ah, hello?" he said.

"Is that...you? You break your voice box?" asked a man.

What? The caller had a bit of a southern accent. And an attitude. Did Pepper recognize the voice? "What're you calling for?" Pepper asked, trying to out-attitude the caller.

"Job #1 is all set. I thought you'd want to know we're almost ready for the big show. Did you take care of the list yet?"

List? "Ah, we should meet to go over that," improvised Pepper. "Do you know Roger's Lighthouse parking lot? Let's meet tonight, nine o'clock, don't be late."

The man on the other end clicked off.

Was he spooked by something, or was a meet-up all set? The whole conversation felt sneaky, but was Pepper missing some innocent explanation?

Pepper typed the man's number into his own phone. He didn't really know whether the call had anything to do with the cases he was working, but his blood was pumping hard. He was about to put the phone back in the penguin but stopped when he saw the tiny glassine envelopes again. Maybe twenty or so. Each was sealed shut and held a small amount of white powder that looked like salt. Opium or some variation?

Pepper activated the flashlight on his phone and held one envelope up to its bright light, but that technique told him nada. And he wasn't going to do a taste test. So he took the envelope and slipped it into an evidence bag in his backpack, sealed it. Let a lab figure it out. He carefully placed the blue phone back in the penguin, put its head back on and gave it a little pat. Had the head been on perfectly straight before he lifted it, or had it been slightly to one side? He had a nagging sense, maybe slightly off-center? But to which side? If he didn't guess right, would someone know the penguin had been tampered with?

The man stirred in the bed, muttering unintelligible words that sounded vaguely panicked. Had Pepper's phone call or the flashlight app disturbed him?

Fuck it, leave the head straight. Pepper quickly checked the rest of the bedroom but didn't see anything else that caught his interest. Other than the decorative penguin, the room was strangely lacking in personal effects.

He cracked the door and peeked out in time to see a man in a blue blazer checking a doorknob across the hall, walkie-talkie in hand, electronic voice quietly squawking. Pepper pulled back his head, slid the door almost closed, held his breath. The man in the bed behind him was muttering louder, half shouting as if in a nightmare. Pepper closed the door, locked the knob and leaned against it.

A moment later, Pepper heard the doorknob creak and rattle as it was tried from the other side. Did Blazer Man have a key?

Pepper pressed himself against the wall and hoped not.

The door didn't open and the knob didn't rattle again. Pepper counted to fifty, then eased the door open again and stuck his head out far enough to see the hall was now clear of blazers and walkie-talkies. Pepper quickly went door to door on the ocean side of the hall, checking rooms. A few were locked. A few were unlocked but appeared to be unused bedrooms. The fifth door that Pepper tried was different. It was unlocked and looked lived in. He quickly went inside, saying a firm but quiet, "Hello?"

It was a large bedroom—much larger than the others on the hall. Maybe the largest Pepper had ever seen. A billionaire's bedroom, seemed like. A lot of furniture but even more empty space. A big bed with sheets and blankets pulled back a bit like someone had been sleeping there. So why was Acker Smith tucked away in the other, smaller room?

Pepper saw French doors at the far end leading to a balcony. Off to the side was a mahogany desk with a large flatscreen monitor for a desktop computer.

He quickly went to the desk, hoping for anything relevant to his investigation. Maybe Keser's picture with a red X across his face? At that point, Pepper would have settled for naked pics of Smith's assistant. He felt like he was taking risks but getting nowhere.

Pepper tapped the keyboard to wake the monitor but then it required a password. He tried 'madeline'. Then 'Madeline'. And then 'MADELINE'. Nope, nope, nope. Pepper was worried if he failed too many times the computer would lock and give away that someone had tried to hack in.

The desk drawers were unlocked. He rifled through them. The drawers were full of documents and other odds and ends, like any desk. But what else? Time was running out. Someone could come in any minute—what would he say? That he needed a safety pin for his swimsuit?

A neat stack of documents was perched on the desk's corner. None looked like a will, but Pepper quickly took a picture of each document's top page. He didn't have time for the other pages...

As Pepper hastily patted the documents into a stack, a little yellow post-it note kicked free from the pile. It said 'Scoter' and 'BLACKHAM' with a phone number. And an exclamation note below that. Hmm... Pepper took a picture of the note then tucked it back into the stack.

He opened the French doors and stepped onto an enormous balcony. It appeared even larger because there was very little furniture. Just two oversized chairs, wood frames with sleek gray cushions, and one little white table.

The view was impressive. The massive lawn rolled past the blue pool and down a gentle slope. The lawn blended away into a seagrass jungle which led to the beach. A billionaire's backyard. And the *Madeline Too* yacht hunched at the horizon's edge, unmoving, but dominating the view. There weren't as many other craft as usual, due to the restricted zone around Eagle's Nest due to the president's vacation. A few Navy boats were patrolling back and forth across the bay.

He could see Maddie and Justin down on the beach and the twins picking their way through a path in the tall seagrass to join them. Justin was lying on his back just above the high tide line, vigorously making what appeared to be a sand angel. Maddie was about forty feet from shore balancing on a paddleboard. She was wearing an ocean blue strap bikini top and lighter blue swim shorts. Pepper saw her balance her forearms against the flat of the board, then push herself upward into a kind of forearmed handstand. One leg scissored forward, the other back, as she struggled to find balance. But after a little wavering, she found her pose. Her caramel-tanned arms and legs shone with water and light. Girl had some core strength.

"Who're you!?!" demanded a voice behind him—high, hard, female. "What're you doing in Mr. Smith's bedroom?"

Lizzie Concepcion was standing in the middle of the bedroom. Acker Smith's right-hand woman, and maybe more.

Pepper gave her his super most charming smile. Almost

overdid it. "I'm Pepper Ryan! Here with the twins, you know... And Maddie... She said I could put on my board shorts and this was the only open door in this castle. Mind if I?" Pepper jerked his head toward a master bathroom off to the side, past the mahogany desk.

"Mr. Smith's on his way upstairs! If he finds you here, he'll have you arrested! And me fired!" The woman was shaking.

"Whoa, fired?" he said. "Maybe I should get naked somewhere downstairs?"

"Lizzie, call security." The voice came from the doorway, thin but firm. Like it'd been squeezed through two pieces of sandpaper, but under high pressure. A gray-haired man stood there, glaring at them both. Imperious. This was Acker Smith—the disapproving mouth was undeniable. Smith was just as sick as the other man sleeping down the hall—wicked pale with a yellow-orange tinge. A similarly sunken face and sparse, white hair. Radically thinner than years ago.

"*CALL SECURITY!*" Not much louder, but with as much force as the old man could muster. Smith twisted to the side, bent over, and violently vomited on the floor. Lizzie Concepcion rushed to his aid.

Pepper didn't wait for security—he knew how to throw himself out.

Back in his truck, he exited through the Secret Service checkpoints. He expected their phones to ring, for them to point their weapons, to order him from his vehicle. But leaving was much quicker than entering. He was given back his I.D. at the nearest checkpoint. Barely had to stop at the next two. He was soon driving back along Shore Road, a free man, his heart working harder than a one-legged tap dancer.

Why had Smith and Concepcion just let him leave? Too

distracted by Smith's sudden up-chuck? Of course, Pepper was only standing there, in what had to be Smith's bedroom, when he was discovered. He didn't have his hands in the underwear drawer, thank God.

He'd have to see what his document photos showed. Great luck that security or the Secret Service hadn't grabbed him and found all that! But more importantly, what should he do about the mystery meet up at Rogers' Lighthouse at 9 PM? Show up alone? Or try to set a trap, with a full backup of local cops and Secret Service? How would he explain to the General and Alfson how the meeting had been set up? And that he had absolutely no real idea who'd be there? The relationship might be completely, innocently legal. Pepper pulled over to the side of Shore Road. Sighed. Took his phone and scrolled to the mystery number he'd copied from the blue phone. His gut told him he knew that voice, but he just couldn't place it.

Pepper dialed the number.

The call connected but with no greeting. Pepper could hear breathing, no words.

"Just calling to confirm your order," said Pepper in his peppiest voice.

"Who's this?" asked the same voice as earlier.

"Broken Dreams Antiques and Pizzeria... Did I, you know, fat finger the wrong number?" tried Pepper.

"Have a nice fucking day," said the man, disconnecting.

Hmmm... The man's voice was teasing Pepper, like he'd heard it somewhere other than those two calls. Or maybe it was the attitude that seemed so familiar? So many assholes, so little time...

Why would the sick man in the guest bedroom at Smith's mansion have been calling that person anyway? What could be the connection? He'd have to ask Maddie who the sick man was and why he was holed up at Eagle's Nest.

And should he tell Alfson yet? No, still way too many questions...

* * *

Oliver and Croke were hunkered down at the Sanddollar Motel on that Saturday, waiting until they got a further assignment or else the 'all clear' to split. Sitting in Croke's room, each on one of the twin beds, watching crap on TV. Sitting up like those puppets on Sesame Street. Ernie and Bart?

"I think some of these rooms are being rented by the hour," muttered Croke.

"Huh? Who cares?" Croke was getting on Oliver's nerves, clicking through the TV channels aimlessly.

"It's just a lot of traffic. Couples checking in for a few hours, taking off. More people to see us. Maybe remember us." Croke finally stopped clicking when he saw baseball.

"*Those* people aren't dropping a dime. What'll they tell the cops? I was giving my mistress a nooner and I saw two shifty guys at the Sanddollar? Live and let live, that's what I say. Unless someone pays me otherwise."

"I'm getting a bad feeling about Cape Cod," said Croke. "Kinda real bad. Maybe we should take off, huh?"

Take off, and leave the big money and glory that Oliver was certain would soon be his? Not damn yet... "Let's go to that burger place with the fat pickles you like. Talk it over."

Oliver had him at pickles. "Okay," said Croke reluctantly. "But first I gotta piss." Croke slid off his bed and shadow-boxed into the bathroom. One of his quirks, showing off what he claimed had been pretty good boxing skills, back in the home country, in his youth. Just ask him, he'd tell you. At length.

Another of Oliver's annoyances with Croke was the man was a slow pisser—he took longer than anyone Oliver had ever met. He needed one of those medicines from the Golf Channel. Oliver didn't want to loiter outside among the adulterers so he just lay there on the spare bed, closed his eyes and tried to close his ears. The Croke situation was getting on his nerves and giving him a headache.

When they finally went outside to get in the Taurus, they found their way blocked by a woman. A woman in what appeared to be a bathrobe. She stopped Croke with an angry gesture. "This *your* car?" she asked.

"Is something wrong?" asked Croke. Looking a little confused and maybe amused.

"You're parked in my spot." She gestured to room thirteen.

Croke was staying in room sixteen and Oliver was in ten. Croke had split the difference when he'd parked last night, smack in front of room thirteen. Had done it most days since they first arrived at the Sanddollar Motel. He remembered that earlier in their stay someone had rubbed the word *ASHOLE* in the dirt on the back window of their last car, but when Oliver had noticed it he'd just wiped it away, assuming some stupid kid had been showing off his bad language and worse spelling. Maybe instead it had been a stupid woman? Whatever...

"These are not reserved," said Croke to the woman. He waved an arm. "People just park."

Two kids, maybe between four and six years old, had spilled out of room thirteen and were watching.

The woman gave Croke one of the most murderous glares Oliver had ever seen. Pure hatred. Oliver thought he saw Croke waver a bit, but then Croke brushed past the woman. "Excuse *us*, ma'am," he said, all mock politeness.

Croke started the car and slowly backed from the woman's spot and away they went.

"It's not anyone's spot," Croke suddenly said a few minutes later.

Oliver's head was hurting even more now so he didn't reply. There was no simple solution except murder.

TWENTY-SEVEN

"Is this a good idea?" asked Officer Larch, again.

Pepper had been sitting with his colleague in Larch's personal ride—a Kia Sedona—for three hours. It was almost 8 PM. They were staking-out the New River Front house, making a few notes of people's comings and goings, but mostly trying not to die of boredom. The NRF weren't the liveliest bunch. He'd have to pull the plug soon if he wanted to keep his 9 PM rendezvous with the cell phone mystery man.

Pepper's instincts were playing a light drumbeat in his veins. He believed this was enough of a lead to focus on, but not enough to lay out for Chief Eisenhower or Lieutenant Hurd, yet. And definitely not enough to call Special Agent Alfson. Pepper was gambling that these NRF shitbirds might be the shitbirds who abducted Marcus Dunne. Because either Pepper's charm or FBI Deputy Assistant Director Edwina Youngblood—bless her heart—had gotten FBI assets to assist. Thirteen files had arrived in Pepper's email from analysts at the FBI's National Security Branch, full of good, juicy info. The analysis mentioned only one activist group on Pepper's list who'd engaged in kidnapping in recent years: the New River Front. The same shitbirds with sandy shovels on their porch. And who *may* have been seen by the teen witness at Dill Beach lot, that night. So who better for Pepper to focus on? And Pepper knew time was running out to locate Marcus Dunne alive...

While they waited, Pepper had texted his dad the photos he'd taken at Eagle's Nest. He knew his dad was still doggedly (and semi-unofficially) running down the paperwork and people trail to figure out who was behind the house demo. Not to mention the seafood angle of the clambake homicide. But hopefully his dad could take a look at the photos, let him know his thoughts? And could he get Dr. Anderson—the local general practitioner—to look at the medical chart pictures, translate what they said, as a favor? But not to discuss them with anyone else, please... Pepper had reviewed them and hadn't concluded anything helpful, but was hoping the risks he took at Eagle's Nest weren't a complete waste.

"So I'm in the middle of a graveyard shift," Officer Larch was saying. "Real quiet. The Cape in March quiet. I'm cruising past the Rockland Trust branch when I see someone suspicious in the outer lobby, where they got the ATM machine. He's not standing at the ATM, punching in numbers on the keypad like a regular citizen. He's facing the other way, squatting down, with this anxious look on his face."

"Uh-oh," said Pepper.

"Right. The guy's taking a numero two, right there in the ATM lobby. So I put on gloves and bust him, right? He's drunk but otherwise pretty good-natured, now he's taken care of business. I book him for breach of the peace."

In his side view mirror, Pepper saw a light blue Ford Focus pull up close behind them and cut its engine.

"Of course the papers get wind of it somehow,"

continued Larch. He didn't seem to have noticed the Ford Focus. "Personally I suspect the lovely Zula. She's got a mischievous streak. So the Herald's crime beat reporter gets my report, runs it as one of those wacky crimes. So what do you think their headline was?"

"Man Arrested While Making Deposit?"

"No. It was... Dammit, that would've been better. Why didn't the Herald think of that? Now I forget the real headline. Fuck you, Pepper!"

A man came up to the driver side window. Pepper's partner—Special Agent Alfson.

"Mind if I get in?" he asked with a scowl.

Officer Larch clicked the locks and Alfson slid into the back seat. All the way to the middle. Leaned forward, one forearm on each headrest. "Your phone not working?" he asked Pepper. "Because if my partner was staking out a house, I'm sure he would've called me. I couldn't believe it when my team in the bungalow across from the NRF called and reported there was a *second* stakeout group on the street."

Oops. "We got a lead the NRF might be holding Dunne," said Pepper. "And since he's only tangentially related to the Keser case, as a witness, I didn't want to bother you."

Alfson snorted. "Dunne may be more than a witness. I still think he could have been the goddamn killer. Or one of them. His co-conspirators might have grabbed him, maybe afraid he'll rat them out. So what's the deal—you trying to be the hero again?"

"Well, this is awkward," said Larch. "Want me to take a stroll, so you two can kiss and make up?"

Mercifully, right then the front door opened and two men came out and crossed the lawn to the driveway. They opened the rear of a Ford Expedition and wrestled a very large duffel bag to the ground. After a little stretching and tentative tugging, one tried to lift the bag. It was too heavy.

Quick conversation with accusatory gestures. Then they each grabbed an end and began half dragging, half bumping the bag along toward the middle house. They paused to rest twice on the way.

A third guy came out the front door and appeared to be giving them shit. But then the third guy grabbed a corner and they hauled the bag up the front steps and into the house. One man went back to the Expedition for a smaller bag, big enough for maybe a set of golf clubs. He carried that inside too and the house's front door closed.

"Do you think Dunne was in the bigger bag?" asked Larch.

"Looked about the right size and weight," said Pepper. "But who knows? If it's him, hopefully he's just unconscious... I'd better take a peek in their window, to check."

"No, no, no..." scowled Alfson. "I need to touch base with my SAIC before we start raiding private property. Speaking of which, Pepper, I hear you showed up briefly at Eagle's Nest today?"

"We can chat about that later. And we don't have time for a warrant—these are what the DA would call exigent circumstances," said Pepper. "Clearly. Besides, Westin invited us back, remember? Told me to bring more muscle than you."

Larch grinned. "But maybe we should call for backup anyways?"

If Pepper didn't fear the NRF might be about to kill Dunne he'd have said yes. Get a warrant. At least call for backup. But he couldn't wait, not after what he'd promised Trish. He could imagine her face, and little Kaylee's too, if their worst fears were confirmed. "Sit tight and call whoever you want. I'll be back in a minute, no worries. It's not my job description that requires jumping in front of bullets," winked Pepper. "Trust me."

Pepper and Alfson hadn't seen anyone standing lookout or any security cameras on their prior visit to the house, but Pepper decided to assume there might be some. He circled around the block and came at the NRF house from the yard of the house behind it. No dogs started barking. No suspicious senior citizen shot at him. All was going well.

He climbed over the low picket fence bordering the NRF's backyard and flattened himself on the ground. He slowly crawled to the house. Pulled himself up to the kitchen window. A shade was down but one edge had curled forward, leaving enough of a gap for Pepper to view a sizable wedge of the room.

The big bag was on the kitchen floor. Unzipped. And three men were unloading an arsenal of assault rifles, piling them on the kitchen table. Looked like M16s. They also pulled magazine after magazine--long, curved and black. Thirty rounders? And other gear--body armor? So, not Dunne, living or dead. But a whole different kind of trouble.

Then three things went wrong, all in a row--

A siren broke the evening silence.

Then a second later he heard Larch yell, *"Tom...Jones...!"*, loud and long from far away down the street.

Then the shade pulled back and shot up and he was face to face with Brian-Edward Westin. Who was holding a handgun.

Pepper threw himself to the left, away from the window and the light. Then he ran back toward Larch's Kia as fast as his legs could go.

TWENTY-EIGHT

Pepper was almost to the car when he heard a handgun fire six or so times in a quick burst. Heard bullets zipping past, impacting trees and the Kia. He tore open the passenger door as Larch fumbled to start the engine. Larch yanked the shifter into reverse and floored his way out of there. Immediately hitting Alfson's Ford Focus.

"Fucker!" shouted Larch, pulling forward briefly then reversing around the Ford Focus and down the street about fifty yards. He barely missed a police car coming around the curve towards him. The officer slammed his brakes and stopped nearby. Larch parked in the street at an angle.

Pepper saw a man in the street in front of the NRF house, firing down the road towards them. Looked like Brian-Edward Westin.

"Somebody...somebody called in they saw a peeping tom!" gasped Larch. "But I didn't think it was about you—Dispatch said on Robin Street!"

That was the next street over--the row of houses Pepper had cut through to sneak up on the NRF house's rear.

Pepper unholstered his Glock as he climbed out, running around the Kia's rear to the protection of the driver's side. He waved at the uniformed officer--the redhead Dooley--

who was also getting out of his car while trying to figure out what the hell he'd driven into. He had his firearm out and up too, but recognized Pepper. Alfson and Larch also piled out on the Kia's protected side, their handguns drawn.

The man in the road--who definitely appeared to be Westin—had put in a new clip and was firing down the road at them again. All three officers opened fire in return. The distance was around 100 yards. The man suddenly stopped firing, fell, got up and ran back towards the NRF house. They saw at least two other men on the front porch, but all went inside with Westin.

* * *

That began what was later called New Albion's own little Waco Incident.

A flood of local and federal officers secured the area's perimeter. The New River Front went right to their siege playbook--barricading the house and rebuffing the negotiators who called them on the house's land line. The NRF needed to keep the landline open to phone the media. They also sent out text messages, tweets and Facebook posts begging others to come to their defense, peppered with their top pet peeves against President Garby and federal authorities.

Pepper stayed at the front line with Officers Larch and Dooley. Special Agent Alfson had disappeared a block further back to update his SAIC Hanley and Chief Eisenhower.

Seven media trucks descended, staked their turf in a cluster as near as authorities allowed and raised their satellite dishes.

An hour passed—boredom with a side of caged violence.

"The house wants to talk to an Officer Ryan?" said the crisis negotiator who'd arrived from the Mass CNU. He held up the phone questioningly.

Ryan raised a hand, stepped over, took it.

"This is Ryan."

Pepper didn't recognize the voice that replied. The man was hysterical, almost unintelligible, saying, "*It's bought and paid for—*"

"Let me talk to Westin," interrupted Pepper.

Another burst of words. That Westin wasn't coming to the phone, but the voice didn't say why. Was he dead? Or had he escaped before the perimeter was set up? "*That dirty bird—*" Then the line went dead.

The negotiator tried to reestablish contact, then again five minutes later. But the NRF had gone silent.

"Let me go up near the house, try to talk them out," said Pepper. "Maybe their phone died."

Nobody liked that idea. Not Chief Eisenhower, who'd joined the forward cluster of law enforcement officers. Not the staties or the feds. Maybe the first time all those agencies had ever agreed on anything. But no one had a better plan.

So Pepper and two SWAT officers slowly worked their way closer to the house, dressed head to toe in protective gear. Pepper already had sweat running into his eyes. They also carried big ballistic shields with POLICE stenciled on them.

"These shields completely bulletproof?" asked Pepper.

"Should be," said one of the SWAT officers. "They're the third most expensive this company makes."

They halted at the lawn's edge. It was very quiet until Pepper began yelling to the house. That it was him. Could they talk? That they needed to come out, one at a time, hands up.

The answer was the front door burst open. Three men ran out, firing M16s. Pepper and the SWAT officers huddled low behind their overlapping shields as what sounded like hundreds of bullets banged off them. Then Pepper heard the boom-boom-boom of SWAT snipers answering fire from way behind him. More firing came from the other side of the street—the agents who'd been on surveillance in the bungalow. All three NRF men went down, then regained their feet. They were wearing body armor too. One resumed firing at Pepper and his two companions. More booms from the SWAT sniper rifles and all three men went down again, writhing on the ground.

"Dumbasses didn't put on leg protectors," said the SWAT guy to Pepper's left.

One of the NRF men struggled to his feet and careened back toward the house. The SWAT team didn't fire again.

But as the man reached the front porch's top step, his leg skidded out forward and he tumbled backward down the steps, arms windmilling. He hit the concrete walkway with a deadened thump, slid a bit on his own blood-slick, then was still.

TWENTY-NINE

Two of the three NRF men had bled out on the lawn
and the third had been taken by helicopter to the hospital.
And those were the only remaining NRF members at the
house when the shootout had happened. A much larger
group—five men and three women—had driven to the
Golden Fork for its "10% off" weeknight special buffet.
They'd been finishing up dessert when they were taken into
custody by a few dozen local, state and federal officers.

Those members had no idea yet that anything had
happened back at their rental house. They hadn't seen TV
and hadn't gotten a phone call because the shopping plaza
where the Golden Fork was located was a dead spot for cell
reception. They had nothing to say about the big bag of
assault rifles, or the missing smaller bag, or what their leader
Brian-Edward Westin was up to or where he would have fled.
No idea about anything. Even the dumbest knew to ask for a
lawyer, then clam up.

Only Westin was missing. They found a pool of blood
in the kitchen. But he was gone and so was the smaller carry
bag. The ex-Army Ranger must have slipped away through
the backyard during the initial chaos before a perimeter was
fully set up. A BOLO was broadcast for him. Was he

injured enough to require medical attention?

Based on the Secret Service's surveillance after Pepper and Alfson's original visit to the NRF, the feds believed at least three other men and two other women from NRF remained at large in the area. Was Westin hiding with them?

After an expedited warrant, the Secret Service, ATF, state and local law searched the rental house. They found two android phones in the kitchen, which the Secret Service considered a lucky break since those models aren't usually encrypted. The Secret Service would be able to hack them after getting another warrant, for caution's sake. Hopefully, there would be text messages, phone messages and emails explaining what the hell the NRF had been up to.

* * *

"This is gonna sting," said Zula Eisenhower, with a hint of a smile cracking her pretty lips.

"No shit," said Pepper, gritting his teeth. It was late evening and he was back at the station, waiting for Chief Eisenhower and Lieutenant Hurd. Waiting to explain what the hell had happened.

Zula splashed rubbing alcohol on a long scrape on Pepper's chin, where he'd hit himself pretty good with his SWAT shield. The alcohol felt like fire. She gave Pepper's scrape an extra firm rub with a paper towel. Then she carefully covered the raw spot with a loose bandage, then tape.

She patted his hand and smiled. "Good enough for you," she said. "You'll probably be in the Emergency Room for one reason or another in the next few days. They can hit it again more professionally."

"But not half so gently."

"Baby! But I finished researching that name you gave me—Fulmar Limited? Not much to it. Turns out it's a Cayman Islands corporation. Acker Smith's an officer, plus a bunch of other people I didn't recognize except one: Elizabeth Concepcion. Here's the list."

Pepper gave it a glance but didn't recognize any other names.

"And I found that Fulmar Limited's the registered owner for a lot of Smith's assets. Eagle's Nest. His vehicles. His Gulfstream. Two yachts."

"Hmmm. Maybe for tax reasons, estate planning?" Might be totally legit. And would it be normal to have an assistant like Concepcion as an officer, to handle the administrative crap?

"Can you also do a background check on Lizzie Concepcion," he asked, "Just to be thorough?" He *definitely* wasn't going to tell Zula the Concepcion research was at the request of the lovely Maddie Smith…

Zula looked at him like that didn't make sense. "Lizzie Concepcion? For the Keser investigation?"

"Leave no shell unturned, that's my method." Pepper doubted Lizzie Concepcion was a gold digger and didn't know whether anything shady was going on at Eagle's Nest anyway. The whole thing might be a waste of time.

But that reminded Pepper of something else. He took the evidence bag with the little glassine envelope of mystery powder from his pocket and handed it to Zula. "Can you send this up to the State Police Lab?" Hoping she wouldn't throw it back in his face.

But Zula just held it to the light, peering through the plastic bag. "What is it?"

"My guess? Coke. Or maybe heroin."

"Where'd you get it?"

"In the course of my comprehensive investigations. But please ask them to expedite it. ASA frickin' P."

Now she was glaring at him. "So how am I going to pull off *that* favor?"

Pepper had some immature suggestions to offer, but luckily the General and Hurd came into the room. Faces hard, grim. Pepper saw Zula palm the evidence bag and lower it to her side. What a sweetheart!

But the General's face reminded Pepper that some things skip a generation. "We'll have to review your actions that led to the firefight," the General growled. "But at this point, I'm keeping you, Larch and Dooley on active duty—I'm too short this week to pull three officers."

"That might change after the review," added Hurd. "No warrant! What do—"

"Westin invited me on his property when we met five days ago," interrupted Pepper. "He said to come back anytime. Check my report. And there wasn't time for a warrant. I believed Marcus Dunne might have been inside that duffel. His life was in danger. What if--"

Chief Eisenhower stopped Pepper with a glare. "We'll get to all that."

Pepper bit his tongue. And he didn't think it was a great moment to mention the Rogers Lighthouse parking lot rendezvous that he'd set up on that phone call, since Pepper had missed it due to the NRF firefight.

The General seemed to take that for contrition. "You're a good cop, Pepper. You'll be an excellent one, if you stick with it...like your dad and your brother. But you have to know your limits."

"And obey orders," snorted Hurd. "Because your insubordination's going to get one of us killed."

The General gave Hurd a look, then continued. "But we

had some helpful news. The NRF member who survived the firefight talked for a while, in his hospital bed. He admitted that he and a few buddies dug the clambake hole at Dill Beach last week but swore he didn't have anything to do with killing Keser. He said he'd have heard if anyone in the NRF had done it, and he hadn't. Then he stopped talking, asked for a lawyer."

"Shit," blurted Pepper, his mind racing. "If the NRF didn't kill Keser, we've been looking at this Red Starfish threat all wrong."

"What do you mean?"

"We've been chasing individual groups, assuming one must be our threat. What if there are multiple, separate bad actors, each carrying out their own piece. Like separate arms of a starfish."

"So, a conspiracy."

Pepper just grunted his agreement. His brain was already racing forward—they had to find Westin—where would he have gone? And where was Marcus Dunne? But to stop the plot to kill Garby, Pepper knew they'd have to chase down more than what were essentially the arms of the starfish. Does a starfish even *have* a brain?

Because Pepper feared they had to find that brain—the mastermind—to prevent the assassination.

THIRTY

Pepper Ryan woke to banging on his trailer door. He creaked it open. Zula Eisenhower was standing there—she took a step backward when she saw he was wearing only boxer briefs, but quickly recovered. Her face was a mask of seriousness.

"Pepper, does this tin can have power? You ever charge your phone? Marcus Dunne's body washed ashore. Hogan Beach. A lifeguard found him half an hour ago. Pop thought you'd want to look things over for yourself."

Shit! The news was like a punch. All his efforts, and promises to Trish, had been useless...

Pepper slipped into t-shirt and jeans and accepted a ride over in Zula's jeep. On the way, Zula updated Pepper on the research she'd completed for him on Scoter, Inc. She said it was a Cayman Islands-registered company. One of its officers was Wayne Garby—the President of the United States! Its secretary was Isabel Bumpers and its treasurer was John Bumpers, but she hadn't found any further information about them. They may be Cayman nationals—sometimes local people served on Cayman corporations to handle any administrative tasks that arise. She didn't know for sure though.

Pepper thought Zula sounded distracted, like she wanted to talk about something else. But she said nothing after completing her brief info about Scoter, Inc., just let the wind ripping through the open Jeep fill their silence. Which was fine with Pepper—he was still reeling from the tragic news about Marcus Dunne and his own failure to prevent it.

They joined Chief Eisenhower, Lieutenant Hurd and Sergeant Weisner who were questioning the teenage lifeguard who found Dunne's body. She was sitting in an oversized Celtics sweatshirt, hands pulled into her sleeves, pale under her summer tan.

"I was jogging the beach to my station like we're supposed to," she said softly. "I saw him floating in a few inches of water. I pulled him on shore as far as I could and checked for a pulse, you know? But I could tell he was dead for hours... Do I need to stay for my shift?"

Pepper hated the little shake in her voice.

Weisner took her to sit in a police car, away from the breeze and the body.

"So how would they have done it?" asked the General. "One man charters Dunne's boat, goes out to sea with him? Kills him? Then an accomplice shows up in a separate boat, gives the killer a ride back to shore?"

"Maybe the killers own a boat?" said Pepper. "Supports the theory the unsubs are locals. Unless they stole it?" Some lead—searching for a small boat, no description, in Cape Cod. No choice, but a needle in a haystack might be quicker...

But Pepper had to say what he was really thinking. "I can make this one easy, Chief. I know who did it."

"Who?" demanded Hurd.

"We did. It'd have been more merciful to just put a bullet in his head, once the Secret Service announced they had a witness in the clambake case."

"We don't even know if he was killed before or after you started a firefight with those militia nuts," said Hurd with a shake of his nose. "So maybe *we* aren't to blame, Ryan. Maybe it's all on you."

You know that's bullshit, thought Pepper. *But it's definitely my fault too.*

* * *

Pepper was sipping coffee at Aunt Anney's Kitchen, trying to get Dunne's bluish-red face and swollen body out of his mind. He was mentally fried but still had lots of work to do. Reports to file. The bureaucratic garbage which almost made it all not worth it. What would his reports say? Just a mishmash of facts that didn't tell very much?

This was all just temporary madness. Pepper would solve whatever the hell was going on, including catching whoever killed Dunne. Then he'd be out of here. New Albion could go back to the way it was and Pepper would get out of the way... That'd be a fair plan for everyone.

He decided to pursue one of his few tiny loose-ends instead. He pulled up the photo of the yellow post-it note from Smith's desk. BLACKHAM. An exclamation point. Then a phone number. A bit above Blacklock's name was the word SCOTER.

Pepper dialed the number.

"Blacklock!" a man's voice said, brusquely.

Pepper gave his name and title. "Sir, I'm calling to ask you a few questions about Acker Smith. And...Scoter?" Whatever that was.

"What? My call to the feds was anonymous. How'd you get my name?" Loud, belligerent.

"Nothing's anonymous anymore," Pepper assured him, while thinking *Blacklock called a federal agency? What for?* "So you should cooperate fully, for your own protection."

"Fuck *that!* I'm not blowing the whistle on *anyone* without guarantees, in writing. I'm not even sure what I know...I need to talk to someone first... What's Scoter? I called about my Cayman account, Turnstone. What're you trying to pin on me? Maybe I need to chat with a few dozen of my lawyers, then call you back."

Pepper's blood was racing. He'd have to ask Zula to fire up her databases again, dig deep on the two mystery names: Turnstone and Scoter.

"Mr. Blacklock, you don't have anything to worry about. How can we get together, as soon as possible?"

* * *

Pepper's dad called, his voice a bit too loud and excited. "If you're still trying to figure out where the assholes bought that shellfish for their clambake, you can stop."

"What?"

"I found the place! Larry's Fish Market, up in Bourne."

"Bourne? That's an hour away."

"Yep. Either they were trying to be pretty careful or else the feds' theory they're locals is shit. They may have stopped off on their way to the Cape. And bonus points, there's video!"

"What!"

"Kinda grainy and the two jokers are wearing hats and maybe long wigs. Even sunglasses. But the timing matches the purchase we've been looking for."

So, two people. And despite the disguises, maybe the Secret Service could use their technological wizardry to get some other helpful details to ID them. Height, race, that sort of thing. "Nice score Dad! You want to tell Eisenhower?"

His dad laughed. "Why don't you take the credit on this one, tell your Secret Service pal. Probably keep me from getting arrested!" But Pepper could hear the triumph in his dad's voice.

"Helluva job, Dad, thanks."

Then Pepper filled him in on almost everything that happened since they'd last talked, finishing with his conversation with Brandon Blacklock.

"Did you check out the pictures I sent you?" Pepper asked. Sent, but hadn't specifically said where they'd come from. And Pepper was glad his dad hadn't asked...

"I did. Was that a joke?"

"No, why?"

"Son, I won't even ask how you legally got Acker Smith's medical records... But the chart shows better news for him than I'd been hearing. I had Dr. Anderson take a look, on a no-name basis. He said it showed pancreatic cancer, but not final stage. The patient would potentially have one to two years to live, and with further treatment, maybe longer... Hold on, that's Eisenhower on the other line."

In a long minute, his dad clicked back. "Goddamn it Pepper!"

"What happened?"

"Lieutenant Fucking Hurd had the balls to complain to Eisenhower about me! I was following the paperwork on the home destruction and saw he'd assigned that Phillips kid to traffic detail at a bum address that was almost the same as ours. So I went to Hurd who processed the request for a detail officer, asked him if he remembered anything strange about it, right? And he got all crusty with me! Told me to butt out and leave it to the real police. I was catching bad guys in this town before he was potty trained. I told him to go fuck himself and reminded him he's supposed to be heading that investigation and hasn't come up with squat. And I may have said something about his nose probably being bigger than his dick."

"Dad!"

"Hey, with a nose as big as his, he could still be pretty hung. But he went crying to Eisenhower—what an asshole!"

Pepper wouldn't want to be in Hurd's shoes—caught between the new chief and the old one. Didn't Hurd know they were best buds?

His dad continued. "It was bad luck for Hurd, I'd just gotten some other lousy news and was a little less tolerant of idiots than usual. The mortgage company sold my loan and the new holder's forcing my hand. They want our family land sold."

Holy shit! Pepper was speechless.

"Of course I'll try to delay them, but..."

"I'm sorry, Dad," said Pepper quietly. "We'll figure something out."

THIRTY-ONE

The Tuckers had changed their beachcomber routine. Sherry had been more than a little spooked by finding the poor dead man in the clambake pit. Ever since, she'd refused to take their early morning walk along Dill Beach. Not with some maniac on the loose! No, she'd stick to mid-day strolls on busy stretches of beach.

Bert? He felt ten years younger. At least five. He'd become more than a bit of a celebrity at the Knights of Columbus, having to retell his story endlessly. And he thought the Wolsons and the Fischers might even be jealous—they'd been unavailable for cocktail hour all week.

It was early Sunday afternoon at Hogan Beach, a popular stretch of sand in New Albion. Which was fine with Bert. From the corner of his large, wear over sunglasses (which he thought make him resemble Arnold Schwarzenegger) he was watching three foxy teenaged girls attempting to toss a Frisbee. The beach was crowded with sunbathers, kids digging futilely in the sand, and even some swimmers braving early July's cool waters.

And then all hell broke out.

* * *

Bert Tucker would have run away, but, as he explained later, that wasn't his Marine Corps training.

Actually, the Tuckers just froze where they were.

They saw one group, very organized, with signs and fists, entering the beach area from the parking lot. Maybe thirty people, mostly men. Their leader had thick black hair, gelled hard, like a helmet. A number of their signs mentioned the Church of Peter Weeping. They were chanting, blowing whistles and one guy was giving it his best into a megaphone. Bert had heard of those Weepy assholes and their protests at veteran funerals.

A second group was coming south along the beach, ebbing and flowing around the families and their blankets and chairs. A few dozen protesters, a pretty even mix of men and women, chanting passionately, waving signs and banners. Some banners and signs protested the depletion of fish and other natural resources. Bert usually spent a good part of every morning at the Dunkin' Donuts shooting the breeze with other retirees and reading whichever newspapers had been abandoned there, so he knew President Garby had managed to piss off everyone on the fishing topic. The feds had closed part of George's Bank and some groups wanted that reversed, other groups wanted more closures. It was a hot debate across Cape Cod—were the closures necessary and would they wipe out a generation of fishermen?

This group also carried signs supporting wind energy and protesting President Garby's failure to support it. They were even toting a mannequin dressed as President Garby, hung in effigy. This bunch was what Bert would lump into the broad category of 'tree huggers'.

And then, for flip's sakes, he saw a third group arriving! Looked like commercial fishermen, the way they were

217

dressed. They didn't have signs. They had weapons—pieces of pipe and 2x4s, lengths of chain. They'd appeared from the marina's direction and laid into the tree huggers without so much as a how-do-you-do. The tree huggers fell back stunned, then regrouped and started to defend themselves, using their signs as shield and weapon. And their fists, the women too. When the first group—the Weepy a-holes—reached the battle, the two other groups laid into them as well.

The families and other folk caught in the path of the violence tried to flee. Parents grabbed children, boyfriends grabbed girlfriends. Fights spilled into the blankets and chairs and fathers joined the fight. And some mothers. Bert had his bride by one hand, and his other arm up defensively. But they stayed frozen. Sheltered in place, he'd later describe it.

Bert witnessed a police officer—the youngest one from the clambake murder crime scene, Phillips?—calling in the riot on a shoulder radio. The officer then pulled his baton and ran toward a man who was sitting on one of the Frisbee teenagers and banging her head on the sand. Officer Phillips gave the man a full whack to the back of the head, knocking him off and motionless. The girl sat up, red-faced, hysterical, shaking. She crawled to her feet and stumbled off toward the parking lot.

He saw the officer run to a scrub pine tree. Get it to his back. He was trying to use his shoulder radio again but was having problems. And now finally there were sirens filtering in from all directions. The law, descending to kick ass and take names. Most of the rioters were getting in a few final licks and then trying to escape up or down the shoreline. The families and sunbathers were still streaming toward the parking lot.

Bert gently tugged his wife's hand, reassuring her and trying to get her slowly headed up to the parking lot, as well. The news trucks should be there any minute.

THIRTY-TWO

Later that afternoon, Chief of Police Eisenhower spun his laptop around, showed the headline at *boston.com* to SAIC Hanley and Special Agent Alfson. Pepper Ryan and Lieutenant Hurd weren't close enough to read the smaller print, but they didn't need to. They'd already seen it, plenty.

CAPE FEAR! said the headline. The photo below it showed New Albion Officer Jackson Phillips, arm back, baton descending toward the head of a man on his knees. The bottom of the scene was cut off, but the photographer had caught quite a moment--officer in the foreground, arm raised, a half smile on his face, with miscellaneous mayhem and violence in progress in the rest of the photo.

"That should ease your parking problems," said Alfson. But no one laughed.

"I was hoping we could brainstorm a bit about what the hell's going on here," Eisenhower said. "The way the trouble's all tying together. So many outside groups. So aggressive. And they seem to be coordinating with each other. I was interested in your opinions and maybe a little more sharing than we've done so far."

"Sounds good," said Hanley.

"Well, the chief asshole for the Weepers, Reverend

McDevitt, ended up briefly in the hospital. Probably just long enough to support his lawsuits. But one of our officers saw something interesting. McDevitt had one of those fancy blue phones—he had it out for a second when he was pulling himself together to be discharged."

"Maybe just a coincidence," said Hurd.

"Unlikely," said Hanley. Since they're Black Wing II phones. It's a model approved for Department of Defense work. Top of the line privacy features and top of the line price."

"Pretty fancy for a preacher, even a rich fake one," said Eisenhower.

Hanley asked Alfson to recap the investigation's progress. Sadly, it didn't take long.

"We've enhanced the surveillance video from the seafood market," added Alfson. "Their disguises limited the results, but we're comfortable that they're both Caucasian, a younger male about 5'11" and an older male about 5'8"."

The recap went downhill from there. There was little promising physical evidence at the crime scene. One witness dead, and the others who could only say there'd been two men, which fit with the seafood market video. The Secret Service research team believed that Keser and Dunne were killed by the same unsubs, due to the patterns of the crimes, and apparently the same party was behind the unsuccessful poisoning of Freestyle and Funsize at that nightclub. Particularly due to the red starfish messages left at each incident. The Secret Service had also developed a psychological profile but felt it was incomplete, contradictory. The mix of professionalism and personal animus didn't make sense as a whole.

The group digested, glumly.

"There's five days left in the POTUS's vacation

schedule," Hanley reminded them. "Security-wise, every day's gotten worse. I got a call this morning from the FBI's Joint Terrorism Task Force, notifying me they're sending a team to ride herd on the domestic terror groups in town. They've been hearing the reports and don't want to look like they missed the boat."

That didn't surprise Pepper. New Albion had become ground zero for too broad a range of high-profile chaos. He wondered if the beach rioters and other bad actors in town were somehow connected to the red starfish killer? Or was the whole mess just an unrelated convergence of President Garby's enemies, sharing nothing but their hatred for the president?

"But the worst part for me?" continued Hanley. "This red starfish wacko's playing with us. He's right nearby but he's invisible. He kills then disappears. And kind of mocking us at the same time, with that crap about wanting his candy back... It's like he's following some loony playbook developed over a long time and we're only reacting. And mostly just chasing our own fucking tail for his entertainment."

"We'll get him, boss," said Alfson.

"No doubt. But we have to get him before he gets the POTUS. And right now I don't feel too damn confident."

* * *

"Did I pay for that?" Mr. Smith asked weakly, pointing at his laptop with a shaky finger. The billionaire was sitting at his desk in his shadowed bedroom in his bright burgundy bathrobe. Lizzie Concepcion noticed he was still losing weight. She'd have to bring in his tailor to fix up some clothes right away.

She had already read that riot story online. The press was wallowing in the chaos. Gushing lots of blame on local law enforcement's inadequacies, as well as President Garby's poisonous presence... "Well sir," she answered with a smile he probably couldn't see. "You wanted the president to have a miserable vacation...it looks like you're not the only one who feels that way!"

Lizzie knew that despite Mr. Smith's painful decline, he still got a kick out of being in control. And that included seeing the president suffer. Yesterday Mr. Smith had spent a few minutes alone with the president and Mr. Smith had told her everything later, in rich detail. The President had very quickly shifted from pleasantries and small talk to begging for money. He'd asked Smith to contribute $90 million for super PAC financing and $10 million for Garby's presidential library. Smith had been teasingly noncommittal, making the President of the United States beg and beg. Then Mr. Smith had left him in limbo to wait for a decision. So, the more misery the better, right?

"What a weasel!" laughed Mr. Smith—a thin, sandpaper squeak.

Lizzie jumped on his good mood to share some less happy news, which she accompanied with a light shoulder rub. "You got a call from Brandon Blacklock," she said. The star portfolio manager had demanded to speak to Smith but Lizzie had lied, said he was asleep. The fat slob had been his usual belligerent, condescending self with her, but his voice had had an unusual urgency. Almost a panic. "He said he needs to talk to you in person. Said he'll fly up tomorrow."

"Did he say what about?"

"He wouldn't tell *me*. But I hear he's been fighting with the trading desk, so maybe he just wants to vent."

Smith coughed. "Fly here to vent? No, he wants to see

for himself how close I am to dead. And maybe if there's anything he can do to speed me along. Count on it, he'll be the next traitor trying to grab my company..."

Blacklock and Mr. Smith hadn't been on good relations since the presidential election when Mr. Smith had heavily backed Garby and Blacklock had very publicly—and financially—supported Garby's opponent. It'd caused quite a fuss within Smith Enterprises and also in the financial press. It didn't help that Mr. Smith probably realized by now that Blacklock had been right about that weasel Garby. "Well, we'll see when he gets here." Lizzie gently changed the topic by sliding onto his lap a small pile of documents for signature. Actually, Blacklock *had* said what about. The slob had threatened to drop a dime to the feds about Turnstone Fund's recent wire activity unless Smith agreed to two things. One, to implement operational changes on the development fund, specifically so there'd be no future wire activity unless authorized by Blacklock, as portfolio manager. And two, the real bullet—to publicly name Blacklock as Smith's successor at Smith Enterprises, with transition to begin immediately.

Well, there was no way Lizzie was going to deliver *those* ultimatums to Mr. Smith herself! She'd told Blacklock to hop on the jet and come to Eagle's Nest himself. She hadn't gone so far as to call him a traitorous coward, but she said enough, in a pretty obnoxious tone, that it *may* have been implied...

Let him try his darn blackmail face-to-face with Mr. Smith, if the arrogant whale actually showed up. Because Lizzie was betting he wouldn't...

* * *

"What the fuck do you mean, cancel the Fourth of July?" asked President Garby.

Today he'd been golfing but his drive back to Eagle's Nest had been messed up by another damn illegal protest. Five semi-truck trailers displaying large pictures of Americans killed by illegal immigrants had been parked blocking Shore Road 400 yards short of the first Secret Service checkpoint. The drivers had disconnected their trailers and sabotaged the hookup mechanisms. Each trailer was guarded by dozens of activists. It took two hours to clear the mob and haul the trailers away.

And not a mile away, a riot had broken out on the beach right when he was supposed to be driving past in his twenty vehicle caravan. The press had split in half to cover both the blockade and the riot. This shit was red meat for those jackals.

Garby's limousine, The Beast, had been re-routed to Chatham Municipal Airport, where he was picked up by Marine One and helicoptered back to Eagle's Nest. He was beyond pissed. And he was still raw from the jerking around he'd gotten from Smith after he took the time to present those financial support opportunities.

Now Garby was sequestered with his core presidential staff and Special Agent in Charge Hanley. He glared at Hanley with his full Leader of the Free World wattage. Who did this punk think he was?

"Not cancel the Fourth of July, sir," said Hanley. "Just your attendance at the fireworks."

Acker Smith had paid for a fireworks display to be held tomorrow night off New Albion that would be bigger and better than anywhere else in America. Around 55,000 shells. And all in Garby's honor. It'd been trumpeted in the press and huge crowds were expected to swarm to the area to watch.

"So you're saying the only place you can keep me safe is

locked up here? Is that what you told your bosses?"

"A package arrived at Eagle's Nest in today's mail, addressed to you. Again with a copy of the Declaration of Independence, with tomorrow's date printed on it and *RIP Garby* again. And the sentence: *I want my candy!* The package held one high-caliber bullet, a .308. And another red starfish. I gave my assessment to Deputy Director Lawrence. Then to Director Kerpitki. Our best assessment is we have a very specific, very credible threat of an assassination attempt to be made on your life sometime during the Fourth. My recommendation is you shouldn't appear in public tomorrow unless we've arrested the unsubs. For your safety, and your family's."

Garby felt an icy finger of fear slide up his spine. He could almost feel what a .308 bullet would be like, tearing into his chest, ripping him apart, killing him. Who was this red starfish wacko—one of those wack-job activists? And why hadn't they caught him yet?

Deep breath.

I'm the most powerful man in the world.

I'm the most powerful man in the world.

His mantra didn't completely thaw the ice that'd spread up his spine to his neck, but it helped a bit. Frankly, the whole thing was bullshit. Some shithead wanted their candy? Garby didn't even eat sweets, he didn't know what the hell that could be about. And Garby had never even *seen* a red starfish before, except maybe on a school trip to the aquarium? He faintly recalled that as a lowly senator he'd dated a redhead with a fish tattoo at the very top of her thigh... No, that had to have been an octopus, in that private spot, right? He smothered a burst of horniness and set his face in a mask of boredom and disgust. "Well, let me give you some advice," he growled at Hanley. "Do your job. It's to protect me, isn't it? Is that too much to ask?"

That'd shut Hanley up.

What kind of a man would Garby look like, hiding away, scared of his own shadow? Was that how they wanted him to be seen? He pressed his hands in his golf grip and made a mini-swing. Muscle memory. That was the key to running the world and being able to shoot in the high seventies at the same time.

"Just so we're clear," said Garby digging deep for his most presidential timbre. "I'm not changing any plans. Not canceling any public outings. Smith's fireworks'll be the most expensive goddamn display since the Beijing Olympics. He'd be pissed if I blew it off, rightly so. But I have a solution—Smith offered us his yacht for the show. You can sweep it from stern to poop deck, whatever security you think necessary as long as your folks don't ruin the party. And I don't want to read in the papers or goddamn Twitter about this so-called threat. No leaks. If you're not with me, step aside for someone who's up to the job, got it? Lucky for you I'm an optimist."

"Yes sir," said Hanley, but still looking like he'd sucked a lemon.

What an asshole!

THIRTY-THREE

Zula Eisenhower was headed out the front door to work when she was almost bowled over by Pepper's dad. Gerry Ryan was fired up, almost non-verbal.

But he apologized, explained. He'd just gotten a call on his cell phone, from Reverend McDevitt. The man had said if he came over to the property the Weepers were renting in New Albion, the Reverend would tell him who'd destroyed the Ryan family house.

"Since he's a snake, sounds like he's setting you up somehow?" said Zula.

"Of course it's a setup. But he knows I'll show up anyway, right?"

God, the Ryans. "I'll drive you," she insisted, but looking at her watch. "You'll need a friendly witness, in case you knock him out again."

So they drove in Zula's red Jeep Wrangler to the waterfront address that Gerry Ryan had been given. On the way, she called her pop, told him where they were going and could he tell Barbara she'd be late to Dispatch? Her pop insisted on talking to Gerry Ryan, apparently trying to talk him out of confronting McDevitt. Too quickly, the call ended. *Man, Gerry Ryan looks just like Pepper, right now…*

But Zula was otherwise enjoying the drive in her Wrangler—sunny Fourth of July, no top, no doors. They passed Hogan Beach and were slowed by thick traffic. The beach area was full to beyond bursting. The Hogan Beach riot was apparently forgotten. It was a peaceful swarm of families, coolers and sand buckets--the whole mess of casual fun which defined her summer world. The main reason she came home every summer when her friends were now getting jobs in Boston or New York.

"Chief Ryan, do you have any old favors waiting at the State Police Lab?"

"Up in Maynard? I do, if the tech I know hasn't retired."

Zula told him about the white powder that Pepper asked her to have analyzed ASAP and that she wasn't having any luck. They'd told her they were swamped. Her civilian title hadn't impressed them either.

"Why didn't Pepper have the Secret Service analyze it, if it's such a rush?"

"You know Pepper—he says little and explains less. Maybe he wants to one-up that Alfson?"

"That's probably the most innocent excuse… If you give me the control number, I'll give my friend a call."

They passed St. Jude's Cemetery. Then Zula was detoured away from the ocean for two miles to avoid the area closed to traffic due to the president's stay at Eagle's Nest. She cut back down and rejoined Shore Road on the other side.

"None of my business," said Gerry Ryan, "but what's going on with you and Pepper?"

Zula had been wondering the same thing, wished she knew. "Nothing. He's day and night with the Clambake investigation."

"And that Maddie Smith, right?" But saying her name like he wasn't too impressed.

Zula felt her face turning hot. Mercifully, they'd arrived at the address so Zula didn't have to answer.

The Weeper rental was an impressive oceanside vacation estate. Long driveway from the road to a large, split-level house. Maybe a $5 - 10 million property? If Zula owned a place like this, she'd never rent it out, especially to insects like the Weepers.

A large, handmade sign by the road said 'Free Clambake Today!'

"Shit," said Gerry Ryan.

There were cars parked in a long line up and down both sides of the driveway. Even three television trucks, parked on the lawn. Nothing on the street, it was all self-contained to the property.

A tall, skinny guy in his twenties with too much brown hair waved them in, gesturing theatrically toward the end of the row of parked cars.

"Funny the Weepers rented a fancy house like this," commented Zula. "Their home base is only a couple hours away, I'd have thought they'd commute to cause their trouble."

Gerry Ryan snorted. "McDevitt's gotten filthy rich from his hate crimes—let's hope he's only renting..."

In the backyard, a picnic of sorts was in full swing. It was a classic Cape Cod scene. A long lawn led down to the shore, where there was a light blue boathouse, a pier and a large motor cruiser. The lawn was thick with a good-sized crowd—100 people? Many were sitting in circles on the grass, eating. Others were milling around. Half the crowd was standing close to a low stage, and a man was addressing them, microphone in hand. It was Reverend McDevitt. He was flanked by five women, ranging in age from mid-teens to forties. Was one of them his wife? Some of the teens, his daughters? They were all hanging on his speech, leading the clapping and cheering. Cult cheerleaders?

Zula saw three TV teams with handheld cameras, shooting footage.

"And now the President of the United States is among us, in this very town!" McDevitt was saying. "The sinner-in-chief! But does he stand with us?"

Loud jeers from the crowd. Everyone had something to hate about President Wayne Garby.

"Does he stand up for what's right and just? *Whoremongers and adulterers, God will judge!*"

Even louder cheering from the crowd.

"Brutality!" Reverend McDevitt continued. "*Surely oppression maketh a wise man mad!* And in this town, the poison passes down from father to son. Police brutality by their Chief of Police Ryan, who resigned in disgrace. And his son, Officer Pepper Ryan, killed a suspect nine years ago in the most reckless fashion. Of course, the son paid no price. Look it up!"

"Shit," said Gerry Ryan. Clenched jaw, clenched fists. Looked like he was going to rush the stage.

"And ladies and gentlemen. God's children. Look who now stands among us! There in the back. It's former Chief Ryan. Look at the anger, the devil's fingerprints on his face!"

Most of the people turned to Gerry Ryan and Zula. The cameras. All of the crowd's energy.

"He comes here in anger. His house was destroyed recently and revenge is on his face. But the Bible tells us who tore down this sinner's temple! *The Lord destroyed the house of the proud,* and blessed is the word of the Lord. So it was written in Proverbs!"

Zula had Pepper's dad by the arm now, physically holding him back from moving toward the stage. He was talking to himself, quiet but hard, too low for Zula to catch the words.

She saw a dozen or so Weepers moving from the stage front toward them, threading through the crowd.

"Time to go," she said in Gerry Ryan's ear, jerking his arm. And miracle of miracles, he followed.

* * *

Zula had reached her desk, taken a quick thirty-second verbal beating by Barbara for being late, and logged in before Lieutenant Hurd descended on the Dispatch pen.

"Hello, Zula."

"Oh, hey Lieutenant." Keeping her voice chill.

"We got a call this morning from the Federal Bureau of Investigation's Financial Crimes Unit. They're interested why a local police station queried FinCEN's database about an entity called Scoter and its associated persons. They'd like to hear more about our investigation. I said I didn't know anything about it, so I probably sounded pretty stupid…"

Shit. She'd feared the entity Scoter, Inc. might be a time bomb since the President of the United States was a listed officer… What the hell'd Pepper gotten her to step in this time? "Well, it's for the Keser case."

"What's up with it?"

"Nothing much yet. Nothing to report."

"Well, maybe you can be a little more open with your father how FinCEN's database is relevant to a Secret Service agent's murder. Especially since he told you not to spend any time helping Pepper on that investigation? Can you tell him what you're up to, before one of us loses our job?" Hurd shook his head, left. More muttering and abuse from Barbara followed.

Double shit.

And then of course, a few minutes later, Pepper cornered her too.

He gave her that smile and it worked. Made her chest tighten, like a silly schoolgirl. Idiot!

"Hurd's on the warpath about me and I saw him poking his nose over here," Pepper said, keeping his voice quiet. "He wasn't giving you crap for helping me, was he?"

"Pepper, you don't need to..."

"No. You've been great. And your father too, supporting my dad's footwork investigating the house demo."

So she had to tell him about the Weeper clambake, McDevitt's public slandering of him and his dad, the TV crews, the whole thing.

"Thanks for going with him...my family can't stay out of trouble, looks like." He looked humbled and she was surprised to realize that she didn't like that look on him. She wanted to hug him right there and then. Instead, she came back too snappish.

"Pepper, you're kind of right. But around here, your dad was the man. Then your brother--sure, he was up in Boston, but we could see his shadow all the way down here. He was all over the Herald."

"I never wanted to be like them," said Pepper. "I just wanted to do my own thing. Maybe play a little guitar..."

"You don't fool me, Pepper," said Zula. "First punch to the nose and you came up swinging. That's your DNA." She wanted to either kiss him or choke him, so she changed the topic. "But I've gotta get focused here. Barbara gets a little testy. Buy me breakfast tomorrow and I'll have some info about your list of corporations and their officers that'll make it worth your while."

"Can you get Barbara to stay on for a few minutes, maybe finish up that research for me now?"

He has the patience of a three-year-old. "Barbara wants to go see the big show tonight. And I'm already in trouble today. You don't think you've been acting a little out of control? Doing things your way, no matter who gets hurt?"

"Is it about the NRF shootout?"

There's no line a Ryan won't cross when he thinks he's on the path of the righteous. Especially Pepper. "All I'm saying is, take a deep breath. You ever try practicing mindfulness?" *Or even think a little bit about others?*

Pepper smiled at her. "Not all who wander are lost," he said.

Asshole. Zula had a t-shirt with that quote on the front. She thought it was part true, part funny. And it didn't hurt the t-shirt was just the right amount of snug up front. She'd worn it last week and Pepper must have remembered. And now the jackass was teasing her about it?

"Don't patronize me, Pepper! I predict two things. First, you'll eventually do the right thing. And second...you'll still be an idiot."

"Well, at least I'll finally do the right thing. So good for me." Now smiling a little.

Ya, good for you Pepper. That's what's important. And she dismissed him with a flip of hair before she'd say or do who knows what else. His jackassery must be contagious.

THIRTY-FOUR

Special Agent Dan Alfson didn't personally care much for the pomp and bullshit of the major holidays. Occupational hazard. But Alfson was a patriot so the Fourth of July was probably the least annoying holiday. Especially while on a superyacht half a mile offshore with the President of the United States, keeping him safe.

That morning, Alfson had gotten a call from Pepper Ryan that surprised him. Ryan asked if Alfson had heard of a Cayman entity called Scoter, Inc. and some individuals named as officers—John and Isabel Bumpers. Ryan claimed Wayne Garby had been an officer too but had resigned shortly before his election as POTUS—did Alfson know the specifics of the POTUS's past involvement with Scoter?

Alfson didn't know what political mud Ryan was digging into. But he was sure it had nothing to do with the Keser investigation and the Secret Service's protection of the POTUS and he said so to Ryan. Surprisingly, that'd shut him up pretty quickly. Which was good, because Alfson's gut still said don't trust Ryan and he definitely didn't have time for his partner's maverick grandstanding. The kind of nonsense that could quickly trash the careers of people in Ryan's splash zone if they weren't careful.

That afternoon, Alfson had personally joined the technical security team's sweep of the *Madeline Too* and its crew. So thorough, the crew would be able to skip their next proctological exams. The Navy did a similar sweep around and under the yacht. All was clear.

The day's end came fast, with lots of buzz. Everyone across America knew about the personally-funded fireworks extravaganza in honor of the First Family and way too many had driven down to see the historic spectacle in person. Law enforcement was reporting that New Albion's shoreline was crowded with hundreds of thousands of spectators, ready to witness history. Except within the Eagle's Nest security perimeter, of course.

The POTUS and his family were on the *Madeline Too's* upper deck, being entertained by Smith's daughter Maddie— her father had begged off due to his illness. Little red dress, long tanned legs, blonde hair flowing like the sea breeze was her own personal wind machine. But a hell of a brat—she tended to either ignore the Secret Service agents or treat them like servants. What'd she see in Ryan? She was *way* out of his class. (As was Ryan's other flirtation, the sassy Zula...) The POTUS also was accompanied by a small group of platinum donors, executive hangers-on and other core West Wing staff. The yacht was surrounded by a loose perimeter of Navy craft.

As dusk arrived, a Blue Angel squadron flew low along the coast. Smith had paid for them too. Alfson felt his bones shake from their engines' force.

Then the first salvo of fireworks lit the sky, followed by muffled booms. Smith had reportedly guaranteed his show would last exactly three times as long as Boston's. And was ten times as expensive. Children would talk about those fireworks long into old age.

But in law enforcement circles, they would talk about the

assault on the Eagle's Nest compound that went down right in the middle of the fireworks show.

* * *

Pepper had been driving in his truck back to his trailer around dusk on the Fourth of July. He had just put in a follow-up request to Edwina Youngblood at the FBI about the two entities Pepper had been bumping into: Scoter, Inc. and Turnstone. Any recent activity or unusual registrations, that sort of thing. Pepper had begged for quick results but she'd made no promises, with thin staffing on the holiday.

As Pepper hung up, something Zula Eisenhower had said to him earlier clicked in his head: *Barbara wants to go see the big show tonight.* The day Pepper had searched Eagle's Nest, the anonymous voice on the cell phone hidden in the ceramic penguin had used the same term. *The big show,* maybe referring to Smith's gigantic fireworks show? And that voice had also asked about a list.

Could the voice have been talking about the security checkpoint authorization list?

Pepper felt a tingling down his spine. He did a u-turn on Shore Road, headed toward Eagle's Nest at high speed. He tried to call Special Agent Alfson, but his call immediately went through to Alfson's voice mail. Pepper left a hurried message as he drove, saying he had a strong hunch some bad actors might try to attack Eagle's Nest by road during the fireworks show. Pepper didn't say why he thought that, since he hadn't told Alfson about his search of Eagle's Nest or the phone call he'd had with the unknown man. And now was definitely not the time to come clean.

As Pepper neared the Secret Service's first checkpoint, he saw a dozen or so cars and trucks waiting in line. The vehicle at the head of the line was a bakery truck with oversized pictures of bread and cakes on its large rear door.

Pepper didn't wait his turn. He pulled over to the shoulder and kept driving, honking his horn every couple of seconds, his hazard flashers on.

Pepper was only halfway to the front of the row of vehicles when he saw the bakery truck driver's head crane out to look back at Pepper's approaching pickup truck, then the bakery truck suddenly drove off, kicking up a cloud of dust and knocking back the Secret Service agent who had been questioning the driver.

The bakery truck hit a row of tire spikes that were in place just short of the second checkpoint. Blew all four tires, but the truck continued at high speed. Pepper saw an agent at the third checkpoint empty a submachine gun into the bakery truck's engine and windshield. Completely shredding the truck's front and windshield, as well as the driver.

Pepper also heard the *boom, boom, boom* of a rooftop sentry firing a Win Mag rifle, but later it couldn't be verified whether that agent's shots struck the bakery truck because at that moment the vehicle veered into a temporary concrete barricade and exploded in a fireball. The bakery truck was— *yep*—toast.

* * *

The forensic reconstruction team determined later that the bakery truck's driver—a woman—was wearing an explosive vest with a deadman's switch. The truck's rear had contained an ammonium nitrate fertilizer bomb—a smaller version of the one used in the Oklahoma City bombing. The agent who had been interviewing the woman at the first checkpoint before she panicked said she had appeared to be sedated. Separate legwork using video footage from the first checkpoint confirmed the female driver was a known associate of Brian-Edward Westin and the New River Front.

But the driver and the bakery truck were not on the checkpoint list for admission to Eagle's Nest. Had Pepper been flat out wrong in his guess about an imminent attack related to the mentions of a 'big show' and a 'list' during the ceramic penguin phone call?

And how would Pepper explain the coincidentally accurate warning message he'd left for Alfson on his voicemail?

THIRTY-FIVE

The Secret Service, the ATF, the State Police and every local police department within 100 miles were hunting down Brian-Edward Westin. Pepper's offer to stay at Eagle's Nest and help out with the crime scene had been bluntly rejected by Secret Service agents at the scene. They had a lot of work to do but didn't need any local help to get it done right.

But Pepper knew that after his dear partner Alfson listened to his message predicting a vehicle attack, the Secret Service would want to interview Pepper. And he knew it would be a very awkward interview...

So, fine—Pepper would leave the mess at Eagle's Nest to the Secret Service. Tomorrow would be soon enough to explain himself... And maybe they'd weathered the storm and the Red Starfish attacks were done?

So while the Secret Service did the dirty cleanup work, Pepper would go clear his debt to his pal Angel Cavada. Pepper owed him, big time, for his disappearing act three years earlier. And for having been too preoccupied with his investigations since returning to get up onstage at Angel's joint. So Pepper had offered to perform that night at Malecón's holiday blowout. Pepper had promised to see if he could drive the crowd to break Malecón's one-day booze sale record. Angel had been immediately, fully excited. He'd happily paid off his scheduled band, sent them back to Boston.

The ultra lounge trappings were long gone, restoring Malecón's patio to a simple, seaside oasis. But still with party music and shots, shots, shots. And there *was* a line outside. Two bouncers, both local kids, trying to keep control at the door. Scarface must have flown home to Miami.

So Pepper kept his promise to Angel and it felt awesome to be back on stage again. Pepper was gleefully breaking in a guitar that Angel had bought him as a gift. It was an acoustic-electric Fender, a beauty. He'd felt like he was missing an arm since his guitar was destroyed with the Ryan house.

He started with a string of the most popular island party songs. Then branched out a bit. Hit them with "Bang Bang (My Baby Shot Me Down)"--the Stevie Wonder version, not Cher's. He was really enjoying the feel and tone of the guitar Angel had given him—it felt like a natural fit in his hands. Pepper kept mixing it up, but always pushing the party vibe. He slid in a few of his original songs and they went over well too. A lot of the crowd had migrated to the dance floor and their energy was building. No sign of Maddie, the First Daughters and their entourage, yet. But he believed Maddie, who'd promised they were coming despite the attack at Eagle's Nest. He didn't want to even guess how agitated the Secret Service would be about Freestyle and Funsize going to a public venue that same night as if the attack had been no biggie. Wild.

After an hour, Pepper took a break. When he came offstage and headed to check in with Angel by the bar, a blonde woman, probably late forties, cut him off. Pepper instantly recognized her as one of the women who'd been onstage at the **ecó** event, when DJ ChilEboy spun his final tune! One of the women who'd been whisked away by Special Agent Alfson before Pepper could interview her...

"Hey, great voice!" she said laughing. "But aren't you a cop or something?"

"Yes, but music's his true love," said Angel, arriving at their sides. "One of them." He quickly had one arm around them both. The gracious host, with a flirty side. Angel introduced himself as Malecón's owner and Pepper as his oldest friend.

The woman was eating it up. "I'm Alexis. I'm staying with a friend nearby but I'm soooo bored... How long can you sit by a pool?"

A woman joined Alexis as they talked. It was the redhead—disappearing witness #2 from the ChilEboy homicide. A little older and a little heavier than Alexis. She had Alexis by the elbow, was leaning in, breaking things up.

"Come back every night and bring all your friends," said Angel. "I'll make sure Pepper's ready and waiting."

"Really?" the blonde smiled. And then she grabbed Pepper's forearm. She had strong fingers, probably a tennis player. "Do you know who I am?" she asked.

He shook his head but smiled. Should he?

"Well, if you want to find out...give me a call some time," she said. And with a little smile she pressed a balled-up cocktail napkin in Pepper's hand.

"Lexie, you're the *worst*!" said her friend. "Time to go!"

As her friend led her away, Alexis glanced back over her shoulder, gave Pepper a wink.

"You see how I was letting you have her?" said Angel.

"Pimping me out now?"

"*Mano*, I would if I could. But I know I'd get too many complaints..."

Pepper uncrumpled the cocktail napkin. She'd written her name and phone number. Must have had it ready when she came up to him?

And then it hit Pepper who she must be—President Garby's mistress! He'd heard all about an Alexis from the Secret Service guys. They'd been cracking about her secret service codename: Flame. Which she'd been named because she used to be a redhead. And they thought wasn't it funny, now she was suddenly a blonde? And the worst kept secret on Cape Cod. No wonder Alfson had hustled her and her friend away before getting witness statements. Pepper had heard from the agents that she got kid glove treatment from them—for example, at Eagle's Nest checkpoints they didn't take her ID and didn't search her car, despite the obvious security risks that caused. It was mandated by the highest level of the Secret Service... But the agents all said they liked her. She was always polite and friendly, always had a smile for them.

But fucking Alfson. Holding out on his own dear partner...

* * *

Pepper had been back on stage for a few songs when Maddie Smith and the First Twins arrived, with an entourage. Causing a ripple of head turns. Lots of pointing and the chatter level went up. The crowd split for them as they headed toward the bar, with more Secret Service agents in tow than previously.

Internet king Justin Case was with the ladies, in white cutoff shorts with ragged fringe. A pale blue tank-top showing just enough chest muscles. A shell necklace he'd probably picked up on Main Street that morning, or in Bora

Bora last month.   Arrived in flip-flops, but was quickly barefoot.

For a guy who'd perfected being lazy, he sure was getting around tonight. He was always in motion, but slowly. Shots at the bar with the ladies. Then mini-mobbed by a little flood of cyber fans. Took a little time for pics and vids with them, milking his signature shrug.

Moments later he was out dancing with Maddie. Pepper realized she was the kind of beautiful that made everyone around her seem younger, better-looking. Like it rubbed off, or they somehow lived up to her. She waved up to Pepper, locking eyes with him mid-song, making him stumble over the lyrics. Then she blew Pepper a big, fat kiss.

Which Justin saw. He stomped off with Maddie in tow and Pepper could see them arguing. Maddie shrugged, headed for the ladies' room. Moments later, Justin was back on the dance floor with the First Twins, one in each hand. For a slug, he sure had energy. And the sonofabitch could dance.

But Pepper turned his focus from Justin back to the crowd. He was having a blast performing for an audience again, just him and his guitar, singing his guts out. He went for another full hour before he took a second break. He flipped on some recorded music to try to keep the patio's party energy going. The reality is the buzz would dip some, which was fine—he'd crank it up quickly again when he got back on stage in ten minutes.

Except Alfson ambushed him the minute he came off stage.

"Ryan, have you seen the twins?" he asked, his pretty blonde haircut a bit unruly and sweat beading on his forehead.

Pepper couldn't tell whether he was angry or upset or

what. "I just saw them over by the bar, with Justin Case."

"Well, they've disappeared. I haven't seen Case either."

"Your agents have been on them like snow on Santa. I'm sure nothing's wrong."

But two agents—a man and woman—were shoving their way through the crowd, obviously searching for the girls. Their faces showed panic.

"Ryan, let's go!" Alfson pulled his phone, tried to make a call despite the music's volume.

Had someone managed to kidnap the First Daughters?

He found Angel talking to Maddie. Pepper's blood was pumping and his face was flushed…Angel was going to kill him.

"Have you seen Justin?" she yelled to Pepper. "And the twins?"

He shook his head no. "But I've gotta help find them! I gotta go!" yelled Pepper to Maddie and Angel over the loud music.

Angel was shaking his head like he couldn't hear right. "Go? You joking, *Mano*? You're the entertainment! What am I gonna do?"

Angel was right--Pepper was completely screwing him over. Again. But he had no choice. "Buddy, I'm sorry!" Pepper felt like shit, but maybe he'd be right back?

Why did Pepper always have to do something wrong when he needed to do something right? He left, running outside to catch up to Alfson. They had to find the twins!

All the Suburbans were still in the lot. The drivers hadn't seen Freestyle or Funsize. But they'd gotten the distress message from their colleagues—their necks were craning, they were sweating too. Every agent's worst nightmare.

How had someone gotten the twins out and away

without being seen?

"Did any of you see Justin Case leave?" asked Pepper.

No, no one had. Why—did he believe Case was in on it?

* * *

An hour later, social media blew up. First, selfies by Justin Case and the twins. Thank God, they were alive! But then, video snippets. The three of them, skinny dipping! And yeah, it was nighttime, but the full moon and lack of cloud cover meant the video was only dark enough to be slightly mysterious.

Pepper thought he recognized the scenery in the background and took an educated guess, directing the Suburbans to Dill Beach. They located the missing trio waterside, ten minutes later. The Secret Service agents politely but firmly bundled the girls into a Suburban, with the loan of two agents' blazers as towels. A little less politely— and more than a bit roughly—they left Justin Case there at the top of the beach path, naked except for his shell necklace and a wounded pout.

Pepper got back to Malecón ninety minutes after he'd run off. It was past last call and the crowd was streaming out the door. A TV truck was parked in the lot and a red-haired Channel Ten reporter ran over, caught Pepper by the arm as he was about to go inside. She was an artist at it—looked like she was just resting her fingers on his arm, but actually was holding him firmly in place. Her cameraman was a couple of steps back and to the side, catching them together in his bright light.

"Officer Ryan! What happened here? Were the First Daughters in danger? And is it true the fugitive Brian-Edward Westin is a suspect in tonight's attack at Eagle's

Nest?"

"No comment. Contact the Secret Service." He tried to gently wiggle his arm free from her pincer fingers.

"But officer, the public needs to know! Public safety—"

Pepper was tired and pissed off. "Okay, tell your viewers this. I know who's behind all this chaos and I personally guarantee they're going down, ASAP. Everyone else should sleep tight." And he winked into the camera.

Pepper pulled loose and quickly disappeared into the refuge of Malecón. Instantly mad at himself for his comments on camera. Already knowing who'd be upset— Pepper's bosses, Alfson and *his* bosses, it'd be a goddamn long line of people ready to spank him. Why hadn't he just shut his cake hole!

But first, Pepper had to find Angel and face the heat for running off, again. He imagined what Angel must have had to do to keep the party going once his entertainment disappeared. On probably the tourist season's biggest night. No apology was coming to Pepper's mind that'd make things right with Angel.

Pepper knew how the fireworks felt, after their explosions were done.

THIRTY-SIX

Oliver thought something stunk.

He'd just driven back from the Chatham Public Library where he'd checked the chat site for instructions from their bosses in Queens.

An ominous message had been waiting for Oliver:

FBTW. Charlie in coma. You hadn't heard, right? Go home kids... HAGD

Have a good day? Their bosses liked using the chat room but it didn't mean *they* were good at it. But *they* seemed suspicious that the client had been talking to Oliver and Croke directly. One thing *they* absolutely were good at was being suspicious. And vindictive.

Then, of course, on the drive back to the Sanddollar Motel, the special blue phone had rung and Oliver had received a garbled, cryptic instruction from the client: they should meet someone today at noon at somewhere called the High Seas Ice Cream Hut to receive a special package. Their assignment would follow.

And, frankly? The money had been too lucrative to say no. So Oliver was going to ignore *them* (keeping *their* chat room message a secret from Croke) and take the next assignment. Even though the setup reeked. Oliver didn't even trust Croke. Why was Oliver going to walk into a blind meeting? Well, he wasn't.

When Oliver got back to the motel, he went straight to Croke's room.

Croke was watching TV, as usual. "That Pepper Ryan was on the news earlier," he said. "Talking big about how close the cops are to catching us. Said he knows the whole setup, even more than we do. The reporter looked like she was going to kiss him, right there on the news."

"He said that? Must mean they're desperate. Some kind of bluff."

"Or maybe not. He winked, right at the damn camera. Maybe we should get off Cape Cod, right now?"

"Croke, do you know what 'fuck you' money is?" Oliver explained as simply as he could.

Croke was visibly impressed, so Oliver decided to push him. "And good news, you'll soon be one step closer to a big fat retirement fund. The client wants you to collect a package at a place called High Seas Ice Cream Hut, today at noon. Then we'll get the details of another very profitable assignment."

"Me?" asked Croke. "What package?"

"You. And the client didn't say. I don't know why he thought *you'd* do a better job. But hey, the client's always right, huh? I suggest you wear a new disguise to the handoff. I got it—maybe a smile?"

* * *

Oliver had read recently that a car is stolen in the United States every forty-five seconds. So Oliver felt it was statistically in his favor on that Tuesday that he'd find a car to drive to High Seas Ice Cream Hut. He wanted to monitor the handoff without anyone's knowledge, including Croke's.

Oliver soon located a Toyota Corolla behind a dumpy apartment building a few blocks from the motel that was just volunteering to be borrowed. The car was heavily dusted with green pollen, making Oliver guess it wasn't driven daily. But best of all, the owner had left the driver's side window down an inch.

So Oliver took the invitation. He stuck in his fingers and gripped the window tight. Then he rocked it back and forth until it popped from the track. That left enough room for him to reach in and unlock the door.

And the universe was smiling at Oliver that day because the owner had left a valet key in the unlocked glove box with the owner's manual. Karmic groove, baby! Or maybe the owner was too dumb to even know the key was in there. Whatever--away he drove.

Oliver arrived across the street from High Seas Ice Cream Hut wearing his favorite disguise to make sure no one--including Croke--could identify him. Sadly, Croke still looked like Croke, despite Oliver's honest efforts. Dark baseball cap and sunglasses. Fake mustache. High neck fleece pullover with a shark on it. Unfortunately, he couldn't do much to change Croke's potato-like torso and cauliflower ear.

Besides, if it was a setup by the client to clean up the operation for some reason, the plan would be to kill whoever showed up to collect the package. It wasn't to put his face on a wanted poster. Oliver would watch whether Croke met that fate, and if he did, Oliver and his pollen-crusted ride would head on up Route 6 and disappear forever.

He saw Croke sitting on a wooden picnic bench, eating

an ice cream cone. He looked self-conscious and very warm in his fleece pullover. He kept taking his hat off and waving it at his face, and the ice cream was like a big brown O of lipstick around his mouth, gumming up his fake mustache. It wouldn't be the end of the world if Croke did get shot.

Croke also stood out because the other customers were in family clusters. So when a newish brown Honda Accord pulled in and a single man got out, stretching, the solo man and Croke made eye contact pretty much right away. SoloMan was more than a bit overweight and he was wearing sunglasses and a bucket hat, plus a windbreaker. He seemed kind of familiar...

Oliver watched the handoff from across the street in the anonymity of his stolen Toyota. The green dust covering the car was almost like window tint, protecting his privacy. He saw Croke get up and drop his half-finished cone in a garbage barrel. Croke went over and shook hands with the man. Shook hands, who does that for a handoff? Oliver saw the other man recoil a bit, then surreptitiously wipe his hand on his dark pants. Was the man one of those guys whose pictures were splashed all over the news? One of the militia group that the feds were trying to hunt down? Oliver thought so...

The man popped his trunk, pulled out a golf club travel bag, all zipped up. Didn't appear to be too heavy, by the way the man lifted it. He handed it to Croke, clapped him on the back, got in his Honda and drove away. Like one creepy guy giving another creepy guy back his golf clubs. And that was it. Croke watched the man depart then put the bag in the trunk of their Ford Taurus.

But there was another reason Oliver had come to watch—paranoia. When Croke turned onto the street, Oliver merged into traffic a few cars later. Traffic was the typical soul-crushing bumper to bumper Cape Cod mess and Croke was easy to follow, just going with the slow flow. Oliver maintained his position for five or six traffic lights, then slowly dropped further back.

And then, aha! A black Toyota 4Runner—a nice, new one—passed Oliver's beater and settled in three cars behind Croke's. Oliver didn't get a good look at the driver. The 4Runner maintained that distance, but carefully forcing itself through intersections to not be left behind.

Then a Chevy hatchback passed Oliver and he recognized the driver. Oliver laughed—it was the lead asshole from the militia group. The main guy whose face was on TV, the biggest target of the big manhunt—Brian Something Westin? Pretty ballsy or stupid to be out and about in traffic. Maybe trying to figure out who his flunky had handed off the package to and where it was going?

So first vehicle, Croke. Then the 4Runner. Then Westin's Chevy. Oliver followed them all at what he hoped was an extra-safe distance, all the way back to the Sanddollar Motel.

Croke pulled into the lot like usual, but the 4Runner pulled over at the curb on the street. It waited while Croke parked, got out of the Taurus and went into room sixteen. Then the 4Runner drove away. The Chevy rejoined traffic moments later, from where it had waited in an oil change shop's parking lot, a bit further down the street.

Oliver followed them both from a very, very cautious distance. The two vehicles made a left onto Rogers Folly Road and Oliver had to run a stale yellow. Who was Rogers, and what was his folly? Oliver wondered the same thing every time he took this road. He could probably research it at the Chatham Library. Or he could get the hell off Cape Cod before his brain melted any further...

Oliver followed the 4Runner and the Chevy right into downtown New Albion. More stop and go traffic, for jaywalking pedestrians and cars swooping into parking spots which had been abandoned a split second before. Then the 4Runner turned right and pulled into one of the only empty parking spots in town because it was in front of the New Albion Police Station and was reserved for police parking. The Chevy kept driving and disappeared around the corner. A man climbed down from the 4Runner and sauntered into the police station as Oliver cruised past, carefully nonchalant but otherwise soaking the guy in.

Oliver recognized Mr. 4Runner— it was the police lieutenant with the big nose who got beat up by the tweaker fisherman in that bar! The situation was all too interconnected to be a coincidence—both the militia guys and the lieutenant somehow in on this handoff?

But the thing that bugged Oliver most—why the hell was a cop monitoring the package drop? To provide some shady security oversight, or something more? The call from the client had—as usual—been electronically garbled, the voice unrecognizable. Had it been someone else on the line—a cop? Was the whole thing some kind of setup? It worried Oliver to be on the defensive. He didn't want to be the prey, ever.

Still a little rattled and confused, Oliver drove back to the Sanddollar Motel's neighborhood. He carefully parked his borrowed Toyota Corolla in the same spot behind the apartment building where he'd found it. Nobody was around, nobody came out to start a fuss. Oliver wiped down everything he thought he might have touched. He'd already popped the driver's window back in its track and now lowered it to the same careless inch as when he'd found it. Oliver locked the door and strolled away, pocketing the valet key in case he needed a set of wheels again. Always good to have a personal Plan B.

Oliver noticed Croke had parked the Taurus in front of room thirteen again. That stubborn bastard had obviously decided to carry on his simmering feud with the murderous-looking woman with the two brats. Like it was now a point of honor for Croke not to back off and park in one of the motel's other open spots instead. So much for a low-key hideaway—they'd come out some morning and find their vehicle on fire.

Still anonymous and invisible in his disguise, Oliver picked some shade across the street from the motel and sat down, watching to see whether maybe the golf bag would draw a swarm of police cars to Croke's room. That was the only reason Oliver could imagine for a cop to monitor its handoff to Croke.

But nothing happened. All was quiet. Families came from their rooms, stumbling under armfuls of awkward beach gear, and departed. Self-conscious adulterers slunk in, then slunk out forty-five minutes later. The two little kids from room thirteen came outside and played within earshot of their room. Then their mother's head poked out of the room, saw their parked Taurus and grimaced terribly. Then she bellowed at the kids to come inside the room. Thirteen's door closed with a slam. Just another postcard afternoon at the Sanddollar Motel.

Croke came from room sixteen a couple times, made his way six doors down to Oliver's. Knocked, waited, then went back to his own room. Oliver could see Croke's lips moving in what was likely a traditional Eastern European curse.

But Oliver needed alone time, to think. Why the hell was a cop monitoring the client's package?

After an hour or so, Oliver went back to his room and

removed his disguise. Packed it carefully away. Then he wove through the two kids from thirteen, who were outside again and chalking up the concrete. He knocked on Croke's door.

The golf club travel bag was lying open on the tile floor surrounded by four blankets which must have been included for padding. Croke said he'd checked the bag for any tracking devices and found no problem, but Oliver gave it the once over again.

"So?" Oliver asked. "What was inside?"

"Christmas present."

"I love it when you try to joke."

Croke gave him a glare then reached under the bed and pulled out the coolest rifle. Black and green. Scope on top. A sniper rifle? But smaller than any sniper rifle Oliver had ever seen—maybe two feet long. "Bullets too," said Croke. "Special made."

"Were you followed back?" Oliver asked, knowing Croke would expect the question.

"Of course not!"

Right. One more vehicle it would have been a parade. "Well, maybe let's ditch the Taurus and get different wheels again—just in case?" Oliver knew for a fact at least one cop knew the Taurus—the mysterious lieutenant. They should probably change motels immediately too.

And why the hell had the militia group delivered them a sniper rifle?

The special blue phone buzzed. Their client's garbled voice gave them a clear, simple assignment—to shoot that local cop, Pepper Ryan. Payment would be made within the hour. Biggest payment yet.

So, that's why the sniper rifle... The motel change would have to wait—duty called!

THIRTY-SEVEN

Chief Eisenhower was wicked pissed, again. "Pepper, what the hell were you thinking last night, holding your own press conference!"

Pepper had finally shown up at the station to face the heat.

Sgt. Weisner came around the corner, saw him, started clapping. "Congrats Wonderboy, you're famous again! And your wink—an instant classic. You know the press is calling you Flirty Harry? I'll bet those bad guys haven't stopped running yet."

Eisenhower wasn't sharing the humor. "Pepper, don't do *anything* until I talk to Hanley and we decide how to fix this! Stay out of trouble!"

But later on Tuesday morning, Pepper's cell phone rang--Maddie Smith's name flashing on his screen. She was all tears, Pepper couldn't really understand her. She was at Eagle's Nest and had fought with Justin Case. The rest he couldn't make out.

"I'll be right there," he promised. Chief Eisenhower had only ordered him to stay away from *work* trouble, right?

It took Pepper longer than before to get through the Secret Service roadblocks. As his truck crunched down the long driveway to the main mansion, he remembered he had to ask Maddie about the other sick man tucked upstairs—who the heck was he?

Maddie was waiting for him by the naked nymph fountain. She was wearing white capri pants, a pink t-shirt and flip-flops. Casually lovely, despite red eyes and messy hair. Her pretty mouth was twisted in a thick pout.

"Where's Mr. Skinny-dip?" asked Pepper.

Maddie scowled at him. "Gone! We had a big fight and I kicked him out! He thought their midnight swim was no big deal. Just a way to get more exposure. And right when I was screaming at him, his manager called—a production company wants him for a new show!"

"Oh yeah? Something lazy and easy?"

"It's a reality show called *Love Raft Cancun.*"

Pepper didn't spend much time watching reality shows--weren't they pretty much all the same? "Love Raft? Like, the sharks aren't all in the water? Doesn't sound too lazy-style."

She gave him a face. "Don't be an asshole, Pepper. I *liked* him."

"So did Freestyle and Funsize."

"He just can't help sharing himself with the world." She scowled some more, but it changed to laughing. "Sorry, I know. It sounds stupid. And he embarrassed me, running around naked with the First Daughters. Sluts! I know he's a self-absorbed, playboy flake. But he made me happy, some of the time." Then she gathered herself. "But let's forget about him. Tell me *everything* you've dug up on that Lizzie Concepcion... She's trying to steal Daddy's money, right? Is she a career criminal?"

Her topic change tripped Pepper up. He almost suggested they go inside together—maybe he could search the big house more successfully on a second attempt? But what were the odds that Smith and his assistant would be safely out of his way again? Slim to nil, right?

"Let's take a drive and we'll talk," he said. He took the keys to her yellow Porsche and away they went, the car fighting his slow pace like a tightly wound spring, stuck in second gear.

* * *

Zula Eisenhower's pop needed to talk to Pepper Ryan ASAP and of course he'd disappeared from the station. And wasn't answering her calls. When Zula saw a pic on Instagram of Madeline Smith with Pepper at the Fudge Castle, she volunteered to hustle right over.

The first thing Zula noticed as she approached their table was Maddie eating from Pepper's dish. Then wiping a drop of chocolate sauce off the corner of Pepper's lip. Laughing, licking her finger. Putting on a show.

"Oh hey," Maddie said with a little smile, seeing her before Pepper did. "It's Zula, right?" She looked like a Ralph Lauren model, little nipples sticking through her pink t-shirt, and blonde hair back in braids all cool. Does that girl even wear makeup?

"Hey, Little Ike!" Pepper said, voice cracking, sitting up straight. "What's up?"

"Pop just scheduled a 2 PM with the Secret Service about your little, ah, press briefing and where things stand with the Westin hunt. And you didn't answer your phone...your battery die again?"

"Damned cell phones..." he said, coughing. Actually appeared kinda embarrassed.

"Sorry, he's been taking care of me," said Maddie with a sleepy smile.

Zula felt her face flush.

"But if you've got *something else* to do?" she asked Pepper.

"No, no, I'll be there. Thanks kid."

"Right, well I've gotta get back to the Desk," she said stupidly. Self-conscious in her khaki work pants and white blouse. And mad at herself for not playing it more chill— Pepper could hook up with whoever he wanted to. But did it really have to be that super-rich, smug blonde? Fuck.

And maybe mad at herself for being his frickin' errand girl. No wonder that's all he thought of her.

* * *

Pepper wasn't going to get smacked around by Chief Eisenhower and the Secret Service until 2 PM. And Maddie was demanding not to go straight back to Eagle's Nest, almost throwing a mini-tantrum. So Pepper drove them back down to Shore Road and snaked their way slowly along the New Albion coast toward Chatham, killing time.

Traffic was thick and Pepper had to focus on keeping the Porsche moving smoothly at such a slow speed, easing the clutch in and out. Maddie was going on and on about Zula. What's the deal with her? Is she dating anyone? So *exotic*, right? Except for her clothes...

Pepper didn't really want to get into the Zula topic with Maddie, so instead he filled her in on the Lizzie investigation, the little he'd learned. Told her about the Delaware entity called Fulmar Limited that owned Eagle's Nest, the yachts, etc. And that Lizzie is an officer.

"I *knew* it!" Maddie shouted triumphantly. "That *bitch!* Can't you arrest her?"

Jeez. "No, no...it might be totally innocent," warned Pepper. "Just tax planning for rich people. But you may want to ask your dad what's up. Tell him what you're worried about, the whole Lizzie thing. Family first, right?"

Pepper saw St. Jude's Cemetery on their left and he pulled off the road and parked. "Did I ever bring you here?"

"This may be the one place we *didn't* park," Maddie giggled. She seemed to have forgotten all about Justin Case and her worries about Lizzie Concepcion.

Pepper led her down the crushed oyster shell path into the cemetery. He stopped to show her some beach rose hips, an odd plant which looked like it had bright red apples and octopus legs. Then he led her up the rise, to the right. Stopped at two gravestones separated by empty grass from the plots around them. The first said *Mary Maureen Ryan and Kevin Mullaney Ryan. Mother and Son, Together In Eternal Rest.* The second said *James Michael Ryan. Forever Duty.*

"Did you know my mom died after giving birth to my little brother, Kevin? You hadn't moved to New Albion yet. I was four years old so I don't even remember her funeral. Then baby Kevin died, two weeks after mom. Something was wrong with his lungs. So my dad had mom's grave opened up so they could rest Kevin's body in her arms. Buried her again.

"Their grave was in the cemetery's oldest part—low down, near where we parked. A year later, a hurricane hit the Cape. It happened at high tide and a lot of the coast flooded. A bunch of graves closest to the beach were washed out to sea. For weeks after the storm, boaters came across half submerged coffins. The one with my mom and Kevin was found by a fisherman names Daniel Dunne. So my dad buried her for the third time, way up here on the hill."

"That's sad but it's creepy too," said Maddie. "And so *tragic*, your dad, raising you boys alone." She put her arm around his waist, snuggled close.

Pepper closed his eyes when Maddie's sweet, light perfume filled his nose. Flowers and grass and sunshine. He didn't know what he felt about the mother he couldn't remember. He remembered her more from that story than anything else. The woman buried three times. And he didn't want to think about his dad, how his badge came first, Jake came second and Pepper a distant last place.

"My mom's buried in the south of France," said Maddie quietly. "In Bonnieux, where she grew up. I went back to her grave a few years ago. It's tucked up on a hill too, a cozy village cemetery in Provence. And I stood there and couldn't cry. Like it could have been anyone's grave. I didn't last ten minutes. Totally sad, right?"

Pepper just nodded gently. He was no philosopher or wordsmith, except maybe when writing a song. He slipped off his sneaker and dumped out a few shoe-venirs which had found their way in during the walk. "This is my first time here since I got back. Last time was when we buried Jake."

And he told her about the day Jake died, the real story. How he and Jake had been fighting on the phone. They were always fighting in those days, with words and sometimes fists. Neither willing to give an inch. Pepper down in New Albion, working for Chief Eisenhower but raising hell on and off duty. How Pepper had dared Jake to come down from Boston and straighten him out. That Jake was on his way to New Albion when he heard a call on his scanner about a jewelry store robbery in East Sandwich as he was driving by. How he'd responded, jumped right in, was first to arrive. How he was shot by the store robbers, believed to be two undocumented gangbangers from Mexico. Neither of whom had ever been apprehended.

"So you like, blame yourself?"

"Sure. I think about that day all the time, what I could

261

have done differently, if I hadn't been such a self-absorbed dick." Pepper blamed everyone. Himself, because Jake wouldn't have been near East Sandwich if Pepper hadn't taunted him into coming down to the Cape. Obviously the jewelry store robbers, for shooting Jake and never paying the price. And Jake, for putting himself in their path, no bulletproof vest, no backup. For thinking he was invincible, or for not caring enough that he wasn't.

"So sad, on such a sunny day!" she said. "You know, thinking too much, that's a kind of self-torture."

Then two completely unexpected things happened. Maddie thrust herself down on Pepper, pressing him to the ground for a kiss. And mid-press, Pepper heard an intense slapping noise and saw the corner of his family headstone explode into fragments.

"Christ!" screamed Maddie, and Pepper saw blood. Was it from her head? Her arm? Was she hit?

Pepper grabbed her and pulled her down even lower on his family grave. *Slap!* A second bullet whizzed past, hitting a tree beyond them in an explosion of splinters.

That was no regular handgun. It was something more powerful. A rifle?

Pepper drew his puny Glock 23, tried to look for the gunman while keeping his face as low to Maddie's chest as he could. Would have been a pleasant experience if not for the blood, bullets and Maddie's hysterical attempts to jerk away from him.

"Don't move," he hissed, pulling her down harder, rolling her to the side.

Maddie's eyes were enormous and blood was flowing down her forehead, past her nose, to her open mouth.

Slap! A huge lick of dirt sprayed them. They had to get out of there. The Porsche was waiting by the road at the bottom of the hill. Could they reach it? What if the attackers had followed them to the cemetery and saw where they left the Porsche? They might anticipate Pepper and Maddie trying to escape to it, downhill. If there was a second gunman that's where he'd be hidden.

Pepper whispered instructions to Maddie, shaking her when she objected. He knew she was heading into shock, would soon be hard to control.

Pepper squeezed off three quick, wild shots uphill, toward where he believed the gunman was positioned. At least Pepper was making it clear they weren't completely toothless.

"Crawl," he whispered. He pushed her ahead and they began crawling left, parallel to the hill and away from where Pepper believed the sniper was positioned. They moved from headstone to headstone as quickly as they could. After fifteen feet, Maddie started to get up. Pepper grabbed her feet, dragged her flat. She shrieked.

Slap! Another headstone took a direct hit about ten feet ahead, sending another shower of stone shrapnel at them. Pepper felt a sting across the top of his head. Shit! He ducked lower. Then he blindly pointed his Glock uphill and fired six more times.

Leaving him with only four bullets, he quickly calculated. They had to keep moving. He whispered to Maddie again, pushed her trim butt forward, urgently. Her white capri pants were covered in dirt and blood.

But Maddie seemed to have a burst of adrenaline. She crawled forward so fast Pepper had trouble keeping up. Reached a small cluster of trees at the edge of a little road that wound through the cemetery.

He pressed Maddie as low as she could get at the base of the trees. Shielded her with his body—his Glock up and ready in case the sniper came into sight. Whoever moved next was going to die.

Then Pepper heard sirens in the distance.

* * *

"Missed!?!" shrieked Oliver. "How can you miss an unsuspecting target with a sniper rifle?" They'd rendezvoused back at their latest swiped vehicle, a maroon Buick LaCrosse, two streets away from the cemetery and were now driving at the speed limit as far away from the damn cemetery as they could get. Oliver had been waiting down where Ryan and the girl had parked their fancy convertible, ready to ambush them with a handgun if Croke failed, but they must have escaped in a different direction. Damn local knowledge!

Of course Croke was defiant. "You wouldn't let me practice with it," he grumbled.

"Practice? There wasn't time, once we saw where they were on Instagram! At that distance, you should be deciding which eyelash to hit. It's automatic. I should have done it myself."

Oliver suspected Croke's eyesight wasn't 20-20, based on his driving. Fucking Croke! Now they'd have to do it the hard way.

But first, Oliver made the phone call to the client to break the bad news. The client was—no surprise—super pissed.

Oliver let him vent in his garbled voice for a bit, then cut in. "We'll take care of Ryan tonight," he promised. Then inspiration hit him. A plan, coming from the surveillance he'd already done and the burning desire to not just kill, but to kill spectacularly, notoriously. To take his slaughter up a notch, Hollywood-style. "But we need you to arrange some special—and clean—equipment."

More venting from the client...with an increased volume of curse words.

Oliver waited it out, then interrupted. "This time? We're gonna need a bigger boat."

A long, long pause. Oliver hoped the client wasn't a movie fan, didn't think he was being made fun of... Then the scrambled voice gave grudging agreement, with the warning that time was of the essence. The job had to happen tonight and it had to succeed.

Oliver smiled. This'd actually be a chance to become even more infamous. "Good news," he said to Croke. "We're going to drown that bastard."

"Okay," said Croke, slowing for a yellow light. "Which bastard?"

THIRTY-EIGHT

After the cemetery gunfight, Chief Eisenhower ordered Pepper Ryan to *stop* and to *stay out of trouble.* Lay low—don't shoot anyone, don't get shot. The New Albion police department would process the cemetery as a crime scene. He and Pepper would meet in the morning and Pepper would have a chance to explain himself, before the General made any final decisions.

Final decisions? That sounded predetermined, somehow...

Pepper had called Zula to see if she'd learned anything helpful during her research for him about the list of corporations and officers. But also to ask if she wanted to grab some dinner...he realized he missed hanging out with her. But she hadn't picked up—he must be on her shit list too.

But Maddie? Getting injured by headstone shrapnel had oddly been a bit of a turn on for her. She'd only had a scratch on her arm, which she'd allowed paramedics to treat on the spot and refused to go to the hospital. She was giggling, flirting, exhilarated by her brush with death, drunk on adrenaline and attention. When he returned her and the Porsche to Eagle's Nest, she'd fiercely kissed him goodbye, insisting she would bring the damned First Twins to Malecón again that night. "The crazy thing is Daddy absolutely *hates* President Garby, called him a weasel and there's nothing that gets him madder these days," she'd said with a laugh. "And I'd like to strangle those twins instead of hugging them...but that's politics and money, right? But tonight I'm going to *live*...so you'd better be there tonight too. I won't take no for an answer!"

So, sidelined by the General anyway, Pepper took an Uber to Malecón that night with the single-minded goal to let off steam. He was hoping a series of Jack Daniels shots and beer chasers would reboot his brain, shake off his near-death encounter and the threat of his meeting the next morning with the General. Pepper wasn't playing around with daiquiris or margaritas. Pepper was just planning to get drunk—no need to make a circus of it.

Two guys and a woman were onstage, doing a serviceable but somewhat mellow set. The dance floor was empty. It was somewhere around 10 P.M.

Then, comfortably buzzed and hanging near the bar, Pepper got waylaid by Angel. As his buddy pointed out, Pepper owed him after running out again the night before. So before Pepper knew it, he'd jumped in with the group on stage. A couple songs later, when the band headed to a break, he asked if they'd mind him playing on, solo. And they didn't mind at all. Pepper was still floating along on the rush of booze and performing and switched to his original songs.

Which were a little rowdier than the tunes the trio had been playing. The crowd seemed to love his stuff. One song blended to the next, his old showmanship flowing too, whipping the crowd into a party mood. When the band finally came back from their break, Pepper stayed to accompany them. Now they were playing more up-tempo radio stuff, songs everyone knew, but Pepper was still having a blast. It was great to just be doing what he loved again, for the fun of it, no baggage.

Then there was a surge and a fuss by the patio entrance. A large group of buzz cut heads, serious faces. Then too-loud laughter, hands in the air. The First Daughters had arrived again.

And Maddie Smith. He saw her smiling at something one of the twins said. Laughing. Like she hadn't almost been shot that afternoon. She looked about twelve years old tonight, her blonde hair back in braids again. She was wearing a peach colored bandeau top and a white skirt almost to her knees, an ensemble marred only by the white bandage on her arm.

The twins worked their way through the dancing bodies to claim a space right below Pepper. They each had a drink in their hand and were dancing with practiced abandon.

Then Maddie was up front too. Then she was on stage, twirling, toasting the crowd, shimmying to the song with Pepper. It was a romantic Luke Bryan song with a great groove and she made it even better. Now the twins were on stage too, and it was getting past capacity.

But Pepper let things go on because he saw Angel by the bar, beaming. His arms wide to say, "Told you kid!"

Two more songs and then Pepper bowed out, handing the show back to the band, getting one last roar of applause. He didn't even feel the steps as he came off stage. Angel gave him a full body hug by the bar and then Maddie and the twins swept over with a few other people. Angel stood them all a round of Patron shots. Or was it three rounds?

* * *

Justin Case wanted his Maddie back, bad. He didn't care that she'd been a C U Next Tuesday. He wanted back into her world. He felt like he'd been kicked in the nuts, kicked to the curb, kicked like a —

What was the word he was looking for?

He'd gone to that Cuban bar again to confront her. To take her by the hand and the heart. But after he arrived, he'd stayed in the background, low key for once, sucking down mojitos and Moscow mules, waiting for his opening. Seen Maddie arrive with the cocktease twins from hell. Seen Maddie dancing on stage with that cop, Ryan. Maddie laughing and flirting like a slut, like Justin had never existed.

He decided to confront his girl and Ryan in a place a little more...private. He'd borrowed a pepper spray keychain from a female fan, which Justin thought would help convince the cop to fuck right off, get his own girl. So Justin caught a Lyft to the cop's address, but only found a silver trailer there...cop pay must be shit. And Justin caught a break—the trailer door was unlocked. He went inside, stood facing the doorway. Angry and drunk. Pepper spray at the ready. Then he got the humor of it—ambushing Pepper Ryan with pepper spray—it was going to be so fucking apropos! He knew they'd be coming there to do the deed—he'd seen Ryan's hand on her hip, already proprietary. And he knew they wouldn't go to Eagle's Nest—her rich daddy hated Pepper Ryan even more than he hated Justin, and that was saying something.

As the minutes passed, Justin decided it might make sense to sit down. He pulled out his vape pen. Maybe a few hits of weed oil would take the edge off his drunken state. His head felt thick from the mojitos and Moscow mules, but he needed to be on point, to win back his babe!

* * *

Pepper took a free ride back to Eagle's Nest. They were a sloppy bunch at this point. Laughing and laughing, about nothing in particular, little things someone had said at the bar. Everyone laughing except their sober Secret Service driver.

When they arrived at Eagle's Nest, Pepper and Maddie lost themselves from the group, slipped around the side of the main mansion. So they wandered down to the beach, past more Secret Service. Laughing about how it must look on the surveillance cameras, how many sensors they were tripping.

It was almost completely dark due to thick clouds blocking the moon and stars. Somehow they were both barefoot, but Pepper couldn't remember where they'd lost their shoes. They were down near the inky water's edge. Close enough to get caught by the fingers of the biggest waves, the quick chill grabbing them as they danced upward to drier sand.

"Pepper—" she started. Then stopped, laughed. "Even your name sounds funny tonight. How'd you get that nickname anyway? And don't say because you're SO hot, you've always been called that. Even our first-grade teacher..."

"My name's Peter. But Jake always had trouble pronouncing it when he was young. Dragged me around like a stuffed animal when I was a baby. Peddah, Peddah, eventually became Pepper. So it was Jake."

"That is *too* cute." Maddie stepped close and kissed him.

Pepper could feel her hunger. Her teeth pulled at his lip and her kiss broadened into a grin. If the world could stop, thought Pepper, and be this simple. If he could hold a woman who wanted to be held…kiss a woman who wanted to be kissed.

Pepper realized they were on the beach in front of his family's property. Right below his trailer… Maddie pressed up against him, her back to his front, facing the ocean they couldn't really see in the near darkness, then said in more of a little girl voice, "Pepper, what're we doing?"

He pulled her even closer. "I'd say, heading to second base…"

"No. What're WE doing?" She paused and when he didn't answer, she continued. "When that sniper tried to kill us today in the cemetery…I've never felt so scared! But also so safe, with you protecting me, taking care of me. I was thinking…what would you say to going away with me? Just us?"

"What?"

"We could live anywhere we want. Paris…Buenos Aries…Hong Kong…" Running her leg along his. Her gentle stroking was electric. "You don't need to be a cop, right? Let someone else put their lives in danger for crappy pay. And I can get away from all the parties and craziness, get back to my painting. You and I could have a lot of laughs…"

Pepper started to picture the alternate path she was offering: Europe, South America. A life of exploration, adventure, relaxation. Unlimited financial means, thanks to the Smith fortune, with his long-lost childhood sweetheart. Lunacy, but very tempting lunacy. What'd his job really matter anyway? What kind of cop was he—unable to follow orders, follow procedures? Spending more time in trouble than out of it. Sure, somebody had to do it, but why him? And for all he knew, tomorrow morning he was going to be fired. "Is that what you really want?" he asked.

"What I want?" She tilted her head down, thinking. Was silent for a long time. Then she looked right into his eyes. Even more beautiful in the near darkness...the 99% shadows.

"I want to be happy for the majority of each day," she whispered. "The majority. And if that's too much to ask, I'm talking to the wrong person. All I know is, I haven't talked this way out loud in so long, so fucking *honest*, I don't recognize myself."

Maybe he was the wrong person. She was jet-set, world-class...way out of Pepper's league. Compared to Zula—and why was he now doing that? Zula was beautiful too, but less conventionally. Zula made him feel grounded, home. Maddie brought out the wild teen in his blood and made him second-guess everything about himself since that age.

And Maddie wanted to be with him, right now. Zula wouldn't even take his calls anymore, so damn her for getting in his head right now!

Pepper was conscious that he was thoroughly buzzed at the moment—from alcohol and Maddie, perfectly mixed. It was irresistible. He picked up Maddie and she was light, warm, floral. His left hand happened to cup her soft breast. A perfect handful. His right hand cradled her firm ass, sliding smoothly across the silk skirt. She kissed him again as Pepper started walking toward the wooden stairs that led to his Airstream trailer.

Maddie wasn't making it easy for him to walk. She was kissing him and her hands were under his shirt, running roughly across his ribs, his chest, his nipple. When she happened to press the deep bruise on his left side, he spasmed wildly like he'd been electrocuted. His right hand had somehow worked its way under her skirt and he felt the cool satin of her panties.

As they reached where Pepper believed the wooden stairs should be waiting in the dark, he got clotheslined in the neck by a thick steel cable. He fell backward, Maddie landing on him, startled. But she was still laughing. Then he heard the cable go *thrum!*—and a heavy, rushing sound. He grabbed Maddie tight and rolled away to the side, over and over through the high beach grass.

His trailer just missed them.

It was skidding and bumping along at a high speed and was actually airborne as it passed them toward the sand, toward the ocean.

He felt Maddie clutch up at him, let out a drunken giggle. "Hey, a UFO!"

Sonofabitch.

THIRTY-NINE

Justin Case woke to the mother of all hangovers. He was lying on the floor of the cop's trailer. It was dark. His head was spinning and bobbing like it wasn't even attached to his neck. His stomach...it was even worse. He didn't want to even come up with the words to describe it because if he did, it would definitely make him throw up.

With that thought, Justin threw up.

He finally got to his knees. Then his feet. Grabbed the table, pulled himself to a semi-erect position. And he really, really couldn't see much. Either it was still nighttime or else he'd fried his eyes.

He needed to find water. His mouth was constricted and swollen. He experimented and discovered he could move his tongue around from one woolen corner to the other. But his tongue hurt too.

He let go of the table and almost fell. Flailing, he slipped in his vomit and did fall. His head hit the table and unconsciousness mercifully took him away.

Justin didn't know how much time had passed when he woke again. He struggled to his feet. Feeling at least as bad as before. His head? With the new bump, and maybe a mild concussion to top off his hangover, it felt like an overripe cantaloupe balanced on a frayed rope. What was that, from some song? He fumbled in his pockets to see if he had his vape pen. A little weed would be a godsend. Settle his damn equilibrium. But no, it was missing.

So, water. Water would also be a godsend. He found the trailer's little sink, turned the knob and a weak spurt of water filled his cupped hand. Glorious water.

He struggled his way to the door, gave the handle a twist and pushed, but it didn't budge. He groaned, pushed harder. Nothing. He stumbled to the window and peered out into the slanted glow of faint, faint moonlight.

The heavy clouds had parted a bit. There was just enough light now so he could see water. All around the trailer—dark, calm water.

The trailer was slowly floating on the Atlantic Ocean, toward...Ireland?

Where the *fuck* was his vape pen?

* * *

Pepper and Maddie were waiting up by the road in the semi-darkness for a patrol car that Marty Lane, the graveyard Dispatch clerk, had promised to send right over, through his fits of laughter.

It was an awkward wait. Maddie's offer hung in the air between them, but blurred by the alcohol, their tiredness and the bizarre interruption they'd experienced. They were both in a kind of shock.

Pepper tried a completely new topic. "Maddie, I forgot to ask—who's the other sick man at Eagle's Nest?"

"Lizzie's uncle? He moved in a few months ago and he's dying of cancer too, like Daddy. She's his only family and of course daddy wouldn't say no to *anything* she asks for, these days." She hugged herself tighter.

Pepper got a call back from Marty Lane a while later. A coast guard helicopter had spotted his Airstream floating southward, a mile offshore, in the direction of open water. It was remarkably buoyant. The Coast Guard had sent two boats. They'd found one man inside after cutting straps that trapped the door closed. The man, the big celebrity Justin Case, had been unable to explain to the Coast Guard what had happened. Did Pepper want to arrange a tow?

* * *

"Floated!?!" swore Oliver. They'd returned the forty-six-foot motor yacht right back to its home dock, as the client had firmly instructed, and were back in Croke's room at the Sanddollar Motel. Oliver was staring at the TV early bird news like it had to be a prank. "The goddamn thing's made of metal! He should be on the ocean bottom."

They studied the news image of the trailer, bobbing gently in a hovering news helicopter's spotlight.

"If you'd let me shoot it up, make some holes for water to get in," shrugged Croke. "Woulda sunk like a rock..."

The video cut back to a dock. Showed a man getting off a Coast Guard boat, towel around his shoulders, sipping a little plastic bottle of water. *'Celebrity Rescued'* said the headline below the image.

"That's not Pepper Ryan," said Croke. "Who the hell's that?"

So they'd fucked up times two. Oliver swore an oath to himself, the only person he cared about, the only person he trusted. The client had mentioned one more day of jobs and sure, they'd do that, as well as kill the elusive Pepper Ryan. Pocket that final big payday from the client. Then Oliver would get the hell off Cape Cod. Far away from the thick fog of law enforcement officers who were searching for them. The traffic and insanity. And the bad luck. They were starting to appear fucking incompetent...

"Maybe some help from New York will kinda be good?" said Croke.

Help? What was Croke saying? "Croke, you didn't call Queens for help, did you? Because if *they* find out we've been taking jobs direct from the client, we'll be the next job."

Croke just stared at him defiantly. Silent. Then finally said, "Whatever. But no more goddamn boats."

And for once, Oliver agreed with him.

FORTY

Pepper Ryan had a patrol car drop Maddie Smith at the Eagle's Nest checkpoint, then him at Angel Cavada's house. Angel was still awake, having just gotten home, and had no problem with Pepper bunking there. But thought it was hilarious that Pepper refused to explain why. Pepper was too pissed. Too fried, wiped, done.

The next morning, Pepper spilled the story and Angel laughed so hard he got a cramp. Pepper found himself laughing too—what other response made sense? But when Angel recovered, Pepper asked him to keep his ears open for any local rumors about anyone being out in nearby waters last night with a powerful enough boat to tow a goddamn trailer. Which had set off Angel's hilarity and cramping again...

Angel finally recovered enough to drop him at his truck. Pepper was driving to the station to face Chief Eisenhower when he got a surprise call from Brandon Blacklock. The fund manager from Smith Enterprises was about to get on Acker Smith's private plane on his way to Cape Cod. He had a meeting with Smith and might be willing to talk to Pepper, afterward. No guarantees.

Pepper tried to change Blacklock's mind but no, he absolutely insisted on talking to Smith first.

Pepper believed Brandon Blacklock could be the key to

his investigations coming together into one clear picture. So instead of making his meeting with the Chief, Pepper took a spare patrol car and headed out to Rogers Folly Road. He parked in a blind spot that local cops had used for years as a speed trap. He ignored calls from the Chief. Sarcastic text messages from Zula. He did call his partner Alfson, who confirmed Blacklock's name had been added to the gate list for Eagle's Nest. The Secret Service had resisted the last minute request but Smith's people had shut them down by threatening to call D.C. Why was Pepper asking about Blacklock, Special Agent Alfson asked, voice heavy with suspicion and distrust?

It was so good to have a partner.

Pepper's dad called him with new info about Reverend McDevitt and his thugs. He'd contacted a Fall River detective captain he knew who'd told him the Weepers had built out a hell of a piece of real estate down there in recent years. That most of the cars going in and out were Cadillacs. Business was good for the Church of Peter Weeping. The Fall River police had not been very active at the Weepers' compound recently, other than supporting occasional visits by the state's Department of Children and Families who were following up on complaints about the safety of minors on the property. "But the Weepers' main public activity lately has been in other cities. Ambushing the president at his public appearances, that sort of fun," said his dad. "Or their old favorites, like disrupting soldiers' funerals."

His dad grumbled a bit about the impossibility of getting more New Albion manpower on the home destruction case. The POTUS visit had sucked all the bandwidth from the small department. But the POTUS was leaving in a few days, on July 8th, and hopefully the Ryan case would jump up to top priority. He trusted the General to make sure that it did.

"And I had some other bad news," his dad said, a little louder. "I talked to the insurance company. The adjuster's screwing around—said our policy won't cover the demolition unless their investigation concludes it was an accident. He even said they're investigating whether we did it ourselves, for the money!"

Pepper didn't know what to say, he was stunned into silence. Couldn't they catch just a little freakin' break?

"But don't worry, the angels are on our side," said his dad, with a forced laugh, then abruptly changed the subject. "Any word yet when's Marcus Dunne's funeral going to be?"

"Not yet," sighed Pepper. "His body was just released." Another reason for Pepper to be in a shitty mood. He didn't know if he could pay his respects to Trish and her daughter, with her husband's killer still out there...

A limousine came around the corner, maybe a couple miles an hour over the speed limit. Pepper ended his call with his dad, then hit his rollers and took off after it. Pepper didn't call in his location after they'd stopped on the roadside.

Pepper walked to the driver's window, showed his badge. Confirmed the driver was Smith's chauffeur and asked him to unlock the back doors.

But he found the passenger area empty.

The chauffeur explained he'd gone to Barnstable Municipal Airport to collect a man who never showed up. Mr. Smith's plane had arrived but the man must have taken other ground transportation. Some mix-up, no one at Eagle's Nest could say. Smith's chief of staff—Ms. Concepcion—had told him to come back to the compound. Yes, the missing passenger's name was Blacklock. But the chauffeur's trip had been a waste of time.

So, it appeared, had been Pepper's plan.

Where had Blacklock disappeared to?

FORTY-ONE

Lizzie Concepcion was worried. And scared. Time was running out for her because Mr. Smith was fading quickly. The billionaire was pale as thin, yellow paper. He was weak. He didn't seem to be able to leave his bed.

Mr. Smith was still working every morning, trying to stay on top of his global financial empire. Phone calls to Stamford, to London, to Hong Kong. And she would read him his emails as he sat, eyes closed, probably listening.

But his energy was failing. Lizzie could see it in his eyes this Wednesday morning. And he was in a particularly grumpy mood today because he was experiencing another attack of the pins and needles in his hands and feet.

When she'd told him that the fund manager Brandon Blacklock hadn't arrived as scheduled, he'd gazed at her like he couldn't remember who Blacklock was.

"What about that Reverend McDevitt? The news stories?" he asked. "I'm paying him to stir things up, correct?"

"Yes sir." McDevitt had been rabidly active, had understood what they needed his group to do and had required almost no prompting once the payments had cleared.

"He's a scumbag," wheezed Mr. Smith.

"Yes sir. But he's our scumbag. Which may come in handy again before the president's vacation's over."

Smith laughed. But it devolved into a long coughing fit.

What would she do, if Mr. Smith suddenly died? It couldn't happen! She thought back to the life she used to live, before Mr. Smith hired her. Her D.C. life. She almost didn't remember who she'd been. The romantic roller coaster of her younger days. Her surprise pregnancy. Then her miscarriage. Followed soon by divorce papers from her husband John, like an aftershock. But nothing hurt like the loss of her baby. It'd almost killed her, and definitely killed who she'd hoped to be.

She'd only survived by changing everything in her life. No more husband's accusatory stares. No more K Street office vapidity. She'd found new meaning, new purpose, with Mr. Smith.

And now that Mr. Smith was dying? Of course it scared her, but no one would ever see her fear again.

* * *

Zula Eisenhower was in her pop's office, giving him two Tylenols and a bottle of water. She'd already taken some herself—sad and pissed off about Pepper Ryan not showing up that morning to face her pop. Not to mention the gossip from the night before about him on the beach with that slut Madeline Smith. And someone tried to drown him in his trailer?

More freaking chaos—classic Pepper. And somehow, infuriatingly, it all made Zula want him more. *Stupid, stupid, stupid!*

She knew her pop had been fielding calls from the Secret Service and the ATF. As well as the State Police, the DA, the town manager, and everyone else with a title and a telephone. All reasons why Pop had a heck of a headache going, even before Lieutenant Dwayne Hurd stepped in and interrupted them.

"A second, boss?" Hurd asked, raising his eyebrows, which somehow emphasized his big nose even more.

He looks like an animal, scavenging for food. An anteater?

Her pop waved Hurd in.

"Sir, I know you and the Ryans go way back," the lieutenant said, then paused and glanced at Zula. "But is there any way Pepper's on the wrong side of all the trouble that's been happening? I mean, where was he a month ago? Playing music in some bar in Nashville, he says? What if somebody paid him a lot of money to come back and help screw our shit up? Maybe even put the president's life at risk."

Her pop scowled but waived a dismissive hand. "The Ryans are pretty simple to understand. It's not always pretty, but they're all about duty--to hell with everything else. Even when they can't follow a goddamn order."

"Okay... But what if he's carrying out a different duty than we think? A duty to someone, you know, on the wrong team? I recommend we suspend Ryan, just to be safe, right? We can sort everything else out later."

"I'll think about that," her pop promised, and she could tell he even meant it. "In the meanwhile, how're you holding up, Lieutenant? You didn't even have a chance to recover from that bar fight and now you're shouldering a double load coordinating the POTUS traffic details. Not to mention our share of the Westin manhunt and everything else."

"I'm better than I look."

Her pop wouldn't let it go. "I mean everything you've been through lately. Your divorce, all the extra hours." Zula could see her pop was studying Hurd.

The lieutenant let out a laugh with no humor in it at all. "I'm just taking care of business, boss. But when all this is over, I wouldn't say no to a vacation."

Neither will we.

* * *

Zula made a tough decision. Outside, in the semi-privacy of her topless, doorless Jeep, she called Pepper. Miracle of miracles, he answered. She didn't lecture or yell at him. Instead, she told him everything Hurd and her father had said.

Long silence from Pepper. "Thank you," he finally said.

To change the topic, Zula hurriedly updated him on her research. "I found a marriage certificate for John and Isabel Bumpers, the officers on Scoter, Inc.?"

"Marriage certificate?"

"Yep. In Maryland. And then a divorce certificate, seven years later. But there was one juicy detail on the marriage certificate. The bride's maiden name? It was Isabel Concepcion."

"Concepcion, like Smith's chief of staff? Wow! So, Smith used his girl Friday as a pawn in his Scoter, Inc. venture with President Garby?"

"Unclear. I called John Bumpers in Maryland but he didn't want to talk much. He's a staff accountant in the Treasury Department. He said he didn't know anything about being an officer of any corporations. And he didn't want to talk about their divorce, just said Lizzie'd had a miscarriage and their marriage imploded. And I redid my background searches on Lizzie Concepcion just to make sure I hadn't missed anything and found no criminal history, no hits...under Concepcion or Bumpers."

"Great job, Little Ike, way to dig deep! I owe you another breakfast!"

Be still, my beating heart.

"And if you'll research where I can find Justin Case, I'll throw in a slice of pie. I need to have a personal chat with that joker about why he was in my trailer."

FORTY-TWO

Sometimes a tip can save an investigation. Sometimes, a job. Like maybe the anonymous call Pepper Ryan received on his cell phone, as he drove back to the station. He didn't recognize the voice, but still—how could he not jump?

A few minutes later, Pepper burst into Chief Eisenhower's office, waving his phone at the General. "Sir, I just got a blind call with info where Westin and his last few guys are hiding out! Sorry I'm late for our meeting, I'm sorry about everything. No name, but the tip was specific and I want to hit it. But it's your call..."

* * *

The U.S. Secret Service, assisted by Hyannis law enforcement and other local resources, including Pepper Ryan and Lieutenant Hurd representing the New Albion police, raided the Sanddollar Motel at 1 PM. The General didn't join them—for the sake of his blood pressure he was going to be off for a few hours that afternoon. First time in weeks.

Special Agent Alfson wasn't available to join the raid. He'd explained to Pepper by phone that he was 'out of pocket'. The FLOTUS and the twins were on a shopping trip to Boston—tearing Newbury Street a new one—and with the Westin manhunt sucking up resources, he'd been pressed into protective service.

"Well, avoid Boston's meter maids, they bite if you try to pet them," Pepper had said, and had promised to keep his partner up on any progress. Pepper was feeling giddy and the goodwill even reached his partner.

Ten minutes later, three SWAT vehicles crawled into the motel parking lot and teams simultaneously hit rooms ten and sixteen. Other law enforcement vehicles skidded into every available inch of the lot.

No one was in room ten.

But three men were in room sixteen. Three men possessing handguns with silencers. Which the three men actually had out, but not exactly in hand because they were playing cards. The crash team had all three men flat on the cheap tile floor, arms wrenched up behind them, cuffed and stuffed before they could snatch up their weapons and get off a single shot.

But Brian-Edward Westin wasn't one of them. None of them matched descriptions of the missing New River Front members. It appeared they were... three other guys? Three guys waiting with lights out for the right suspects? Cautious friends, to have handguns with silencers at the near ready. Friends, or an ambush?

When the three men were removed to three separate police vehicles, the scene quickly switched from jacked-up attack mode to the bureaucratic rhythm of a crime scene. A crowd of looky-loos appeared in moments--the sleepy guests in the Sanddollar's other rooms spilled out onto the walkway in various levels of dress. A perimeter of passers-by. The majority holding up cell phones, capturing everything, hoping for something exciting to happen. But actually just capturing Pepper's latest failure. He stood among the other agents and cops, chagrined. Had they been played?

A Secret Service team led the effort to process the two rooms. The first pass yielded nothing dramatic. Small duffels, some basic clothing. Junk food wrappers. No physical evidence that anyone staying in the room had been plotting to kill the POTUS or had committed the other murders. They would run fingerprints and DNA, of course, and hopefully they'd get a real hit among the endless people who'd come and gone from the two rooms in recent months. Something to tell them specifically who they were chasing.

Pepper rubbed his temples--he felt the beginnings of a pretty good headache. Pepper also hoped for pictures of the rooms' occupants, but unfortunately the Sanddollar was one of the few remaining motels in America without security cameras. The desk clerk had shrugged helplessly in lieu of explanation—nope, he just worked there. Pepper guessed that maybe some guests didn't want their presence at a local motel on tape... Hyannis officers were canvassing nearby businesses to see whether anyone else had joined the 21st century and had picked something up on a security camera.

Then, maybe two breaks?

First, a Hyannis sergeant and one of the Secret Service agents brought over a woman to talk to Pepper. Lieutenant Hurd had disappeared somewhere. The woman on the larger side and pretty tough looking. Maybe in her forties. Or fifties. Or sixties? Bathrobe on, but untied. Showing that she was wearing a Disney t-shirt, but not, unfortunately, a bra. With a little kid firmly in each hand, little white faces-- intent on everything that was happening.

"This lady's been staying in room thirteen for a while," said the Hyannis cop. Didn't say it, but everyone was thinking it: Section Eight housing.

The woman gave a thin smile. "Two other assholes were staying in those rooms, not the ones you caught. The real assholes? They parked in my spot. Every goddamn day this week. I complained but that doorknob," she pointed at the reception desk clerk who was being interviewed nearby, "was too chickenshit to do anything." She just glared at Pepper, kind of defiant, like she had nothing to lose.

He nodded, taking her gripe seriously. "What'd the men look like?"

"The older guy was like that old actor with the smile who sells gold coins. William Devane? But fatter. And he talked like a foreigner. The younger one looked regular."

"Regular?"

"Just a regular guy. But with glasses."

Pepper gave her a second. Trying to be patient.

"But I got them on video on my phone. And pictures, parking in my spot."

Pictures? Video?

"Three different cars, but it was definitely the same assholes every time," she said. "I knew those fuckers weren't tourists. Oh, and the younger one might be a crossdresser."

"Pardon?"

"The younger one. He came back a couple days ago dressed like a woman. Or maybe a wizard. I didn't get a picture of *that*, I wish! But who should I text the videos to? And what's the reward?"

"Let's start from the beginning," said Pepper. "Do you know the makes of the three cars?"

She nodded smugly. "A blue Impala. Then a green Taurus. Then some reddish Buick. All the cars were dirty because they were slobs. The Impala even had a word writ in the dirt on its back window."

Pepper thought about something he'd heard days ago, thought it was worth a guess. "Did the word say '*Asshole*'?"

The woman looked surprised, then pleased. "That's the one!" She crossed her thick arms. Pride of authorship?

So Marcus Dunne must have seen that same car when Keser was being snatched. But the Secret Service agent and the Hyannis sergeant were looking at him funny.

Pepper pulled up Westin's picture on his phone, mixed in with pictures of five other men. Pepper scrolled through them for the woman, asked if any were a match to the two men.

"Nope," she said, certain. "But I saw that guy on the news." Pointing to Westin's picture. So the tip had been a dud?

But then came the second break. The Secret Service team processing room sixteen came out displaying a plastic bag. Lieutenant Hurd was with them and he was beaming. Snapping off his latex gloves triumphantly.

The bag held a small, thin water bottle.

"Look what they found wedged behind the nightstand!' crowed Hurd. "Looks like one of the water bottles missing from Agent Keser's jogging belt."

And one of Alfson's female agents—Parkins?—held up an evidence bag with one large cartridge in it. "This was under the bed, tucked right against its leg," she said. "Maybe a .308... what you'd use for big-game hunting. Or worse."

Like for a sniper rifle. "I bet it matches the casings in the cemetery," Pepper said. He felt adrenaline wash through him, blushing away his headache. So maybe Westin and his crew hadn't been using the Sanddollar Motel, but some other arm of the Red Starfish conspiracy had!

"Any of you know when Special Agent Alfson's due back from Boston?" Pepper asked the agents.

"Boston? No, Alfson's been at the compound all day, he wasn't on the team that went to Boston. He had something more important at Eagle's Nest."

More important than this raid? It took some of the euphoria out of Pepper—what was his sneaky partner up to now?

* * *

Oliver and Croke *really* needed to find themselves a new place to stay.

Earlier that day, they'd handled a last-minute job from the client. That wasn't Oliver's professional style but this time it worked out. Simple and clean, the guy never knew what hit him. As directed by the client, they'd stashed the body in a particular boat shed on the New Albion/Chatham line. Because the client didn't want any publicity *this* time.

Then Oliver and Croke had done a scouting drive-by of two veterinary clinics in the area for Oliver to choose one to drop in on, after hours, to borrow some more atricurium besylate. Atricurium was his go-to method for immobilizing targets. It made life simpler, causing their target's muscles to relax almost instantaneously. Followed by short-term paralysis, which gave them plenty of time to secure the victim with zip ties or handcuffs and get away to a quieter location to finish up.

At the rate they were going, Oliver needed to replenish his supplies as soon as they could take a minute from kidnapping and murdering people...

Business was really piling up.

Then, as they'd arrived back at the Sanddollar Motel, Croke had been about to hook a left into the lot when Oliver—paranoid and watchful at this point—saw the goddamn curtain in Croke's room slightly move. It had definitely moved, it was not his imagination.

Oliver had nudged Croke to pull over at the lot's far end, nowhere near their rooms. It wasn't a maid—they stick their cart in the door, prop it wide open. And he and Croke had put their crummy *do not disturb* signs on their rooms' knobs that morning.

So they had company. Cops? Or worse, people sent up from Queens by *them*? Oliver could think of no innocent explanation.

They'd gotten the hell out of there. Made one stop at an old-fashioned pay phone, where Oliver put in a brief call to the famous police officer, Pepper Ryan, and lied that he could find the New River Front fugitives at the Sanddollar Motel in their rooms. Oliver and Croke had circled back close enough to wait and see an avalanche of police arrive seventy-five minutes later, then they'd driven away with big, smug smiles. Because whoever had been waiting in Croke's room to ambush them got exactly what they deserved...

Oliver was surprised to be sad that the Sanddollar Motel was dead to them. But they needed something a little more private anyway. Cape Cod had too many cops and too many cameras in public places... Now they were cruising along in the Buick LaCross with the sniper rifle and ammo in their trunk (Oliver having decided not to leave it under the bed, a genius move that Croke would *never* congratulate him for).

They were arguing about their next move but avoiding the big accusation Oliver wanted to hit Croke with—did he fucking talk to *them* behind Oliver's back? Not a conversation to have while driving down the road, since it would probably end with one of them shooting the other.

One more day and Oliver was getting the hell off Cape Cod, no matter what *they* or the client said. Fuck him. The temperature was just getting too high for Oliver and Croke and they were going to slip up eventually, get taken down by one side or the other.

It didn't help that now Croke was talking to himself under his breath in his coarse Eastern European mutter. Checking his rear view mirror every few seconds. Kinda freaking out. Oliver was concerned about their situation but he was still feeling his karmic groove. Everything would work out, at least for him...

And of course Croke had it in his head he wanted a cheeseburger for a late lunch. Oliver said what the hell, sounds good. Humor the fucking bonehead—he didn't seem to be acting like a guilty traitor. They parked briefly to shift their disguises. Then they stopped at a little nothing diner in the town of Orleans, on a road actually called Cranberry Highway.

When their food came, Croke started grousing about his cheeseburger not coming with pickles. Who serves a cheeseburger that way. On and on.

But Oliver didn't commiserate with him—he was totally focused on a thick, old TV on a shelf behind the counter. Its sound was off, but he could see it was on a news channel. The footage showed three men in police custody in the Sanddollar Motel parking lot, being perp walked to police vehicles. They could have been pulled from central casting of a Godfather movie. The cops too. A subtitle on the screen called the three men Persons of Interest. One of the cops crowding into the camera shot was the big-nosed lieutenant, grinning like a fool!

But those three fuckers lying in wait in Croke's room? Oliver's best guess was Croke had carried out his idea to call the bosses in Queens himself. *They* probably offered to send someone down to discuss the situation. By someone, *they* meant three men with weapons. And by discuss, *they* meant kill. Which Croke had not twigged to.

Oliver's thought process was derailed when the picture on the TV changed to grainy, still pictures of Oliver and Croke. *Shit. Had his manipulation of that Pepper Ryan backfired?*

Then the news cut back to video footage again, another shock—the Chatham librarian! She was being interviewed, probably blabbing about every visit Oliver and Croke had made to her library. And by now the cops were undoubtedly digging into the computer Oliver used, which better have no traces of his chat room activities. What's the world coming to when you can't even trust librarians? He didn't tell Croke to turn and check out the TV since he wasn't sure how Croke would handle the news. Luckily, at that moment the special phone buzzed in Oliver's pocket.

Of course it was the client, again bypassing Oliver and Croke's bosses. Which seemed completely fair, now that their bosses had tried to have Oliver and Croke whacked. Screw *them*!

The client didn't even mention the Sanddollar Motel situation or the rest of the bad news. Maybe he hadn't seen it yet? The client was just calling with their next job—an oldie but a goodie—to kill Pepper Ryan right this time. Oliver was truly embarrassed by their fuck-ups and what he'd just seen on the TV screen and so didn't even acknowledge the client's sarcasm.

The client went on to share some special information about Pepper Ryan that would make catching and killing him *so* easy. Oliver wrote the details down on his cheap placemat depicting seashells of Cape Cod. And then, icing on the frigging cake, the client volunteered to double their pay for the Ryan hit.

What could Oliver say but yes sir!

FORTY-THREE

"*Too bad* about the NRF motel thing," said Special Agent Alfson. "And I'd love to answer your many questions but as you know, my job description requires jumping in front of bullets. I'm tied up on protection the next while. Nothing I can do. How about we meet later tonight, maybe?"

Pepper still believed, deep down, that Alfson was hiding important secrets at Eagle's Nest. And he believed it was time to confront his dear partner, right there at ground zero, that afternoon. He would tell Alfson all about Blacklock. And demand access to the whole Red Starfish file from Alfson. The whole truth about the Secret Service's part of the investigation. His gut told him he was missing key info and that Alfson held it, even if the skinny know-it-all didn't know how important it was.

So Pepper hung up and did the only logical thing. He headed to Eagle's Nest to catch Alfson in his lie. And hopefully get immediate answers to some other questions that had been evaded too damn long.

* * *

No one was taking a chance that the assassination threat

hadn't ended with the failed attempt on July Fourth. Security was even tighter now, as Pepper slowly advanced into Eagle's Nest. The list and database check at the first checkpoint. At the second, the canine unit was twice as thorough as before. And at the final checkpoint, they took away his ID again and interviewed him—what was his business today?

He said he was there to touch base with Special Agent Alfson. To synergize, move the needle. Gave them a full measure of Alfson's typical mumbo-jumbo. And that of course he was expected. Which was kind of true—Alfson was smart enough to expect that Pepper wouldn't be snowed *that* easy and definitely wouldn't take no for an answer, right?

Pepper eventually made it in.

As he climbed from his police car near the fountain, he saw Acker Smith's employee Lizzie Concepcion hustling across from the president's guest house to the main mansion. Her color-coded pin from the Secret Service for vetted staff was prominent on her blouse lapel. She was sweating and breathing heavy. The loyal worker bee.

"Oh," she said, putting her hand to her throat. Must be his handsome uniform. "What are *you* doing here?" She snapped then unsnapped her purse in agitation. So maybe she wasn't overcome by his looks, maybe only had debated pepper-spraying him?

"Official business. How's old Mr. Smith today? Maybe I could talk to him for a minute? I have a couple questions for him about one of his fund companies. Turnstone?"

She stared at him, frowning. "Mr. Smith's terrible today. If you call tomorrow, I'll see if he's able to talk to you."

"Thanks, Ms. Bumpers."

She recoiled slightly, but didn't otherwise acknowledge Pepper's use of her old married name.

"But right now I'm looking for Special Agent Alfson—

have you seen him?"

She studied him. Partially like he was dog poop on the driveway, partially like she didn't have time to be dealing with dog poop. Finally, she smiled. "He went out to the *Madeline Too,* about half an hour ago. More security work, before the president goes onboard," she said. "You'll have to call Captain Vinter. He'll probably send someone in the tender to pick you up, eventually." Then with a final condescending look, she hurried off.

Pepper headed down to the shore, passing another Secret Service agent positioned on the lawn. Had to give his name again, wait for confirmation.

Free again, Pepper walked down to the dock. The tender wasn't there, as Lizzie had said. But a sleek speedboat was—with a fat, powerful outboard motor. Another billionaire's toy. Why bother Vinter, and ruin dear Alf's surprise? So Pepper hopped in and fired up the outboard. Revved up the big motor as he pulled away in a quick, powerful arc and headed straight toward the big yacht. Ignored the Secret Service agents running down the beach towards him.

But Pepper wasn't able to ignore the two gray and blue zodiacs zipping across the water on a path to intercept him. Again, federal officers--Navy or Secret Service? Each with two men. One steering, the other shouting and gesturing but Pepper couldn't hear over the engines and distance. They were also pointing semiautomatic machine guns at him, which he did understand. The universal language of impending death.

So Pepper shut down his motor. He was two-thirds of the way to the yacht. The two zodiacs converged on him in seconds, one on each side. Men boarded his boat, still screaming orders Pepper wasn't processing. They pig-piled him. Wrestled him face down on the floor of his boat, none too gently. His hands and feet were quickly and efficiently bound with zip ties, and one officer—the heaviest in the group?--knelt squarely on his back.

Thirty minutes later, they perp-walked Pepper through the front door of his own goddamn police station. Didn't even do him the favor of taking him to the county sheriff's lockup instead.

Lieutenant Dwayne Hurd was there waiting, a tight smile on his face that said *I told you so*. Pepper saw Zula Eisenhower's face, eyes wide in shock, as they led him through. Hurd escorted the agents down the yellow tiled hallway into the lockup area and secured Pepper in a holding cell.

* * *

Zula was in shock. What had Pepper done this time? But she instantly called her pop, told him the little she knew. After a short burst of swear words followed by an apology to Zula, he was on the way.

Lieutenant Hurd had rejoined the New Albion officers and staff in the outer area. He told them to settle down, get back to work. But he also listed possible charges the agents had mentioned Pepper could be facing for unlawfully entering a restricted perimeter around the President of the United States. Assaulting, resisting or impeding Secret Service agents. Making threats. A handful of felony charges and probably some misdemeanors, as icing on Pepper's farewell cake.

FORTY-FOUR

Pepper had been in the cell for an hour when Chief Eisenhower arrived, with Lieutenant Hurd at his side. So he'd had plenty of time to think about how much trouble he was in and what he was going to say. Fuck. Pepper understood he'd screwed up, but no one had yet been willing to explain his offense. Some protocol about the POTUS protection?

"Golfing. With your dad," said Eisenhower.

"What?" asked Pepper.

"I'm sure you were wondering where I was on my first afternoon off in three weeks, when you got yourself arrested for storming the President of the United States. And I had a good chance to break 100. Four holes to go, so who knows what kind of shit I'd get into. But on track for the high nineties." And Eisenhower just stood there, waiting as if there was something he expected Pepper to say.

Pepper stayed silent.

"So, starting with the bad news," said Eisenhower. "You're suspended. I'll need your badge and firearm. The good news for you? The Secret Service's going to treat this as a misunderstanding. No charges. They don't want a lot of noise about whatever was going on with President Garby, out on Smith's yacht."

"President Garby?   What was he doing on board already?"

Hurd glared at him. "It isn't clear who was on the yacht with the POTUS, except it's classified and so none of our fucking business."

Eisenhower put up a hand, cutting off Hurd. "But you're suspended anyway, Pepper. And your carry license is revoked. Failure to follow Secret Service orders? Resisting arrest? What the hell were you thinking?"

"I was thinking the president hadn't gone to the yacht yet," Pepper said quietly. "Because Acker Smith's goddamn assistant told me so."

* * *

Zula figured she'd find Pepper heading out the police station's back door. Knew he'd avoid the staff and media circus out front.

And here he was. But not alone--he was chin to chin in the narrow back hallway with Lieutenant Hurd. *This can only end badly...*

"You've got no respect for authority or your badge," Hurd was saying. "Just like your old man. What'd you really come home for, huh?"

"Put down your badge and gun and step outside and I can take care of all your questions."

Hurd stuck a finger in Pepper's face. "You stay far away from police work. And the president, his family, the whole mess."

"I'm off the job but it's still a free country."

"Fuck you, Ryan."

Time to go. "My pop's looking everywhere for you!" she

said to Hurd. Then she grabbed Pepper's arm and pulled him out the back door.

"Hey, thanks," said Pepper. "But you probably don't want to be seen with me. Just another Ryan failure."

Then she slapped him. A good hard slap--surprised them both. Her hand was instantly tingling pins and needles and she hoped his face was too.

"I don't know exactly what you think you're doing," she said. "And not just getting arrested. You won't follow orders. You won't report what you're finding, what you're up to."

"I've been investigating, not pushing paper. The goal's justice, right? Even when the laws don't make it easy to get there..."

She snorted. "So that's it, the old 'end justifies the means' shit? It doesn't matter how many rules you break, as long as you get to be Wonderboy? How far would you go?"

Pepper just looked at her, said nothing.

"Tell me, what's your good reason for not listening to Pop? Your boss? Cause you're making it really easy for the people around you to get hurt." *Stupid, stupid Pepper.* He took her from caring about him so badly to being pissed off, so fast. She had to get out of there or she didn't know what she'd do.

"Hey Ryan! Didn't you used to work here?" said Sergeant Weisner as she came out the back door, headed to her cruiser. "Shouldn't you be off doing the beach body boogie with the Smith girl? Or maybe the First Daughters?"

Beach body boogie? "You know, Jake was great," said Zula, softly enough so Weisner couldn't hear. "We all loved Jake. But you were always better."

And then, with a disgusted shake of her head, she left him.

* * *

Lizzie Concepcion was with Mr. Smith on his balcony. Standing at the railing. He'd told her he was actually not feeling too terribly that afternoon.

But Lizzie knew Mr. Smith would have been weaker—and very quickly—if she'd let Pepper Ryan harass him with questions. Lieutenant Hurd had told her *all* about Pepper Ryan, every dirty detail. Dangerous, out-of-control and arrogant. Lizzie had dealt with people like Pepper Ryan all her life. People who let their emotions get the better of them. The way to handle people like that is to bug them. Irritate them. Then sit back and watch them defeat themselves. So yes, she'd sent him into trouble by pointing him out to the yacht...and was proud of herself for the result.

She stepped inside to call her police lieutenant chum, Dwayne Hurd, for an update. He confirmed Pepper Ryan was in deep shit.

"Are the feds charging him?" she asked.

"Unfortunately no. But he's off the force. He'll probably disappear somewhere, that's his M.O. A quitter... But I gotta go, Lizzie, someone's coming. We can't talk about confidential stuff anymore. And I definitely can't do you any more little favors until the president leaves town. My boss has been kicking asses all over the police station this week, including mine. Did you tell anyone about me helping you out, telling you things I shouldn't? My life's gonna be over!"

He sounded *beyond* stressed—dangerously ready to snap. Lizzie spoke to him for a bit—low voice, calm, flirty. Talking him down. Then she insisted she had to see him later. "No talk tonight..." she promised. "Just a private, special reward for my hero."

Back on the balcony, she found Mr. Smith gazing out over his estate and muttering loudly about the President of the United States, his continuous preoccupation in recent months. Garby's betrayal, Mr. Smith had essentially funded his successful election! How Garby had reversed course on a number of tax and regulatory policies dearest to Smith-- policies Smith believed would ensure the brightest future for America and his financial empire. Garby had looked right into Smith's eyes and promised to deliver on Smith's priorities, only to flip-flop as soon as his poll numbers began to fall. So, a spineless, poisonous traitor.

Muttering, but also chuckling about how miserable Garby's vacation had been so far. With the biggest humiliation yet to come...

Then, as was more and more typical of Mr. Smith these days, he changed topics without warning. "Lizzie, why is Brandon Blacklock flying up to see me?"

"Sir? Remember I told you yesterday—he was coming, but then didn't show. Maybe he changed his mind."

"I saw the email from two days ago—he wants to meet about a new fund, Turnstone..."

"The new developmental fund? It's International Special Equities, ex. Europe. We set it up as master-feeder, for tax purposes. Remember? What did he say was his issue—no compensation? We never pay portfolio managers on developmental funds—the only assets are your seed money. He has to prove the strategy so we can take in investor money before he gets even a nickel. Greedy—"

She was interrupted by her phone's ring. It was Captain Vinter on the *Madeline Too*. She stepped inside again.

In his slow, stubborn Norwegian accent, Captain Vinter was questioning his orders to prepare to take Madeline Too over to Nantucket for the night. Who will be on board as guests? There was weather coming and it might be an uncomfortable stretch. If they could move it up by six hours, the seas would be calmer. On and on…

"Captain, I'll check and we can touch base later. I can't trouble Mr. Smith with this right now, but I'll follow up with you as soon as I can talk to some people. And that's a promise." *If she didn't have a mental breakdown first…*

FORTY-FIVE

Oliver and Croke were hunkered down at the boat shed near the New Albion/Chatham line. It was very industrial, very basic. Concrete floor strewn with odds and ends of boat repair projects and Dunkin' Donuts cups and bags. Metal benches along one wall. Dirty skylights. A big water well led out through a door into the ocean. A small battered dingy with a tiny motor was floating in the water well, tied to a cleat. It had a couple inches of greasy water in its bottom. Luckily they wouldn't be needing to ride in that. They'd spruced up the place with a couple folding beach chairs, a white Styrofoam cooler and two air mattresses. Tolerable, for the very, very brief time they'd remain on Cape Cod.

Oliver was on edge. The drumbeat of his blood seemed to be encouraging him, begging him—forget any more assignments, just get the hell out of town. Hogs get slaughtered, wasn't that the saying? And Oliver had enough money to disappear for a good while. But his savings weren't quite F.U. money, yet. He'd have to get back to work sooner than he liked and he'd probably need to find new bosses, using a brand new name. And he felt like infamy was so close, he could almost smell it...

A call from the client interrupted Oliver's worrying and

made him glad he'd stuck around, when he heard the new assignment. The job was someone Oliver knew by sight— and well enough to dislike: the police lieutenant, Dwayne Hurd. The fisherman's punching bag at that bar fight. And who'd been in the 4Runner, tailing Croke from the ice cream stand handoff back to the Sanddollar…

The client emphasized the target had to be killed that night, after midnight but before dawn. No earlier, no later. And the client emphasized: make it messy. Which worked for Oliver—he figured the lieutenant might have tipped off the bosses in Queens if he was dirty, resulting in the three-man mafia death squad at the Sanddollar Motel. Or if he was straight, he'd probably been waiting for the right time to raid the motel anyway. Karma's long, deadly hand, coming back to bite the lieutenant in the keister.

And what about the elusive Pepper Ryan? The client confirmed Ryan was still on the to-do list, but first things first. So they would take care of the lieutenant—messily!— then handle any final assignments from the client in the next day or so, if the pay was fat enough. Easy, sneezy. The client said don't kill him until after midnight, but that didn't restrict when they grabbed him, right? So why not get right to it a few hours early, maybe before the lieutenant arrived home?

Oliver's karma was rocking—the lieutenant wasn't home when Croke dropped him at the address the client had given. The dumpy little house didn't have an alarm so it was quick work for Oliver to pick the back door. Oliver wandered around a bit, enjoying his home invasion. Kinda voyeuristic. The house was mostly empty of furniture. The guy seemed like a loser.

Oliver went into the larger of the two bedrooms. One dresser, one nightstand. A metal bed took up most of the rest of the space. Oliver pawed through the dresser drawers and found nothing interesting except some tighty-whitey underwear—who wears those anymore?—and a passport with a picture of Hurd, staring glumly straight into the camera. Oliver tucked the passport into his pocket.

Oliver was pleased to find that the metal bed had just enough room for him to hide underneath, like a childhood nightmare, so he did. With a chuckle, he soon fell asleep.

He woke to the sound of someone walking into the bedroom. That person—Hurd?—changed his clothes, walked out. From his spot under the bed, Oliver heard more noises from the direction of the kitchen.

Sounds from a television. Then of a beer can slishing open. Was Oliver going to have to hang around all night? Then, faintly, a door knock. Then voices—Hurd's and some woman's. Oliver could only make out snatches of conversation. Something about eagles. Something about a yacht.

Then something about...the motel raid? Oliver definitely heard motel and Secret Service. The woman's voice was flirty and interested but too low for Oliver to hear. Hurd's voice was just loud enough to make out snatches of what he was saying: *hadn't caught the suspects just yet... had some good leads... found some evidence... high caliber bullet...*

Under the bed, Oliver's mind was racing. *A bullet?* What'd that idiot Croke done—fool around with the sniper rifle, drop a bullet? Did it have Croke's fingerprint?

The tone of the conversation changed, more flirty now. More giggling from the woman. And soon after, footsteps coming back into the bedroom. The wet smacks of overly passionate kisses, punctuated by more bursts of sexy talk from the woman. Soon the light went out.

And then Hurd and the woman began doing the dirty deed. Yes, with Oliver tucked right underneath the bed.

Their moans mingled, grew. The woman, higher pitched, louder. Somebody's nose was whistling too—had to be the lieutenant's? How'd they ignore *that*, keep focused? The bouncing, grunting and whistling intensified quickly.

The back of Oliver's head was pressed against the dusty hardwood floor and the mattress smacked his forehead and stomach as it rose and fell... It was dirty under the bed and all the activity was generating a little dust storm around Oliver. He felt the electrifying tingle in his nose that signaled he was about to sneeze. Disaster! He pinched his nose and smothered the explosion, which popped his right ear. *Ouch*! Then he pulled up his shirt to cover his nose and mouth.

Hurd and the woman carried on much longer than Oliver expected. He snaked his other hand down into his pants, to make some adjustments. The situation was both ridiculous and erotic. Finally, with a burst of moans and whistling, the couple's activity climaxed, then petered out. Oliver's forehead was tingling where it'd been pounded on by the mattress.

Oliver heard more gentle talking, some light laughing, and feet shuffling back and forth to the bathroom. Over the running water, Oliver could make out one little snatch of the conversation, Hurd saying, "I mean it. I'm out." Sounding both adamant and panicky.

Then the woman's answer—softer and calmer but Oliver couldn't hear the words. More kissing noises.

Was the woman going to sleep over? Oliver hadn't brought two needles. Stick him, then silence her with the knife? Oliver could improvise... But Oliver heard them leave the bedroom, a little more laughter, some muffled goodbyes and more lip-smacking. The front door opening, closing.

So the woman was gone.

Hurd returned, futzed around in the bathroom for a while, then finally climbed into bed. He was soon snoring in rhythmic, tortured gasps and squeaks.

Oliver waited for another half-hour, just to be sure. Then he scootched slowly and silently out from under the bed. Uncapped the needle. Shot the Atricurium right into the sleeping lieutenant's neck. Held the man's shoulders down to make sure the dose took him. Called Croke to come get them the hell out of there.

* * *

The police lieutenant woke slowly. Badly. His hands were zip-tied together behind his back around a metal pole built into a sleeve in the boat shed's concrete floor. He was wearing his ridiculous white undies, a t-shirt and one sock.

"How do you feel?" Oliver asked him.

The man suddenly leaned to one side and threw up. Almost splashed on Oliver's foot.

Oliver knew Atricurium packed a wallop, so wasn't surprised.

"Let me introduce myself," he said, giving the lieutenant a sharp kick, carefully avoiding the puke zone. "I'm Oliver."

Croke chuckled. He was pacing back and forth, impatient. "And you don't need to know me," he said, stopping to lean in close to the man. "But I bet we owe you one for that motel raid."

Not to mention having to hide under the lieutenant's sex romp, thought Oliver. Which he was *never* going to tell Croke about.

"You know I'm a cop?" said Hurd, still sounding very groggy. "Maybe we can work something out? I'm tight with someone with a lot of money."

Oliver laughed. "You know, I think maybe that's who paid us already."

Hurd cleared his throat and spat at them, but his meager spittle didn't get further than his lower lip. Just hung there. "Alright you dickless wonders," he said. "Do your goddamn worst."

So Oliver and Croke did.

* * *

Oliver was pretty relaxed the next morning, despite having spent a sweaty night on an air mattress in the boat shed. Made him almost miss the Sanddollar motel.

He was waiting with Croke at a pier in Chatham to pick up a man. Their next gig. They waited in their newest stolen ride, a large Lincoln sedan. Perfect for a fake limo service.

And Oliver was feeling pretty invincible. Not like a dickless wonder, at all. More like a deadly ghost, moving around the area. No wonder law enforcement hadn't really come close to catching them yet.

Oliver was also in a giddy mood because he was picturing the reaction in the Queens cheese shop (such a terribly thin cover for their bosses' criminal activities) when later that morning *they* would open the small package that contained a severed hand, carefully arranged prior to *rigor mortis* to deliver a one-finger salute. Worth every damn penny for the private courier. In a way, the 'hand delivery' simplified Oliver's future decisions—he had to get big money now because he would absolutely have to take off, far from *them* and their inevitable attempt for vengeance. Because seriously, they had no sense of humor.

It also helped Oliver's mood that he and Croke could handle this job on dry ground—even the sight of the ocean brought up bad memories. The man they were waiting for was easy to recognize when he finally arrived, exactly as described—nautical uniform and bushy mustache. Oliver and Croke were *not* easy to recognize—both were heavily disguised due to the grainy but accurate pictures of them being blasted on the TV news. The pictures must have been from the Sanddollar? Were there security cameras Oliver hadn't seen?

Oliver held the door as their job climbed into the backseat. Then he discretely uncapped his needle and gave it a flick.

FORTY-SIX

Lieutenant Dwayne Hurd reappeared later that Thursday morning. At least, partially.

The Boston Globe received a package by private courier containing Hurd's left arm. They knew immediately it belonged to a man named Hurd because it was accompanied by a polite note identifying him. Signed only with what appeared to be a drawing of a starfish. Red ink.

His right arm (handless) arrived at Fox News.

His head was found by two German tourists on the top step of Rodger's Light.

The media went apeshit. Every news outlet--nationally-- was showing a map of the eastern seaboard, labeling the various locations where Lieutenant Hurd's body pieces had popped up. The only parts unaccounted for were his torso and his right hand. And what was with the red starfish— some kind of tag for the serial killer? Why wouldn't the police comment?

The New Albion police station--deep in shock--became the epicenter. *Everyone* was freaking about Lieutenant Hurd. News trucks surrounded the police station, digging for information. And gore.

Then it got worse, after about an hour. Reporters were

asking, could the Chief of Police confirm or deny the new allegation that Hurd was dirty? And word had leaked that Officer Pepper Ryan was suspended—could the Chief confirm that action and whether Ryan's suspension related to Lieutenant Hurd's dismemberment?

* * *

Pepper was sitting in civilian clothes and his Red Sox ball cap in Broken Dreams Antiques and Pizza, mechanically toying with a couple of slices. He couldn't eat—he was too sick to his stomach about Lieutenant Hurd. Even if the rumors were true and Hurd had been taking money under the table and spilling confidential info. If he was dirty, what else that'd gone wrong in the last couple weeks could be his fault? Maybe it explained Hurd's obstinate lack of effort on the home demolition case? Maybe it explained things that were even worse. Pepper needed a pause to rethink recent events in light of Hurd's involvement but events had been unfolding too fast and time was clearly running out.

But what could Pepper do to help—suspended and disgraced? He was overdue at the police station, where he was supposed to turn in his Glock that he'd retrieved from his truck's lockbox. He'd also received a voice message from Edwina Youngblood at the FBI—to call her back about the research he requested on Turnstone and Scoter. If he called, what would he have to tell her about his new job status? Pepper was procrastinating from both those opportunities for high embarrassment when his phone rang.

"Officer Ryan?" The voice was a little high. A bit cracked. "Guess who?"

Perfect. Guessing games while his pizza was getting cold. "I wouldn't know where to start," he replied. And at that moment Pepper saw Zula enter Broken Dreams and begin to weave her way back toward Pepper's table.

"Then you lose again! It's Rowboat Willie. You said call, right? I think I can help you out, if maybe there's a little cash in it for me?"

"Help me?" How could the looney homeless guy help him?

"I bet I can take you to the dudes who chopped up that lieutenant from the bar. And you know I don't lose bets!" Laughter, high and thin. "But it's gotta be right now before we're too late. Down at the Rogers Lighthouse parking lot. Just you. It's hard to know who to trust these days, you know?"

Pepper pondered a second. What's the worst that could happen--fifteen minutes wasted? And whatever lead Pepper got, he could pass it to Chief Eisenhower when he surrendered his handgun. Make some tiny amends, right? "I'll be right there. Let me just toss the rest of my dinner in the trash."

"Hey—eat, drink and be merry," advised Rowboat Willie. "For tomorrow you may diet!" Rowboat's laughter was cut off as he hung up.

Zula had reached his table and was staring at him, hands on her hips. "Pepper, you're not stupid enough to be working cases, right? Not while suspended?"

Pepper stood and looked into her big, accusatory eyes. Gave her a gentle hug. "Little Ike, how could I forget that? I gotta go."

"Hang on, what'd you think I came here for, a calzone? I got a call from the State Police Lab. Your dad helped get that little envelope of white powder tested in record time. But you guessed wrong—it wasn't some recreational drug. It was arsenic trioxide!"

Arsenic?!? Why would Smith's cancer patient guest have an arsenic stockpile? Who was he poisoning? Or who was he about to poison...!

Zula continued. "Your sample was way less than a lethal dose, the tech said. But still...where'd you get it?"

"I'll tell you tomorrow over dinner, my treat. I promise." Pepper hurried out.

* * *

Pepper's dad called as Pepper drove toward the meet-up with Rowboat Willie.

"Son, are you okay? I heard what happened at Eagle's Nest, some of it! Where are you?" His voice quick with panic.

Pepper couldn't recall ever hearing his dad that way and it scared him. "Dad, I'm fine. Off the job again, so someone in the office pool won that bet. But I'm 100% okay."

"Glad to hear it. Don called to say the feds backed off, so that's a good break. But I didn't know where you were. And I got a phone message about the home demo investigation that might lift your spirits. Didn't you say a few days ago that your whistleblower mentioned an entity called 'Turnstone'? I just got the bank's info on the wire payment to A&M Demolition and it came from some offshore outfit with that same name! They've got to be our scumbags!"

Pepper was stunned. How could Brandon Blacklock and Acker Smith be connected to the Ryan home demolition?

"Dad, I think I've got to tell you the longer version of that story—can I meet you at the General's house in half an hour? I have to make one quick stop."

"Okay. You near the water? I'm just getting static... Can you hear me, Son?" The call disconnected.

Pepper pulled into the lighthouse parking lot and saw Rowboat Willie standing by himself way down at the end of the lot, where many cars were parked but no other people were nearby at the moment. Willie was facing away toward the water, apparently talking on a cell phone. And his purple hat was missing—he was wearing some kind of trucker's cap instead. But he otherwise looked like his old grubby self.

No bars on Pepper's own phone, of course. Disgusted, Pepper left it on his truck's seat. He locked the door, walked over.

"Still good," said Rowboat Willie into his phone, now facing Pepper. And his voice wasn't high and thin. The trucker's cap had a lime green front and an Interstate Batteries logo.

Pepper drew the Glock he didn't have a permit to carry anymore. "Hang up and hands behind your head, Willie," he said, pointing his firearm.

Rowboat Willie just smiled. "If I did that, your nephews would be executed immediately. Patrick and Jake, right? My partner's sitting with them right now with a very sharp knife. If I don't tell him the magic words every thirty seconds...hold on.

"Still good," said Willie into the phone, then lowered it. "And your nephews live another thirty seconds, unless my call ends first. So drop your gun and kick it away. Then put on these handcuffs. Hurry up, my cell coverage is lousy down here."

"Don't you hurt those kids," said Pepper, still pointing his Glock.

"My friend, that'll be on you, if you don't do what I said. Immediately." Then, into his phone, Willie said, "Still good." Then, his attention back on Pepper, he said with a little shrug, "And I'm not going to say those words to him again if you're not in cuffs. In thirty seconds they'll be dead and it'll be your bad." Willie tossed the handcuffs and they landed at Pepper's feet with a clatter.

No time to think or argue. No options. Pepper gently placed his weapon on the pavement, kicked it toward Willie. And snapped on the cuffs.

"Still good," said Willie into the phone.

"Okay, Officer Wonderboy, turn around and kneel down. Cross your ankles."

Pepper did, and a moment later felt a burning sting in the back of his neck. Then, nothing.

* * *

Pepper woke to an almighty headache. Like his head had been split right down the middle. He was sitting with his legs out and his arms handcuffed behind him, around a metal pole. In a single bare bulb's light Pepper could see he was in a small metal building or shed.

"How do you feel?" asked Rowboat Willie. He was sitting in a chair in front of Pepper. He was now wearing Pepper's Red Sox cap. In his hand was an aluminum baseball bat with what looked like a bloodstain on its barrel.

"You'd better not have hurt the boys," said Pepper.

"Ah, sorry about that. I was given their info to help this go more smoothly. Truth is, they were never in danger. And I'm not being paid to kill kids--the fee's not quite high enough. But a pretty good bluff, no?" Willie scooted closer. "But now game time's over." And Willie tossed Pepper's hat on the floor. Then pulled off his long hair. "Let me introduce myself for real. I'm Oliver."

FORTY-SEVEN

Oliver was pumped. He was absolutely in control of the man, the myth—Pepper Ryan!

And Oliver was also an absolute sensation—everyone in America had heard of his creative, murderous work. The splashy distribution of the lieutenant's body parts was the clincher. The buzz over every form of media was more than terror. It was fascination—who was this mysterious, savage Red Starfish killer? The video clips by news reporters on CNN's website made the killer sound so sexy.

And even better, Oliver was almost done.

Their orders from the client were very specific: kill Pepper Ryan, ASAP. The client had emphasized how super important it was this time, which gave Oliver the idea to renegotiate his fee. Oliver had a strong theory that their client was the local billionaire, Acker Smith, despite the voice distortion device that the client used. And if he was right, the client could absolutely afford to pay triple the offered rate, without any difficulty. Especially if Oliver only demanded *his* cut be tripled... Which was fair, since he had to put up with Croke.

Triple. A number which would allow him to disappear immediately for a long, long time. Get far away from his

318

bosses in Queens, who had probably already sent another carload of maniacs in the direction of Cape Cod to eliminate Oliver and Croke in the most excruciating way *they* could think of.

The law was closing in too. They couldn't go out in public anymore without new disguises and Oliver was running out of variations. And now they had to change cars like what—every five minutes? No, it was time to go. Which meant Oliver had only this one last chance to negotiate a monster payday.

Oliver didn't have a personal beef with Pepper Ryan. Really, the opposite. Kinda felt like they were kindred spirits—rebellious men of action. And Pepper had been respectful in their earlier encounters when Oliver was playing the down-and-out Rowboat Willie. He decided when it came time, he'd finish Ryan with a smooth stab to the heart using his razor-sharp Gerger blade. Professional courtesy for a worthy but vanquished foe.

Oliver was extra confident about getting triple pay because he suspected the client planned to ask them to carry out one final, epic hit—to assassinate the President of the United States. Because when they'd last talked, the client had asked Oliver whether he still had the sniper rifle and ammo. When he'd said yes, the client had said good, to hold onto it for a bit.

Oliver had even daydreamed about the thrill of such a kill. The rush from putting a bullet through the brain of the most powerful man in the world. And it was fun to guess what mega, mega fee would accompany such a request.

But Oliver knew he would never take that contract because it'd be impossible to escape after pulling that trigger. There was no percentage. Not even Oliver wanted the infamy that would end with himself dead or—worse—buried in some federal hellhole for life.

But kill Ryan? No problem, once the client upped the ante.

Oliver wasn't able to get a signal on the so-called expensive blue phone in the boat shed. Not even on the dock outside. He'd have to drive up toward town until he got a signal, then call the client. Negotiate. Confirm the triple payment's delivery. Move the funds to his other, more secure offshore account. Then they'd kill Ryan.

And *then* Oliver was gone, gone, gone, no matter what final job and payday the client offered…

"Recognize your friend?" Croke was asking Pepper Ryan, who appeared half awake but was otherwise none too bad, yet. Still handcuffed securely to the pole. Oliver saw Ryan looking at a body halfway across the floor.

"No, not *that* dead guy," hinted Croke. "The shorter one." Croke gestured toward the dead lieutenant's bloody torso in the corner, laughing like he'd made some joke.

What a weirdo!

* * *

Pepper's vision was still swimming, but he was trying to focus on a clothing heap where the older guy had pointed. Pepper gagged from the sweet, thick rotting smell, drifting from that direction… But Pepper didn't see a head. Didn't see any limbs.

Shit. Pepper felt a chill wash from the back of his head, down his neck, down the center of his back. Was that what's left from Hurd? The parts that didn't go in the mail?

The body of a very fat, gray-haired man in a seersucker suit was sprawled a bit closer to Pepper…some man he didn't recognize. He'd been dead a while, based on his coloring.

Flies were moving in a mini-cloud, near his head and his hands.

Another body was a bit further away, but it faced Pepper, with a purple gash across the man's neck and a red bath of blood on his shirt. Pepper recognized the uniform, the face, the bushy blonde mustache: it was Vinter, the captain of the *Madeline Too*! Why the hell'd they kill him? Had Vinter stumbled on their activities and been killed for what he saw, like Marcus Dunne? Or was he in cahoots with the murderers and they double-crossed him? Vinter's body was getting attention from the flies too.

Rowboat Willie—no, Oliver—was talking to the older guy now, seemed to be giving him instructions. The older guy wasn't liking it, they were kind of arguing, but trying to appear like they weren't, like a married couple squabbling in a crowded restaurant. Oliver was gesturing at the older guy with one of those fancy blue phones...

"That's *it*," Pepper heard Oliver hiss. "I'll be *right back*." The older guy made a rude gesture at Oliver's back as he left the shed. Made two fists, bobbed and weaved a bit, threw some jabs and an uppercut. Actually pretty smoothly, like maybe he had some ring experience.

Pepper groaned, tried to stretch. Failed. Remembered his Red Sox hat was missing. Sonofabitch. He was still sitting against the cold metal pole, his arms looped around it. Held there by the cold handcuffs. The good news was his head was clearing. The bad news was the more fully he regained consciousness, the more his head hurt.

"So hey, can we talk about this?" asked Pepper. The older captive was the guy that the motel witness described as looking like the actor William Devane, and Pepper could see the resemblance.

The man chuckled, stepping close. "Oh, you wanna buy

us off too? You see how that worked out for your buddy over there? No, our client is one rich bastard and we're getting 'fuck you" money. And it's you who's fucked..."

Pepper saw a fist's blur, then felt a shooting pain as his head snapped back against the metal pole. He was sliding into a hole so fast, so far, that his mind went black like a broken light bulb.

* * *

Zula Eisenhower was with Pepper's dad at Aunt Anney's Kitchen, praying for any word from Pepper. He was supposed to have been back at the station an hour ago. After Hurd, everyone was thinking Pepper was next. If he was safe, he'd have been in touch. They both knew, without any further info, that Pepper was in deep trouble.

Zula and Gerry Ryan had fled the station and the predatory herd of reporters in Zula's Jeep. They'd ordered food but hadn't taken more than a couple bites each. Zula was systematically calling everyone she could think of, trying to locate Pepper.

"It's gotta be bad. He'd answer his phone if he could," said Gerry Ryan, uselessly. His face was heavy with worry and fatigue. His eyes were frantic.

"Sometimes it's him, sometimes it's his damn phone."

"Well, I've got a signal. And I've got a terrible feeling...I keep expecting to get the call they just found Pepper's body, all chopped up—"

Gerry Ryan cut off himself when an old lady in a red felt hat at the table behind Zula turned and gave him a stern glare. His grisly talk was overshadowing the ladies' supper conversation...

"I'll tell you, that sucks," said the old lady in the red felt hat. "The Nine's is open, but it's too loud. There's no reason." Another pointed glare back over her shoulder at Chief Ryan. "And we can drive to Mahans, but that sucks too. Last time I had the chicken and they didn't put cheese on it. Eleven bucks. Worst sandwich I ever had."

Zula tried to concentrate on her phone's contact list, scrolling through names uselessly. Nobody made Zula madder than Pepper, but nobody got her going more, either. As a kid, Zula had made her pop take her to every one of Pepper's high school hockey games. Then drove up with her pop to see Pepper play for Harvard. Nobody took him down--he was like a crazy, dumb warrior with a mullet. Sure he had the scoring touch of a quadriplegic. But he'd never quit. *But this time I know he needs help.*

In the booth behind them, the other lady was sniffing now to emphasize her displeasure. "I never finish a meal at Mahans. It's a sin."

"Well, that's why God created doggie bags. But eleven bucks and the fries were cold. Sucked."

Zula had spilled some raspberry jelly onto the white laminate tabletop and when she wiped it with her napkin it just spread, making the mess worse. The tabletop even seemed to be absorbing the stain. Goddamn it. "Pepper has a good head on his shoulders," she said to Gerry Ryan. "He gets into trouble easily, but he's even better at getting out of it." *So where the hell are you Pepper?*

Gerry Ryan had stopped pretending to eat too. "I shouldn't have let him take the badge again. I should have twisted your dad's arm. But Pepper wouldn't have listened. He's a chip off my damn block, and paying the price for it. But I can't lose him too..."

Tears came to Zula's eyes. Pepper *couldn't* be dead. "I never even told him how I feel," she said, with more than a little anger in her voice. *Did she just say that out loud?*

Pepper's dad took her hand across the table, gave it a squeeze. But said nothing.

Now Zula was anxious, scared *and* embarrassed. She decided there was no way she was going to eat any more. "Let's go. I've gotta get back to the station. Or anywhere but here."

Then Zula's phone rang.

It was Angel Cavada. "I think I've got a lead on Pepper," he said. "Just maybe. Somebody might be holding him, down by the shore."

FORTY-EIGHT

The first thing that came to Pepper Ryan's mind, when he eventually regained consciousness, was *no more riling up William Devane.* Pepper's vision was choppy gray, sliding painfully to black, then slowly unfolding back to color. He had a brain-splintering headache. And he was still handcuffed to the pole.

The Devane guy was sitting in a folding chair, over near the door. Reading some book. Pepper had the impression they were both waiting for Oliver to get back. And that his return would be bad news for Pepper.

The man had said their client was some rich bastard. That statement solidified Pepper's instinct, his suspicion— *Smith!* Pepper had never been close to actually proving it. And now it was too late to do anything to stop whatever he was planning. Were Oliver and Devane (as Pepper now thought of him) going to be carrying out a plan by Smith to kill the president? What'd it matter now, what more he knew? He was cuffed up, busted up, done.

No way to keep going, right?

Pepper tried to get fired up. Mad. He felt a feeble burst of anger swell up, then be swallowed by his pain. But he wasn't dead yet. So, what could he do to fight on?

His hands were still cuffed behind his back, around a metal pole. Obviously, step one was to get the handcuffs off. That'd be as simple as picking the lock. Pepper had heard it was fairly easy to do if you have two little pieces of metal. Which of course he didn't. The only way he was getting those cuffs off would be with his abductors' key.

So what about the pole? By leaning back he could see it extended up about six feet and had a sign at the top. He couldn't read it from that angle--probably said something like No Handcuffing To This Pole. Twisting his neck, which almost caused him to lose consciousness again, he saw the pole was seated in a metal sleeve built into the concrete floor. Very sturdy. It was held in the sleeve by a heavy duty metal screw with a thick head that his wrist scratched against when his hands sagged to the floor.

Could he undo the screw?

He could try. Or he could sit here and wait for them to kill him.

Pepper arranged himself for maximum leverage over the screw. Wait--lefty loosey, correct? So which way was left in this position?

He thought it through, slowly. It'd be the opposite of if it was on his side of the pole. So what felt like righty tighty would actually be the correct way to loosen the screw. Right?

He twisted himself again to find a better angle and was able to arrange a thumb and forefinger around the screw. How much torque would he need? He gave it his best possible squeeze. Tried to give it a twist in the direction he hoped would loosen it.

Nothing. Didn't budge. His fingers held for a second, then slid across the unmoving screw. He felt pain in his fingers where his skin snagging on the screw. Sonovabitch. But Oliver could reappear any time and whatever they'd do to him would hurt a lot more.

So right back to it. Fumble, squeeze, twist, slide, pain. Again. And again. Pepper counted each attempt as if to convince himself that the bigger the number, the more progress he was making. *Just don't quit again.* Time to prove everyone wrong, including himself.

He could feel the wet chill as his fingers began to bleed. This made the effort seem even more like a waste of time. The blood made the screw slick, so the twist went straight to slide and straight to pain. Less likely he'd actually turn the screw.

Then Pepper got the bright idea to pull up the back of his shirt and slip it over the screw. It seemed to soak up some of the blood and gave him a bit better purchase. Squeeze, twist, slide. The pain was constant now, not just a punch line at the end of every failed attempt.

FORTY-NINE

Pepper lost count of his efforts to move the damn screw somewhere north of forty tries. And he kept laboring long after that. He didn't want to rest because he doubted he'd start again, it just hurt too much.

The William Devane guy was still sitting in a folding chair over by the door, engrossed in some book. Then he suddenly stopped, looked over at Pepper. "You're awake!" the man said, chuckling. "That was my money punch..."

"Yeah, nice K.O." Pepper tried to smile and keep the guy settled where he was so he wouldn't glimpse Pepper's bloody struggle behind his back. "What's the book?"

The man looked delighted. "I hoped you'd ask, *Pepper Ryan*. 'Cause it's called *Salt!*" And the man laughed and laughed like it was the funniest coincidence ever. "Oh, man...*Pepper, it's called Salt...* Anyways, you think it's just about the history of salt, but it's *really* about money and fertility and smuggling..." The man launched into a long, scattered recap of the book. It was almost more painful than the punch.

Pepper kept working on the screw behind his back. Still twisting fruitlessly. Still bleeding.

After summarizing and editorializing for more than five

minutes, the man ran out of steam. "So that's where I'm at so far." The man grunted, heaved himself to his feet. "But let's check you over."

Crap. "Hey, that book sounds good. Did you know, ah, the first millionaire in America was a Cape Cod salt maker?" lied Pepper.

Devane paused. "Oh, yeah?"

"But he died from salt poisoning. He must be in that book."

The man went back and picked up the book, flipped the pages in a disgruntled way. "I read all that part, about Cape Cod. I don't remember any millionaire."

"Oh, yeah, yeah. His name was Barnstable. They named the town nearby after him, you know it? Any serious book about salt must have mentioned him a bunch. Check the index."

Devane flipped to the book's front, then jumped to the index at the back. But of course didn't find any Barnstable listed there. He was getting more irritated. He tossed the book back on his lawn chair.

"I think I remember that guy, I'll find it," Devane promised. "But I gotta piss, so sit tight." He chuckled, headed toward the door.

And then Pepper was alone with the dead bodies and the screw.

* * *

Oliver was annoyed. The client hadn't answered when he called on the blue phone. Oliver leaned against the stolen car, parked on a residential street just outside downtown New Albion. Full cell signal. Waited five minutes, called again.

No answer.

Oliver called again every five minutes, getting madder and madder.

On the fifth try, the garbled voice answered. Sounding robotic but also…tired?

"Good news," said Oliver. "We have Ryan. But it took extra overhead and extra risk. So the price to kill him's gone up."

Garbled swear words. Garbled anger.

"The payment to this account—" Oliver recited his own offshore bank account number "needs to be…quadrupled." Fuck him—the extra was for making Oliver sit there like a putz, redialing… Long silence from the client. Long enough for Oliver to wonder, was he wrong about their client's identity and wealth? And the likelihood of being asked to do the one final, mega assignment?

Then…laughter. "Quadruple, just the one payment? Does your partner know?"

Oliver kept silent, sat on his anger. Waited. Thought about the F.U. money.

"Okay," said the client finally. "I'll call when it's wired, then you kill Ryan. Immediately. Or I'll have *you* killed."

Oliver slapped his leg in victory. Hung up and smiled.

Five minutes later, the client called back to confirm the money had transferred. Which Oliver was able to verify for himself on an app on his own phone, then transfer it all to a different account in the Bahamas.

"You still there?" demanded the client. "When you're done, sit tight in that boat shed for an hour, then call me. I have one final contract to offer that'll make everything so far look like pocket change."

"Whoa, sounds great!" said Oliver, and hung up.

Then he tucked the special blue phone under his car's

front tire and drove back and forth over it until it was an expensive, secure clump of plastic splinters.

* * *

Angel Cavada's intel was razor thin.

Pepper had asked Angel to put out the word a couple of days earlier about any boats in the gray area between owned and stolen, in connection with Marcus Dunne's death. Anything borrowed, or loaned, or wink wink nudge nudged. Angel had now called that entire network again, a ton of people, hoping for any scraps of info that might lead to Pepper's location. After sorting through a lot of irrelevant gossip and rumors, Angel finally thought he had a lead, validated through a few different sources. Might be completely jack shit, but he was telling Zula just in case...

A large motor cruiser had been moored at a rental property for the past week, at a private dock that was usually empty. The house was the property occupied by the Weepers church group. A night kayaker had seen the motor cruiser—around fifty feet with powerful twin engines, a real beast—returning to its dock the night Pepper's trailer had been dragged into the ocean. The big cruiser had come in hot, almost taken out the dock.

Also, a neighbor to the Weepers property—and pretty pissed about it—had been watching them with binoculars, hoping they'd do something the neighbor could report to the law and hopefully get their hateful asses run out of town. A couple hours ago, she'd seen two people come from the boathouse next to the dock where the big motor cruiser was docked. The people were having some kind of confrontation. Maybe even a bit of a fight. One had pretty much dragged the other onto the big boat and below deck then things became quiet again. So, Angel had wondered, was Pepper being held there?

Pepper's dad was getting red in the face from the news and he was shaking from some mix of anger and fear. "I have to check it out," he said firmly. "It's the only tip we've got, even if it might be a big nothing...but if Pepper's in danger..."

"No, absolutely! I'll drive," promised Zula. Her stomach had tightened like a fist, squeezing her spine. Pepper might already be dead! Or could be, any minute...

The tip was probably even too thin to justify police backup. But they did call Zula's pop as the Jeep sped toward the Weepers' rental property.

"You two stay put," commanded her pop, predictably. "I'll send a car to check it out."

But Gerry Ryan was still red-faced, still shaking. "Don, I can't wait, my boy might be in there. We're here and every minute might count!"

"Gerry—"

Pepper's dad clicked off. Despite the heavy stress evident on his face, he grinned at Zula. "Pepper would laugh." Then he tried to get Zula to stay in the car but she refused. Who knew how many people were on the boat? How many were armed?

Zula unlocked the toolbox in the rear of her Jeep and took out her twelve gauge shotgun. "End of discussion," she said.

"Where the hell'd you get that?" asked Gerry Ryan.

"From you. On my sixteenth birthday and don't pretend you forgot."

They walked swiftly but alertly around the house's side to the back lawn. Saw no one. As they approached the private dock they could see a boathouse on one side of the dock and on the other side a huge Sundancer cabin cruiser, close to fifty feet long, with enormous twin engines. No one was in sight.

They went to the boat first. Zula peeked through a tiny opening in the blinds. She could see what must be a stateroom: a thin sliver of bed, and part of a person's body outlined through a blanket.

She whispered to Gerry Ryan what she'd seen.

"Fuck this," said Gerry Ryan. He stepped onto the boat. Zula pulled herself up the side of the boat too as a man came from the cabin doorway. The man and Gerry Ryan saw each other at the same moment—it was Reverend McDevitt! His black hair was smoothed up and to the side, like a burnt, squashed beehive.

"Freeze, police!" shouted Gerry Ryan. He pointed his big Smith & Wesson at the man.

After a brief moment, McDevitt darted back below deck.

"I said *freeze!*"

Then the top of McDevitt's beehive head reappeared, and just the tip of a handgun, like he was gearing up for a fight. From McDevitt's blind spot behind the hatch, Zula stepped up and loudly racked the 12 gauge shotgun and pointed it at the back of McDevitt's head—just a foot away.

"Hear that, asshole?" she asked.

This time the reverend did freeze. Gerry Ryan took McDevitt's weapon and quickly had him flat on the boat's deck.

Zula was already headed below, shotgun in front of her, to free Pepper. But she didn't find Pepper. She found a teenage girl, cheek with a purpling bruise, in bed. Tears running down her cheeks. Looked kinda numb but also kinda panicked by the shouting.

A few used condoms and wrappers littered the floor.

"She was here of her own consent!" yelled the reverend from on deck. "Her own consent! And you—"

"Sweetie, how old are you?" Zula asked.

The girl didn't want to answer. Zula could see her eyes moving as she thought furiously, weighing the situation.

"How old, sweetie?"

"I'm sixteen."

"Sixteen?"

"Almost—fifteen and a half."

Zula called her dad, briefly explained they hadn't found Pepper but had interrupted the sexual assault of a minor. She asked him to send it all. EMTs and backup to process the scene so that the Reverend McDevitt could be prosecuted for statutory rape. And to request assistance from the Rape Crisis Center in Hyannis and the state DCF.

Back on deck, McDevitt was getting his bluster back. "You're trespassing, and you've assaulted me, in front of a witness!" he yelled at Gerry Ryan. "This is an illegal arrest! I'm going to... Anyway, *you* can't arrest me! You're no cop anymore, Ryan, I already took care of that!"

No, you didn't, he'll always be a cop.

Pepper's dad just smiled, pulled his wallet. Showed the shield pinned there. "County deputy. Nothing fancy, but enough to take you into custody. You have the right to remain silent..." he said, as he pulled his cuffs.

And they sounded like the sharp grinding of metal jaws as Gerry Ryan squeezed them tight on McDevitt's hairy wrists, looped through a metal railing.

Gerry Ryan and Zula ran to the boat shed, hoping that Pepper was there instead. Zula turned the doorknob and Gerry Ryan kicked it wide open. He moved inside, gun up, screaming *'police'!*

But the shed was empty.

Zula was crushed—Angel's tip hadn't gotten them any closer to saving Pepper.

* * *

Alfson was with Hanley in the Eagle's Nest guest house's command post, reviewing logistics for the POTUS's planned dinner that evening on the Smith yacht. He was trying to push to the back of his mind the call he'd gotten from Zula Eisenhower telling him that Pepper had disappeared—had he seen him? He hadn't. Alfson instantly pictured Lieutenant Hurd, all chopped up. And Arnold Keser, in the clambake pit. But Alfson's duty prevented him from running off to look for Pepper. Hopefully, the maverick was somewhere innocent—holed up with a bottle or a girl or both, some crazy story—and would turn up any moment.

Then Hanley received a call from a woman named Edwina Youngblood forwarded through the Secret Service's Joint Operations Center. Youngblood identified herself as Deputy Assistant Director in the FBI's Criminal Investigative Division. Hanley put her on speakerphone so Alfson could hear.

"I wanted to notify you I have a missing FBI agent in New Albion," Youngblood said. "His name's Peter Ryan. I'd appreciate it if your agents could assist in locating him."

Peter Ryan? Peter Ryan... Was there any goddamn chance...? Alfson could feel his face get flushed.

Youngblood continued. "You may know him as Pepper Ryan. He grew up in New Albion, so I borrowed him from another FBI unit to assist the Financial Crimes Unit with an investigation in that area. He's been undercover as a member of local law...collecting intelligence on money laundering activity and a criminal conspiracy....wire transfers tripped red flags, so a bank filed a SAR..."

Youngblood rambled on, but Alfson had stopped listening. Stunned. Pepper Ryan was an undercover FBI agent?

Alfson's mind raced. Recalculating all of his judgments and decisions. So Ryan wasn't an out-of-control local cop, wasn't in bed with the domestic terrorists? Maybe wasn't even nuts?

"Ryan volunteered a few days after the POTUS announced his vacation plans. We agreed it was a great opportunity, worth pulling him from an assignment in central Tennessee. He's been posing as a member of local law enforcement... We feared one or more members of local law enforcement might be involved in the criminal activity, so no one locally was informed..."

Alfson thought for a good while before he spoke. Both about the new information as well as his long, beloved career aspirations. Then he said it because it needed saying. "Is there any possibility Ryan's gone to the other side? That he's been compromised?"

One of Alfson's team members entered the room and interrupted. "Sir?!?"

"Just a second, please," Hanley said to the FBI.

"Sir, we just received a tip on the main number at headquarters. It was anonymous and the caller was using an electronic device to disguise his voice. But the caller gave us a specific location where Pepper Ryan's being held."

"Did you hear that?" Hanley asked Youngblood on the phone. "We're rolling."

Hopefully not too late, thought Alfson, whatever hole Ryan had dug himself into...

FIFTY

Squeeze, twist, slide....maybe the screw gave? Pepper Ryan couldn't be sure, he might have hallucinated it.

The William Devane guy hadn't come back into the shed yet—was he *still* pissing?

Squeeze, twist...yes, the screw gave a little.

Energy flooded through Pepper's fingers, his arms, his chest. Tried again and the screw gave a little more.

But his shirt seemed to be snagged on the screw, was it impeding the turn? Pepper tried to picture the screw, his bloody shirt, the whole puzzle. And he gently tried to unwind the shirt. It took a bit of time, but the fabric fell free from the screw.

Okay, back to twisting the screw. It moved a bit every time now, maybe his blood was working like oil, lubricating his effort?

How many turns would it take? He kept making little tugs, one after the other without more than a tiny pause. The screw froze, resisting his twists. Then it broke free again, easier than ever. He had to be close. Finally, the screw actually wiggled in its hole. Pepper kept twisting until it fell free and clattered lightly on the concrete at his hip.

He celebrated by resting half a sec. Deep breath. Had

his efforts been worth it? Would the pole lift from the support sleeve? And would his captors come back through the door first?

Pepper scootched himself up into a squatting position, his feet flat on the floor for leverage. He twisted his hands into a chokehold on the pipe despite the screaming pain in the hand that'd battled the screw. Well, this would be a leg exercise.

He tried to push himself upward and lift the pole from the sleeve. Nothing. The pole didn't budge. But on the third heave, Pepper shot to his feet, the pole tipped sideways. He lost his grip on the pole but since it was threaded through his arms, the weight of it slammed into the back of his shoulder and threw Pepper onto his side. Pain shot through his shoulder and he screamed silently.

But the pole's clatter on the concrete floor had been noisy--had the peeing Devane heard?

* * *

The next step was easy for Pepper--scootch away on his butt until his arms came free from the pole. That fucking pole. Not as bad as that fucking screw, but close.

Then Pepper stood, leaned against the wall, bent his knees and passed his handcuffed hands down below his butt. Slid to the floor and awkwardly slipped his hands around the heel of one shoe, then the other. His hands were still cuffed but now they were in front. Usable.

Pepper heard a rattling noise from the shed door and reacted quicker than he would have believed. Up on his feet, two steps to pick up the bloody baseball bat where it was leaning against the wall. As Devane stepped through the doorway, Pepper hit him in the gut with the bat as hard as he could.

The man jackknifed forward with a howl.

Pepper pushed past him, ready to attack his partner. But Oliver wasn't there, must not be back quite yet. So Pepper yanked the door closed and gave Devane three hits more hits with all his remaining strength. The man screamed and fell flat, then shuddered and was still.

Searching Devane, Pepper caught a break that the guy had the handcuff key in his pocket. Pepper also found a Walther semi-automatic. Pepper confirmed it was loaded and its safety was off, then he slipped it in his own pocket. Pepper uncuffed himself, then drag the semi-conscious man over to a thick metal table leg. He cuffed the man around the table leg after checking it was firmly cemented into the floor. With no fucking screw.

Then Pepper slapped Devane to full wakefulness. He didn't have the time or the inclination to fool around with this guy. Pepper had to find out anything the man knew about the presidential assassination plans and then get out of there. And shit, the assassination might be happening right now, or have already happened while Pepper was captive if that's where Oliver had disappeared to!

The man was sitting up against the table leg, blinking, spitting blood and swearing in a language Pepper didn't recognize.

"Your turn, tough guy," said Pepper. He hefted the baseball bat, smiled. "I need to know everything about the assassination plan. Where are you planning to kill the president? When?"

The man swore louder, spat blood on Pepper's leg. "Fuck you cop! I want my lawyer..."

Pepper drove the baseball bat's butt end into Devane's nose. His neck snapped back and blood erupted.

"They took my badge, you didn't hear?" said Pepper. "So we'll do this by your rules instead." And he swung the bat down as hard as he could on the man's right knee, shattering it. The man convulsed like he'd been electrocuted and screamed a broken curse.

Pepper glared at him with cold murder in his eyes. "In the next thirty seconds you'll answer every question I ask or I'm gonna beat you to a paste, starting with your other knee. So next question. Where's my Red Sox hat?"

FIFTY-ONE

Pepper Ryan made his escape in the old boat waiting in the shed. Absolutely a crappy boat—with a scummy slosh of water in it, but hopefully not from a leak. He managed to start its little outboard motor and back it out the shed's sea door. He didn't know where he was, but he could parallel the shore and get away faster than he could walk in his current state. And the quickest route to Eagle's Nest had to be by boat, right? He steered to head around a small outcropping of sandbars, toward where he thought civilization was. Or maybe he'd come across another boat and could get a more reliable lift.

But Pepper soon regretted his decision. The late afternoon weather had gotten worse. The wind was up, the water was very choppy and the little boat was bucking and plunging. Pepper was holding the outboard motor's handle with one hand while trying to bail water out of the bottom of the boat with a soup can because water was washing over his ankles. A cut on his lower leg was stinging and bleeding in the oily water.

The tiny engine was sputtering along, sounding like Pepper felt. He heard a dull thump and felt his boat twist.

The soup can slipped from his hand into the water. Leaning over the port side, he was horrified to see a shark's dorsal fin disappear under the waves. The largest dorsal fin he'd ever seen—had to be a great white shark, right? Maybe the fourteen-foot monster that'd been getting all the press over in Chatham? He slid back to the middle of the boat. Had it been attracted by Pepper's blood mixed in the water he poured over the side?

After about five minutes, the engine conked out. Nothing Pepper did could get it to turn over again. He'd taken the William Devane guy's phone but hadn't been able to get a signal at the boat shed. Couldn't get one out here either. The bad guys must have the same provider as Pepper… He had nothing else but his old Sox hat, which he'd located where it'd been tossed in a far corner of the shed, behind the bodies.

Pepper slumped back, defeated again. He had no way to steer or propel the boat. The water level in the boat was slowly rising. He just lay back and did the only thing he could still do. Think.

Thinking about what Devane had said when Pepper terrorized him. What little the old guy knew about his and Oliver's client. About the fancy blue phones. That they'd gotten the sniper rifle from a stranger, in a handoff. He didn't know anything about Brian-Edward Westin. Not the Weepers either. But the man said he knew for a fact that today was the final day. Had Oliver gone to kill the POTUS—was that why he hadn't come straight back? Devane had whined no, but then admitted that Oliver hadn't shared everything he was up to. A distrustful partner, like Alfson.

What Pepper had been able to piece together was yes, they had a very wealthy client and yes, Oliver had said they might have one final job—the job of a lifetime—then they'd be leaving the Cape that night.

Pepper was in the foggy zone. The client had to be Smith, the target had to be the POTUS, right? Pepper was finding it hard to concentrate. To not pass out from pain and fatigue...

He startled awake. There was definitely more water in the boat now. Was it coming over the side, or was the boat leaking? There was no land in sight. Where was that damned shark?

Pepper didn't often think about death. Not think so hard as to imagine it, his own death. Fading to black, like going to sleep, like he'd never existed. No trace of himself, whatever he was, and he'd gotten pretty darn attached to existing...took it for granted most of the time, but he really appreciated existing.

Really? No consciousness...dead? His personality and memories, wiped out? His ears tingled, spreading down his spine. If he didn't stop he'd really freak himself out, bobbing and sliding along in a leaking boat on the choppy waves.

So Pepper just was. He floated. He could tell his brains were still muddled. He felt beyond the pain now--a calmness--felt himself the way he always pictured. He was happy to recognize himself again, even if he was dying. He felt clean and knew what he needed to do if the little boat didn't sink under him. Where the heck were any other boats? Anyone? A few birds were overhead but nothing else alive was in sight. Better if he hadn't lived past infancy, like his poor little dead brother Kevin, than to be one final embarrassment to his family. To his dad.

'*You quitting again?*' asked his dead brother Jake with his little half smile on his face. "*Just one more Ryan failure?*" Jake sat in the front of the boat, facing backward. He looked good. Fit. And completely relaxed.

"I wasn't talking about you," said Pepper. It's not all about you, Jake.

"*Who then, Dad? He ever explain why he's mad you put on the badge again?*"

"Not really."

"*Well, you ask him, then decide if he's mad or just scared to lose you too. If you get back to shore alive. You never were the sailor in the family.*" True, Jake was the better sailor too. Jake, who was always best at everything except humility...

"*And hey, nice hat. But it looked better on me.*" Sure, the Red Sox hat had been Jake's... But it was really the same as every other Red Sox hat in New England, right? Millions of them. Somehow Jake knew and had to bust his balls about it. Pepper thought of it as his lucky hat now. The only thing left from Pepper's youth, since he was wearing it at Fenway when their house was demolished.

"*So, Pep, you can be honest now, right? What made you run that brown van off the road? How'd you know?*"

Pepper laughed to himself. People would never stop wondering, so fuck it. "The truth? I was driving home and I'd decided to get thrown off the force. I didn't actually figure out it was the right van. I just figured if I stopped that van recklessly, Dad would have to fire me. There'd be no way I could ever be a cop again. I'd be free."

"*But you saw part of that backpack in the high grass, near the sidewalk. You saw the van had just pulled back on the road and that the driver was sitting back stiffly, driving extra slowly? You saw something smug in the driver's eyes when he looked over at your police car at the red light, watching you too stiffly, when he turned? You sure it was 100% about sabotaging yourself? Or maybe just doing what that girl needed done before it was too late, to hell with the rules.*"

Fucking Jake. Even when Pepper spilled his guts to his

older brother, Jake wouldn't let him be right. Yes, all those details were true. And as the years passed, Pepper thought back about some other details he may have taken into account at the time, at least subconsciously. The unprofessional finish of the van's paint job. The two rear windows covered inside by white cardboard. Maybe enough probable cause for Pepper to have only been acting wildly reckless and not just like a self-absorbed, self-destructive brat. Maybe enough probable cause to pull the van over, check his license and registration, interview the driver. But not enough to do what Pepper had to admit to himself he'd really done— running that van off the road into a tree as soon as the situation escalated. Unless he had reason to believe the van was about to get away...

"*Nothing wrong with listening to your gut,*" laughed Jake. "*Like what's your gut say about the yacht captain? Why those assholes killed him too?*"

Pepper's head was swimming. Had Captain Vinter seen something, like Marcus did—wrong place, wrong damn time? Or maybe he was just unlucky enough to be in the way of whatever they were up to next?

"*What could he have seen? No, I'm with you, the good captain had to have just been in the wrong place at the wrong time...hey, happens to the best of us, right?*"

The little boat was rocking aggressively because Pepper couldn't keep it facing into the waves. And the most powerful force was the invisible pull of the tide. Was it pulling him toward land or further out to sea?

"*Toward land, Pep,*" said Jake. "*You always were the luckier one.*"

And then Pepper was alone with his thoughts. Alone with his half daze, half fever. More unconscious than awake. But not too far gone to hear the light sandpaper of his boat running ashore. Just too far gone to get up and do anything about it.

* * *

Pepper woke he didn't know how much later. The boat was still motionless, stuck on the sand. He groaned, tried to stand up, the boat shifting beneath him. His head was still in a fog.

So he crawled instead. To the edge of the boat closest to land. Hauled himself slowly over its edge, then too far, tumbling suddenly into the shallow water. The cold slap of the salt water on his face and chest woke him further. His head went under, but his knees found themselves, and his head came up. He finally stood. Slowly waded ashore. Saw Rogers Lighthouse, looming over him. After all that, he was back where he'd parked.

Of course, the Devane guy's cell phone was now soaked. First things first. He had to get his hands on a phone. Call Chief Eisenhower. Or if he had to, even call his partner Alfson. It was darker now, the wind clawing at Pepper as he walked up the beach. He followed the thin slatted wooden walkway, getting raked by the high grasses swaying in the wind. It smelled heavy too, like a dump of rain was coming.

He reached the parking lot. It was much more empty now due to the lousy weather. But there, at the far end, waited his sweet old truck.

Pepper reached into his pocket, dug around. Tried his other pocket. Gripped the cool awesomeness of his keys.

* * *

Special Agent Alfson led a mixed team to the blue boat

shed where the tipster said Pepper was being held.

A tactical team went in first, like ghosts.

They found only bodies. Four total. One unidentified male in a suit. Another in a boating uniform, a dead ringer for the *Madeline Too* yacht's captain? Was he missing? Alfson had an agent call back to Eagle's Nest to check and word came back, no, the yacht captain was on board.

The third body was just a torso—head and limbs chopped off. Maybe that missing Lieutenant Hurd? The fourth was an older male with a smashed knee and a cut throat who looked like one of the unsubs in the pictures from the Sanddollar Motel raid. His body was freshest.

They also found a compact, expensive sniper rifle.

It would take investigators and ME's a while to make full sense of the scene. Blood everywhere. Presumably, someone had walked away from the carnage mere minutes before they'd arrived. Pepper Ryan, if he'd actually ever been there? Or others? This was going to take time—did they have it?

FIFTY-TWO

Pepper Ryan drove far enough from the lighthouse to get a strong signal, then called his boss in the FBI's Criminal Investigative Division in D.C.

Edwina Youngblood sounded relieved to hear his voice. She listened to him babble about what had happened. And that he was convinced the POTUS was in imminent danger from his host, Acker Smith. What should Pepper do?

His boss paused for only a second. Then she told him to stand down. She'd run with it, notify the Secret Service. If they had any concerns, they would act to protect the POTUS, of course. She said she'd talked to the SAIC on location already when trying to hunt Pepper down. That the POTUS was remaining at Eagle's Nest. Dinner with his family on the yacht, then remaining at the compound. But the Secret Service had concerns about Pepper's behavior. Questions whether he was undercover for the FBI or had actually joined one of the domestic terror groups. She said again for Pepper to stand down. Reminded him his assignment was the money laundering investigation against Smith and he was now jeopardizing that whole case. That it was an order. That she-

"The yacht?" interrupted Pepper. "Ask them what

happened to the yacht captain's mustache. It's not Westin—it's Oliver. Willie! He's working for Smith, with that William Devane!" Then disconnected the call.

Pepper now realized there was no way anyone was going to believe him quickly enough to stop Smith. If he was even right. Was there still a plan to assassinate the POTUS? Or did everything end with the other murders, what'd already taken place?

Pepper's gut told him the threat was not over. Another assassination attempt was about to take place. But was Pepper willing to sacrifice himself, his career, his family name on the long shot theory that feeble, terminally-ill Smith was really about to kill the POTUS? Could Pepper take the gamble? When it wasn't his job, anyway?

He debated calling Chief Eisenhower. Or Zula? She'd at least believe him...

What options did he have? The Secret Service was definitely not going to let him into Eagle's Nest. He knew he'd been crossed off the lists and wouldn't get past even the first checkpoint, let alone all three. After Pepper's arrest, there were probably new orders to specifically prevent him from getting near Eagle's Nest and the POTUS. His impulse was to storm Eagle's Nest. But this time, they'd probably shoot first, then arrest whatever was left of him. He took a deep breath. Channeled a little Zula-mindfulness shit. Breathed out.

Which choice was shittier—obey orders to walk away, knowing in his gut that the President might be about to be assassinated, or disobey orders and try one last time, likely at the price of his career. And maybe result in a trip to prison or the morgue...

Pepper thought as hard as he still could. Past the pain and the fog.

And remembered Maddie Smith. Remembered the alternative life she'd dangled in front of him just before they were almost decapitated by his Airstream trailer—no duty, no risking his life anymore. Just travel and sunshine and laughs. Bloody, beat-up and exhausted, Pepper thought as hard as he still could...what was the downside of taking the easy way out?

* * *

Special Agent Alfson was still at the boat shed when he received a call from his SAIC Hanley. His boss told him that the FBI's Edwina Youngblood had called again. She'd sounded stressed out. And a bit embarrassed or apologetic.

She'd told Hanley that Ryan was alive. That she'd just talked to him but didn't know where he was, exactly. But he'd sounded injured, that he might be concussed. He'd been saying things she couldn't understand, like maybe that old actor William Devane was part of the plot. That guy from *Knot's Landing* reruns who does the gold coin commercials? And telling her to ask what happened to the yacht captain's mustache... But that he was convinced the POTUS's host, Acker Smith, was planning to kill the POTUS imminently. She'd said she told Ryan to stand down, but thought the Secret Service should be notified since the POTUS's safety was primarily their responsibility.

Hanley had dispatched a team to the Eagle's Nest main mansion. They'd found Smith in bed. Semi-conscious. A dying man. Couldn't hurt himself, let alone the POTUS. Several of the agents had interacted with Smith before and confirmed to Hanley without a doubt the dying man in bed was Smith.

Alfson winced, knowing there'd be a cyclical backlash for

that action. From Smith's people, to the POTUS's inner team, to the top of Secret Service senior management. Negative consequences for Hanley. It is what it is... But Alfson hoped he'd have had the balls to give the same order his boss had done, if his own career was on the line.

Hanley also confirmed the POTUS's protection teams were on high alert, but all was in order. Smith's yacht had recently returned from ferrying the Smith girl and the First Daughters over to Nantucket for shopping and some day drinking. A double team of agents had accompanied them on the yacht, then stayed glued to them during their hours ashore. The yacht arrived back just in time for the advance team to again inspect every corner of the yacht. And twice the usual number of agents would be on board for the POTUS's family dinner, which again the POTUS had refused to cancel. Yes, Captain Vinter was there—agents had talked to him not ten minutes ago.

Alfson requested Hanley to put out a general order for all agents on protection duty to be alert for Pepper Ryan. To take him into custody, that he might be armed and dangerous. Ryan might be concussed or otherwise mentally unstable-- what'd he said about that old TV show? And the yacht captain's mustache? But crazy didn't mean that he couldn't be deadly.

FIFTY-THREE

Sorry everybody, thought Pepper as he drove slowly along the coast. *But duty calls. Then maybe prison...*

He parked his truck and called President Garby's mistress Alexis, using the number on the crumpled napkin she'd given him at Malecón. It had fortunately remained in his truck, behind the seat where he'd tossed it. Pepper pretended to be Garby's chief of staff. He said the President would appreciate the pleasure of Ms. Alexis's company on the *Madeline Too* superyacht for a sunset cocktail. If she could pull herself away? In a half hour? She could, she would. Pepper could hear the excitement in her voice.

Then he pulled up Wikipedia on his phone, searched for arsenic trioxide. Skimmed past the chemistry equations to simply confirm it was a deadly poison. Even nasty in non-lethal doses. Brutal digestive problems. Convulsions, inflammation of organs, changes to skin pigmentation. Maybe worst of all, hair loss. Good thing Pepper didn't taste test the sample he'd stolen...

Then Pepper called Special Agent Alfson. "Partner, where are you?"

"I'm at a crime scene in a boat shed," said Alfson. "Does that ring a bell? I'm wading through a heap of bodies expecting one of them to be you. Ryan, where the hell *are* you?"

"Oh, I'm driving. I might lose you. Can you still hear me, I'm moving into a bad signal area. It's not Brian-Edward Westin! He was just a distraction. It's Oliver. It's Willie! They're all working for Smith. But Oliver doesn't have the sniper rifle, so he must have a different plan. Maybe arsenic! You've got to—"

"Whoa, slow down Miss Marple! Arsenic? Where are you? Head to the police station and I'll meet you there. We can talk this through."

"No time. But I'll meet you in fifteen minutes at Eagle's Nest. Trust me!"

"Trust you?" laughed Alfson. "Every time you say that, someone gets killed. And Ryan, no way they're letting you through our checkpoints!"

Pepper parked, still talking. Started jogging down the street, looking for a particular car. "Don't worry partner, I've got a driver who'll get me inside. All it takes for a free pass is the right bleach blonde hair and pretty face." Then Pepper hung up.

Too obnoxious? Pepper had realized that nobody was getting into Eagle's Nest without their name being on the damn official list. That and a quick proctological exam. But he was gambling on exploiting the system's one Achilles' heel—a forty-something-year-old blonde who got notoriously special treatment. Alexis the First Mistress. AKA, Flame!

Pepper spotted the car he'd been searching for. And it was unlocked, as he'd hoped. He quickly popped its trunk and climbed in.

Pepper heard the noise of someone approaching the car. He pulled the trunk closed the final inch, made it click—he couldn't have a warning light on the dashboard blinking...

Pepper fumbled in the dark to locate the emergency trunk release, if there was one. He knew most newer cars have an emergency handle in case someone locks themselves in their trunk. Another reason bad guys drive older model cars?

The car jerked into motion, picked up speed quickly. Pepper kept feeling slowly and carefully along the trunk's dark interior for anything which might be a release handle. If there wasn't one, someone would have a hell of a surprise waiting when they eventually popped the trunk. Tomorrow? The day after? Or maybe days later, to figure out why there was a dead body smell coming from the trunk?

Soon the car stopped. A traffic light along the route? Or had they reached the first Eagle's Nest checkpoint? Pepper couldn't hear any conversation, but he could imagine it. He held his breath and prayed the Secret Service wouldn't open the trunk.

The car rolled forward. It stopped two additional times—more breath holding and praying by Pepper. Then the fourth time the car stopped, its engine turned off. Was Pepper inside Eagle's Nest, or was he about to be arrested? Pepper waited, barely breathing. Expecting the car's trunk to pop open any second, and to have bright lights and weapons in his face.

* * *

Special Agent Dan Alfson had made it back to Eagle's Nest from the boat shed at top speed, breaking at least a dozen traffic regulations and, thanks to a quick heads up call en route to Hanley, shortened stops at the checkpoints. Record time. He parked at a bad angle near the main turnaround as Hanley came from the Guest House and they jogged back to the first checkpoint together, collecting the canine team from the second checkpoint on the way. The first checkpoint would be the most strategic place to ambush Ryan.

So Alfson was calmly waiting when Alexis' red Lexus halted at the first checkpoint, two minutes later. The blonde gave a big smile and friendly wave. Happy and relaxed. No idea she was smuggling someone into Eagle's Nest.

Alfson joined the male agent who was chatting lightly with Alexis. His boss had taken out his handgun but stayed off to the side, under the white tent with the other agent on post. "Please turn off your engine," Alfson said to Alexis with a smile. "And I'll just need to have a peek in your trunk."

"The trunk? It's pretty much empty," said the woman with a cute, confused frown. He knew—and she knew—it was unwritten gospel to hassle Flame, the First Mistress, as little as goddamn possible, including skipping the regular procedure of searching her vehicle's compartments.

"We appreciate your cooperation." Alfson drew his Sig Sauer P229. He didn't know whether Ryan was armed but he was always dangerous. Alfson stood next to the car's rear quarter panel and pointed his weapon at the trunk as Alexis pulled the release. The other agent was watching him quizzically but had also drawn his firearm.

Alfson hooked the trunk lid's corner with a finger and pulled it up quickly, weapon pointed inside. It was empty.

Huh?

What had Ryan been talking about? Alfson had been sure Ryan was planning to smuggle himself into Eagle's Nest in the trunk of the POTUS's mistress—he'd basically bragged that on the phone, hinting about Alexis' blonde hair and pretty face, no? What'd Ryan been talking about? And why was Flame here anyway? Hanley had confirmed again to

Alfson that the POTUS's plans hadn't changed at all—he was having dinner on the yacht with his wife and daughters. *Nobody* wanted the POTUS's First Mistress and First Lady to cross paths...

Alfson holstered his weapon, clicked shut the trunk and casually went back to the driver's window. But then Alfson had a whispered conversation with Flame about the POTUS's family dinner plan that night.

The woman twisted her mouth in annoyance and called the POTUS's chief of staff on her cell phone. Talked briefly. And very quickly got red in the face. "I'm gone," she said. She did a five-point turn right there in the driveway, then spun her tires, kicking up oyster shells as she drove away. An angry woman. No yachting for her today...

Hanley had stepped out to join them and was looking at Alfson quizzically. Alfson felt the same way.

"Has anyone else driven through this checkpoint in the past twenty minutes without you checking their trunk?" Alfson asked the checkpoint agent, who'd also re-holstered his firearm.

"No sir, absolutely not," said the agent, confused, but squaring his shoulders. "No one but you."

FIFTY-FOUR

Pepper Ryan still hadn't found the emergency release handle. But then he remembered his cell phone--maybe the signal sucked, but it made a hell of a flashlight! And there at the hood's top rear was a cheap-looking green handle. Never in doubt.

Now, how long should he wait before pulling the handle? Could he get into the main mansion? Where would he find Smith and would Oliver somehow be there too?

But Pepper had no more time to waste. He climbed out of the trunk of Alfson's car and limped into the Eagle's Nest main house, trying to appear as natural as possible. Alfson was probably going to shoot him when he figured out how he'd been tricked, but the POTUS's life came first, right?

Then Pepper labored upstairs with the Devane guy's Walther pistol in hand. He brushing past two surprised staff coming down the staircase, not pausing when they shouted. He burst into the master bedroom, where the bed was tousled but empty. No one in sight. He ran through the French doors onto the balcony.

Acker Smith was to the left, leaning against the railing. His dirty-trick-playing assistant Lizzie Concepcion was there too, a bit to his right. They'd both been focused on the

357

ocean and Smith's yacht on the horizon's edge. Another boat—the tiny tender—was slowly approaching the enormous yacht. Five other boats floated nearby—Navy?

But they'd both turned when Pepper slammed through the doors. Smith's eyes went wide when he saw the weapon in Pepper's hand.

Pepper saw Lizzie back a few steps from Smith, reach into her purse and now she had a handgun out too. Pointed pretty much right at Pepper, but shaking back and forth, which scared Pepper even more.

"Don't you hurt Mr. Smith!" she screamed. "Don't shoot him. Please!" Her gun moving frantically back and forth between Pepper and Smith. The assistant was almost hysterical.

Pepper tried to focus on Smith. He looked even worse than last time—paler and waxy. And like he barely had the strength to stand. "Nobody's going to get hurt," said Pepper. "As long as Smith stops his plan to kill the president."

Smith pulled himself to his full height. "Kill him?" His thin voice was mocking. "Why would a sex scandal do that?"

Pepper was thrown off, tried to regroup. "What do you think's going on?" he asked Smith. "That you'll have photos taken of Garby with his mistress on your yacht tonight, leak them to the media? Disgrace him? Get revenge for him screwing you on his campaign promises?"

Blood was flushing Smith's face, but his eyes looked disoriented. Like he was only partially awake and trying to gather himself. Like what Pepper had said made sense, but he couldn't remember why.

"You don't know what you're talking about," said Lizzie, her gun still shaking.

But Pepper stayed facing Smith. His mind was working as fast as it could, trying to sort out the truth. "If that's what was really going down, why are Garby's wife and daughters in the tender with him?" asked Pepper. "And your daughter, Maddie. It doesn't make any sense."

"Madeline went with the Garby women to New York this afternoon," said Lizzie, waving her handgun for emphasis. "Another frivolous shopping trip."

The tender was nearing the yacht, but it was too far away for anyone on the balcony to identify any individuals. Smith pulled out his cell phone, dialed.

"Maddie dear? Where are you?" He listened and ended the call. Smiled weakly. "Ryan's right. She's with the Garbys, they're having a dinner party onboard. You didn't know?" The last question addressed to Lizzie.

The tender had reached the yacht and Pepper could see little people making their way onboard.

"The yacht's not a love nest tonight," said Pepper. "You're not going to get that kind of media scandal." He was still pointing his handgun at Smith who didn't seem to care. Didn't seem to be processing the developments. "I'll bet it's a floating bomb. You're going to blow the *Madeline Too* into little splinters, right Smith? Kill him for betraying you? A last act brave act before you die too?"

"You're nuts," wheezed Smith.

"The Secret Service has combed the yacht every day this week," scoffed Lizzie. "Every inch, with the best equipment in the world."

"I'm guessing they didn't. Up until this afternoon, they searched the *Madeline Too.* But that yacht out there now is its sister ship, the *Madeline, right?* When did you switch the yachts—in Nantucket a few hours ago? Tell the staff you were pulling a little joke, but Captain Vinter had raised too many questions so you panicked, had him killed too? Let me guess—the second yacht has explosives buried in its hull, which a more rushed security sweep this evening wouldn't detect?"

They all looked over at the yacht, where all the tiny people had now climbed from the tender to the yacht and it was pulling away.

Lizzie's lips formed into a tight, hard line. "You're delusional! But now I'm glad Mr. Smith's been ruining your life too. He had me arrange to have your cheap little house destroyed. He had me send you out to the yacht when Garby was with his new slut, to get you jailed and ruin your career. We even arranged to have you shot. All of it. So what are you going to do now—shoot Mr. Smith? Because with all our lawyers, that's the only chance you have to get revenge!"

She was now pointing her handgun at Smith, as if she was going to shoot Smith for him.

"You're both crazy," said Smith. He was now slumped against the thick stone railing. He looked like his strength was fading. His skin color looked terrible and his scraggly hair was askew. His hand was across his stomach as if he had indigestion. Then Pepper realized that Smith's problem *wasn't* indigestion...!

"Maybe a bullet's what you deserve," said Pepper to Smith. "But speaking of crazy, I've got some good news for you—you're not dying from cancer. You're being poisoned to death."

"Poisoned?"

"There's one man at Eagle's Nest dying from pancreatic cancer but it's not you. Your body's shutting down from arsenic poisoning." And in that instant, the answers clicked into place for Pepper. "Your loyal assistant's been killing you, just like she's about to kill President Garby."

"Lizzie?" Smith gasped.

Lizzie Concepcion's face changed. A few tears remained on her cheeks, but the weakness was gone. It was replaced by an icy coldness.

"I was Garby's lover when he was a senator," Lizzie said. "But he betrayed me, just like he betrays anyone or anything that jeopardizes his ambitions. My pregnancy? My marriage? He destroyed them and never looked back."

She took a step toward Smith. "When your heart stops, your pacemaker'll send a signal to the bell tower. They'll ring just like you ordered. But that signal will also trigger explosives on the *Madeline*. And Garby'll get what he deserves—the lying, cheating *snake*! For what he did to me and our unborn baby. My poor sweet little candy! For what he did to *lots* of women," she screamed, taking another step toward Smith, and pulled the trigger.

But Pepper had already leapt. No time to think. An instinctive lunge—half block, half tackle. Pepper heard the loud smack of Lizzie's handgun discharge and felt her bullet hit him, as his momentum carried him into Smith.

But that explains about the freakin' candy, was Pepper's last thought, before he and Smith crashed against the stone railing, flipped over it and fell to the flagstones below.

FIFTY-FIVE

They both hit hard. Acker Smith got the worst of it because Pepper landed on top. But Pepper felt instant pain in his left arm and across his chest. Maybe from the bullet, maybe from the impact of the fall. And the concussion with the ground knocked Pepper nearly senseless. In a way, the pain seemed to help, to keep him conscious.

Pepper was also aware he was bleeding, again...

Smith wasn't moving, except maybe for the shallowest breathing. Pepper clawed at Smith's suit jacket, was his cell phone still there? Not in the first side pocket, or the second. He found it in an inside breast pocket.

Pepper clicked it on. It was still working and thank God the screen wasn't locked yet. He hit redial.

When Pepper heard Maddie Smith's voice, he yelled, "Maddie! Maddie! Get everyone off the ship! It's gonna explode any second!" Pepper couldn't hear her reply clearly. He shouted his message again, then again, in an insane loop. He couldn't hear much—was the problem a weak cell phone signal or his ears? The world was drifting to spotty black. Pepper's head was spinning and thick.

And had Smith stopped breathing? Would Smith's pacemaker actually trigger a device on the ship, or was that another lie? Pepper crawled up, began mouth to mouth and chest compressions with his one good arm. Practically pounded on Smith's chest, feeling Smith's ribs crack. All Pepper's frustration and anger fueling what little strength he had left. But Pepper was getting weaker, fading. And he just had to rest his eyes for a second.

* * *

Pepper was awakened by an explosion. Even from half a mile away, the bright light and concussive wave of the explosion hit him a hard smack. And despite his scrambled head, Pepper realized the explosion meant Smith was dead, his body still half beneath Pepper. A moment later, the bells in Eagle's Nest's tower began to ring, slow and heavy.

But the bells also tolled the death of U.S. President Wayne Garby. Of everyone on board the yacht. Including Maddie. A dark wave of sorrow and pain washed over Pepper. He'd done everything he could and failed. As pretty much everyone who knew him best would have bet.

Pepper was exhausted. Every time he breathed too deeply, it felt like a sharp kick in his chest. Blood was running down his head into his left eye. And his shoulder was numb.

Pepper heard people running toward him. Then he saw Special Agent Dan Alfson with his Sig Sauer in hand. And two other Secret Service agents, carrying MP5 submachine guns. The SAIC Hanley was a little further back, but with his handgun out too.

And there was Lizzie Concepcion. Also with her gun in hand at her side, which no one but Pepper seemed to have noticed.

"He killed Mr. Smith," screamed Lizzie, pointing her

empty hand at Pepper where he lay against Smith's body.

All the Secret Service agents except Alfson were now leveling their weapons at Pepper.

"I was trying to save the POTUS," said Pepper. I'm sorry, I failed... And I was wrong, the assassin wasn't Smith...It was her!" Gesturing at Lizzie with his only working arm.

"Move away from Mr. Smith," said Alfson, slowly stepping closer. His handgun was now up and pointed at Pepper.

Pepper heard sirens begin their approach from far away. "Trust me, Alf," he said. And winked.

Alfson paused his advance, glanced over quickly at Lizzie and seemed to notice for the first time her handgun. He started turning toward her.

Lizzie stepped back, mouth open. Her arm came up in what seemed like slow motion, her handgun lining up on Pepper.

He heard one shot.

As Pepper felt himself sliding back into the cold pool of unconsciousness, his last sight was Lizzie falling backward, her red mouth open and her dark hair stretching from her head in a wild pattern around her face. Kind of like a starfish.

FIFTY-SIX

Pepper Ryan woke in the hospital.

He was smiling despite his momentous failure, so he knew he was full of painkillers. His left arm was in a sling. His torso felt like it was in a cast, or maybe the cocoon of a wide tensor bandage. Otherwise, Pepper felt nothing but a light happy buzz in his ears from the drugs.

The room was pretty crowded. His dad was there, sitting on the windowsill edge by the bed, where morning sunlight was peeking in. Did his dad have more lines on his face? Chief Eisenhower and Zula were sitting by the window.

"The President..." said Pepper, his throat so dry he could barely rasp out the words. "I tried to warn them. I called Maddie. There wasn't enough time..."

Zula smiled. Flipped her long black hair back off her face. "You did it, dummy. Relax. They got off the yacht in time."

Pepper pushed back in the bed against the industrial grade pillows. What? Had he heard her right? "They all got off?"

"Full evacuation, just barely," said the Chief. "But then that yacht went up *hard*. Right at dusk—they say it looked like a goddamn sunset. And Lizzie Concepcion's dead. Or

Isabel Bumpers. Whatever we should call her. And they took her bullet from your shoulder."

"She was always there, but I didn't figure her out until almost too late," admitted Pepper. "I still think Agent Keser must have asked Lizzie something during his interview that spooked her, so he was chosen as her first victim. Maybe about her old married name."

"Makes sense," agreed Zula. "She had a bunch of Smith Enterprises employees fired when they raised questions about that Turnstone fund. And had Blacklock killed when he flew up to confront Smith about it."

Pepper recalled the mystery body from the boat shed—the fat man in the seersucker suit, covered in flies... He shuddered.

"And poor DJ ChilEboy too..." said Zula. "The Secret Service now thinks Lizzie tried to poison and expose Garby's current mistress Alexis with a GHB overdose at the **ecó** party, although at the time we thought it was the First Daughters who'd been targeted. It was just bad luck for ChilEboy, guzzling all those shots."

"But who was that other sick guy at Eagle's Nest?" asked Pepper.

"Lizzie brought in another man actually dying from pancreatic cancer," explained Chief Eisenhower. "When doctors came to Eagle's Nest to test and treat Smith, she had them examine that man instead. And we believe Smith had been pushing Lizzie for a sexual relationship before he got sick, so she probably figured he deserved what he got. But her main target was Garby, just good old-fashioned revenge. Garby dumped her when his presidential run started and she probably thought he somehow induced her miscarriage to keep a love child from blowing up his candidacy. So poisoning Smith was just a bonus for her."

"Smith's what brought me home in the first place," admitted Pepper. "I was undercover with the FBI's Joint Terror Task Force in Tennessee—I had an offer from them when I took off a few years ago...I'd screwed up here but still wanted to fight the good fight, you know? They loaned me to another division to go undercover here to build a case for money laundering and other financial crimes against Smith and maybe President Garby. They hoped if there was any real involvement by the president, that it'd come out when they squeezed Smith. There was an FBI team in Connecticut building the case too. My assignment was to get inside Smith's compound where he was working these days to substantiate the anonymous tips, to boost probable cause for a warrant to go deep at the Stamford office—tear the lid off what we believed was *his* scheme."

"So *that's* why you were sniffing around Maddie Smith?" asked Zula. "I mean, I knew you weren't *that* dumb..." Then she stepped over to the bed, took his hand. Squeezed a little too hard. "What were you thinking, trying to stop the assassination by yourself?"

"There wasn't enough time to get anyone to believe me. But maybe it's like you said. Blame my DNA."

Then Pepper's dad filled him in about the Reverend McDevitt arrest. Amazing. But not surprising, for a scumbag like McDevitt. "Zula's the one who got him to surrender, held her twelve gauge right to his toupee," concluded his dad with a chuckle.

Zula laughed too, light and proud and, apparently, deadly.

His dad rubbed Pepper's head. "And the Ryans had some good news too. Since Smith's company Turnstone paid to have our house destroyed and Turnstone was also holding our mortgage, there's not a judge in the country who won't cancel the mortgage for their misconduct. The debt'll be voided, we won't have to pay them a penny. Not only that, our insurance company's paying out on the house destruction and they're going after the Smith estate to recover the amount. I'm thinking of overseeing the rebuild myself."

Pepper liked the energy and pride in his dad's voice. "Maybe if I stay around for a while, we can rebuild together?"

His dad took Pepper's only working hand and shook it. Which turned into a full hug, just gentle enough that Pepper didn't pass out. But it felt great.

"I'm proud of you, son," his dad said softly in his ear.

Words Pepper hadn't heard since...practically forever? "And I'm sorry I scared the hell out of you, again," Pepper replied, just as quietly. He was the only one close enough to see—was that a tear in the corner of his dad's eye?

There was a knock at the open door. Pepper craned his neck, a move which hurt like electrocution, and saw Special Agent Dan Alfson standing in the doorway with a frown on his pretty face. "I have a bone to pick with you, Ryan," he said. "You made me look like a jackass with your trunk stunt..."

Was he seriously still pissed?

Then Alfson broke into a half smile. "But we'll take that offline sometime soon, over a beer. Tell me about your showdown with Lizzie Concepcion—how'd you figure out there were explosives on the yacht?"

Pepper's dad handed him a miniature can of apple juice. Pepper took a sip, then explained about finding Vinter's body in the boat shed. "Since your agents confirmed a Captain Vinter was still on board the yacht, I figured both yachts had to be nearby. And why get rid of one Captain Vinter unless you were swapping yachts after the deep security sweep had been completed? It had to be a switcheroo.

"I thought Smith was the mastermind. I thought he was dying and planning some last-ditch revenge against President Garby for going back on all the campaign promises he'd made to buy Smith's financial support. But when I confronted Smith on the balcony, he misunderstood me. He thought he was setting up the president for a sex scandal after humiliating Garby all vacation with the activists and other things he was able to pay for. But Smith was just a puppet.

"And I found a stash of arsenic trioxide at Eagle's Nest, but I thought Smith was the poisoner, not the victim...I didn't guess Lizzie was the real mastermind, and that she was poisoning Smith to weaken him, so she could control him and his resources for her plot."

"Well, when *did* you figure it out?" asked Alfson.

"Almost too late—on the balcony, when Lizzie watched the boat with President Garby approaching the yacht. Once he reached the yacht, she moved her gun from me to Smith. And she even tried to push me to shoot Smith myself, saying everything bad that'd happened to me was caused by him."

Alfson was frowning. "So you actually threw yourself in front of Lizzie's shot at Smith? I thought your job description didn't require jumping in front of bullets?"

Pepper laughed a little painfully. "I'm glad you trusted me."

"I had to pull a Ryan—follow my gut. Just this once."

"By the way Pepper, I talked to your other boss—Edwina Youngblood, in D.C.?" said the General. "She's definitely not as proud of you as we are. She said you're suspended without pay."

Winning was one thing, embarrassing the FBI was something else. Pepper was not surprised he'd pissed off his supervisors. He'd failed to follow FBI procedure. Failed to follow orders. Insubordination. They were probably scrambling to verify what involvement he had with all the carnage in the boat shed. And they'd probably think of a few more procedural violations which would soon put a final bow on his time with the FBI.

The General stood. "Well, if your FBI career is toast, I'd be honored to hire you back for real, this time. Unless you have some other secret job to get back to?"

"Thanks, sir."

"I'm going to check in on the hunt for Brian-Edward Westin," said Alfson. "He's probably halfway across the country by now...but we'll get him. 110%. But we'd better let you rest. The Service'll need to formally interview you. And every other federal and state agency you can name, but I'll hold 'em off a few more hours."

Zula stepped over to the bed, leaned in and gave Pepper a hug. Her long hair tickled his cheek and she smelled like sand and exotic flowers. Maybe orchids? Her hug was definitely a little harder than necessary, given his injuries. And lingered a bit long. But at the moment it felt damn great.

So Pepper turned her chin and kissed her on the lips. Her momentary surprise changed into a great kiss back. Long and electric.

Their dads maybe pretended not to see.

As the room emptied, Pepper remembered something else. "But hey," he yelled after them. "What happened to the other hitman--Oliver? The guy who kidnapped me?"

FIFTY-SEVEN

Oliver gazed out the airplane window and smiled.

Funny how things work out. You find that lieutenant's passport, right in his dresser drawer where it belonged. And he was a reasonable resemblance to Oliver—white, medium height, brown hair. The only mismatch being the lieutenant's nose like a goddamn Pinocchio. But luckily in the passport photo they'd caught the lieutenant dead on straight, minimizing the monstrosity. The half-asleep lady at the Logan Airport security checkpoint hadn't even mentioned it. It was totally fate--the universe was his wingman. And who was Oliver to question fate?

And so there he was on a direct flight to Tokyo! Who'd expect a hitman on the run to head to Asia? In goddamn first class? The economy seats would have been too embarrassing if the cops caught his trail--hauling him off past the clogged rows of families and general mouth breathers. And Asiatic Airlines had by far the best last-minute price for first class. Fate giving him the cosmic high five, one more time.

He hadn't understood half of what the little Asian stewardesses had said since he'd taken his pod-like seat numbered 4A. Bowing and smiling. Oliver's first-class meal came. He'd selected the western option with beef. Even so, there were lots of Asian vegetables and exotic sauces. Oliver ate slowly, savored every bite. He only left some strange looking broccoli.

Oliver's feet were cradling his carry-on bag, which held around $50,000 in little bundles of hundred dollar bills, carefully packed in manila envelopes to resemble thick documents. His emergency fund. And he had over two million dollars in a Bahamian bank account, which he could have wired to...wherever. So, where would he head next? Maybe Australia. Or maybe...Thailand? Oliver had seen a show once about a Bangkok red light district the size of New Orleans. Cheap weed, beautiful young women eager to please. All the pleasures that a third world country could offer a man with heavy cash and a smile. Maybe get some plastic surgery? Hide his trail and boost his looks, Hollywood-style. Maybe become more rugged-looking like that cop, Ryan?

Oliver wondered what eventually happened to Pepper Ryan. He didn't know the entirety of his client's plan, but he suspected it was to kill the president and anyone who got in the way. Smith seemed as relentless as he was rich, so Ryan was probably toast. Not that Oliver would bet against the cop. Ryan was maybe a little too good to be true, a bit of a boy scout, but he'd turned out to be pretty tough. And kinda respectful even when Oliver was in his scraggly Rowboat Willie costume. He decided Ryan would get what he got, but he kind of hoped Ryan kicked his client's rich ass.

Oliver thought about when he'd returned to the boat shed and found Ryan gone and Croke lying in his own blood, with a smashed knee, barely conscious. Croke had started in on those Eastern European cuss words, directed at Oliver. Oliver had seen white. Took out his Gerber folding knife and slit Croke's throat, mid-curse. He remembered the surprise, then fear, which had flooded Croke's face as the knife did the job. No more pickles for you!

The decision to kill Croke had been a little hot-headed, but in hindsight was still the right call. Croke had definitely needed a hospital, which would have meant cops. And Oliver didn't think for a second Croke would keep his mouth shut once that fun started. Better the way it went. When the cops eventually found Croke, they'd also find so much blood from Croke--from Ryan too--that they wouldn't know who'd done what to whom. Maybe they'd think Ryan had offed Croke and would cover it up for their brother-in-blue? Whatever, but it'd be one less chance to track it all back to Oliver.

And Oliver's mob employers? *They* wouldn't know what to think, except that all hell had broken loose, one of their contractors was dead and the other missing. And Oliver planned to stay missing.

But a few hours later Oliver got a nasty shock when the pilot crackled on the overhead speaker and announced they were approaching Los Angeles and would be on the ground in thirty minutes. He flagged down his little Asian stewardess and asked kind of casually, "Isn't this flight direct to Tokyo?"

She explained, in heavily-accented English, that the flight was direct, not non-stop. The airplane would stop briefly in Los Angeles to let on and off some passengers, but those continuing through to Tokyo were welcome to stay on board.

Oliver felt a chill down his spine, wondering if the cops had somehow figured out he was on board this flight and would storm the plane in L.A.? How long would it take for them to figure out his disappearing act?

Oliver hated to feel like the prey.

The plane landed and some passengers got off and others got on. But law enforcement hadn't been waiting and after a routine forty minute stop, the plane was airborne again and headed toward Tokyo.

Eleven and a half hours later, it landed gently at Narita Airport.

But then the flight attendant made an announcement requesting all passengers remain in their seats to keep the aisles clear for a brief delay. When the plane door opened, six small but serious-looking uniformed police boarded, followed by a salt-and-pepper-haired supervisor with his hands folded across his protruding belly. They turned left, into first class and stopped at Oliver's seat.

Which was empty.

"Where is your passenger from 4A, Mr....Dwayne Hurd?" the police supervisor asked the flight attendant, polite but hard.

She gave him a nervous little bow. "Mr. Hurd left the plane in Los Angeles. He told us he had a stomach problem. Then he did not board again when it was time."

The supervisor shrugged and gave the signal for his men to leave. Whoever Mr. Hurd was and whatever bad things he may have done, it seemed he was still America's problem.

FIFTY-EIGHT

A couple of days later, Pepper Ryan was sitting on a big towel on the beach below the Ryan property. His hands were sweeping little fans in the sand, feeling the light scratch of warmth. His finger snagged against a small seashell and he plucked it, wiped it free from sand. It was a perfect spiral, and golden in color. Score! He'd keep it to show Zula and if she liked it, he'd give it to her.

Pepper was soaking in the warm Cape Cod sun. Trying to heal. Wearing Jake's old hat and listening to the Red Sox on a little portable radio turned down low. The Sox were winning but Baltimore had loaded the bases with only one out in the seventh. And Baltimore was riding a five-game win streak.

Pepper saw his buddy Angel walking down the beach toward him.

Pepper stood. But gingerly. Every joint in his body protested even normal movement. The stitches on Pepper's temple felt like he had a toothache on the side of his head.

"Hey *Mano*!" said Angel. His broad smile was infectious. "I heard you were still alive!" Then the big laugh--an eruption of mirth. And relief.

He gave Pepper a gentle hug. Then he held Pepper at

full length, inspecting him. "FBI?" asked Angel, with a quizzical head tilt. "Tell me that means you're a Female Body Inspector! Which reminds me—what happened to Maddie Smith?"

The thought of Maddie still bugged Pepper. She would always be an impossible mix for him. The bitchy, manipulative jet-setter who'd tried to use him, but still showing glimpses of the seventeen-year-old girl he'd maybe loved once, before the adult world had turned them each into very different people. He wondered if she'd meant her offer for him to run away with her, that night—a fantasy that had momentarily seemed better than his messy reality.

Pepper just shook his head and told Angel about Maddie's voice message. She'd said in case he didn't already know, he'd blown his chance. His loss! She needed to clear her head so she was taking her Gulfstream to Cancun with Justin to see his new reality show in production. Lawyers would clean up the mess at Eagle's Nest, arrange her daddy's funeral, and she'd be back for that. But she never wanted to see Pepper again.

"Tough one *Mano!*" frowned Angel, but he couldn't hold it—his frown quickly slipped to a smile and his booming laugh. "But if there's one thing I know about you Pep, you were *never* meant for the easy life!"

Pepper could only laugh too. "Hey, you feel like hanging a while on the beach?"

"Long as you don't suggest a clambake!"

Too soon, Angel...

Pepper could see an elderly couple meandering along the tide line, coming their way. Was it the same couple who'd found the clambake pit with Keser's body? The Tuckers? The old woman picked up something and showed it to the man. Then she shook her head with a grimace, flipped whatever it was into the water. Clearly not up to their standards...

Angel plopped down in the sand, kicked off one flip-flop to the left, the other far to the right. Lay flat and gave a loud, contented sigh. "You see the Globe today? They still had four pages about the assassination attempt. The feds are still trying to hunt down that Brian-Edward Westin from New River Front and that crazy homeless guy, Oliver—I can't believe they haven't caught 'em yet! And hey, they said Lizzie Concepcion had a red starfish tattoo way down by her *cha cha*, did you know? Pretty hot, right? Maybe I should get a tattoo..."

Angel kept babbling but Pepper didn't respond, he was still focused on the shoreline. That elderly couple could have been Pepper's dad and mom someday not too many years from now, if his mom hadn't died so young. Growing old together, the fairy tale. The old man could even be Pepper someday, far, far in the distant future, if he could avoid getting shot or blown up first... He squinted at the elderly couple and tried to guess—if that were actually him someday, who'd be that woman at his side? Impossible to tell.

So for now Pepper surrendered, lay back on his towel. Tuned out Angel's chatter and the Sox play-by-play guy. Listened to the soft percussion of waves stroking the shore like drum brushes. An island song floated to his mind and he sang along softly to the Atlantic's lazy tempo. He tilted his face to the sun—he soaked in its perfect, Cape-Cod-in-July heat—and buried his feet in the sand until he hit a depth still wet and cool from high tide.

And the world finally let Pepper be, for longer than he would have guessed.

<<<<<<<<<<>>>>>>>>>

THANK YOU for buying this book. Pepper Ryan and his friends (and some enemies) will be back for new adventures very soon.

To receive special offers, bonus content, and info on new releases, please sign up for my email list at:
http://eepurl.com/dzcDa9

If you have any comments, send me an email at tim@timothyfagan.com. I'm always happy to hear from people who've read my work. I try to answer every email I receive.

If you liked this story, please write a short review for me on **Amazon** at:
https://www.amazon.com/Beach-Body-Boogie-Pepper-Thriller-ebook/dp/B07F3SSNJR/

and/or

Goodreads
https://www.goodreads.com/book/show/40667903-beach-body-boogie?ac=1&from_search=true

I greatly appreciate any kind words, even one or two sentences go a long way. The number of reviews a book receives greatly improves that book's visibility on Amazon.

ACKNOWLEDGEMENTS

Thank you to my first and best early reader, Karen Fagan. To Jim Fagan, Paul Donahue, Rob Lendrum, Sheridan Leinen, Kate Fagan, Mike Fay and the original (Bill) Smith for their early reads and valuable feedback.

And to all my other beta readers and project supporters: Erin Fagan, Matt Fagan and Anna Fagan. Mary Martinez, Anney Ardiel and Patrick Fagan. Anne Fagan. Bill McCall. Linda Parkins and Dave McCall. Liz Coker. Cindy and Paul Bohne. Joe Reck, Kevin Jordan and Geoff Wadsworth. Sean O'Keefe and Greg Fruno. Tom Museth and Craig Hutcheson. Dan Keser. To Brian Leary for his logistical guidance. To John Raffier for the shoes joke. To Paula Moon and Bruno Massat for the inside scoop on veterinary anesthetics. To everyone else who read, encouraged or pushed me along the way to get this book completed.

To independent editor John Paine, for his developmental editing wisdom. To Damon, Alisha and the rest of the team at damonza.com, for their striking cover design.

To Matt Kurlansky, author of *Salt, A World History* and Ronald Kessler, author of *The First Family Detail: Secret Service Agents Reveal the Hidden Lives of the Presidents*, for their fascinating books that caught my imagination.

And thank you to MFS, a terrific investment management company with even better employees, for your kindness when I quit my day job to write novels. Both times.

ABOUT THE AUTHOR

Timothy Fagan has always loved to read suspenseful books that make you laugh out loud in public. Now he loves to write them.

He previously spent twenty years as an attorney and executive in the financial services industry, focusing on securities regulatory matters across North America, Europe and Asia-Pacific. He was born in Los Angeles, California, grew up in British Columbia, Canada and currently lives near Boston, Massachusetts.

Although his focus is full-length fiction, he also publishes poetry and song lyrics. *Beach Body Boogie* is his first novel.

For more information about Timothy Fagan, his upcoming books and other projects, please visit his website: www.timothyfagan.com

Or follow him at the usual social media sites:

https://twitter.com/TFaganWriting

https://www.instagram.com/timothyfaganwriting/

https://www.facebook.com/timothyfaganwriting/?modal=a dmin_todo_tour

Made in the USA
Lexington, KY
02 January 2019